The WIFE, the MAID, and the MISTRESS

The
WIFE,
the
MAID,
and the
MISTRESS

ARIEL LAWHON

DOUBLEDAY

NEW YORK LONDON TORONTO

SYDNEY AUCKLAND

Copyright © 2014 by Ariel Lawhon

All rights reserved. Published in the United States by Doubleday, a division of Random House LLC, New York, and in Canada by Random House of Canada Limited, Toronto, Penguin Random House Companies.

www.doubleday.com

DOUBLEDAY and the portrayal of an anchor with a dolphin are registered trademarks of Random House LLC.

Jacket design by Emily Mahon
Jacket photograph © Underwood Archives / The Image Works

LIBRARY OF CONGRESS CATALOGING-IN-PUBLICATION DATA
Lawhon, Ariel.
The wife, the maid, and the mistress / Ariel Lawhon. — First edition.
pages   cm
ISBN 978-0-385-53762-9
1. Crater, Joseph Force, born 1889—Fiction.   2. Judges—New York (State)—New York—Fiction.   3. Missing persons—Fiction.   I. Title.
PS3601.L447G66 2014
813'.6—dc23
2012049724

MANUFACTURED IN THE UNITED STATES OF AMERICA

1 3 5 7 9 10 8 6 4 2

First Edition

For Marybeth, I owe you one.

And for Ashley, I owe you everything else.

CLUB ABBEY

GREENWICH VILLAGE, AUGUST 6, 1969

There is, in the city's sun-blistered canyons of concrete, a storied section known as Greenwich Village. And into it on August 6, this tall, stately woman walks, utterly disregarding the heat, on a pilgrimage out of the past. She isn't alone. She is accompanied by a ghost. Her name is Stella Crater.

—*Oscar Fraley, preface to* The Empty Robe

We begin in a bar. We will end here as well, but that is more than you need to know at the moment. For now, a woman sits in a corner booth waiting to give her confession. But her party is late, and without an audience, she looks small and alone, like an invalid in an oversize church pew. It's not so easy for her, this truth telling, and she strains against it. A single strand of pearls, brittle and yellowed with age, rests against the flat plane of her chest. She rolls them between her fingers as though counting the beads on a rosary. Stella Crater has avoided this confession for thirty-nine years. The same number of years she has been coming to this bar.

At one time, this meeting would have been a spectacle, splashed across the headlines of every paper in New York: WIFE OF MISSING JUDGE MEETS WITH LEAD INVESTIGATOR, TELLS ALL! But the days of front-page articles, interviews, and accusations are over, filed away in some distant archives. Tonight her stage is empty.

Stella looks at her watch. Nine-fifteen.

Club Abbey, once a speakeasy during the Jazz Age, is now another relic in Greenwich Village, peddling its former glory through the tourist guides. It sits one floor below street level, dark and subdued. The pine floors are scuffed. Black-and-white photos line the walls. An aging jukebox has long since replaced the jazz quartet. The only remnant is Stan, the bartender. He was fifteen when hired by the notorious gangster Owney Madden to sweep the floors at closing. Owney took a liking to the kid, as did the showgirls, and Stan's been behind the bar ever since. He's never missed Stella's ritual. His part is small, but he plays it well.

Two lowball glasses. Twelve cubes of ice split between them. Whiskey on the rocks. Stan arranges napkins on her table and sets the glasses down. Her eyes are slick with a watery film—the harbinger of age and death.

"Good to see you again, Mrs. Crater."

Stella swats him away with an emaciated hand, and he hangs back to watch, drying glasses with a dish towel. It's the same thing every year: she sits alone in her booth for a few minutes, and then he brings the drinks. Straight whiskey, the way her husband liked it. She'll raise one glass, saluting the empty place across from her, and say, "Good luck, Joe, wherever you are." Stella will take her time with the drink, letting it burn, drawing out the moment until there's nothing left in her glass. That is when she'll rise and walk out, leaving the other drink untouched.

Except tonight she does none of these things.

Fifteen minutes she sits there, rubbing the rim of her glass. Stan has no script for what to do next, and he stares at her, confused. He doesn't see the doors swing open or the older gentleman enter. Doesn't see the trench coat or the faded gray fedora. Sees none of it until Detective Jude Simon slides into the booth across from Stella.

She lays her palm on the table, inches from a pack of cigarettes, and sits up straighter. The booth is hard against her back, walnut planks pressing against the knobs of her spine. "You're late."

"Stella." Jude touches the brim of his hat in greeting. He takes stock of her shriveled body. Tips his head to the side. "It's been years."

"You were here the first time—makes sense that you'd be here the last." Stella lifts her glass and takes a sip of whiskey. Shudders. "Call it a deathbed confession."

Jude surveys the room through the weary smoke. The regular Wednesday night crowd—a few women, mostly men—scattered around in groups of two and three drinking longnecks and griping about the stock market. "This isn't exactly a church, and I'm not much of a priest," he says.

"Priest. Detective. What's the difference? You both love a good confession."

His shoulders twitch—a doubter's shrug. "I'm retired."

Stella draws a cigarette from the pack and props it between her lips. She looks at him expectantly.

He reaches into his pocket and pulls out a tarnished silver lighter.

Something like a smile crosses his face and then melts away. He stares at it, cupped there in his palm, before striking it with his thumb. Jude used to be handsome, decades ago when Stella first met him, and the traces are still there in the square line of his jaw and the steel-blue eyes. But now he looks tired and sad. A bit wilted. It takes three tries before a weak flame sputters from the lighter. Perhaps his hand trembles as he holds it toward her, or it could be a trick of the light.

Stella tips her cigarette into the flame, and the end glows orange. "You would be here tonight even if I hadn't asked you to come." Her eyes shift toward the bar, where Stan pretends not to eavesdrop. "You have your sources."

"Maybe." Jude hangs his fedora on a peg beside the booth and pulls a pad and pen from his coat pocket. He waits for her to speak.

Stella lured him here with the promise of a story—the real version this time. He has been like a duck after bread crumbs for thirty-nine years. Pecking. Relentless. Gobbling up every scrap she leaves for him. Yet the truth is not something she will rush tonight. He will get it one morsel at a time.

Stella Crater picked her poison a long time ago—unfiltered Camels—and she takes a long drag now, sizing up her pet duck. Her cheeks collapse into the sharp angles of her face, and she holds the smoke in her lungs for several long seconds before blowing it from between her teeth. Oh, she'll tell Detective Simon a story all right.

Thirty-nine years earlier . . .

Chapter One

BELGRADE LAKES, MAINE,
SATURDAY, AUGUST 2, 1930

STELLA slept with the windows thrown open that summer, a breeze blowing back the curtains. The sounds of nature lulled her to sleep: frogs croaking in the shallow water beneath her window, the hum of a dragonfly outside the rusted screen, the call of a loon across the lake. She lay there, with one arm thrown across her face in resistance to the burgeoning sunlight, when she heard the Cadillac crunch up the long gravel driveway.

Joe.

Stella sat up and threw her legs over the edge of the bed, toes resting against the cool floorboards. She pushed a tangle of pale curls away from her eyes with a fine-boned hand. Yawned. Then grabbed a blue cotton shift from the floor and pulled it over her tan shoulders. She hadn't expected her husband to come—hadn't wanted him to—but there was no mistaking the familiar rumble of that engine. She went out to meet him wearing yesterday's dress and a contrived grin.

"You're back."

Joseph Crater leaned out the open window and drew her in for a kiss. "Drove all night. We beat the Bar Harbor Express by an hour!" He clapped their chauffeur on the back. "We'll have to paint a racing stripe down the side of this old thing."

Stella pulled the car door open and saw two things at once: he'd brought her flowers—white peonies, her favorite—and he wasn't wearing his wedding band. Again. The sight of that naked finger stripped the grin from her face.

Joe climbed out and reached for her with one arm, but she took a small step backward and looked at his pants pocket. The imprint of his ring pressed round against his cotton trousers. The question that sur-faced was not the one she really wanted to ask. "Did you have a pleasant trip?"

He nodded.

"Where did you go?"

Joe's answer was cautious. "Atlantic City. With William Klein."

Her voice was even, almost carefree. "Just the two of you?" Joe hesi-tated long enough for her to rephrase the question. "Were you and Wil-liam alone?"

He glanced at Fred Kahler, stiff behind the wheel, eyes downcast, and responded with a single sharp word. "*Stell.*"

It took a moment to find her breath. All that fresh air and she couldn't pull a stitch of it into her lungs. "Must you be so *flagrant* about it?"

"We'll talk about this later."

Stella heard the warning in his voice, but didn't care. She rose up onto the balls of her feet, the gravel digging into her bare skin, as anger ripped through her voice. "We have *nothing* to talk about!"

His eyes went small and dark.

Stella grabbed the car door and, with a rage that startled them both, slammed it shut, crushing Joe's hand in the frame. She heard the crunch before he screamed, and when he yanked his hand away, two fingers were bloody and mangled.

STELLA waited for Joe on the deck of the Salt House. It was Belgrade Lakes' only fine-dining establishment, and they'd been late, thanks to his difficulty dressing with one hand. She had refused to help him.

Joe hadn't yelled at her after the incident. Hadn't called her names or lifted a hand to strike her. All he said was, "I'll need your help with this mess." Almost polite. Then he soaked his hand in the kitchen sink and waited for her to gather ointment and gauze. She had wrapped the bandage tighter than necessary, angered anew by his cavalier attitude and the way he expected her to accept that a man of his position would have a mistress. As though some skirt on Broadway was the same thing as a membership in the City Club.

By the time they arrived at the restaurant, he'd created a plausible fiction for his injury. "Had a beastly run-in with a Studebaker," Joe explained to their waiter, wiggling his fingers for effect. "Damn thing tried to eat my hand for lunch." And then, shortly after being seated, he excused himself to make a phone call.

Stella ordered their meal from a menu of summer fare: grilled fish, steaks, roasted vegetables, and fruit. A pleasant breeze rolled off the lake, rocking the Chinese lanterns that were strung around the deck. The red-and-yellow globes sent dancing spheres of amber across the linen tablecloths. Only a handful of the tables were occupied, and the diners leaned close over the candles, lost in conversation or in silence as they enjoyed the view. The longer she waited for Joe to return, the more they sent sympathetic glances her way.

The meal arrived with wine and bread, and Stella shifted candles and silverware to make room for the ample dinner. She waited until their server departed with his tray before taking a long drink of merlot. Steam rose from the pan-seared trout with lemon-caper sauce on her plate, and she wondered what sort of mood Joe would be in when he finished his call.

Minutes later, the door banged open on loose hinges, and Stella forced a smile as Joe strode toward the table, shoulders rounded forward like an ox. It was a look Stella knew well. Fury and determination and arrogance.

He yanked his chair away from the table with his good hand. "I'm leaving in the morning."

"Why?"

"I have to go back to the city tomorrow. Straighten a few things out. I'll be back on Thursday, in plenty of time for your birthday."

"But—"

"Don't snivel. It doesn't become you." Joe unfolded the crisp black napkin and spread it over his lap. "You shouldn't have waited. Food's getting cold."

STELLA stayed in bed when Joe pushed back the covers at six the next morning. She stayed there while he bathed—the water turning on with a groan of rusted pipes—and when his toothbrush tapped against the sink. Stella stayed curled around her pillow when he rattled through the dresser and yanked his clothes from the closet. Didn't move when he nudged her shoulder or when he cursed or when he brushed dry lips against her temple—a rote farewell—his freshly shaved chin rubbing against her cheek. Not until she heard his footsteps on the stairs did she open her eyes. And only when the Cadillac roared to life outside did she sit up. Four steps brought her to the window. She wiped his kiss from her temple. "Goodbye."

The last Stella Crater ever saw of her husband was a glimpse of his shirt collar through the rear window as Fred eased the Cadillac down the gravel driveway.

MARIA and Jude lay in a breathless tan-
gle, watching the sky lighten to the color of ash outside their bedroom
window. *Wanton,* he called her, throwing an arm above his head and
dragging air deep into his lungs.

Maria pressed closer. "Our marriage is doomed to fail."

Jude tugged at her earlobe with his teeth and buried his face in her
hair, inhaling the scents of lemon peel and lavender. "Why's that?"

"We are totally incompatible."

"You've been saying that for years."

Maria's father considered Jude profane, and her mother interceded
daily for his inevitable visit to purgatory, but their different religious
beliefs—or his lack thereof—had never been an issue for them. Despite
the fact that she'd chosen an agnostic husband over her parents'
objections.

"When the baby comes, we'll fight."

Jude moved the sheet away, exposing her flat stomach. He circled her
navel with the tip of one finger and then placed his palm on her belly. The
hope in her copper-penny eyes was too much for him. He turned away.

"We never fight."

"But we will. Because I *will* be pregnant. One day."

"When is your appointment?"

"Fourteen days." She breathed the words against his skin.

"And you think this doctor can help?"

"It's a start."

In the distance they could hear the rumble of the El where Park Row
met the Bowery. Jude groaned and pushed the sheet away.

"Don't." Her breath was warm against his neck.

"I have to."

"You should stay."

"Tell that to the sergeant."

Maria curled into him and wrapped her leg around his. His pulse throbbed against her thigh. "I could convince you."

"You could convince the pope to take a mistress."

"Don't say that." Her hands flew over her chest in the sign of the cross. She grabbed her rosary—pale blue beads on a silver chain—from the bedside table and slipped it around her neck. It hung between the swell of her breasts, carnal and reverent.

"It's true. If Pius the Eleventh saw you right now, he'd reconsider his vow of celibacy." Jude sat up, reluctant. "I could lose my job."

"Is that such a bad thing?" She regretted the words as soon as they were out. A shadow crossed his face, and Maria crawled toward him. She slid her hand along his thigh and offered a coy smile. "Consider the alternative," she whispered.

Jude laughed and dropped back to his elbows. "You're wicked."

"Stay there."

Maria leaned over the bed and reached for something underneath. The heavy silver cross around her neck clanked against the floor as she stretched farther, balanced precariously on her hips. She could feel the heat of his gaze on her spine, could almost sense its caress in the small of her back. Finally, she felt the square edge of the box she'd stashed the night before.

"For you, *Detective*." She handed him the small brown package.

Jude took the gift and peered at the hastily tied string. "Is that my shoelace?"

"We were out of ribbon."

"What's the occasion?"

"I wanted to give it to you back in March, when you got the promotion." She smiled, embarrassed. "It took a while to save up."

Too excited to wait for her husband, Maria ripped off the paper and held up a cigarette lighter.

He took it and flipped the lid. A bright orange flame leapt up.

She pointed to the side. "Your initials."

The letters J.S. were engraved across the metal in script and filled with black patina. Jude ran a thumb across them.

"Do you like it?"

Jude cupped the lighter in the palm of his hand. It was warm against his skin. "I love it."

"Then what's wrong?" She tapped the sudden crease between his eyebrows.

"You shouldn't have to work two jobs. It's not right."

She pulled away to better see his face. "You know Smithson won't hire a woman tailor full-time—too big of a hit to his pride. So I'll keep the housework for now. Besides, we need the money. Rent just went up."

"Not *again*?"

"The notice came in the mail yesterday."

Jude sat up and stretched. He looked like a kitten, tongue curled and back arched. She laughed.

"Not so fast." Maria caught him off balance and tipped him back onto the mattress. She pinned him down with her hands and knees and kissed him with the deep warmth known only to seasoned lovers. He didn't resist.

MARIA slipped through the entrance of 40 Fifth Avenue and paused to catch her breath. She twisted her watch around her thin wrist and noted the time. Eight-thirty. She winced and rushed toward the elevator. Her lust and Jude's shoelaces had made them both late for work, but she could always blame the incessant construction-induced traffic along Fifth Avenue. There were over seven hundred buildings under construction in Manhattan that year, turning her well-laid route into a maze of cracked concrete and cordoned-off streets. It seemed every building, cellar, subway, and foundation was undergoing some sort of alteration to make room for the relentless swell of people. The air was a broken symphony of shovels, rock drills, jack-hammers, and cranes pecking, breaking, and thundering New York City into the twentieth century.

Maria wiped a bead of sweat from her upper lip and leaned against the cool wall of the elevator as it rose to the fifth floor. Her uniform, a black rayon dress with lace collar and cuffs, stuck against her back with the humidity and chafed her skin. She fished for the keys to apartment 508 inside her purse, thankful that the owners were on vacation in Maine and wouldn't know she was late.

She let herself into the apartment and eased the door shut. Four times the size of the efficiency she shared with Jude, the Craters' home spread before her, wood floors and cream-colored walls dotted with oil paintings in gilded frames. The living room was anchored by a stone fireplace with a stained mantel and a painting that cost more than she made in six months. Mrs. Crater had beamed the day they won the Monet at auction, confiding that it would be worth a small fortune in a few years—not that they hadn't parted with a decent sum, mind you, but it was a luxury now that Mr. Crater had his seat on the bench. She had shown Maria the signature in the bottom right-hand corner, insisted she trace it with her fingertip to *feel* his name on the painting. They both knew it was the closest Maria would ever come to a Monet.

The rest of the apartment was compact. A small kitchen and dining room were off to the side, an empty pewter fruit bowl and place settings for six on the table. Vacant elegance. Maria stood in the entry and inhaled the smells of oiled furniture and floor wax. The heavy must of velvet drapes. One day she hoped to have a home as lovely. Jude's promotion brought them a step closer, but the reality was that even if he made sergeant in a few years, they would never be able to afford something like this. She pushed aside a swell of envy and got to work.

The Craters kept the cleaning supplies beneath the cabinet in the guest bathroom, and she was about to collect them when she heard the Victrola playing softly in the master bedroom. Mr. Crater often left it on—a habit that irritated Mrs. Crater to no end—and must have forgotten to turn it off when he left for Maine on Friday evening.

Maria pushed open the dark wood door that led from the living room into the master bedroom. It was furnished, as was the rest of the apartment, thoughtfully and expensively. Sturdy walnut furniture. Red-and-cream bedclothes. Curtains puddled on the floor.

But stretched across the bed was a naked woman, twenty years younger than Mrs. Crater and a great deal more buxom. She and Maria stared at each other for one horrified second. The woman screamed and hurried to cover herself as Joseph Crater emerged from the bathroom, dripping wet, a towel around his waist. Maria gasped an apology and shut the door. She stood, paralyzed, listening to the tumult in the other room.

"The maid," Crater said.

A whisper. "What is she doing here?"

"Cleaning, obviously." He tripped over something. Cursed. "I forgot to tell her not to come."

"You *forgot*?"

"Stay here."

Maria looked at the front door, wondering if she could grab her purse and leave before he came out. Mr. Crater charged from the bedroom, holding on to his towel with one hand. Barrel chest. Pasty skin. And behind him, the woman, pushed up against the headboard with the bedspread yanked up to her chin. The look on her face was desperate and ashamed. Pleading. Maria shifted her gaze to the floor. She backed up as Mr. Crater strode toward her.

"I'm so sorry. I thought you were in Maine. That's what you said Friday, that you'd be gone." The words tumbled out, and she was afraid to meet his furious gaze.

"Get out!" He pointed at the front door.

Gladly. She stumbled backward, eyes still on the floor.

"Don't come back until Thursday when I'm gone, you understand?"

"Yes."

"One word of this to my wife and you're fired."

"Of course."

Mr. Crater leaned in, his voice hoarse with anger. "You know what I did for your husband. I will take it all away if you don't keep your stupid mouth shut."

Maria couldn't look at him for fear the hatred would be evident on her face, but she gave a quick nod and blinked hard.

"It's not her fault. She was just doing her job." His mistress now stood in the doorway, hair mussed, eyes large, and ample curves hidden by the bedclothes. Maria startled at the protective note in her voice.

Mr. Crater shifted his gaze between the two. "Stay out of this."

Maria grabbed her purse from the side table.

"You won't say anything? Please?" she said in a stage whisper, and took a step toward Maria. *Don't start trouble with him,* the look said. *Please go.*

Mr. Crater had hired Maria three years earlier as a gift to his wife. She cleaned their home and cooked their meals and ran their errands. Mr. Crater signed her paychecks and gave her a small Christmas bonus every year. He had once pinched her bottom when his wife wasn't home. Maria felt no loyalty to him and didn't care to guard his secrets. But there was a depth of sadness in the girl's hazel eyes that she could not turn from. An unspoken agreement passed between them.

"I have nothing to tell," she said, and left the apartment, locking the door behind her.

FIFTH AVENUE, SATURDAY, FEBRUARY 15, 1930

"Thank you, Mr. Crater!"

"For?"

"Putting a good word in for Jude with Commissioner Mulrooney. He's got an interview with the detective bureau next week."

He glanced up from his paper, impassive.

Maria twisted the cleaning rag in her hands and shot an uncertain look at Mrs. Crater. "If he gets the promotion, he'll finally get off the vice squad. We want to start a family, and that's a hard job for a father to have."

"I do wonder," Mr. Crater said, rising from the table with a sneer, "how the daughter of Spanish immigrants managed to snag one of New York's finest. It's an odd match, don't you think?" He folded the newspaper in half, tossed it on the table, and retreated to the bedroom to dress for work.

Maria busied herself with his dirty breakfast dishes so Stella wouldn't see the shame spread across her cheeks.

"Ignore him," Mrs. Crater said. "He's all piss and vinegar because his own promotion looks a bit tentative right now."

"He's right." Maria swallowed. "I married above myself."

Mrs. Crater placed a cool hand on the back of Maria's neck. She patted. "Your husband is obviously a wise man. Look at you, lovely thing!"

"I'm a maid."

"*You*," she said, "are smart enough to know that a woman is only as good as her husband. The better off he is, the better off you are. Many women don't understand that."

Maria turned and peered at her. "You convinced Mr. Crater, didn't you?"

"He's never been good at telling me no." Her eyes crinkled at the corners. "I'll listen to the back channel and see how things go for Jude. How's that?"

"Back channel?"

"The political wives, dear. Chances are, I'll know something before Joe."

Maria smiled, bright and grateful. "Remind me never to get on your bad side."

"We're in this together. Where would women be if we didn't look out for one another?" She returned to the living room, where her novel waited, cracked open at the spine.

"Mrs. Crater?"

"Yes?"

"Jude would be furious if he ever found out I did this. He wants to succeed on his own merit. Not on favors. Certainly not those begged by his wife."

Mrs. Crater spread her skirt across the couch with a flourish. "Well, that's silly. Everything in this city is based on favors. In one way or another."

MARIA opened the door to Smithson Tailors and reached up to steady the bell. To her left, she could see the city's newest structure, a monolith dubbed the Empire State Building, dwarf the skyline. The papers said it would be a mind-boggling 102 stories when finished. Construction began less than six months ago, and already the building was fifty-five stories high. Over three thousand workers were employed full-time. Maria could not imagine anyone wanting to be that high above the ground.

Donald Smithson glanced up in his office. Tapped his watch. "Your appointment will be here in five minutes," he said.

Maria nodded and wove her way through the bolts of fabric in the showroom, gray wool and brown tweed, pinstriped cotton and, most popular during the brick-oven summer months, linen.

She took her sewing bag to a small alcove set into the front window. When she'd inherited the job from her father, she had no intention of becoming the store display. It happened by accident. With square footage in high demand on Fifth Avenue, Smithson could not expand as he'd wished, at least not without securing a second mortgage. So he set his new tailor in the window behind a small desk until space could be made for her in the back with the others. But he soon found an increase in foot traffic as people stopped to watch her nimble fingers work a needle with rapier accuracy. Once settled into her space, she became a living advertisement for the quality offered by Smithson Tailors.

Maria's real genius, however—and the reason she'd secured a position in the all-male establishment—was her dual talents as both cutter and stitcher, a rare combination on Savile Row, much less in New York City. Though she could never explain it, Maria could *feel* the fabric. Not only the texture and the thread count beneath the pads of her fingers, but the proclivity of the material itself, whether it wanted to bunch or snag, whether it would hang well on a particular frame. A natural intuition allowed her to make adjustments in a pattern for a client with a pronounced stoop, a paunch, a barrel chest, a limp, or some other physical quirk that wasn't taken into account by standard measurements. The warp and weft of fabric softened beneath her touch, like strings for a cellist. Her chalk lines were light and fluid, almost a language of her own, a dot here for buttonholes, a line there for slanted pockets, a streak to allow for extra material that would form the inlay. Nuanced as her cutting skills were, it was in her stitching that Smithson made his real profit. She produced no less than five thousand stitches per suit—she counted—every one equal in size. A straighter hem or tighter seam could not be found in Manhattan. Smithson knew this, of course, and monopolized her abilities for himself. Yet he would not give her the dignity of a full-time position—and therefore the salary that would accompany it—or a referral that would send her to a competitor.

Donald Smithson stuck his head out from his office. "This client is priority, Maria. I expect you to behave accordingly."

Maria forced herself to respond with a smile. "Of course." *Priority*, she knew, meant wealthy beyond the normal standards of their clientele. It meant a man willing to buy five or more suits at one time. It meant a level of flattery by Smithson that would nauseate any human with a shred of dignity.

"I suggested he use one of our more *experienced* tailors, but he insisted on you. Requested you by name, as a matter of fact."

Smithson pulled a tin of Altoids from his pocket. He placed one mint on the tip of his tongue and drew it in with a grimace, straightened his tie, then said, "Get the fitting room ready. And unlock the humidor. Top shelf."

Maria grabbed her sewing bag and inspected the contents: measuring tape, pins, cushion, chalk, pinking shears, scissors, and needles in three different sizes. Then she made her way across the showroom and through a side door. What expense her employer spared in her work area he made up for in here. Heavy green carpet covered the floor and the dark paneled walls were adorned every eight feet with a mannequin dressed in the latest menswear. Between each mannequin was a mirror almost seven feet tall, self-admiration available from all angles. In the middle of the room, a round mahogany platform was positioned directly beneath the chandelier. Two leather chairs rested off to the side, an end table between them. Tiffany lamps in masculine shades of blue, yellow, and green and a gold ashtray completed the opulent decor. Along the back wall sat the built-in humidor. Maria unlocked the doors and swung them open, revealing a generous display of cigars behind a glass case. Her fingers trembled slightly, nerves still on edge from finding *that* woman in Mr. Crater's bed. She closed her hands into fists and took a deep breath before she slid the glass open and pulled out the top shelf. The Cubans—Romeo y Julieta being Smithson's preferred brand. He paid extra for the personalized silver band embossed with the company logo, but he never smoked them himself. She made sure they were straight and that the cigar clipper was clean and polished.

Panatelas, she called them, the saboteurs of fabric. "Can't get the smell out of wool," Maria had complained to Jude more times than she could count. "Ruins a suit every time."

She unloaded her sewing bag and set the contents on the edge of the platform. Even in this she was orderly. Pins placed in a perfect swirl around the red cushion. Tape folded in eighths. Scissors laid out neatly. As she finished, the door swished open behind her. She took a quick breath and turned to see the wide eyes and cleft chin of her client.

"Maria, this is Owney Madden. Owney, Maria Simon."

He swaggered the five steps between them, grabbed her hand, and rattled out his greeting in an almost incomprehensible Liverpool accent. "Your reputation precedes you."

Coming from one of the city's most notorious gangsters, the comment could easily be applied to him as well. "Mr. Madden." A quick nod and Maria lowered her eyes.

"Have we met before?" His studied her face. "You look familiar."

"No. I don't see how that's possible."

"It must be the name, then. I hear you're the best tailor in the city."
He paused. "Seamstress? What exactly are you?"

Maria caught the waver in her voice and forced it back. "*Costurera.*
There is no English equivalent. *Tailor* will do just fine."

"Are you as good as they say?"

She answered the question as honestly as she could without sounding
arrogant. "Yes."

Owney looked at Smithson. "I like her."

A bored smile. "Her talents are unrivaled."

Heat crept up Maria's face as Owney's eyes traveled down her body
and paused at her breasts. "I'm sure they are."

Smithson leaned forward eagerly, clipboard in hand. "How can we
serve you today, Mr. Madden?"

The Liverpool accent, derogatorily referred to as Scouse by most,
sounded to Maria's untrained ears like the bastard child of Ireland and
England, and though she'd often heard it mocked, Owney was the first
person she'd ever met who had one. She tipped her head to the side,
intrigued and slightly unnerved. Given his reputation, the accent only
made him appear that much more sinister.

"I need a new fall and winter wardrobe. The latest styles. Top-notch,
hear?"

"Of course." Smithson practically trembled with joy. "Why don't we
look at our newest trends? Maria, go get the fabric. Bring the hand-
finished wool. Chocolate and charcoal. The merino wool." He paused to
think. "In navy and black. The gray tweed. And the vicuña."

Maria parted her lips to speak but then pressed them together again.
She nodded and walked toward the door.

"What were you going to say?" Owney asked.

"Nothing."

"Yes, you were. Go ahead."

Maria avoided Smithson's gaze and debated for a moment before she
said, "The vicuña doesn't hang well. Especially in winter. And I doubt
it would suit a man such as yourself." She cleared her throat. "It's a bit
effeminate."

Owney looked from Smithson to Maria and grinned. "What would
you recommend?"

"A classic English wool would drape better across your shoulders."

The suit he had on looked worse for the wear, wrinkled and stretched. Typical of cotton. Certainly not up to her standards of craftsmanship.

Smithson stepped forward with a little cough. "She does know her fabrics." A sharp glance in her direction. "Fetch them. Would you?"

"Yes, sir."

"But leave the vicuña."

Maria nodded and left the fitting room. Vicuñas, like llamas, had long woolen strands that were wonderful for weaving but terrible for holding shape. Smithson knew this but did not care. The fabric was rare, so he could charge three times as much as for standard sheep's wool. She'd worked with it on a number of occasions and resented its defiance. It fought against her as she sewed, bunching beneath the thread. It took a great deal of tension on the stitch and patience on her part to make vicuña cooperate.

Glad for the chance to escape, Maria went to the showroom, running her fingers over the bolts as she searched. She collected all the samples that Smithson requested, in various colors, and also grabbed three shades of satin for the lining to save herself a trip later. He would ask for it. She was certain of that.

She slid back into the fitting room, holding the door open with one foot, while they discussed the latest fashion in men's suits. Owney held a newly lit cigar between thumb and forefinger, puffing out small bursts of smoke.

"There she is," Smithson said. "Let's get your measurements."

She set the fabric bolts on one of the leather chairs and stepped up behind Owney on the platform. "Jacket, please." He shrugged out of it and she laid it aside. "Stand still if you can. The more accurate your measurements, the better the fit."

"I heard you go more on sight and feel than numbers."

His words came so quickly that she had to sort through each syllable after the fact, disentangling them from one another. "The numbers never lie, Mr. Madden."

"Well, feel free to look and touch all you like regardless."

Maria turned her face away to hide the furious blush that swept across her cheeks. She tapped his elbows quickly. "Arms up."

As Owney raised his arms above his head, she wrapped the tape around his chest. Smithson recorded the measurements on the order form as Maria called them out. "Chest, forty-three inches." She stretched the tape between her fingers and stood back. Owney was well muscled but not lean. "Make that forty-four. He'll want the extra room for movement. He's broad through the torso."

"Was that a compliment? Or a complaint?"

Maria placed her first and second fingers on the protruding bone at the top of his spine and did her best to ignore the innuendo. "Chin down, please—your sleeves are next." She set one end of the tape against the bone and ran the rest over his shoulder, down his arm, and all the way to his wrist, then added another inch for the shirt cuff. "Sleeve, thirty-three inches."

Owney raised his arms again as Maria stepped in front and brought the tape around his waist. He tried to catch her glance, but she did not look at him. "Waist, thirty-six."

There were few things more awkward in her experience than measuring a man's inseam. The near groping aside, her position—kneeling at crotch level—was compromising. It was a rare client who did not squirm beneath her touch or make an off-color remark. Owney did neither. He stood, hands on his hips, searching her face with a curious expression.

"How did you end up here? Aren't most of your kind sewing scraps down in the garment district?"

Her embarrassment was replaced with a sudden anger, and Maria clenched her jaw to suppress a sharp retort. As though there were much difference between his kind or hers: limey or grasa. They'd all crossed the Atlantic the same way, penniless and desperate. At least she'd been born on this continent. Owney clearly had not. He couldn't have acquired a dialect like that anywhere but the docks in Merseyside. Maria sniffed, unwilling to dignify him with a response.

"She replaced her father when he went blind," Smithson explained when the silence stretched on longer than was comfortable. "An unconventional arrangement, to be sure, but there is no doubting her abilities."

Maria sat back on her heels and looked up at Owney Madden. "Inseam, thirty-four."

"Sure you measured that right?"

She didn't blink. "I was generous."

"Maria!" Donald Smithson stepped forward.

Owney laughed, a deep sort of thing that left no doubt as to his humor.

"It's my fault. I provoked her. Just wanted to see if she'd bite back." He grinned. "Nice sharp teeth on that one." He stepped off the platform and grabbed his jacket from the chair. "Now, why don't we talk style?"

"I think what you want"—Smithson walked Owney to the nearest mannequin—"is the drape cut. Or the London drape, as they call it on Savile Row. It has a softer silhouette. Extra fabric in the shoulders for movement, and a narrowed waist. We have found this style to greatly enhance a man's figure."

Maria laid out the fabric bolts on the platform and stepped aside, waiting.

"What do you think?" Owney asked, looking over his shoulder at her. "You're the expert. Or so I've been told."

"And what friend referred our services, Mr. Madden? I'd like the opportunity to write and thank him." Smithson made a note on the corner of his clipboard.

"Simon Rifkind, an attorney downtown." He prodded Maria again, undeterred by Smithson. "Go on."

Simon Rifkind. The toothy, obnoxious associate of Mr. Crater's. It made sense that the three of them would run together. Maria kept her voice steady, nonchalant. "I think the London drape looks pompous. I prefer a simple double-breasted suit with a waistcoat and a strong, bold tie in an accentuating color. A matching fabric square in the breast pocket for evenings. Classic. Nothing showy."

Smithson forced a laugh. "Leave it to a woman to try and get out of hard labor. The London drape requires more craftsmanship than the double-breasted. Why don't we look at those fabrics?" He cupped Maria's elbow in his palm and bent closer. "What's wrong with you?"

"He asked my opinion."

"Your *opinion* is irrelevant." Smithson released her and stepped away. "Thank you for your help, Mrs. Simon. I will take it from here. I put some piecework at your station."

She placed her sewing materials back in her bag and gave Owney a courteous nod. "Mr. Madden."

"A *pleasure* to meet you."

Again, she thought as she turned away. Maria had the distinct impression that he watched her backside as she left the room. In the last few hours, Maria had found Joseph Crater in bed with a woman half his age and herself measuring the inseam of one of New York City's most reviled gangsters. She was overcome with a sudden need to wash her hands. After a quick trip to the restroom, she returned to her work area and dropped into her seat. She set her face in her hands. *What have I gotten myself into?*

RITZI and Crater sat at a small table in a corner of Club Abbey and listened to the jazz quartet. She slipped one shoe off under the table and rubbed a blister on the side of her big toe. Rehearsal ran long that afternoon and her feet ached, but she hid it with a smile. Crater couldn't stop looking at her. Couldn't stop touching her.

"Where is she?" Ritzi asked, looking at his wedding ring. "This wife of yours?"

"In Maine, at our lake house. She spends summers there."

She brought her bare foot up the front of Crater's leg. "That must be nice. A vacation home. You should take me there sometime."

He caught her gaze, still on the ring, and spun it around his finger. "I can take it off if it bothers you."

"Doesn't make a difference, I suppose."

He slid the ring off and put it in his pocket.

The room smelled of pipe smoke and wood polish and anise. Area rugs and lamps with red shades were scattered around the bar. Warm. Seductive. Flickering candles cast halos of soft light across the center of each table. Young couples lounged close together, arms draped over shoulders and hands resting on thighs. The nuzzle of a neck. A brazen kiss. On the other side of the room, Owney Madden sat in his corner booth. He nodded at Ritzi and continued to study Crater. She shifted a little closer to the judge.

The bartender arrived at their table, a fresh-faced young man with red hair and a wrinkled apron. He still looked to be in his teens. "What'll you have?"

"Bring her an absinthe," Crater said. "And one for me as well."

Although Joseph Crater always imbibed in the evening—straight whiskey on the rocks being his drink of choice—this was the first time he ordered absinthe. Perhaps he was feeling a bit cosmopolitan, or maybe just giving in to the trend. It arrived several minutes later on an elaborate silver tray with two reservoir glasses, slotted silver spoons, a bowl of sugar cubes, and a carafe of ice water. The bartender set the paraphernalia on the table and was about to slip away when Crater asked, "What's your name, kid?"

"Stan."

Crater tucked a dollar bill into his hand and said, "Keep them coming."

"Sure thing, mister." He stuffed the money in his pocket and went back to the bar.

"I don't want to drink tonight," Ritzi said.

Crater dismissed her with a glance. "I don't care."

Fine, then. Ritzi lifted her glass and would have taken a swig had Crater not grabbed her wrist.

"Easy. You'll be on the floor in two minutes if you take it like that." He took the glass from her and held it up to the candle. "Let me educate you."

"By *educate,* you mean corrupt."

"Semantics."

Crater lifted a sugar cube from the bowl and set it on the slotted spoon. He rested the spoon on the glass of absinthe and poured a small amount of ice water over the top. "Look," he said. The liquor was the color of green apples, and the sugar created a small white cloud as it dripped into the glass. He stirred the absinthe with the spoon and then handed it to her to taste.

Ritzi wrapped her lips around the spoon. It tasted of licorice. Her tongue curled away from the bitter alcohol. "How can you drink that?" She coughed.

"I just wanted you to try it." Joe laughed, seemingly delighted by her naïveté. He poured more ice water into the glass, filling it two-thirds full. "You don't drink it straight." He handed it to her again.

She sipped. "Better." Ritzi took another, and then another. The sugar replaced the bitterness with a sweet tang, and the absinthe slid down her throat in a cool rush. Her head felt a bit light before the glass was half empty.

According to the Eighteenth Amendment, this was illegal. And therefore highly desirable. For a decade, Owney Madden had taken advantage of the Volstead Act and added bootlegger to his list of lucrative careers. Prohibition was good for business, and those with enough clout to get through the doors could quench a variety of thirsts at Club Abbey.

By the time William Klein joined them at the table, Ritzi was nursing her second absinthe. *Pompous prick,* she thought, knocking back her glass to avoid his lewd gaze.

Crater ran a finger under Ritzi's chin and tipped her face upward. "Why don't you go powder your nose?"

"But—"

"Now." He squeezed her chin between thumb and forefinger, pinching just enough to make her eyes sting.

Ritzi grabbed her purse, smoothed the anger from her face, and carefully wound her way through the dance floor, ignoring the appreciative glances that followed her.

The ladies' room in Club Abbey had dark paneled wood and low lighting. Ritzi looked at her reflection in the mirror. It always seemed distorted in there. Like she was a cheap imitation of herself.

Ritzi took her time primping. She adjusted the neckline of her black satin gown away from the deep plunge of cleavage, painted her lips red, and pinned a stray curl behind her ear. Looped the pearls around her neck three times instead of twice so the eye would be drawn to her clavicles rather than her breasts—no small task. Rearranged stockings and garters. Emptied the trash from her purse: ticket stubs, broken cigarettes, and a matchbook with the Club Abbey logo. Then she settled into one of two purple velvet chairs and drew a pack of Pall Malls from her purse. Only two smokes left. Ritzi drew one out and set it in a mother-of-pearl holder. *Eveningwear,* Vivian had said. *Make sure you don't use the silver one after six.* So many damned rules to this gig. She struck a match and cupped her palm around the flame, watching the paper curl and burn black.

God, Mama would die if she saw me smoke. She smiled. Her mother had always said it was a filthy habit, something tramps did in the big city. *Poor Mama. She don't know a thing about the big city. Or tramps, for that matter.*

Waiting was an art Ritzi had mastered in the last three years. Men needed time to talk shop. Return to the table too soon and she'd be dismissed again. Too late and they'd get suspicious. Fifteen minutes was her general rule, long enough for their conversation to turn elsewhere. So she rested her head back on the chair and let her mind wander to her childhood and the farm and days when she could smell the barn from her open bedroom window. She recalled the brown eyes of a dairy cow. Long lashes and a knowing gaze. Udders full and dripping in the predawn chill of morning. One of countless mornings that Ritzi was sent out to milk and feed and gather eggs, her fingers numb and red from cold. The rough patches on her hands. It had taken her months to pumice away the calluses. She was careful that first year in Manhattan how she shook hands. A delicate greeting, all fingertips and none of the crushing grip Daddy had taught her to give. Three years in this place and she still had the pad of muscle between thumb and forefinger earned from years in the milking stall. She'd grown her fingernails long and kept them painted, but they were still farmer hands. Strong hands. Not pretty and slender like the rest of the girls' in the chorus line. But she made up for that lack with a multitude of other things. And Crater didn't complain at night when she kneaded his shoulders and back and thighs with her farm-girl hands.

Legs crossed and eyes closed, Ritzi finished the cigarette and prepared herself for what would surely be a wretched evening. A few more minutes and she stubbed out her cigarette in the sink and washed the ashes down the drain.

Time to get back out there.

Ritzi caught fragments of their hushed conversation as she approached the table. "Do you know how close Seabury is to figuring this thing out . . . And that damn reporter George Hall . . . Could kill whoever tipped him off . . . Have to leave town for a while." Crater went silent when he caught sight of Ritzi.

Crater shoved another glass of absinthe into her hand as soon as she sat down. Ritzi already felt dizzy and nauseated, and what she really wanted was a steak and hot rolls with butter and then a piece of chocolate cake as big as her fist. Real food. Something she rarely got the chance to consume.

Ritzi wrapped her hands around the absinthe to stop them from trembling. She winked at Crater. "Look at Billy licking that glass."

"Never heard him called that before."

"I nickname all you boys. Isn't that right, Billy?" Ritzi had caught the *ain't* on its way out of her mouth and swallowed it with a sip. She set her glass on the table. Grimaced. Wiped her palms on her lap and then laced her fingers together.

Klein slid a littler closer and patted her thigh. "You can call me whatever you want, baby doll. But for the record, it's not the glass I want to lick."

"What do you call me?" Joseph Crater asked.

Uncircumcised donkey pizzle. Ritzi grinned, lopsided and charming. "Your *Honor.*"

Crater waved for the bartender. "Put this on my tab," he said when Stan arrived.

Stan shot a glance at the corner booth. "Did Owney clear you for that?"

"Do I look stupid enough to try a stunt like that if he hadn't?"

Stan smiled apologetically. "Just checking."

Ritzi followed Crater and Klein out the front door and up the steps onto the sidewalk. They stood in the waxy light and searched the street for a cab.

Crater tipped his hat to Klein. "Probably won't see you until session starts. Headed back to Maine first thing in the morning."

"And tonight?" He spoke to Crater but looked at Ritzi.

"We're off to see *Dancing Partner.*"

"Again? It wasn't that great the first time."

"That was Atlantic City. Thought I'd see if they worked out the kinks for the Broadway run. Besides, it wasn't *that* bad."

Depends on who you ask, Ritzi thought.

Crater stepped into the street to hail a passing cab. The whistle was shrill, and heads turned up and down the block.

Klein pulled Ritzi in for a hug as Crater's back was turned. "Why don't you come over to my place when Joe's done with you?" He ran a finger down her spine, and slipped it inside her open-backed dress, seeking territory farther down.

"You're not my type."

"Word on the street is that you have a price tag, not a type."

She stepped away, repulsed. "Apparently, you spend too much time on the street."

"With the right connections, you could lead on Broadway. A girl like you is too pretty to stay in the chorus line." Klein shifted away as Crater came back to fetch Ritzi. "Keep that in mind."

HEAT still radiated from the pavement in waves, even though the sun had set almost two hours earlier. The temperature neared one hundred degrees that day, and with nary a breeze, fire hydrants were loosed, turning streets into shower baths. Fountains were commandeered citywide as adults and children alike rolled up their pants and splashed with mass indignity.

"To the Belasco Theater," Crater told the cabdriver. He slid into the backseat next to Ritzi, their thighs touching.

The cab eased away from the curb and melted into traffic, keeping in the right lane. Several minutes later, it rolled to a stop in front of the Belasco. A black Cadillac pulled up beside them and emptied its passengers onto the sidewalk. Ritzi watched the pale disks of two straw Panama hats disappear into the theater. People rushed by on the sidewalk, all of them dressed for a night on the town.

"Wait here," Crater told her.

Ritzi watched him jog up to the ticket booth. He leaned in, exchanged a few words with the teller, and took an envelope. Crater glanced back at Ritzi and frowned. Then he searched his wallet, slid a bill across the counter, and waited. Light from the marquee across the street bounced off the ticket window, reflecting STRIKE UP THE BAND backward. Somewhere behind the glass the teller must have refused Joe's offer, because he took the money and stuffed it back in his wallet. Crater returned to the cab.

"What was that about?"

"I only had one ticket at will-call." He lifted the envelope. "But they're sold out and I couldn't get another. Bribery aside."

"You could stay. I'm tired. I can take the cab home."

"No." Crater tapped the ticket against his bandaged hand, then reached over the seat. "Change of plans, cabbie. Take us to Coney Island."

"Why don't we go back to your place? Get some sleep?"

"Not after what happened Monday." Crater shook his head. "We don't sleep at my place again."

The air inside the cab was warm and still, and Ritzi mumbled her displeasure at the change of plans. As they swung into traffic, a car behind them washed the cab in its headlights, and Ritzi squinted at the glare that bounced back from the rearview mirror. Her eyelids resisted efforts to open again. She was asleep before they reached Brooklyn.

She woke to the smells of salt air and fried food. They parked near the Boardwalk, in front of Nathan's Famous. She stretched and yawned as Crater helped her from the cab. Her sleep-addled brain skipped from one sound to another while he paid the fare.

"A nickel, a nickel, half a dime! Come get your frankfurters—red hot, red hot!" The vendor stood on the Boardwalk outside Nathan's, wearing a grease-stained apron and waving a hot dog in the air.

"Shoot the chutes for a dime!"

"Boiled peanuts. Get 'em while they're hot!"

The calls bounced and tumbled around her. She blinked into the chaos. Though it was ten o'clock, the party at Coney Island showed no signs of slowing down. Crater took her elbow and escorted her along the Boardwalk. Luna Park loomed before them, flashing lights and spinning wheels, a cacophony. Behind the gates rose the Cyclone. The roller coaster chinked and rattled up the wooden frame, and they stood, eyes locked on the cars as they hovered in a moment of suspended gravity. Then they thundered down at a stomach-lurching angle to the delighted shrieks of their passengers. Ritzi could feel the rumble in her feet.

A barker, somewhere deep in the park, shouted into a microphone, "Never take your wife on the roller coaster. It's every man for himself!"

Ritzi lifted the hem of her dress and looked at her three-inch heels. Surely he didn't expect her to ride the roller coaster dressed like this?

"Maybe tomorrow," Crater whispered, pulling her close. "We're over there." He pointed to a hotel, right across the street from Luna Park. Five stories tall, it reflected the garish lights of the amusement park in its many windows. She was too tired to read the name. He took her hand and wove through traffic on Surf Avenue. As they neared the hotel, she felt exposed and vulnerable, as though standing beneath a spotlight. *You could end this right here.* But she had long since passed the point of no return. Sally Lou Ritz let Crater lead her toward the revolving glass door.

The lobby was empty, and she stood off to the side as he secured a room. They crossed the tile floor and slid inside the elevator. His lips were on her neck before the doors were closed. She shut her eyes, willed herself to relax. To respond.

Several long seconds later, the doors opened to reveal the burgundy-carpeted fifth-floor hallway. Their room was at the end, facing the Boardwalk. He took the key from his pocket and slid it into the lock.

Six windows spread across the wall in front of them, looking down at the spinning display of Luna Park. He pushed back the curtains, and lights from the Ferris wheel danced red, blue, and green on the ceiling. The rumble of the roller coaster vibrated the walls. Ritzi stood next to the window, fingertips resting against the glass. She could feel Crater's breath on her neck.

For once she allowed herself to wonder what it would be like to walk into this hotel as his wife instead of his mistress. But the thought tumbled down as soon as she'd constructed it. The truth was, she didn't even want to be here as the other woman, much less the only woman. She didn't want to be here at all.

Crater touched the base of her neck with one finger, tugging at a curl, and then ran it down her spine, to the deepest plunge of her dress. She fought the shiver that swept over her skin.

The question popped out before it had fully registered in her mind, and she would have taken it back had it not hung in the air between them. "Do you love her?"

His finger drifted to a stop. "Who?"

Ritzi struggled to collect the words, to say them aloud. "Your wife."

A long silence, and then, "What's it matter to you?" The tip of that one finger rested at the base of her spine, like a red-hot poker.

Crater never discussed Stella except in passing and never in a personal way. As though she were a notch, an accomplishment. An irritant.

She took a deep breath and spun to face him. His eyes were pinched. "I'd like to think that you love her." She shrugged. *I'd like to think that you're sorry about this.*

Crater looked out the window behind her. "She's a good wife."

Ritzi could hear the edge in his voice. She reached up and loosened his tie. Her voice was a hum, deep and sultry. "Does she know?"

He lifted his bandaged hand. Turned it as though waving in a parade. A what-the-hell-do-you-think motion.

A perverse sort of pride erupted inside Ritzi. *Good for her.* She kissed the tips of his fingers to hide the smile that threatened to spread across her face.

"I'm going back to Maine first thing in the morning," Crater said, tugging at the straps of her dress. It dropped to the floor in a puddle of inky satin. "I don't want to talk about my wife."

RITZI lay on her side, the sheet bunched beneath her chin. Crater was sprawled next to her, the rise and fall of his breath rhythmic. One arm thrown over his head and the other resting against the soft skin of her back. He twitched in his sleep, limbs responding to some dream. *Just like a dog.* Ritzi lay there until she was certain he'd dipped into heavy slumber. Then she slid away from his reach and out of bed. She gathered her things and tiptoed into the bathroom. She stood, garter and hose dangling from her fingers, and willed herself not to be sick.

God, I hate that man.

Time to leave. She did not want to be there when he woke up. Ritzi pulled on her lingerie and slipped the dress over her head. She reached for her shoes but startled when someone banged on the hotel room door. A heavy fist pounded, one, two, three times. She sucked in a sharp breath and listened.

Another knock. Louder. More insistent.

She instinctively flipped off the bathroom light and tugged the door shut with a soft click.

Somewhere on the Boardwalk below, a big band trumpeted show tunes. She could feel the music vibrate through the floor and into her bare feet.

Her mama always said that God gave women a way to know when something wasn't right. A sense. An intuition. It rushed in on her then, a whoosh right up the spine. She spun around the small bathroom looking for a place to hide. There was no linen closet, only a cast-iron tub, a toilet, and a small cabinet beneath the sink, hardly large enough for a child, much less a buxom woman on the edge of panic.

Out in the bedroom, Crater mumbled something in response to the knocking, but he didn't get up. He was too far beneath the weight of sleep. Ritzi stuffed her purse and shoes into the cabinet even as she heard a shudder followed by splintering wood.

Someone kicked the door open. Crater, now awake, was groggy. "What? What is it?" She imagined him blinking into the darkness of their room, eyes slowly focusing on the silhouette in the doorway.

Ritzi ran a hand along the base of the cabinet and felt nothing but toilet tissue. Whatever sense of foolishness might have caused her to hesitate, to reconsider, was abandoned when she heard the scuffle on the other side of the door. The thud of fists on flesh and the low groan that followed. Then an order: "Close the door." More voices. And footsteps inside the room.

Sally Lou Ritz dropped to the floor and maneuvered into the cabinet, tucking the hem of her dress around her ankles. She had to press her chin against her collarbone and pull her knees into her stomach. She wriggled and squirmed, drawing all her limbs into the cabinet, praying that she couldn't be heard outside the bathroom.

On the other side of the door, Crater let out a bovine grunt. "Son of a—"

"Court's in session, Judge. My court." The voice was low, controlled. "And you don't speak unless called upon."

The sound of Crater being dragged out of bed.

"Get him up." Had she been able to pull herself smaller and smaller until she was a mite of dust, Ritzi would have at the sound of that voice. "And find the girl he came in with."

"Nothing on the balcony, boss."

"Check the bathroom."

The door banged open and Ritzi froze. The light popped on, an L-shaped wedge of yellow light appeared around the cabinet door, and there, at the bottom, a small corner of her dress peeked out. The trash can toppled over, followed by silence until she heard the rustle of a belt and the whiz of a zipper. She had plenty of time to anticipate the worst before hearing a splash in the toilet. He approached the cabinet with a heavy tread. One ear was pressed against the pipes beneath the sink, and she heard the rush of water as he washed his hands. He stood at the sink for a long time and Ritzi could clearly see the brown leather shoes in the crack of the door.

"She ain't in here."

Crater groaned out in the bedroom.

"What'd you do with the girl?" the intruder asked.

Crater's voice was thick, confused, as though stuffed with cotton. He spit something onto the floor. "She was here."

A pause. "Well, she ain't here now. Did she go home?"

"I don't know where she went."

Stuffed in that cabinet like a coat in winter storage, Ritzi's muscles began to cramp. Her feet, bent at irregular angles, tingled as her circulation slowed.

"Wrap him up."

The sound of the bed being stripped, peppered with Crater's pleas. "Don't. This isn't necessary."

The beating began in earnest then, and Ritzi trembled inside the cabinet unable to block out the sickening screams of Joseph Crater. He thrashed and howled like the tourists on the Cyclone outside. After several minutes, he begged, "Please, whatever you want, I can make it happen." A short gasp, and then, "You know I can. I've pulled strings before. Settled that last mess."

"Seems you been causing trouble for my friends, Joe. And they don't appreciate that. Then they come asking me questions, which I don't appreciate. Don't like it when Samuel Seabury starts sniffing around. Way I see it, you're the common denominator."

"We can sort it out." Crater's composure was gone, and Ritzi heard the terror in his voice.

"That deal we made with Martin Healy was supposed to be taken care of clean and quiet. But now"—the slap of a newspaper across Crater's face—"it's front-page news. How the *hell* did George Hall sniff out that story?"

"I don't know shit about that. Nothing."

"You're taking a ride with us, Joe."

"No—"

"Clean the place up, boys. No one needs to know we were here."

Chapter Four

BELGRADE LAKES, MAINE,
THURSDAY, AUGUST 7, 1930

THURSDAY dawned dark and angry, and Stella woke to the lash of tree branches against the metal roof. A summer storm had blown in during the night. It was a sudden, full sort of wakefulness that dragged her from sleep, and she sat up, grasping at the edges of a dream she couldn't quite remember. After a moment, she slipped from bed and padded down the stairs in her bare feet to rummage in the kitchen for a tin of coffee. She stood at the window, arms crossed, watching gray water slap across the pier. The lake looked furious. As the smell of coffee started to warm the air, she heard a knock at the kitchen door. Fred Kahler, crouched on the stoop, soaked to the skin. Hands cupped to his face, he peered in the window.

Stella wore nothing but a cotton nightgown frayed thin from use.

They realized this at the same time. Fred was about to leave when she held up one finger. *Wait,* she mouthed, and ran back up the stairs, face crimson.

Her dressing gown hung on the bathroom door, and though she wouldn't normally wear it in front of a man other than her husband, Stella didn't have time to get dressed. On her way out of the room, she grabbed a towel and slipped on a pair of socks.

Fred stared at his feet when she opened the door. "I'm so sorry. I—"

"Come in."

He ducked inside, streams of water running from him in at least four different places, and offered her a grateful smile. Stella handed him the towel, and he wrung himself out while standing on it.

"Coffee?"

The puddle by his feet crept toward the potted fern. Fred stared at the trail of water. She could tell he was about to politely refuse. And suddenly the kitchen felt dark and lonely, so she said, "Just drop your jacket on the floor. It's only water." Stella picked two cups from the cabinet and poured him some coffee.

Fred scooted across the floor with the towel beneath his feet, trying not to make a bigger mess. It was considerate. And funny. She laughed. "Cream or sugar?"

"Black." He took a gulp of the hot liquid and sank into a chair with a sigh. He stared at her sock-clad toes.

"Cold feet," she said.

Her feet were fine, actually. She'd thrown them on because there was, by and large, nothing sexy about socks. And juvenile as it may be, Stella felt the need to counteract the sight he'd glimpsed through the window. She searched the icebox for milk and the cupboard for sugar. After Fred drove Joe to the train station on Monday, Joe had told him to stay behind. Fred had spent most of the week in his apartment behind the garage or tinkering with the car. The consequences of the situation were awkward, however. It had been years since Stella had been alone with another man.

She stared at the coffee grains floating at the top of her cup. "Do you think he took the night train?"

"I don't know."

"He didn't tell you what time he'd come back?" She looked over the rim of her cup at Fred.

"No."

"Did he say anything," Stella balled her fist and pointed to it for emphasis—"you know, about what happened?"

He inspected the bottom of his cup. "I like you far too much to repeat what he said, ma'am."

Stella nodded and rubbed her eyes. They sat in silence for a few minutes, drinking coffee and watching the downpour. When the minutes stretched long and Fred had drained his cup, he looked at the clock over the stove.

"The next train will be pulling up any minute," he said. "I'd better get going. Just in case."

"Probably best." Stella forced a smile. "We wouldn't want to keep him waiting."

Fred set his cap on his head and tapped the brim as he walked out the door. "Back in a few."

Stella finished off the pot of coffee but didn't make another. Joe wouldn't be on that train. Not today or tomorrow—or the next day, for that matter. She was certain of it. This was her punishment for what she'd done.

RITZI stood in William Klein's office like a beggar. The Schubert Association had not officially opened for business, but Ritzi implored the doorman to let her in. As usual, William Klein was in the office early, and he'd been only too pleased to see her. Until she made her request. There was no hiding the desperate note in her voice. "Do we have an agreement?"

"I'm not saying shit about being at Club Abbey last night. That's just asking for trouble."

"Then don't. Say we had dinner at Billy Haas's Chophouse. Crater goes there all the time."

Klein jerked at the knot in his tie, and his face was flushed. Angry. "I still don't see how this is my problem."

She didn't want to be close to him, didn't want his sweaty hands anywhere near her, but she leaned over the desk anyway, her best act of intimidation. Ritzi was scared enough to be convincing. "I will make it your problem the second the cops come looking for me. I went home with you last night. That's the story."

"I could take it to Owney, tell him you're blackmailing me."

The threat landed like a fist in her rib cage.

"Joe is your *friend*." She choked out the words.

"So?"

"So your friend—a damned supreme court justice, I might add—was dragged out of a hotel room in Coney Island last night. You don't think that's going to be a *problem*?"

Klein turned to study one of the many black-and-white prints on the wall. Showgirls, every one. Feathered and sequined and leggy. His favorite leading ladies. "How do I know you're telling the truth? That this isn't some racket?"

"I can tell you how they stomped on him. The way he screamed."

Ritzi held on to the lip of the desk as she moved closer. "Is that what you want?"

"Enough."

"They can't know I was there."

"It's your mess, Ritz. I don't want any part of it."

"What if Crater doesn't come back? We're the last people to see him."

"You don't know that."

"But if I'm right, there will be questions. The only thing left to decide is how to answer them."

His eyes, usually greedy, had a calculating look in them now. Ritzi felt them on her like an itch. Last night's dress was disheveled, the satin crushed and one shoulder strap torn. She had swapped her pearls for a cab ride early this morning, and her shoes smelled of vomit. The odor drifted upward, stinging her nose.

"You look like shit," he said.

The anger seeped out of her, and there was a broken-down sort of tired in her bones. Ritzi counted the hours since she last slept and lost track at thirty. "You make it clear that you and I were together last night—lots of nights, for that matter—and I'll keep my mouth shut. Otherwise, I tell anyone who comes asking that you know what happened to Crater."

Klein shifted in his chair and twisted his mouth at the unpleasant prospect of her threat. "So, Billy Haas's Chophouse?"

Ritzi nodded.

There was nothing left to say, so she turned toward the door. The carpet was thick and she didn't hear him approach from behind. His hand on the back of her neck was a small death, and she choked on the strangled sound that tried to erupt. The backless gown felt daring last night, sexy. But now she was exposed. His hand left a trail of shame against her skin.

"I'll keep my end of the deal." He pulled her toward him. His breath, damp on her cheek, smelled of cigarettes and stale coffee. Clammy fingers snaked into her dress and curled around her right breast. "Seeing as how you're with me now."

The muscles in her body went rigid. Klein felt the barrier and grabbed her shoulder with his other hand. "That's my condition," he said, and bent her over the desk.

MARIA would be late to Smithson's if she didn't hurry. Since she'd last been at the Craters' apartment, the judge had reverted to his single ways. Dishes in the sink. Toilet seats up and towels mildewing in the hamper. Books and papers and clothing strewn about. The apartment practically looked ransacked. The bed hadn't been made. Pants on the floor. Jacket tossed at the foot of the bed. Vest nowhere to be seen. The suit probably cost more than she made in a month, and yet he flung it about like so many dishrags. She'd stripped the bed, ironed the sheets, and taken his suit to the cleaners. It took her an hour to clean the kitchen and another to clean the bathrooms. Now, with the clock inching toward twelve-thirty, she tried to finish dusting the bedroom. She would certainly miss lunch, but if she was lucky, she could avoid getting yelled at by Smithson. Maria was mentally calculating her route when someone rattled the handle to the front door. She stood up straight, listening. A key shifted in the lock. Then the door swung open with a heavy, wooden thud.

Maria winced at the thought of facing Mr. Crater again so soon. Two sets of footsteps shuffled through the entry.

"Where is she?" The voice was sharp and cunning and unfamiliar. She froze.

"Gone for the day."

Maria gasped and spun around. She stood holding the dusting rag, arms stretched out in front of her like a marionette, as her mind adjusted to what she heard. She knew that second voice. Knew it and loved it.

Jude.

Maria looked back and forth between the closet and the open bedroom door. She bolted across the room and parted the garments with one smooth movement. Then she slipped inside, drawing them together again with a snap. Maria had the feeling of being a child, caught somewhere she didn't belong. She pushed her back against the cedar-lined wall and scooted over so her shoes weren't visible. Tucked into the shadowed corner of the closet, she peeked out between two pinstriped suits and saw Jude stick his head in the bedroom, followed by a broad-shouldered man in a Panama hat. Leo Lowenthall. Jude's partner in the detective unit.

In one hand Jude held four manila envelopes and in the other Mr.

Crater's house keys—the ones with the key ring made from a silver dollar, the ones he hung by the front door every day. He shoved the keys in his pocket. Maria could barely see him through the louvered slats as he scanned the room.

Jude walked over to the antique bureau on the far wall. A key stuck out from one of the small drawers. He turned it, pulled the drawer open, and placed the envelopes inside. Maria saw him hesitate, his hand hovering above the drawer, as though to lift them out again.

Leo stood in the doorway, staring at the closet. Suspicious. "So that's why you were stalling?"

Jude spun around. "What do you mean?"

"I thought you didn't have the stomach for the job. But really you just wanted to give Maria time to finish work. She was supposed to be here, you know. Owney wanted her to see this."

Jude took three wild steps toward Leo and grabbed him by the lapels. "You leave my wife out of this."

Leo rose up to his full height and knocked Jude's arms away. "How else can we make sure you cooperate?"

"And you think threatening my *wife* will keep me in line? Is that it?" Jude shoved him backward a step.

"I think you're not trustworthy. That you need a little motivation to do as you're told. To stop asking so many questions."

"Don't worry about me. I'm not stupid." Maria knew her husband well enough to detect the fear in his voice, given away by the high note at the end of each sentence. "And don't go near my wife."

"It's not *me* you have to worry about." Leo laughed at the look of strangled panic on Jude's face. "What? You think Owney didn't know she worked for the Craters? That this was all some *coincidence*? Grow up. Nothing in this town happens on accident." He snorted. "Just do your job."

The rest happened quickly, and Maria struggled to remain silent. The rustle of paper. The bureau drawer sliding shut. The small, almost inaudible click of a lock.

"Doesn't matter," Leo continued. "Now you know the rules. You cross Owney and he goes after your wife." He left the bedroom.

Jude shifted into her line of sight, and Maria pulled into her spine, willing herself to shrink farther into the darkness. She could not blink, could not turn away or breathe, as her husband walked out of Joseph Crater's apartment.

"GET UP. You've got an audition."

Ritzi heard the words, but they did not register at first. A cool hand grabbed her bare shoulder and shook. Somewhere at the base of her skull, a deep throb muffled the words into nonsense. She squeezed her eyes shut to block out the light.

"I will drag your bare-naked ass into that shower if I have to."

"Viv?" The word climbed its way out of her raw throat.

"Expecting someone else?" A pause, and then the voice softened. "Owney, perhaps?"

Ritzi jerked at the name and tried to sit up, but the hand forced her gently back to the pillow. "Is he here?"

"Came by this morning. Wanted to know what time you got in. And to make sure you don't miss this audition."

Ritzi's stomach lurched, and she drew a long breath through her nose to quell the nausea. Her voice came, weak and pleading. "I don't want to do this anymore. I want to go home."

"Home isn't an option anymore, Ritz. You know that."

She cracked open her swollen eyes and found herself sideways in the sheet, a worn gray sock clenched in her hands. Vivian Gordon sat on the edge of the bed, primped and pressed as usual. Ritzi blinked at her a few times before she noticed the competing expressions of concern and anger on her friend's face. "What did you tell him?"

Vivian flashed a wicked grin. "The truth, of course. That you stumbled in drunk just after midnight."

Thank God.

Ritzi let go of the sock and eased her eyes shut with the heels of her hands, counting backward—minutes, hours, days—rewinding time first to William Klein, then to the moment she crawled out of that bathroom cabinet, and further to Club Abbey and Crater and details that turned her stomach. The sex. The sound of fists raining down on Crater. She shuddered. "What time is it?"

"Almost noon."

"What day is it?"

"Thursday."

A few hours. Was that all? Sleep had fallen so hard that she felt as though a month could have passed. It took several seconds before Ritzi could remember her middle name, and it was all she could do to form a sentence. "I'm thirsty."

Vivian left the room and returned a few seconds later with a glass of water.

"Thank you," Ritzi said.

"He's a bastard."

"For the water. But thanks for that too."

Vivian leveled her unnerving jade eyes on Ritzi. "What happened last night?"

Ritzi guzzled half the glass of water. Her throat was sore from the relentless vomiting she'd endured early that morning. It had taken twenty minutes for her muscles to stop cramping once she unfolded herself from the tight confines of the cabinet. And all that time, doubled over in agony, she'd retched, first onto the floor and then into the toilet. On and on it went until there was nothing left but bile. It was a long time before she could look at Vivian and say the words out loud. "You don't want to know."

"I can't protect you if you don't tell me."

"And I can't protect *you* if I do."

They stared at each other in stalemate.

Vivian pursed her lips. Looked away. "You'll lose your spot if you don't get moving. You know what they do with no-shows."

Ritzi sat up and drew the sheets around her. So many details about the last twenty-four hours were vivid in her mind, but she could not, for the life of her, figure out how she got into bed without her clothes.

"I burned your dress," Vivian said. "Damn thing smelled of vomit and looked like evidence."

"I don't remember taking it off."

"You didn't. I came in this morning and found you passed out. Didn't think you'd want to ruin the sheets." Vivian stuck her chest out in an exaggerated motion. "Besides, you ain't got nothin' I ain't got." She laughed. "Okay, maybe a little more."

"I'm so sorry."

"Did Crater get you drunk again?"

Ritzi groaned at the sound of his name. "Yes."

"You didn't even roll over. I pulled it off you like a sausage casing." Vivian nodded toward the sock lying next to Ritzi. "You wouldn't let go of that thing, though. What you got hidden in there?"

The sock was knotted in the middle, and she picked it up and clutched it to her chest. It had come with her on the train to New York City and held the one thing she couldn't bear to part with from her old life, the one thing she had no intention of sharing. In recent months, she'd taken to sleeping with it, like a child who wouldn't part with a filthy security blanket. "Nothing."

Vivian shifted closer and tucked a limp piece of hair behind Ritzi's ear. "Fine. Keep your secrets. We've all got them." She walked to the window and pulled back the curtains. Vivian blinked into the sunlight. "I'm sorry, you know, that I ever introduced you to Owney. Should have told you to go back home when I had the chance."

"I wouldn't have listened."

"It doesn't go well for most of the girls who come asking for me. By the look of things, I only made it worse for you."

Ritzi didn't often see Vivian during the day, and the fine lines around her eyes seemed deeper, the corners of her mouth limp. It occurred to her for the first time that the notorious madam Vivian Gordon was starting to look her age. Ritzi set her feet on the floor and tested her balance.

"I did this to myself, Viv. It's not your fault."

She grabbed the gray sock, wrapped the sheet around herself like a corn husk, and shuffled to the bathroom in search of a shower—a rare modern amenity that she took advantage of whenever possible. As she tossed the sheet aside Ritzi realized that she didn't know where her underclothes were. Had she left them in Klein's office? The hotel room?

And that was the tipping point. Ritzi began to wail. Great gasping breaths of air that choked her as the water—first needles of ice and then fire—pelted from above. Her tender body ached from the strain. Stomach sore. Thighs bruised. And a pain in her joints, as though they were all being stretched apart. She closed her eyes and lifted her face to the water, letting it soothe the weariness until she was wrung dry of tears. Ritzi soaped and rinsed over and over, digging at her body with a washcloth, desperate to scrub away the shame.

The air was thick with steam and her skin pink by the time the water finally ran cold. She stepped, dripping, onto the floor. The girl in the mirror with the frightened eyes was sadly recognizable. It was the same girl who got off a train from Iowa three years earlier looking for fame and fortune. For the first time in ages, Ritzi didn't see a stranger in her own reflection.

"Feel better?" Vivian asked when she came back to the bedroom. She'd gone through Ritzi's closet and laid a blue dress on the bed.

"Much."

"You have less than an hour to get to the theater. Clean up good."

"Thanks. For everything."

"I didn't want a roommate, you know," she said, digging around in the bottom of Ritzi's closet for a pair of black heels. She plucked a strand of hair off one shoe and set them next to the dress. "I prefer to live alone. Was none too pleased with Owney when he insisted on this arrangement. But I'm glad you're here, Ritz. I really am."

RITZI swung herself into the backseat of the black Cadillac. "Where's the audition?"

Shorty Petak leaned over the front seat and pushed up the rim of his bowler hat. "The new Broadway Theatre. This'll be the first show."

A Polish thug employed by Owney, Shorty served many purposes: chauffeur, bodyguard, bouncer. He often stood watch outside the dressing room during shows that Owney backed to keep stagehands and riffraff from the performers. Sometimes Ritzi liked him; sometimes he got on her last nerve.

She lifted a compact from her purse and inspected her reflection. Eyes a bit swollen. Nose chapped. Ritzi patted powder onto her cheeks and applied another coat of lipstick. "So this show is a big deal?"

"Jimmy Durante is the lead." Shorty swerved into traffic, and she had to grasp the door handle so she wouldn't tip over.

"The chorus line will be big, then? Twenty or thirty?"

He flashed a look in the rearview mirror. "This ain't for the chorus line. Owney set you up for a solo. You knew that, right?"

If Owney had bothered to relay that information, it had gotten lost in the chaos of the last twenty-four hours. She would have missed the audition altogether if not for Vivian dragging her out of bed. "Of course," she lied.

All her other auditions had been for kickers in the chorus line. She made for a pretty face in the crowd, a good set of legs in the background. But this was something else entirely. She'd begged Owney for three years to give her a shot like this. Had worked hard for it. Done things she would never admit to in the light of day. But after last night, she wanted nothing to do with him ever again. Three years of ambition erased by one night listening to the agonized shrieks of Joseph Crater.

The Broadway Theater was a short drive from her apartment, and Shorty reached it in record time—he loved gunning the engine when Owney wasn't around. He parked illegally and walked her right into the lobby. A crowd of large-busted girls stood with glossy lips, each waiting her turn.

Shorty took her elbow and pushed through the crowd toward a man with a clipboard.

"Name," he asked, not bothering to look up.

"She's on the reserved list," Shorty said.

A murmur of dissent rose around them. Angry whispers. Protests. Someone shouted, "This is an open audition. No reserves. That's what my agent said!"

"Name," the man with the clipboard repeated.

"Sally Lou Ritz," she said.

He flipped a few pages and scanned his list. "Right through there."

Shorty walked her down a side passage. Once they were out of ear-shot, he said, "You're auditioning for the part of May, a prostitute."

"Fitting."

He pinched her arm. "You've got a solo. It's perfect for your range, but tricky. There's only a piano accompaniment. That's what's messing up the other girls. No orchestra to hide the sour notes. Sing it clear and you'll be fine. The rest has been arranged."

The hallway merged left and emptied them into the area backstage. Shorty took her purse and gave her a little shove.

An assistant waved her forward. "This way." He held back the curtain and led her onstage.

A nameless, faceless voice called out from the dark mouth of the theater, "Are you ready, Miss . . . Ritz?" He sounded bored, as though he'd sat there listening to one performer after another butcher the song.

"Yes." She searched for a face but could see nothing past the yellow spotlight in which she stood.

"That's Cole Porter on the piano to your left. He wrote the musical."

"It's a pleasure to meet you." Her voice raised an octave. She cleared her throat. Swallowed.

Porter looked amused at her discomfort. He leaned away from the piano, all eyes and receding hairline. "I'll go through it once so you catch the melody. You'll come in on the third measure."

Ritzi scanned the sheet music as he played. *Shorty gave me a way out of this,* she thought. Everything was arranged, as long as she sang well. She couldn't flub it completely—Owney would know better. Ritzi was consistent. But she could try too hard. Put a little too much emotion into it. That certainly wouldn't be much of a stretch today. Would Owney let her be if she didn't land this gig? One way to find out.

After several minutes, Porter's fingers came to a rest on the piano keys. "Got it?"

Ritzi nodded and he began again. She waited, marking each beat with a gentle tap of fingers against her thigh. At the beginning of the third measure, she joined the melody, her voice deep and lusty and emotional. She could have sung the song straight and high and clear. But she didn't. Ritzi allowed herself to feel it instead of performing it. In her peripheral vision, she saw Shorty standing next to the curtain. His head jerked up at the sound of her voice. Ritzi kept her eyes on the sheet of lyrics. They rang all too true. Ritzi let her voice crack at the beginning of the last chorus, an emotion-filled rasp that would surely cost her the audition.

Appetizing young love for sale
If you want to buy my wares
Follow me and climb the stairs
Love for sale

She brought the last line to a close with a slight waver. This was the opportunity she'd struggled for. Her chance at a real part in a Broadway show. And she'd blown it on purpose. All Ritzi wanted was to go home and go to bed with an aspirin and a hot water bottle and forget that she had ever boarded that train three years ago. She closed her eyes and waited for the rejection.

Damning silence filled the auditorium. Cole Porter rustled his sheet music. She heard whispers. And then, "Rehearsals begin next week, right here. Don't be late."

It took several moments for her to make sense of the congratulations and the handshakes and the pleased look on Shorty's face. Ritzi was given a packet of paperwork filled with scores and scripts and a typed contract stating her role in the production.

Cole Porter graced her with a smile that might have thrilled her had it come a few years earlier. "You're perfect," he said.

She remembered to smile and give thanks, to look pretty and charming and delighted. Ritzi had enough composure left to look the part. It was only when Shorty led her down the dark hallway again that she let her face crumple into dismay.

"That was risky," he whispered.

"Why? I got the part."

"That's not how Owney wanted you to sing it."

"Maybe I wanted to try something different."

"Listen." He stopped and shoved her up against the wall, lowering his voice so no one could hear. Shorty pushed up on his toes to meet her eye to eye. "Keep doing things your way and you'll get a short ride in the trunk of Owney's Cadillac. I'm tired of dumping bodies off the Brooklyn Bridge at two in the morning, Ritz. I sure as hell don't wanna do yours. Got it?"

MARIA inherited kitchen duties at the age of ten. Her mother had passed the mantle, and the family recipes, with austerity and a hand-carved wooden spoon straight from the hills of Barcelona. Caramel colored with a smooth handle that fit in the curve of her palm, it was one of the few things she'd brought with her when she married Jude. Something about the feel of that spoon, the swish it made across the bottom of the pan, was therapeutic, and Maria swayed as she stood at the stove, boiling chutney to go with dinner.

Bifana. The meal her mother made for special occasions. Pork tenderloin with cinnamon, cloves, cumin, and raisins. Maria usually made the complicated Portuguese dish during the holidays. Tonight it was an act of bribery. A way of softening her husband, easing into a conversation she didn't know how to approach.

The apartment was three rooms cobbled together with thin walls and rusty plumbing. A tenement near Chinatown. One corner of the living area was reserved for the kitchen, a nook containing a stove, a sink, an icebox, and a small stretch of counter against which Maria now rested, stirring the chutney in rhythmic circles. The heat radiating from the stove caused beads of sweat to rise along her hairline and lip. She wiped them away with the back of her hand.

Maria had rushed home from Smithson's that day and worked out her anxiety by preparing the meal. She browned the tenderloin. Added spices. Stuck it in the oven to roast. And all the while, she wrestled her fears about Jude. She stacked the questions in her mind, shuffling them like a deck of cards in the hands of a dealer. Muttered prayers. Worried her rosary with puckered fingers. At one point, she lit a cluster of votive candles on the coffee table and tried to recite the doxology, but she couldn't get through five words without her mind wandering to Jude and those envelopes in the Craters' apartment. When Maria heard Jude's key in the lock, there was nothing left to do and she surrendered to the inevitable. She didn't move when the door pushed open or when she heard him stop in the doorway. Instead, she swayed to an imaginary tune and hummed beneath her breath, arm raised to pin a pile of chestnut curls to the top of her head. Maria jumped back when a glob of chutney splashed her arm. She brandished the wooden spoon like a weapon, banging the side of the pot in frustration.

"Don't hurt the cookware," Jude said. "It's no match for you."

Only then did she meet his gaze. She couldn't help smiling when she saw his blue eyes, his hesitant dimples. "You're late."

Jude looked guarded. The words he chose were noncommittal. "Long shift."

Maria set the spoon on the counter. She crossed the room in four steps and wrapped her arms around him. She kissed his cheek. Then his neck. "Come eat dinner."

The small table sat wedged against the open window and was covered with the only tablecloth they owned. There wasn't even enough breeze to startle the lit candle.

She pulled the platter of *bifana* from the warm oven and drizzled it with chutney. The meat surrendered easily beneath the knife, and she sliced several thin pieces for Jude and set them on his plate.

Maria watched him cut the tenderloin into strips, amazed at his left-handed dexterity. Writing, cutting, and eating all required a shift in posture for Jude that looked uncomfortable to her, as though he were tipping to the side to accommodate that left hand. He was fully immersed in his meal, while she swirled each piece of meat through the chutney and chewed more than necessary, trying to find the right question to ask.

Finally, Maria pushed her plate away, appetite gone, and looked out the window. On the street below, a group of boys played stickball during lulls in traffic.

"Do you know anything about Owney Madden?" she asked. "That gangster from Liverpool?"

Jude dropped his fork. He stared at her with suspicion, palms spread flat against the tablecloth. "Why?"

"He came into Smithson's two days ago. And there was something really familiar about him, but I didn't figure it out until today." Not the complete truth, of course, but hearing Jude mention him at the Craters' that morning kept Owney firmly cemented in her mind.

"You've seen him before?" He picked up his fork and stuck the tines through a raisin. "Where?"

"He was at one of the Craters' parties."

"Owney Madden was at the Craters'?" His jaw stretched tight.

She wanted to hear the truth from him. "Who is he?"

"A brutal son of a bitch. Gangster. Bootlegger. Owns Club Abbey. And the Cotton Club. Not to mention half the showgirls in this town. Among other things." Jude gripped his steak knife, knuckles white, and cut a long strip of tenderloin. He dissected it into small pieces before taking a bite.

"I've never heard anyone talk that way. Like he spent his days on a fishing trawler and his nights on the dock."

"He probably did."

"Have you ever met him?"

Maria was startled at how level his voice was. How calm. How he chose such a careful answer.

"He's not someone I want to know."

She turned to the window to avoid the intensity in his gaze.

"Why was he at the Craters'?" Jude asked. His eyes had that curious slant she'd always loved. Until now. Now it unnerved her.

"Celebrating. Same as everyone else."

"What?"

"Mr. Crater becoming a judge."

He mopped a bite through the chutney. "What made you think of him?"

"Nothing, really." She swallowed. "It just surfaced. You know, the way thoughts do."

Jude threw his knife and fork onto the plate, and they bounced, then fell to the floor, leaving a blotch of chutney on the tablecloth. "Don't lie to me!"

His voice was a slap. She recoiled. "What?"

"Did he come to their apartment? Did he threaten you?"

"What are you talking about?"

"Shit, Maria. Do you know what *bad news* that guy is? I could kill the Craters for putting you in the same room with him. And Owney for going anywhere near you."

Maria yanked the *bifana* from the table and carried the platter back to the kitchen. Set it on the counter with trembling hands. "I have never seen you like this."

Jude got up and stood behind her. "You gotta tell me if that guy's been around."

"You're scaring me." Maria placed her palm on the rosary where it hung between her breasts. Took a measured breath. "Why would I lie to you?"

He set his hands on her arms. Panic stretched his eyes wide. "You would if you thought it would protect me. I know you."

"Is there something I need to protect you from?"

"It's my job to protect, okay? *Mine.*" Jude loomed over her, shoulders rounded and the veins in his neck drawn tight with a frightening intensity. Maria stepped away, and he reached for her, imploring, but caught a fistful of blue rosary beads instead. Too eager, too desperate to make her understand, he yanked her toward him. The thin silver chain snapped in half, and beads went spinning across the floor, under furniture, against the walls. The crucifix dropped to her feet.

Fear and shame fought for control of his face. He trembled as he towered over her. "I'm sorry—"

She fell to her knees, scooping up the beads. She chased them across the floor. When she counted them in her hand, over half were missing. Maria could not look at him. She cupped them in her palm.

"It was your grandmother's," Jude whispered.

Maria stumbled to her feet and moved toward the bedroom.

"I went to see Finn this afternoon," Jude called as she reached for the knob.

It took a minute for Maria to register what he said, and then the atmosphere pitched sideways. "Since when do you go to confession?"

"I needed someone to talk to." Jude sounded pained. He pinched the bridge of his nose. "It was a long, rotten day."

In all the years they'd been married, Maria could not remember a single time that Jude had gone to see Father Finn Donnegal on his own. For the most part, he'd insisted on calling him by his first name— a liberty that the priest never seemed to mind. A patient man, Father Donnegal.

"What happened today?" She leaned forward a bit, expectant, hopeful that he'd tell her about those envelopes, about Owney, that he wouldn't keep something of that magnitude from her.

He grabbed a handful of tousled hair and yanked. "Nothing . . . just . . . shit, Maria, it was just a bad day, okay?"

Maria stared at him with mournful brown eyes and then stepped into the bedroom and locked the door. She went to the bathroom and ran the tap so the rush of water would muffle Jude's apology on the other side of the door. Maria climbed into the empty tub and held the broken rosary to her chest.

Chapter Five

BELGRADE LAKES, MAINE,
SATURDAY, AUGUST 9, 1930

STELLA dove off the pier into shallow water. She knew better, really, but there was no feeling like the caress of water against her skin. With a quick arch of her back and three kicks, she came to the surface and then swam freestyle deeper into the lake. Fifty yards from shore, she rolled onto her back and floated, her arms drifting wide. A sky stripped bare of clouds, so blue it seemed bottomless, stretched above her. If only they would meet, sky and lake, and swallow her whole.

Her bathing suit was scandalous. A strapless number in blue and white checks with a satin belt and a skirt so short it didn't fully cover her derriere. She'd bought it this summer, intending to surprise Joe on their first swim together, to show him that she was still willing to be seduced. Stella had imagined the look of pleasure when he took in the bare expanse of leg and the hint of cleavage, had hoped he would take a renewed interest in her. It hadn't happened, of course. Joe was gone again before she could model it for him. Back to his mistress.

Nature had not endowed Stella well up top. But she was long and lean with a small waist and clear blue eyes. Joe was fond of both. She'd turned more than her fair share of heads—including his, all those years ago. There was no reason for Stella to feel ashamed of herself, and yet she could not stop the insecurity from smothering her right there in the water. She was a fool for thinking a trashy bathing suit could mend a rift so deep.

Stella pounded her fist in the water. Squeezed her eyes shut. And pushed beneath the surface. She held her breath until her lungs burned and her lips began to tingle. Finally, she bobbed back to the surface and resumed her floating position.

A small family of loons rose from the shore with a squawk and flew low over the lake. They parted around Stella and then landed on the surface twenty feet away. She watched the female beat the water with her wings, proclaiming her displeasure. Stella glanced toward the cabin and saw a truck backing up to the water's edge. A canoe was tied to the flatbed, candy-apple red and slick with varnish. All the greens and browns of her lakeside retreat were ripped open, exposed by that streak of color.

Irv Bean climbed from the truck, scanned the lake, and waved when he saw her treading water offshore. Stella returned the wave and swam back to the pier. She covered herself with a towel before crossing the yard. Dripping and embarrassed, Stella ran one hand along the glossy finish. She didn't have to ask what it was.

Her birthday present.

"Joe ordered it for you. I've had it sitting in the storeroom for a week. Figured I'd go ahead and bring it up since I haven't heard from him." He looked at Stella, a little sheepish. "Hope I didn't ruin the surprise."

Irv tugged at one of the ropes harnessing the canoe in place and pulled until the tail end rested on the ground. He hoisted it onto his shoulders and trudged toward the dock, where he slid the canoe into the water with a splash, then stood back to admire.

"Sure is a beauty, ain't it?"

"You haven't heard from him?"

Irv had one of those faces that struggled to muster any expression other than jovial. Bright eyes and flushed cheeks and a wide grin. "Sorry, no messages for you. I'll drive up right away if anything comes in." He shrugged broad shoulders in apology. Then he tied off the canoe so it wouldn't drift into the lake. "Best be getting back. Happy birthday, Mrs. Crater."

Stella's eyes filled with the canoe. Long after the sound of Irv's delivery truck was replaced by the hush of afternoon, she hung by the water's edge, wondering exactly what had happened to Joe.

Chapter Six

BELGRADE LAKES, MAINE,
MONDAY, AUGUST 11, 1930

"I WANT you to go back to New York and look for Joe."

Fred sat at the kitchen counter, cup of coffee in hand, watching sheets of rain slide down the window. The rain had returned and with it Stella's dismal mood. "You think it's that serious?"

"I think it's time we do something other than sit around and wonder. I want you to search everywhere you can think of. Especially the apartment. What if he's in there . . ." Stella pulled at a loose thread on her blouse. "What if he's dead?"

"Mrs. Crater, I don't think—"

"This will get you in." She pulled a key ring from her purse and set it on the counter. She pointed at a large brass key.

"You're not coming?"

How could she answer that question? That she only wanted to know what had happened to Joe? She settled for the easiest explanation. "I need to be here if he comes back."

"I'll search for him," Fred said. "I promise."

"Write to me if you find anything."

"Of course." Fred picked his jacket off the floor and ducked out the door, arms over his face to protect from the biting wind. He was lost in the rain before she could see him run around the cabin toward the car.

When Stella was certain Fred had driven away, she went upstairs and dumped out the clothes hamper. At the bottom were the khaki pants Joe had worn to the Salt House. Stella turned the pockets inside out but found only the wrapper to an after-dinner mint. She stuffed the dirty clothes back in and went to the closet. Joe's dinner jacket hung on a peg inside the door. Stella reached into the left pocket and found his cigarettes—unfiltered Camels—and a matchbook with the Club Abbey logo. Stella grimaced. She'd never approved of Joe's patronage of the speakeasy that the papers referred to as a "white-light rendezvous spot." In Joe's right pocket were two business cards: one for Simon Rifkind, a law associate of Joe's, and the other for Owney Madden, proprietor of Club Abbey. Stella tapped the cards against her palm.

"So that's who he called." She changed into trousers and tucked the business cards into her pocket. Then she grabbed her raincoat and galoshes and marched into the storm.

"I DON'T know what you were playing at the other day," Donald Smithson said, laying an invoice on her work table. "But it clearly worked. He paid in advance."

Maria lifted the sheet of paper and saw an order for five suits, along with a check for $750. "Owney Madden?"

"I will grant that your tactics were effective with him—perhaps due in part to his own lack of breeding—but it's not a strategy that I want you to employ in the future. Are we clear?"

"Yes, sir."

Smithson placed his clipboard next to the invoice. On it was recorded all of Owney Madden's measurements and his choice of fabric for each suit. "He will be back in two weeks for his first fitting. Let's begin with the classic cut in charcoal wool. You know what to do."

Maria watched Smithson return to his office. That was the closest he'd ever come to paying her a compliment. But the joy of being vindicated was dulled by the uncomfortable fact that she would have to see Owney Madden again.

IRV BEAN'S general store sat at the bottom of a wooded inlet a little over two miles away. But he had a telephone, which at the moment was the most important thing. Despite endless promises from the public works department, phone service had not yet made it to the Craters' end of the lake, and they were forced to make the trek into town to use the phone. Normally, this was not a problem, given the services of Fred Kahler. But Stella had something to say that she did not want him to hear. So having sent him away, she had no choice but to walk. What would have usually been a lovely trip beneath a heavy canopy of oak trees proved a lesson in misery. Although the branches protected her somewhat from the stinging rain, the little that made it through drenched her head and neck until rivulets of water ran down her spine. It took her an hour to hike down the hill, head bowed and hands tucked beneath her arms. The lights were on when she rounded the last turn in the gravel road. Sodden and dispirited, Stella trudged up the wide plank steps and pushed against the door with her shoulder. The shop bells above her clattered in alarm.

The store was empty, save for Irv himself, stretched out behind the counter on a stool with his back against the wall and his mammoth feet near the register. He had the look of a man lulled to sleep by the sound of rain on a tin roof. Arms crossed. Head tipped to the side. Slack mouth. Scratchy snore. Stella let the door snap closed behind her, and the racket of bells jerked him from slumber.

"I need to use your phone." She gave no other greeting as he stumbled from his perch and blinked the sleep from his eyes.

"Something wrong?"

"Joe never came back from the city."

He pointed a long, knuckled finger at the wall. "Phone's over there."

Stella wove around the barrels of apples and crates of Sunkist soda toward the back wall, where, partly hidden behind a shelf of canned goods, a box phone hung. She waited until Irv was out of sight to lift the business cards from her pocket. Owney Madden first. She lifted the receiver and turned the crank until static crackled onto the line, followed by a tired-sounding voice, then requested an operator in Manhattan. Stella read the Greenwich Village exchange and the five-digit number that would connect her to Club Abbey.

Irv was silent behind the counter, most likely straining to hear her conversation, and she bent closer to the wall. A metallic ringing erupted in her ear. One minute stretched into three before someone answered. He sounded young and half asleep.

"Abbey."

"Who is this?"

"Stan." A yawn, and then, "The bartender."

"I need Owney Madden, please." Stella was surprised at the authority in her voice.

He laughed. "Listen, Owney ain't awake right now, much less here."

"Then give me his home number."

"I ain't got it. And even if I did, I ain't stupid enough to hand it out."

"I need to talk to him. It's important."

"Then you can do like all the other broads. No shortcuts. Come by around midnight and show Owney what you got."

"What I've got, Stan, is a missing husband." She took a deep breath and lowered her voice, mindful of Irv's affinity for gossip. "And seeing as how your employer's card was in his pocket, that's a matter I'd like to discuss with him. Unless he'd rather I take my questions to the police."

She paused, waiting for his reply. He had none.

"So you tell Mr. Madden that Joseph Crater's wife needs to talk. Can you remember that? Or do you need to write it down?"

Stan's voice took on a decidedly more respectful tone when he said, "Joseph Crater. Got it."

"He knows how to reach me." Stella set the receiver back on its cradle, picked up the other card, and gave her instructions to the operator.

This time the phone was answered on the first ring. "Have you seen Joe?" she demanded.

Simon Rifkind did not sound pleased to hear her voice. "Stella?"

"He was supposed to be back last Wednesday, and I've not heard from him."

"Slow down. Tell me what happened." He sounded small and distant on the other end, as though he spoke through a culvert, and he listened in silence as she explained the urgent phone call that had lured Joe back to New York City and how more than a week had come and gone without word. "I'm sure there's nothing to worry about," Rifkind finally said.

"You would let me know if Joe got himself into trouble?"

She wondered what he was thinking in the long pause before he answered. "No need to worry. I'm sure all is well. He likely got caught up with business. You know how Joe is."

"You have to find him." She looked around the shelf and looked back at Irv, who was studying an inventory sheet with exaggerated interest. Her voice fell to a whisper. "I need money."

"I'm sure he'll turn up, Stella."

"You don't understand. There is Fred's salary to pay, and a lot of other things as well."

"Can't you—"

"You know he takes care of all that."

"How about I go by the courthouse and collect his check. I can deposit it for you. Would that help?"

"Yes. Very much."

"Which bank?"

On Joe's insistence, they held accounts at several banks. She had to think of the one for their personal checking. "New York Bank and Trust."

"I'll ask around. You stay put, and I'll be in contact the moment I find something out."

"Thank you."

"And, Stella?"

"Yes?"

"Best not to talk about this in public just yet. Joe's spot on the bench is still so . . . tentative. There's his reelection to consider. You wouldn't want people to think him unreliable."

"Of course not."

"Right, then. I'll let you know what I find out."

A puddle had grown around her feet by the time she slid the cards back in her pocket. When she returned to the counter, Irv stared at her with the sort of curiosity that turns to gossip if left to marinate long enough.

"Your floor." She pointed at her muddy galoshes. "I'm sorry."

"Don't worry about it," he said. "This isn't exactly Saks."

Irv looked out the window at the ropes of rain coming in sideways. "Let me get my coat. I'll drive you home."

"Thank you."

The tree limbs hung heavy with rain, brushing the windows of his flatbed as they bumped along the back road toward the cabin. He was quiet, eyes locked on the windshield, and Stella did not attempt conversation. Irv dropped her off with some trite words of sympathy that she quickly forgot, and then Stella walked through the door of her cabin— the one piece of property in her name—and took in the magnitude of Joe's disappearance.

THE obstetrics waiting room at Colum-
bia Presbyterian Hospital overflowed with women who spoke only their
native tongues. Spanish. Portuguese. Italian. Hebrew. A handful piecing
together questions in German and Polish. All of them straining against
the weight of round bellies or looking weak and pale with nausea. All
of them except Maria. They sat on benches against the walls or huddled
in clusters, whispering and rocking from side to side, supporting their
stomachs. A number of them had small children in tow or infants asleep
at their breasts. Maria stood apart from them, arms wrapped around her
waist, keenly aware of her emptiness.

Seven nurses sat at the reception desk in white uniforms and crisply
pointed hats. Each spoke English and at least one other language and
attended to the patients she could most easily communicate with. As
names were rattled off, the nurses would direct the women to see a doctor. Maria assumed they served dual purposes of attendant and trans-
lator. The numbers in the waiting room never seemed to diminish.
No matter how many names were called, more women trickled through
the door.

Maria inched forward with the line until her turn at the reception
desk arrived. The sign in front of her read CASTELLANO. A dark-haired
nurse with chocolate-colored eyes waved her over.

"*Nombre?*"

"I speak English," Maria said.

The nurse smiled with relief. "Well, that's nice. You're the second one
today." She slid a pen and paper forward. "Please fill this out. Name, age,
address, and how far along in your pregnancy."

Maria de la Luz Tarancón Simon. Thirty-two years old. Ninety-seven Orchard Street, apartment 32. She scribbled the information and pushed the clipboard back across the counter. It always seemed strange to her, that mouthful of a name. Though she had been born and raised in New York City, her parents had stayed true to their Spanish heritage and endowed her with surnames from both sides of the family. Jude found it charming. She'd always thought that she would abandon the tradition when she had children of her own. But now that the very possibility was cast into doubt, she felt sentimental about the custom.

"Are you pregnant?"

Maria looked up, startled. Was her barrenness that obvious?

"You left this blank." The nurse pointed to the section of the form that Maria had not filled out.

"No," she said, "I'm not." Her entire struggle was summed up in the white space on that page. Empty form. Empty womb.

"Let's hope the doctor can help with that." The nurse reached out and placed a warm, wrinkled hand on Maria's wrist. Her eyes were bright with kindness. "Now go through that door and wait on the bench outside room number eight. Set this in the slot on the door. He'll call you in when he's ready."

Maria took the clipboard from her outstretched hand, gave her a grateful smile, then passed through a stark white door to the left of the reception desk. The corridor was long and narrow, with a gray-tiled floor and harsh white lighting. She found room number eight, set the clipboard into a metal bracket attached to the door, and dropped to the wooden bench to wait. She was alone in the hallway but could hear voices rising on the other side of the door.

"We don't provide that here, miss." The doctor's voice, insistent.

"But I won't be able to perform pregnant."

"I am afraid I cannot help you."

A wild sob. "They'll kick me off the show. I'll lose everything."

The sound of compassion in his voice and his choice of words were at odds. "Perhaps what you need is a lifestyle change, not that garbage. It's not even medicine. It's dangerous."

"Can you at least tell me where to go?"

Tense silence, and then, "No. I can't. What you're asking for is illegal."

Her rage was almost palpable. "You think I did this to *myself*? You think I had a *choice*?"

"I'm sorry—"

"No, you're not. You're a man. You're all the same."

The door flew open and Maria jerked. She recognized the young woman at once: soft brown hair and hazel eyes and a panicked, shamed expression. The girl from Mr. Crater's bed. She slammed the door behind her and stood in the hallway trembling. Their eyes met.

Maria eased onto her feet. She extended a hand in sympathy, but the girl knocked it away.

"Don't." Her eyes filled with tears, and she swiped them from her cheeks. The smile she offered was bitter and no words came with it. She rushed off down the hall.

Maria took a hesitant step after her. "You're pregnant?"

For one short moment, Maria thought they might have been friends, that perhaps they had an understanding. The feeling quickly dissipated when the girl said, "Just leave me alone." She pushed through the door and back into the waiting room.

Maria stood there wondering whether to run after her, but then her name was called.

"Maria de la . . ." The doctor paused, tripping over her name, and finally added, "Simon. This way, please."

She followed him into the room. It was small and sparse and neat. Bare walls. An exam table covered by a clean white sheet that still had creases from being folded.

"English?" he asked.

"Yes."

"Thank God. I get so tired of bad translations. No fault of my nurses, of course. They do the best they can, but still. So many people. So many languages." He patted the exam table. "Hop up."

Maria sat on the end of the table and dangled her feet off the edge. She felt like a child.

"I'm Dr. Godfrey." He studied the blank space on her chart. "How can I help you today?"

A blush spread across her cheeks, and she felt foolish for being there at all. Pregnancy should be a simple thing. God knows she and Jude had perfected the art of trying. "I'm not exactly sure," she said.

"Are you pregnant? That is my specialty, you realize."

She tried to smile but the effort fell short. "I can't seem to get pregnant. We've tried."

"For how long? Sometimes it takes a few months. Perhaps a year." He scribbled on the chart.

"My husband and I have been trying for several years."

His head snapped up and his eyes narrowed. "Is this your first time visiting a doctor?"

"Yes."

"Can I do a quick external exam? I'll need you to lie down."

Maria turned and lifted her legs onto the table. She lay on her back, arms at her side, as Dr. Godfrey probed her stomach with two fingers.

"May I?" he asked, indicating the waistband of her skirt.

She nodded, and he simultaneously lifted her blouse and folded her skirt down so that five inches of bare skin was exposed around her navel. He scrutinized her face while he prodded. Maria winced as his blunt fingers pressed into sensitive areas farther down.

"Can you tell me about your monthly cycles. Are they regular?"

"Rarely. They come and go as they please. It makes me hopeful that I've finally gotten pregnant. But I always start."

"Do you have pain or bloating throughout the month?"

Maria pondered. That was like asking a woman if she had breasts. Pain and bloating seemed to come with the territory of being a woman. "Yes. But it usually doesn't stop me from working."

"You're quite thin. Any troubles with appetite? Or fatigue?"

"I work two jobs for very demanding employers," she said. "I don't have a choice but to be fatigued." The expression on his face was troubled enough that she asked, "Is something wrong with me?"

"Not necessarily. But I would like to do an internal exam just in case."

Maria tugged at her waistband. "Will I have to . . . ?"

"Yes. I'll need you to disrobe."

"My husband is the only man who's ever seen me naked."

"Would you like me to get a nurse?"

"If you don't mind."

In many ways, Dr. Godfrey looked like her father. His hair had once been dark but was now run through with silver and receding, and his eyes were a translucent gray. He looked kind and tired and old but truly concerned.

"That woman just now . . ."

"You heard that?"

"I wish I hadn't."

"Yes. I suppose it must seem horrible for a woman in your position to hear another ask me to induce miscarriage."

She looked at her feet and whispered, "It doesn't seem fair."

Dr. Godfrey opened his medical bag and set it on the table next to her. "It rains on the just and the unjust, Mrs. Simon. That's the first thing you learn in my profession. There is no fair. Nor is there the ability to help everyone."

"You wouldn't help her."

He sighed. "Have you ever watched a woman bleed to death?"

"No."

"Or die of sepsis?"

She shook her head.

"Well, I have. And apart from the health risks, I'd lose my medical license just for writing the prescription—not that she could even get it filled. Fem-A-Gyn induces a severe uterine hemorrhage. It's unsafe. And illegal. I sympathize with her. Truly, I do. But I am forced to pick and choose every day who I am able to help. Besides," he said, "I have no doubt she will find what she's looking for. They usually do."

"Can you help *me*?"

He drew a stethoscope and a small metal contraption from the bag. "I hope so. But I'll have to do that exam first. Are you comfortable with me performing it today?"

His clipboard sat on the empty chair. It held a thick pile of forms. Hers rested on the top. "Yes."

"Good. Why don't you undress, and I'll go fetch the nurse." He pulled a sheet from the shelf on the wall and handed it to her. "You can cover up with this."

The moment Dr. Godfrey left the room, Maria jumped off the table and grabbed the clipboard. She found exactly what she was looking for on the form beneath hers: Sally Lou Ritz's personal information. She took the paper and stuffed it in her purse. Then she set the clipboard back on the chair.

When Dr. Godfrey returned, Maria lay on the table, the sheet covering the lower half of her body.

. . .

RITZI took the No. 9 subway at 168th Street and settled in for the ride back to Midtown. She had chosen Columbia Presbyterian Hospital because it was so far removed from everyone and everything she knew. Or at least that's what she'd thought. But now she had a failed errand and Crater's maid to deal with. It was supposed to be a simple appointment. Nothing to worry about. She'd assumed that if the doctor on staff wouldn't provide the medicine, then he'd refer her to someone who would. It happened all the time. Three of the girls on the show had bragged about getting Fem-A-Gen suppositories that year. They would know where to go, but Ritzi couldn't ask them. She couldn't let anyone know she was pregnant. Not yet. They'd all suspect Crater. The affair was a poorly kept secret, and Ritzi's only claim to honor was that she'd refused to discuss him when teased or prodded. Not that any of that mattered now, of course.

Ritzi leaned her head against the window and closed her eyes as the train slipped away from the station. She hadn't known when she first arrived in New York that vinegar and lemon juice on a sponge could be used to prevent pregnancy. That conversation in the dressing room had caused no small amount of embarrassment on her part and a great deal of teasing afterward. The most shocking revelation was learning that most of the showgirls preferred Coca-Cola as a douche. Administered immediately after sex, it was, apparently, quite effective. No need for those extremes, however: diaphragms and condoms were easy enough to come by for the resourceful. Vivian usually kept a small supply of condoms in their shared bathroom. But they'd been out when it counted.

Twenty minutes later, Ritzi stepped out of the train at the Forty-Second Street station. She leaned against a column, one hand clutching her stomach and the other pressed against her eyes. She waited until the train moved on to the next stop, and then she rushed to the edge of the platform and vomited onto the tracks.

STELLA nodded as she read Fred's letter. Less than a page long, and written in quick, legible print, it confirmed her suspicions: Joe's associates intended to cover up his disappearance.

Mrs. Crater,

I looked through the apartment late last night and everything appears to be in order. I haven't seen Mr. Crater but everyone says he's been around and is all right. They don't seem keen on my being here, though. Mr. Rifkind asked me not to hang around too much because it might provoke suspicion among the reporters. They say it could hurt his chances for reelection if we stir up a lot of talk about him being missing. Mr. Crater's legal secretary, Joseph Mara, said there would be possible "detrimental effects" from any undue publicity. I'm not exactly sure what that means or why it would stop them from looking around but I find it curious.

Sorry I don't have better news. I'll return to the lake in a few days.

Fred

Stella wadded the letter into a ball and dropped it to the bottom of the trash can. *No matter now. What's done is done.* She pulled the cold coffee grounds from the pot and dumped them on top of Fred's missive.

RITZI stared at her face in the bathroom mirror. Her skin was translucent beneath the glow, eyes too large, lips pale. Three years ago, when she boarded that eastbound train and left behind the only life she'd ever known, the bright lights of Broadway were all she thought about. But never once had it occurred to her how much work it would be. The long hours and the blisters and the soreness that swept through her muscles. She never anticipated the price of celebrity. Ritzi never imagined the favors she would have to trade in order to get onstage.

Ever since Vivian had questioned the contents of the knotted gray sock, Ritzi kept it in the back of her closet. But its presence grew in her mind daily. She found herself thinking about it at the oddest times: during rehearsal or while in the shower. The memories it brought were disruptive. Bittersweet. Ritzi finished primping in the mirror and then went to her closet and pulled the sock from an empty hatbox hidden behind her winter coat. She dumped the contents into her palm.

A tarnished gold wedding band. She admired it, letting herself remember her first love and her former name and the man who once called her his wife. Ritzi slid the ring on her left hand for old times' sake. She was not prepared for the wave of regret that swept over her.

"Charlie." The sound of his name brought the trace of a smile to her lips, and for a brief second she felt something other than the despair that had overwhelmed her since she and Crater had gone to Coney Island.

"You're *married*?"

Ritzi looked up to see Vivian standing in the doorway.

"Why didn't you tell me?" Vivian demanded, crossing the room in a few rushed steps.

"I was so young," she said with an embarrassed shrug. "Who gets married at seventeen? It was stupid."

They stared at one another, and finally Vivian's face softened. "If you have another life, you should go back to it."

Ritzi slid the ring into the sock and retied the knot. "You said it was too late for that."

"For me, yeah. You?" She glanced at the sock. "Apparently, you have options."

"Not anymore."

"This place will break you. You'll wake up one day and not even recognize yourself."

Too late for that. "Did you need something?" Ritzi didn't want to talk about Charlie. Certainly not with the woman who'd helped arrange her relationship with Crater.

The vivid green of Vivian's dress made her eyes seem even more intense. "Owney's been asking for you again. Thought you'd want to know."

"I don't care to see Owney right now."

"That's the point, dear. He knows that. And he thinks you're hiding something. I'd suggest you put in an appearance at Club Abbey." She shrugged and left the room, calling back over her shoulder, "Or you can always go home."

Ritzi sat on the edge of her bed, sock in hand. She pressed her thumb against the ring until it dug into her skin. Home was a troubling memory that made her ache. But she had to do something to protect herself. No telling where Crater was now. It was only a matter of time before word got back to Owney that she had been with him in the hotel room that night.

Ritzi studied her face in the mirror as she decided on her course of action. Her lips set in a determined line. She would turn the spotlight back on Crater. Sure, it was sleazy, but her options were limited. She would drop a hint to the right reporter. She'd done it before and had marveled at how the city took care of the rest. A missing judge was just the thing to get people talking. And a way to make sure Owney kept his distance.

Out in the living room, Vivian gathered her purse and left to see a client. Ritzi waited until her key turned in the lock, then went to the telephone and dialed the operator. "The *New York World,* please."

"One moment," came the reply. A generic Midwest accent. Ritzi guessed Ohio or maybe Missouri. Most likely another girl like herself, gone to the big city in search of something more than cornfields and dirt roads.

A light static rattled in her ear, and then the polished voice of a receptionist: "The *New York World*. How may I direct your call?"

"George Hall."

"He's busy. Would you like to call back, or may I take a message?"

"How do you know George is busy?"

A pause. "Excuse me?"

"Can you actually see him right now? Or is that what he told you to say?"

"I don't—"

"Listen. You tell George to take my call or he can miss the best tip he's gonna get this week. Hell, the best tip he'll get all year. His choice." Ritzi tapped the phone on the table to make it sound like she was hanging up. She heard the receptionist scramble on the other end.

"May I tell him who's calling?"

"I'm not in the habit of giving my name to the papers, much less the gal who answers the phone. Now, are you gonna put George on or what?"

"Hold, please."

It took nearly three minutes before George cussed his way onto the line. "Who the hell is this?"

"It's not who I am, it's what I know."

"I ain't got time for games, doll."

"If you're not interested in what I know, I can take it to the *Post*. Henry Wilson's always up for a scoop."

"I need a name."

"Just call me a source."

"I got sources coming out my ass."

"Sounds like a personal issue."

"Listen, you think you're the first person who called up today with a tip? Twice someone got through saying Governor Roosevelt is shagging some Ziegfeld girl. I ain't the gossip column. I don't give a shit who pulled his zipper." Ritzi heard George tap his pen on the desk. A deliberate silence, and then, "Go on. Tell me what you got. This better be good."

"I think we should meet."

"And I think you should tell me what is so damned important that I leave work in the middle of the day to chat. With a broad, no less."

"Two weeks ago, you got a phone call from an unnamed source claiming Martin Healy has been selling seats on the bench to any politician with a big enough down payment." She paused; the rapid tapping of his pen had ceased. "I made that call, George."

"Go on."

"Meet me at the newsstand outside Gramercy Park. Thirty minutes."

GLOBE THEATER, ATLANTIC CITY,
SATURDAY, JULY 26, 1930

Ritzi leaned over her armrest and whispered in Crater's ear, "I'm going to the ladies' room."

"It's almost intermission." He glanced down their row. She would have to step over William Klein and ten other people before reaching the aisle. As usual, he had paid agency rates for seats in the third row center.

Ritzi flicked her eyes behind him, toward the box seats on the second floor. "I have to go now."

His voice was an angry hiss. "Can't you wait?"

She squirmed in her seat to prove her discomfort.

"Fine. But hurry. William says the end of this act is supposed to be amazing."

That's what Klein had said about the entire musical. Billed as a "spicy comedy," *Dancing Partner* had failed to deliver, in her opinion. The flash and dazzle was gone for Ritzi when it came to Broadway. She'd been behind the curtains. She'd gone through countless hours of auditions and rehearsals and performances. There was no magic left. Only cold scrutiny. And this particular production fell short. But that was usually the case with shows that debuted out of town. They worked out the kinks on a less jaded audience. There would be many to work out after tonight's performance, and Ritzi did not envy this chorus line in the morning. The pained look on Klein's face hinted that he felt the same.

She lifted the hem of her gown and picked her way down the row, careful to stay on her tiptoes and in a half bend so she wouldn't obstruct the

view for others. Once in the aisle, she hurried to the back of the theater
and out the door into the lobby. The restrooms were to the right, but Ritzi
went left toward the balcony. She tiptoed up the carpeted steps. An usher
waited at the top. He stood against the wall, head lolling on his shoulder.
He jerked upright when he saw her.

"Ticket?"

She flashed it in front of him, obscuring the seat number with her
thumb. "Box seven," she said, and walked past him, confident.

She'd guessed at the number when sitting down below. It was left of
the balcony, almost directly above the stage. And there was only one occupant in the box: Judge Samuel Seabury. She had been assured he would be
there tonight and that he would be alone. Ritzi took a deep breath before
parting the curtain to his box.

Seabury moved forward in his seat, arms on his knees, bored and half
asleep. He jumped when she slid into the seat next to him. Pushed his
spectacles onto the bridge of his nose so that his brown eyes flashed at her
from behind them. His hair was peppered with white and parted severely
down the middle.

"Who are you?"

"A messenger. Of sorts."

"What's that supposed to mean?"

She leaned closer to him but kept her voice low and her face turned to
the side. "It means that I've come to deliver a message from a friend."

"I have office hours, miss. I suggest you make an appointment and that
you return to your seat. I do not conduct business in this manner."

Ritzi could barely see Crater and Klein. They were transfixed by the
spray of bare legs on the stage. She settled back in the seat. Crossed her
feet. "Are you familiar with Martin Healy?"

"I must insist that you leave."

"Are you aware that he's been selling judgeships to the highest bidder?"

"I—" Seabury pulled his glasses off, cleaned them on a handkerchief,
and set them back on his nose. "Excuse me?"

The orchestra erupted below. A man and woman twirled onstage, surrounded by other couples in the background. Round and round they went
in widening circles. Her dress flared out like flower petals, and with the
last burst of music, they stopped, arms outstretched and chests heaving.
The audience gave them tepid applause.

Ritzi brushed her lips against Samuel Seabury's ear. It was the only way he would be able to hear her next words, and it was vital that he heard them correctly. "Tammany Hall district leader Martin Healy has been stacking your court system with jurists of his own choosing."

"I don't believe you."

The audience had risen to their feet now, stretching and talking and looking for the exits so they could find the restrooms. Crater was searching for her in the crowd.

"You should. Because I happen to know that Joseph Crater is just one of the men who paid a year's salary for the privilege of wearing a jurist's robe. And that, Your Honor, should concern you deeply."

"That is preposterous."

"It is nothing but the truth. And it will come to light sooner or later. The only question is whether you'll get the glory for uncovering the most graft-ridden scandal in political history."

Judge Samuel Seabury gazed ahead, silent, as Ritzi slipped from his private box. Patrons were clogged at the top of the stairs, and she had to push her way through in order to get back down to the lobby. She skirted the wall and ran the tips of her fingers through the drinking fountain before joining Crater in the third row.

"Feel better?" he asked.

"Immensely."

GEORGE Hall was a tall, twitchy man, the sort who couldn't seem to find pants long enough. Almost an inch of white sock was visible above his black wingtips. He plowed through the rambling crowd with his sleeves pushed up to his elbows, his tie loose, and the first button of his shirt undone. He snapped his head this way and that, looking for eye contact. After a moment of aggravated searching, George stopped near the south gate, within view of the bronze statue of Edwin Booth playing Hamlet, and leaned against the wrought-iron fence, scanning the crowd.

Ritzi ignored him and finished her corned beef sandwich. Melted Swiss cheese. Sauerkraut. Toasted rye bread. For three minutes, she savored every bite. A meal of her own choosing with no one around to harass her. No salads or ice water or boiled eggs. The rare luxury of real food.

The perimeter of Gramercy Park—the city's most elite private garden—was ornamented with decorative benches, and she sat on one near the newsstand, tucked beneath a large elm, that day's issue of the *New York World* spread across her lap catching crumbs. She swept them off with her fingers to read George's latest article, an investigation into whether judgeships were on the block to the highest bidder. The headline screamed corruption: TAMMANY HALL DISTRICT LEADER MARTIN HEALY INDICTED BY SEABURY COMMISSION. The article claimed that a local magistrate had purchased his robe in an elaborate scheme brokered by members of Tammany Hall and the underworld. So far, three witnesses were pleading the Fifth Amendment. Others couldn't be located. Crater's name was mentioned below the fold as a person of interest.

Ritzi kept one eye on George Hall as he scanned the park. She wore her favorite blue dress with the black satin belt and a wide-brimmed floppy hat that dipped down over one eye. A pair of dark sunglasses and bright red lipstick completed the ensemble. She looked out of place among the crowd, and it didn't take George long to spot her beneath the elm. He paused, uncertain, and then she held up his article in affirmation. Ritzi beckoned him with a little wave. Poor George seemed undone by the smile she graced him with.

He made his way toward her with a hot dog dripping with mustard and sauerkraut and wrapped in newsprint, then settled onto the far end of the bench and ate his meal in four large bites.

"If I knew my lunch date would be this pretty, I'd have dressed for the occasion." He wiped his mouth with the back of his hand.

"This is business, Georgie. Don't flatter yourself." She crossed her legs and rocked her foot back and forth.

He looked mesmerized by the motion, a swinging pendulum of bare calf. "Your phone call created one hell of a mess."

"That was rather the point."

George tipped his head to the side, trying to recognize her face behind the lipstick and hat and glasses.

"Don't waste your time. You've never seen me before."

"Wouldn't mind seeing you again."

Ritzi glanced at his wedding ring. *They're all the same.* She turned away, giving him nothing but her profile. "Ever hear of a judge by the name Joseph Crater? Sits on the supreme court?"

George pulled a steno pad from his shirt pocket and flipped backward through pages filled with slanted shorthand, abbreviated words thrown on the page like nails on a table. He tapped the page he was looking for with the tip of his pen, ready to add to his existing notes on Crater.

"Sure. He's supposed to testify before the grand jury about that Healy mess. They both belong to the same Tammany political club."

Ritzi nodded. She had already relayed that information to Owney, volatile details that they were.

"So what's the deal? Cheating on his wife? Stacking both sides of the deck? It can't be worse than what he's already caught up in."

"He stepped into a cab on August sixth and hasn't been seen since."

She finally had George's undivided attention.

"I haven't heard anything about this," he said.

"That's my point exactly."

"You mean to tell me that a New York State Supreme Court judge is missing?"

"*Missing* would be a polite way of describing his situation."

"Anyone else know about this?"

She gave him a malicious grin. "Not yet."

George flipped to a clean sheet of paper in his notebook. "I don't suppose you're gonna give me a name, dollface?"

Ritzi folded the newspaper and set it on the bench between them. "If you talk about me in your article, if you so much as mention the color of my dress, I'll take the rest of the story to Henry Wilson at the *Post*. Understand? I don't exist."

"There's more to the story?"

Ritzi patted George's cheek. He hadn't shaved in a couple of days. "You have *no* idea."

"When do I get to hear the rest?"

"Get to work, Georgie. Turn over a few stones. Write your story. I know where to find you when it's time." She made sure to give George Hall plenty to watch as she left him sitting beneath the elm in Gramercy Park.

MARIA stood outside the Craters' apartment. She paused, then laid her hand on the knob and twisted. Locked. The key rested in her palm, but she pressed her ear to the door and listened. Mrs. Crater was not due back from Maine for another week. The apartment should be empty. But better safe than sorry. Convinced that all was calm and quiet within, she made the sign of the cross and let herself into the apartment.

"*Superstición.*"

She laughed a little. Perhaps Jude was right and crossing herself was no different from throwing salt over her shoulder. Or spitting three times in reaction to evil. Always the skeptic, he poked and prodded at her faith, searching for thin places where his doubt could push through. Had she possessed a handful of salt just then, she would have gladly tossed it. The lines between religion and superstition were tenuous at best. Today she would take either. Her last two experiences in this home had not been pleasant. Maria locked the door behind her.

She set her purse down and went straight to the master suite. Radio off. Bathroom empty. No one in sight. Maria exhaled for the first time since walking in.

The room looked exactly the way she'd left it the last time she was here. The bed was made and the room straightened. Legal books stacked neatly on the nightstand. Mr. Crater's robe hung on a hook on the bathroom door. The only difference was the thin film of dust that lay across the furniture. It was undisturbed. Maria ran her finger over the bureau and looked at the mark of clean wood left behind. What had Jude hidden in there, she wondered. Maria lifted the red-and-gold brocade bureau scarf. The key stuck out of the lock, right where he had left it. An invitation.

Curiosity roared through her mind, and Maria could not take her eyes off that small gold key. She reached a hand out and let it hover in the air long enough for her to take a breath and decide. One small turn. She couldn't help it. The lock clicked and she slid the drawer open. Four manila envelopes piled on top of each other, with Mrs. Crater's initials written in jerky letters. Maria pulled out the first envelope and balanced its weight in her hand.

Red string was wrapped around two buttons, sealing the envelope. Maria sat on the edge of the Craters' bed as she slowly unwound it, telling herself all the while to put the envelope back, to leave it alone. Even as her mind objected to the work of her hands, she pulled the envelope open. What could be so important that her husband was willing to violate his own conscience? She tipped the answer into her lap. Maria regretted her decision as soon as she saw the pile of money. Thousands of dollars were stacked and bound with string. She gasped and lifted one from her lap, fanning through the bills with her thumb.

Maria jumped when someone pounded on the front door. For one terrible moment, she thought her employers had returned and that she would be discovered sifting through their belongings. She stuffed the money back in the envelope and then locked it in the drawer.

Her palms were slick with perspiration and her pulse raced as she went to the door and peered through the peephole. The man on the other side looked as though he stood in front of a fun-house mirror: neck and legs stretched to a comical length, eyes abnormally large. She hesitated, uncertain. He didn't appear threatening. Maria unlocked the door as he lifted his fist to knock again. She cracked it open but left the chain in place. She waited for him to speak.

"I'm looking for Joseph Crater." The man was young and clean-shaven with a wide grin. Unusually tall. He seemed to quiver with energy, as though he might come bounding through the door at any second.

She cleared her throat. "He's not here."

"Do you know where I can find him?"

Maria wasn't in the habit of telling strangers the location of her employer. But this was general enough. "In Maine. *Vacaciones.*"

He pulled a small notebook from a pocket inside his suit coat and scratched a few indecipherable lines. "When do you expect him back?"

"Who are you?" Maria said, suddenly cautious.

"George Hall, with the *New York World.*" There was barely enough room for him to stick his hand through the crack in the door.

She did not take it. "What do you want?"

"I'm usually the one who asks the questions. This is a nice change of pace. Mind if I come in?"

"Yes."

"I promise I'll only stay a minute. Have a look around." Maria went to close the door, but he stepped back, palms up. "Hey, I'm sorry. Can't blame me for trying."

"I think you need to leave."

"No one has seen your boss in weeks," George said.

Her hand grasped the knob tighter. "He's in Maine."

"Are you sure?"

"Yes." *Maybe.* "We spoke on the fourth. He said he was going back there." Fears rushed in on Maria. Jude. The cash in that envelope. The woman in Mr. Crater's bed.

"Is that the last time you saw him?" George whipped his pen across the pad, quick, blunt strokes that almost tore the paper.

"Yes."

"Did anything seem wrong? Was he upset?"

The image of her boss wrapped in a towel and dripping wet surfaced in her mind. "No."

"One more question. And it's not about him. I promise." George smiled. His pen hovered over his notepad. "What's your name?"

Maria looked at the notes he'd scratched so far, furious with herself. She'd given him a story. None of the information she relayed could incriminate her employer or the girl he'd brought home or, most important, Jude, but it was still too much. There was no way her name was going in that article. She thought of the first name that came to mind. Her mother's. "*Amedia.*" She cleared her throat, and then, "*Mi nombre es Amedia Christian.*"

Maria pressed her forehead against the door when the reporter left. Mr. Crater signed her paychecks. Mr. Crater was gone. His mistress was intent on getting rid of their illegitimate child, while she herself could not get pregnant. Jude was planting evidence and doing God knows what else. She went back to the bedroom and opened the bureau drawer. She removed the cash-heavy envelope.

IT took every ounce of Maria's self-control not to run from the Craters' apartment. She was flushed and uneasy, the money heavy in her purse. Maria started counting when she locked the apartment door. Fifteen steps to the elevator. Twenty-three across the lobby. Only once she was outside in that thick air did she start to tremble. But she took steady, measured footsteps the five blocks to Smithson's. She did not hold the bell when she walked in. Did not raise her head. Her only goal was the small work area. Maria crumpled into her chair. A bead of sweat trickled down her rib cage, and she gave herself the freedom to place her hand over her heart. To close her eyes.

Had her father still worked for Smithson, he would have known with a single glance what she had done. But he'd long since gone blind and been forced out of his job. It was his failing eyesight that pushed her to master the art of stitching in the first place. What his eyes could not see, his fingers did. He counted her stitches with diligence, never letting her skip. It was a game they played in recent years, Maria sitting near his feet on the floor doing stitchwork as they talked. Adding or deleting stitches at random to see if he would notice. Then she'd hand the pieces over for inspection. Without fail, he'd call her out.

"Two missing on the inseam. Seven extra on the hem."

"You shouldn't have quit, you know. No one does this better than you."

"I didn't quit. I went blind. Besides, you do this better than me."

"No."

"Yes. You're faster. More accurate." He raised an eyebrow and turned toward the sound of her voice, one pale eye searching the space where he knew she must be. "Unless you miss on purpose."

"Smithson should have kept you."

"That man hated me."

"He respected you."

"Respect and profit are two different things, *hija*." He patted her head. "And you? Does he like you?"

"He likes my work. But he pays me less than half what he paid you."

Her father sat in silence for a moment. *"El Smithson de los cojones."*

"Papa!"

"It's true."

"Perhaps. But I wouldn't speak it out loud."

"You think God doesn't hear it if you don't say it out loud?" He tapped her forehead with one long finger. "He hears *everything.*"

"Is that supposed to comfort me?"

"Depends on what you're thinking."

That was how it went with them, the banter, whenever they were together. Her marriage to Jude had strained their relationship to the point of breaking at first, but she learned quickly not to bring him on her weekly visits. Once or twice a year, at Christmas and Easter, was plenty. They all got along better if they pretended that Maria had not cast custom aside and married an agnostic.

"Maria." She startled from the memory at the sound of Smithson's voice. "To the fitting room, if you don't mind. Mr. Madden is waiting for you."

She blinked at him. "Oh. His appointment."

"You forgot?"

"No. Just gathering my thoughts."

"Why don't you gather his *suits* and meet us back there?"

"Right away."

Maria had just begun the stitching on one of the five suits. Three others were cut, and the last was only outlined in chalk on a bolt of gray English wool. She grabbed her sewing bag and went into the supply room. She lifted the five long cardboard boxes from a shelf. Each was marked with Mr. Madden's name, measurements, order specifics, and estimated date of completion. Maria balanced the boxes precariously in her arms as she pushed the fitting room door open with her foot.

"Mrs. Simon," Owney said with a nod, his accent blurring the words into one indistinguishable moniker: *Missessimon.*

"Sir." Maria set the boxes on the platform. Her heart raced beneath the thin fabric of her dress, but miraculously her voice was steady. "Thank you for coming in again. I know it can be inconvenient. But we're ensured the best fit if we can put you inside the garment before completion."

His small, dark eyes darted across her face and body as though he were taking measurements of his own. "I don't mind."

Maria looked away. "If you would kindly remove your jacket and trousers, Mr. Smithson will assist you into your suit. I'll step from the room."

"There's no need. I'm not shy."

Maria shut the door behind her softly and leaned against it, struggling to regain her composure. She heard them speaking inside but could not understand the words. Maria took two gulps of warm air to steady herself. After counting to one hundred, she returned to the room.

Owney stood on the riser in his socks as Smithson draped the jacket over his shoulders. Little more than a blueprint, the basted suit still had clear chalk lines and was lightly stitched together so that adjustments could be made if necessary. They rarely were. Where other tailors often had to disassemble a suit to account for additional alterations, Maria did not. Only once had she been forced to recut a suit, and that was after a client gained ten pounds between fittings.

"It looks good," she said. "We will probably be able to finish this in two fittings instead of three."

"You do good work." Owney looked in the mirror and assessed his reflection.

The length, neck points, and cuffs of his jacket were all precisely measured, but Maria thought the trousers gapped a little too much at his waist. She pulled her pincushion from the sewing bag and knelt on the riser.

"Do you ever freelance?" Owney asked.

"Excuse me?"

"Do you ever accept work on your own time?"

Maria glanced at the scowl on Smithson's face. "No."

"So if I wanted to employ you for another project, I would need to go directly through Smithson here?"

"Yes." She pinched the section of excess fabric at his waist and speared it with a pin. "Hold still."

Owney watched her, a curious expression on his face. "Why are you wearing a maid's uniform?"

Maria reached up and touched the cap on her head. She cursed herself. In her haste to get out of the Craters' apartment, she had forgotten to change. A foolish oversight, as Smithson was not fond of her dual employment being known. It made him look stingy.

"Against my advice and better judgment, Mrs. Simon works as a *domestic* when she is not here," Smithson said, as though the admission would discredit her tailoring skills.

"For who?"

What to say? That he had seen her twice before? Once with a tray of champagne at the Craters' apartment. "If you're not comfortable with my services, I'm sure Mr. Smithson would be only too happy to provide a more traditional arrangement."

"Your *services*, Maria," he said, "are a pleasure."

She stepped away from the platform and stuffed the pincushion back in her bag. "The suit fits perfectly. Now, if you'll excuse me, I have one left to cut, and I need to begin if all five will be done by the beginning of November. Have a good day."

"Can I watch?"

"What?"

"I'd like to watch you cut my suit. It's not every day a man has a chance to see that." Owney turned to Smithson and lifted one eyebrow, challenging him to object.

"Of course." He glared at Maria. "I'll help you get dressed, and we'll join Mrs. Simon in the cutting room."

Unlike the fitting room, the cutting room was all function and no form. A square room at the back of the shop with a long table and bright lighting, it boasted a collection of scissors rivaled only by Savile Row's. None were allowed out of the room, and any employee caught cutting paper with them would be fired. Nothing dulled a pair of scissors like paper. To use them for that purpose was an act of sacrilege.

Maria collected the garment boxes and put all but one back on the supply room shelf. The last box she took to the cutting room. Inside was a bolt of fabric with irregular shapes marked out in pale chalk lines along one side. She rolled the fabric onto the table and smoothed it with her hand.

A few minutes later, Smithson and Owney joined her. "A demonstration, Mrs. Simon? Our client is very eager to witness this part of the process."

"There's nothing magical about it, I'm afraid," Maria said. "It just takes a steady hand."

The jovial Owney seemed to have vanished during the short trip to the cutting room, and for the first time, she saw the dark gangster whom Jude had warned her about. He stood beside her, arms crossed over his chest, brooding.

"Go on," he said.

Maria lifted a pair of scissors from the shelf and folded the length of cloth in half. The chalk lines faced up, and she pressed the fabric flat with her palm. She made sure there were no ripples or folds in either layer. A deep breath. And then she cut the first sleeve. Normally, this was the simplest part of constructing a suit. But with Owney Madden standing at her shoulder, she struggled to keep her hand from trembling.

At one point, Smithson tried to offer commentary on the process, but Owney raised a hand to silence him.

After the second sleeve, she could no longer tolerate the silence. "You'll see that I have allowed three-inch adjustments to the inlays for the main body seams," she said, not looking at Owney for permission to speak. "They will be felled by hand, and the vent and front edge will be prick-stitched. You'll notice special features on the finished product— namely, the slanted breast pocket, the left lapel buttonhole with a sewn flower loop, an inlay under the collar, cuffs with slit openings, cross-stitched buttons, and the reinforced pockets and gorge."

Maria turned to explain that he would be hard-pressed to find a suit of this quality anywhere else in New York. But Owney wasn't looking at the suit. He was staring at her.

"You work for Joseph Crater, *Mrs. Simon*," he said.

CLUB ABBEY

GREENWICH VILLAGE, AUGUST 6, 1969

Club Abbey was owned by Owen "Owney" Madden. Madden, a Liverpool native, had been a gang leader in his youth, later a leading bootlegger, an occasional backer of Broadway shows (including Mae West's Sex*), and a fellow with a violent past.*

—*Richard J. Tofel,* Vanishing Point

"I read your memoir," Jude says. He leans across the table to where his coat hangs limp on a peg and pulls a slim book from an inside pocket. The coat has seen better days. So has the book. He lays it, scratched and dog-eared, faceup on the table and slides it toward Stella. The cover is plain: title in red, a byline—Stella and her cowriter—and a poor rendition of a jurist's black robe.

"You weren't impressed?"

"It was two hundred and ten pages of unconvincing."

"So you're a better judge of the facts?"

"I have respect for the facts. That's the difference." He jabs a finger at the book. "You're a lot of things, Stella, but weak and naive aren't two of them. You come across as helpless in this thing. I'd even go so far as to say stupid. I know you better than that."

Stella looks at the book for the first time since he set it on the table. Her eyes scan the title: *The Empty Robe: The Story and Legend of the Disappearance of Judge Crater.* "I suppose that means you don't want me to sign it?"

"If you're of the mind to sign something, a confession would be great. You can borrow my pen. Start with where to find the body."

"Always so obsessed with the body. Haven't you figured out there are more important things?" She flicks her wrist at him, irritated. "You really think I killed my husband?"

Jude plays with the end of his pen, sending a little clicking sound into the silence between them. "I'm certain you know who did."

When Stella sighs, it sounds like gravel in a bucket, all rattle. She points a spindly finger at him. "Your problem is that you always rush things. You show up on a doorstep or slide into a booth and demand answers. But you're no good at listening."

A mound of ashes rests in the ashtray, and her supply of cigarettes has dwindled by half. They lay across the table like bleached railroad ties. She chooses one at random and rolls it between her fingers.

"Forgive me if I'm a little short on patience these days," Jude says. "It's been thirty-nine years."

"You don't have to remind me how long it's been. For you, this was just a case. But it's something I've lived and breathed and suffered through every day since Joe left."

"Still playing the grieving wife? I thought you were long past that."

"Lighter," she demands.

Jude hands it over, and she wrestles with the striker, her fingers weak and curled in on themselves. Stella refuses when Jude offers to help. After a few moments, she succeeds in producing a spark large enough to ignite the fluid. The paper burns orange and then black as a thin trail of smoke drifts toward the ceiling. She puffs on the cigarette a few times and then hacks a wet cough into her palm.

"Suffering and grief are two different things. I don't grieve my husband's passing. But I do suffer the loss."

"That's not what you said in here. Convinced your writer well enough, by the look of things. He painted you as the ultimate victim." Jude flips the book open and thumbs through the pages until he reaches the epilogue. He reads: "'Because work is her only surcease, the single antidote to a sorrow which three decades settled upon but could not bow her slender but proudly squared shoulders.'" He chucks it back to the table in disgust.

"I think he fancied me," she says. "Besides, it was his job to write me as sympathetic."

"He failed. Did anyone actually buy that bullshit?"

"It went into several printings. The *Saturday Review* called it 'absorbing' and 'fascinating.' So, yes, quite a few people *bought* it."

Stella pushes the ice cubes around her drink with the tip of one finger. Only two cubes remain, and they don't have enough weight to clink against the glass when she pokes them. She fishes them out with her thumb and forefinger. Eats them. The four decades since Joe's disappearance have not been kind to Stella, and the smoking in particular has taken its toll. Deep crevices around her thinning lips suggest a mouth too often puckered in anger or craving. Her teeth, once bright and white, are stained yellow, and they grind the ice cubes into shards.

"People wanted to know my side of things. So I told them." Stella turns the book over and sets it facedown on the table. She slides it back toward Jude. "My publishers at Doubleday thought it would be a good touch to hire Oscar Fraley to write the book. He'd recently had all that success with *The Untouchables,* and they believed it would add a certain"—she waves her finger around, searching for the right word—"*authenticity* to the story, given the subject matter. Owney Madden and Tammany Hall and political corruption. The grieving widow gave it a human touch."

"So the book was, what? A way to cash in?"

"We all have bills to pay. Some more than others. Do you know where I've been the last six years, Detective?"

"A nursing home in Mount Vernon."

"I prefer to think of it as a *retirement* home, complete with medical care for the terminally ill." She holds the cigarette up for his inspection. "My doctor found the tumors seven years ago. They took the first lung a year later. Seeing as how I don't have another to spare, I figured I'd make my last days as comfortable as possible."

The sound of the ice dispenser echoes through the bar, and before long Stan arrives at the booth, pitcher and tongs in hand. He drops six cubes into her glass, considers the untouched other drink, and does the same. The once-amber liquid now looks like weak tea. He retreats without a word.

"He's attentive," Jude says.

"He's nervous. I've never had company during this—"

"Charade?"

"Ritual. Stan doesn't know what to make of it."

Jude has another theory, but he doesn't share. It might infuriate her, and he needs Stella content. Chatty. So he spins the lighter in a little circle on the table with his thumb and chooses his words carefully. "I want to know about those envelopes. When you found them. And what was *really* inside."

MAINE. New Hampshire. Connecticut. The states rolled by in a dull kaleidoscope as Stella sat in the back of the Cadillac, ankles crossed and gloved hands limp in her lap. Three times Fred stopped for gas, but she did not get out to stretch her legs or use the facilities. She kept her perch in the vehicle, wintry eyes fixed on some distant point on the other side of the glass. Late in the afternoon, Fred rolled his window down and stretched his arm outside the car. Fresh air rushed over her, tossing the ends of her hair into her eyes. She shut them, rested her head on the back of seat, and was asleep within minutes. Stella woke to the sharp blast of a car horn hours later.

The Manhattan skyline was a dark silhouette against the evening sky as they turned onto Fifth Avenue.

"What time is it?" Stella asked.

Fred turned his wrist up to see his watch. "Almost seven."

"Drop me at home, and you can take the weekend off." She caught his gaze in the rearview mirror. "I'll be fine."

A short time later, Fred rested the Cadillac against the curb in front of the redbrick cooperative at 40 Fifth Avenue. Stella took her small suitcase from him as soon as he lifted it from the trunk.

"We'll drive back to Maine on Sunday evening," she said.

Fred tipped his hat and climbed back behind the wheel.

She went straight up to the apartment, not even bothering to gather her mail in the lobby. After eight hours in the car, her spine ached and her hair was flat beneath her netted hat. She wanted her own shower and her own bed and a sense of familiarity. She turned the key and dropped her bag by the door.

"Joe! Are you here?"

Nothing.

Stella walked through the rooms slowly. She had no idea what she was looking for. A note, maybe? Surely not a body. The very thought made her throat constrict. But she walked through the apartment and looked. In drawers and cupboards. Beneath sofa cushions. Behind the toilet. Part of her could not tolerate having nothing to hold up and say, *See! This is where he went. This is what happened.*

Stella saved the bedroom for last. The closet was exactly the way she'd left it, half empty and smelling of cedar. Nothing under the bed but a few errant dust balls. Nothing behind the curtains or beneath the Victrola. Her dresser was empty, as was her jewelry box—she'd taken the contents with her to Maine, just in case. What little of Joe's clothing that wasn't pressed and hung in the closet was stored in a bureau against the wall. It was an odd piece of furniture. Long and low and top-heavy. Impractical, really, but Joe had taken a fancy to it at an estate sale years earlier. Made of walnut with five drawers. Two stacked on the bottom and three in a row on top. A single streak was visible in the layer of dust on top. Someone had run a finger along the dark wood but had not bothered to clean off the dust. A bureau scarf covered the middle drawer, and she raised the edge. The gold key stuck out of the lock. The drawer usually held receipts and other oddments that Joe took from his pockets. But instead of the paper and loose change she expected, Stella found four manila envelopes.

She lifted them from the drawer.

On the outside of each envelope, in Joe's lettering, were her initials and the word *Personal.* The script was thin and scattered, scrawled across the paper in a hurry. But there was no mistaking the strong slant of the capital letters, as though they were determined to hold their weight. A bit like Joe, those letters were, dogged and brazen.

The first envelope was the heaviest. Stella let it rest on her lap before she undid the clasp and emptied it onto the bedspread. Thirteen stacks of cash, bound with string, and three checks, in Joe's handwriting and made out to himself.

She knew, simply by the size of those stacks, that it was more money than she'd ever held at one time. The bedroom was still, the air thick, and she could hear herself breathe as she untied the string and methodically laid the bills out before her by denomination. On the street outside, a delivery truck rumbled by. A car honked. Someone slammed a door down the hall. Twelve thousand six hundred and nineteen dollars.

The checks were a bit curious, but she counted them as well. One for $500 even. One for $12. And one for $9. These last two made no sense. None of this did. Stella pushed the money aside and reached for the second envelope.

Joseph Crater held four life insurance policies, for a total of $30,000, and each was payable to Stella. These she found in the second envelope. Seeing her name there on the printed page for such an outlandish sum of money rattled her. Three of the policies were with the Mutual Life Insurance Company of New York—two for $10,000 and one for $5,000—and one for $5,000 was with the Fidelity Mutual Life Insurance Company. She stacked them carefully and set them beside the cash.

The third envelope was the most unnerving of the lot, and she swallowed hard after reading the first line:

I, JOSEPH FORCE CRATER, residing in the Borough of Manhattan, City, County, and State of New York, do make, publish and declare this as and for my Last Will and Testament.

As sobering as it was to read those words, worse was the knowledge that Joe had made her role in their marriage clear from the very beginning. Stay pretty. Be proper. Don't ask questions. She continued reading:

FIRST: I hereby revoke any and all Wills and codicils heretofore executed by me.

SECOND: I direct that my just debts and funeral expenses be paid as soon as practical after my decease.

THIRD: I give, devise, and bequeath all my property of whatsoever nature and wheresoever situated to my wife, STELLA M. CRATER, and appoint my said wife sole executrix under this my Will and direct that she be not required to give any bond or other security for the faithful performance of her duties as such executrix.

IN WITNESS WHEREOF I have hereunto set my hand and seal to this my Will at the Borough of Manhattan, on the 4th day of July, 1925.

Joseph Force Crater

The five short paragraphs hit her like warm air from an oven. Stella dropped the paper to her lap and wilted on her spot at the edge of the bed. On Independence Day, five years ago, Joe sat in his office and planned out the legal ramifications following his death. Joe, still in his thirties at that time, writing his will.

"What the *hell* am I supposed to do with this?"

Stella laughed at the abrasive sound of her own voice. Her mother had once told her that only crazy people talked to themselves. *No, Mother,* she'd replied, *lonely people do it all the time.*

The last envelope was the most puzzling to Stella. In addition to her initials and the word *Personal,* he'd added a warning: *Confidential.* A three-page handwritten memorandum gave a startling directive. The letters were large, the pen strokes thick, and the lines straight from one side of the paper to the other, but the hand itself looked distressed. *Confidential* again, underscored on the first page, and then his instructions:

> *The following money is due me from the persons named. Get in touch with them, for they will surely pay their debts.*

He'd listed twenty companies and individuals who owed him money—a roster of every person who had bribed her husband since he took office. Proof of his corruption. Some of the names were indecipherable, as though he lacked the courage to plainly state them in ink. The instructions ended with a word she could not read.

"'Am very *weary*'?" She held the paper close to her face, willing the letters to align in a legible way. "'Am very *sorry*'?"

Weary. Sorry. Those two words spanned a distance so great that a train could pass between them. It was the difference between abdication and apology, and Stella had no idea which he meant.

After that last word, he closed with *Love, Joe.* And then a reiteration of his final warning: *This is all confidential.* The phrase was underlined and the ink went off the page, as though with this last instruction he'd lost the will to control his own pen.

Stella put the contents back into their respective envelopes, which she stacked on the bed. Returning them to the drawer was out of the question. Instead, she went to her closet and knelt down to grab a brown leather satchel that she kept behind her hatboxes. Stella set all four envelopes in her satchel and slid it under the bed. Then she went straight to the phone.

FIFTH AVENUE, MARCH 15, 1920

"Why aren't you dressed for dinner?" Joe asked.

Stella lifted the hem of her skirt. "I wouldn't consider this nudity."

He stood in the doorway, watching her set the table. They dined alone that night, a rare occurrence since Joe had turned an eye toward politics. He called the revolving door of dinner guests "mixers," but Stella found it exhausting at times, never knowing who she'd be entertaining from one night to another. Their grocery bill doubled in the span of months. But for the first time that week, it was just the two of them, and she had taken the opportunity to revel in a casual meal like they used to share. No jewelry. No shoes. Simply a quiet dinner at home.

"That's not what I mean. You've had that dress on all day."

"It's a nice dress."

"It's a day dress," he said, eyes on the paper napkins that she folded into triangles and placed beside their plates. "And it's old."

Stella studied the simple blue dress. It was pretty and feminine, with a lace collar and pleated waist. "I bought it two months ago."

"Why don't you go put on something nice? I'll set the table."

She glanced at the neatly arranged dishes and was about to argue with his bizarre request when she caught the determined look on his face. No point in bickering when Joe set his mind to something. She left the dining room with a scowl and went to rummage in the closet for the violet cocktail dress she'd worn on the few occasions they'd eaten with the members of Joe's Tammany Hall club. It was velvet, with a scoop neck and an asymmetrical hemline, and Joe commented on her figure and the color of her eyes whenever she wore it. For fear of eliciting further criticism, she added jewelry, perfume, high heels, and a fresh coat of lipstick.

"Much better," Joe said when she returned.

He pulled a chair out for her and waved a hand across the newly set table. Linen napkins and silver candlesticks. He'd found a fresh tablecloth and their wedding china as well.

"What's the occasion?"

"If I'm to be a judge—and I believe I will—then we must start acting the part. We have to keep the right company. Shop the right stores."

Stella attempted a laugh, but when she saw the complete seriousness on his face, she cleared her throat instead. "I'm never sloppy with my clothes. Why does it matter where I buy them?"

Joe took the carving knife and cut into the small hen she had roasted for dinner. He sawed back and forth a little harder than necessary, and the tender meat disintegrated beneath the serrated blade. "It matters a great deal. You need to start patronizing the better women's shops in Manhattan. You'll be *seen* there—that's why it's important. All the Tammany men send their wives to Mae & Hattie Green on Fifty-Second. But Dobbs on Fifth also attracts an upper-level clientele. Keep your purchases to those two shops for now. It's the only way we'll be taken seriously." Joe tugged at his collar. "I've found a tailor on Fifth. He's the best around."

"Is that why you've been wearing those shirts?" He looked like a turtle walking upright—stiff collar from shoulder to chin—but Stella couldn't tell him that. Joe was too fond of the price tag and the Smithson label that accompanied his new wardrobe.

He dished a heaping pile of new potatoes and carrots onto his plate. "You know my neck," he said. "Thin and gawky. The collar covers it up. Can't have anyone commenting on the pencil-neck lawyer that wants a judgeship."

The chicken was savory and the potatoes tender, and were it not for the serious turn the dinner had taken, Stella would have thought it one of their more enjoyable evenings.

"I know there are things you have to do," she said—"paying contribution" was the way he'd actually termed it after returning from a meeting at Tammany Hall one night—"but I never thought I'd be going public along with you."

"You're not." He stabbed a carrot with his fork. "Unless I need you on my arm for a function. Your place is right here, in the home. I'd certainly hate to see you sitting around in those smoke-filled rooms at the club debating politics. It's just not the right thing for women."

She bristled at this but hid her frustration behind a cool smile. "It's inevitable, you know, women in politics."

"I don't care if that constitutional amendment did pass last year. You'll never see a woman in government. Mark my words."

"You are hopelessly old-fashioned. It might be fun, you know, to see a woman on city council." Stella needled him with her grin. "Or even on the bench one day. Could you imagine that? A Miss So-and-So for a judge?"

Joe brought his fork down with a loud clank. For a moment, she thought he might have broken the plate. "You can't mean that," he said. "And you mustn't say anything of the sort in public." Joe's view of women's suffrage was not one of his finer points, and this line of talk always irritated him.

"Maybe I'll start the campaign myself. Go down and buy one of those bloomer girl outfits. You know the ones—those militant suffragettes wore them when they'd picket."

"Stell!"

"Oh, come on, Joe. I'm only teasing. You're taking this way too seriously."

"It is serious! Every bit of it. Wagner says he's got me on a fast track for the court. Everything you say and do *is serious*. The length of your hem is serious. Your neckline, it's serious." His voice rose until it was almost a shout, but when he saw Stella with her hands in her lap, spine pressed against the chair, he controlled himself. Joe took a sip of water from the crystal goblet next to his plate and forced a laugh. "You're not like those girls."

"Meaning?"

"You're intelligent. Well bred. Proper. Not like those dames who get off the trains or the boats and end up onstage with low morals."

"That's an unfair comparison, don't you think? Being an activist doesn't make a woman a floozy."

"There's more than one way for a woman to whore herself out."

Stella gaped, appalled. "I can't believe you, talking like that."

"Oh, come off it, Stell. You aren't the type."

"And what exactly do you know of *that* type?"

"I know a lot of things. Chief of which is that you need a good spanking."

Exasperated, Stella threw her dinner roll at him, and he flashed his old mischievous grin. For a few seconds he was the Joseph Crater she met on the dance floor all those years earlier. But then he realized that the French roll had left crumbs on his new suit. He swept them from his lap with a stern look and devoured the rest of his dinner in silence.

MARIA and Jude slid into the velvet-covered seats as the lights dimmed. She took his hand and moved closer, flushed with excitement. The lower floor of the Morosco Theatre was full, and all she could see were heads bent and whispering, the final rush of conversation before the curtain drew back. Only a smattering of empty seats remained in the balcony, and those stuck out like missing teeth, black spots in the theater's red velvet mouth.

"This is amazing," she said.

Jude grinned. "The show hasn't even started yet."

"The entire night has been amazing. Thank you for dinner."

"You deserve it. And I'm sorry."

"You've got to stop apologizing."

The same shadow of sadness that had hovered around him for weeks returned. "I'll get your rosary fixed. Promise."

"I know." Maria tilted her chin and kissed Jude just below his ear. She smiled, dark eyes full of mischief. "I hear this show is scandalous."

He slipped his arm around her lower back, hand resting on her hip. "It has quite the reputation for loosening the corset."

"No wonder you didn't argue when I asked to come."

"The only corset I'm interested in is yours."

"Pity I don't wear one."

Jude made a show of tugging at the neckline of her dress and looking down it. "Even better."

Maria swatted at his hand. "Behave yourself. We're in public."

"It's dark."

"And it's crowded. You'll get us kicked out before the opening number."

Someone shushed them from behind.

"See," Maria whispered.

The crowd gasped as the dim lights dropped into total darkness. The entire theater was temporarily suspended in blindness, and then a single trumpet note lifted from the orchestra below, followed by a French horn. A honeyed glow rose from behind the still-drawn curtain, and the rest of the orchestra began to fill in and complement the melody as the curtain swept aside. And there onstage stood twenty women, linked at the arms, in pink gossamer gowns split right up the thigh. Each dress was fitted with a sequined bodice, and the matching sequined top hats had plumes that swayed in the air as the women kicked in time to the music. They wound into a tight circle, each dancer holding the train of the girl on her left, moving faster and faster until Maria could not see any individual face, only a blur of legs and flashing smiles.

Maria leaned forward, eyes round and lips pressed in concentration. She did not take her eyes off the dancers once during the number, not even as they swooped and spun across the stage, a streaming, orchestrated whirl of pink.

As the circle broke and the dancers spread across the stage in a tightly choreographed routine, Maria saw a familiar face. Her eyes remained fixed on the curvaceous woman, as though tracking her through an elaborate shell game. At the end of the number Maria stood, along with the rest of the crowd, but she did not clap. She rested her hands on the rail in front of her and leaned as far over the balcony as she dared. Yes. She was certain. The young woman on the far left with the sand-colored hair and hazel eyes was the girl she'd come to see. Sally Lou Ritz, pregnant with the bastard child of Joseph Crater.

STELLA spent much of her evening making phone calls and pacing the wall of windows in her living room, waiting for Joe's friends to call her back. Her husband once said that he bought the cooperative apartment—at a mind-boggling sum of $14,000—for the view. A manicured garden belonging to the Church of the Ascension sat right beneath their windows and, depending on the season, guaranteed a bevy of color unmatched by many of the city parks. The groundskeeper for the church was a small, arthritic man of indeterminate European descent. Joe insisted he must be Dutch. *Look at the tulips! he'd say every spring when the garden exploded in white and pink blooms.* But Stella wasn't sure. They had never exchanged words, but she'd often see him bent over some bed, pulling weeds. On days when she left the windows open, his voice drifted up, a soft and lonely melody that translated only in emotion. Stella did not know where he came from, yet she was certain he was a man acquainted with grief. But the garden lay in darkness now, flower beds rounded into shadow. Somewhere below was a cobblestone path dotted by stone markers engraved with the names of generous members of the congregation, but she could not see them from this distance. In the three years that Stella Crater had lived in this apartment, she'd never once set foot within the church. Until tonight, it had not seemed important. What would she do in there? Light a candle? Say a prayer? She might as well turn a cartwheel in her underwear for all the good it would accomplish. And yet she understood the compulsion of the devout right then, the need to *do* something.

The phone rang and Stella leapt for it, banging her shin on the coffee table. *Bleeding hell, that hurts!* "Hello?" She swallowed. Blinked back the pain.

"Stella, it's Martin Healy. I got your message."

"Oh, thank goodness." Her breath came out in a rush. "I can't seem to get through to anyone. Please tell me you've seen Joe." The phone sat on a secretary desk along one wall, and Stella rifled through the top drawer looking for something to write with, the receiver cradled between her chin and shoulder.

"No. I haven't. I'm very sorry. I just wanted to return your call. Make sure you're all right," he said. She could hear laughter in the background. Glasses clinking. Slurred voices. "You'll let me know, won't you, when he shows up?"

She mumbled assent as he hung up, returning to the festivities. Stella slumped into the ladder-back chair next to the desk and rubbed her shin. She could feel the lump rising against her palm. Soon the calls began rolling in, each more unhelpful than the last.

"Stella, such bad news. Wish I had something to tell you. Do keep me posted." Jimmy Walker.

"Nope. Nothing since we last spoke. I've been asking around." Simon Rifkind.

"Term started four days ago. Things can't continue in this manner." Justice Valente. He added a stern warning, as though it were her fault: "It's imperative we find Joe. We have work to do."

She methodically worked her way through Joe's address book, but many of the calls she made went unanswered. Others resulted in messages left with various staffers. She tried three times to call Joe's legal secretary, Joseph Mara, but the line was busy all evening.

It went on like that, call after call, until she had only one number left. And he wasn't in. William Klein. Attorney for the Schubert Association. Joe's closest friend and a theater aficionado. Stella couldn't imagine that Joe would return to the city without visiting Klein. She knew exactly where he'd be, although now was hardly the time to pay him a visit.

It was almost nine o'clock when Stella made her decision. She quickly showered, chose a dress appropriate for the errand, and fixed her hair and makeup.

The city showed no signs of resting as she walked from her apartment building and hailed a cab. "To the Morosco Theatre," Stella said, sliding into the backseat and tucking her dress around her legs.

By the time she arrived at 217 West Forty-Fifth Street, the show was almost over. Stella bought a ticket anyway. Once inside, she approached the nearest usher.

"Can I help you?" he asked.

"I need to have a word with William Klein. I know he's backstage."

The young man twisted the cuffs of his jacket and looked away. "I'm sorry, but—"

"You'll go tell him that Stella Crater is here to see him. He knows me." She pressed a dollar bill into his palm and watched him debate for a moment. He shrugged and then hustled through a side door that led into the bowels of the theater. She waited, gripping her small clutch, for five minutes. She was beginning to wonder if her bribe had worked when he ducked his head back into the lobby and beckoned her to follow.

As soon as the door closed behind them, Stella could feel the throb of the orchestra. It rose through the floor and shimmied up her legs. While walking that twenty feet of hallway, she understood how those girls went onstage and threw themselves around. It was hypnotic. And then the usher opened another door and stepped aside so she could enter the madness backstage. A roiling mass of bodies and ropes and costume racks danced together in a rhythm that she instantly disrupted. Stella fumbled her way across the throng until she reached the far wall. Standing there, behind the curtain, was William Klein. His back was to her, and he watched a string of girls performing a carefully choreographed routine. Their legs bent, lifted, and kicked in seamless motion.

The entire stage was transformed into an elaborate aviary, and the dancers were peacocks, swirling in a show of blue and green feathers. From where she stood behind William Klein, the nearest dancer was only six feet away. Stella was close enough to see sweat drip down her temples. Watching the swirl of movement made her dizzy.

She grabbed Klein's forearm. "William."

"Stella!" He drew her in for a hug. "So good to see you."

"Where is he?" The sound of her voice was startling. Panicked.

William set his hands on her shoulders and leaned toward her. "What's wrong?" And then, "What are you doing here?"

"Joe."

"What about him?"

"He's missing."

William Klein looked at her with dark, mud-puddle eyes, surprise registering a few seconds late. When he finally spoke, the question came out forced. "What do you mean?"

"Joe never came back to Maine. I haven't seen him in weeks. No one has."

A raucous blast of music leapt from the orchestra pit, and the crowd cheered. The swarm of dancing girls gave a final bow and then festooned around them backstage.

"Show's over," Klein said, the young women pawing at him as they passed. They petted and kissed and rubbed him in ways that made Stella's lips part in astonishment. He tried to appear uncomfortable with the attention but could not fully hide his lecherous grin. Klein shooed them away and pulled Stella a step deeper into the shadows.

"I just had dinner with Joe," he said.

"When?"

"A few weeks ago, I guess."

"When. *Exactly.*"

He scratched the side of his neck. "*Dancing Partner* had just opened at the Belasco. That's where he was headed afterward. So it must have been"—he rocked his head back and forth, summoning the playbill from his memory—"the sixth."

Over three weeks earlier.

"You had dinner. Then what?"

"Then we all said goodbye outside Billy Haas's Chophouse, and Joe went on his way."

"All?"

"Me and Joe and . . ." He hesitated before adding, "Ritzi." There was no need to explain who she was, so he didn't. But Klein did glance over Stella's shoulder. Then back to her face. And back again at someone in the crowd.

Stella's eyebrows pulled together in a tight frown. "Have you heard from him since?"

"No. I'm sorry."

"You'll let me know if you hear anything?"

"Of course." He gave her an awkward side hug, mumbled a goodbye, and then shifted his attention to a patiently waiting brunette.

When Stella turned away, she almost tripped over the showgirl behind her and had to step back with a jerk. The girl was tall and curvy and beautiful—the sort that would catch Joe's attention. Stella locked eyes with her for no more than a second. She wore a towering feathered headdress and a sequined costume. Her eyes and lips and cheeks were exaggerated with heavy makeup. Still, she looked familiar. Before Stella could get a good look at the face beneath the makeup, the young woman dissolved back into the crowd.

Stella didn't belong backstage, clearly had no idea how to avoid the traffic that rushed by on all sides, but she stood there anyway, overwhelmed. A stagehand asked if he could help with anything. "Ladies' room?"

"That way." He pointed to her left. "Off the stage and down the hall."

RITZI stood against the wall, breathless. Her chest heaved, heart dancing staccato against her ribs. Around her hummed the orchestrated chaos of *Ladies All,* the last swell of frenetic activity after the final number. Applause surged and then diluted into the rumble of conversation as the audience collected jackets and purses and nudged one another into the aisles. Her legs trembled, and she drew a deep breath through her teeth.

Beneath the feathered headpiece, her hair lay plastered to her scalp. Sweat ran in trickles down her temples and the back of her neck. For the final number, the entire chorus line wore elaborate peacock costumes, complete with sequined bodices and tail plumes. The effect was spectacular when the girls spread across the stage kicking and spinning. But after hours spent in various costumes, Ritzi's lower back ached, and her feet were swollen inside the three-inch heels.

Once Ritzi was certain she could get to the dressing room without stumbling, she peeled herself from the wall and pressed into the sea of performers and stagehands celebrating another successful night. Farther backstage, her stomach lurched. William Klein stood beside the curtain. She hadn't seen him since that morning in his office—had gone out of her way to avoid him, as a matter of fact. Her first thought was that he came to collect payment for his silence. But then she saw that he leaned into conversation with a woman. Tall and blond and . . .

Ritzi stared. The woman was a stalk of grace. She carried herself with an assurance that was unnerving. Radiant in a knee-length navy dress with a scoop neck, her clavicles like the prow of a ship. Pearls twisted around her neck—exactly the way they were in the photo on Crater's bedside table. A wedding ring. Even from this distance, Ritzi could see her eyes, pale blue and startling. Ice water eyes. And then Klein looked up, right at Ritzi. His gaze whipped back and forth between them.

Stella Crater. She had come looking for her husband. Ritzi could read that truth right there on Klein's face.

As usual, he was swarmed by showgirls, vultures in bright plumage picking at whatever scraps he threw them. Some poor girl would end up in his bed tonight and likely be forgotten by lunch tomorrow. Her hatred for Klein was matched only by her fear at the sight of Crater's wife.

After another short burst of conversation, Klein stepped away from Stella and moved toward one of the dancers. Ritzi was not prepared when Stella turned around and their eyes met. She could see the search for recognition scrolling across Stella's face. *Yes, you know me,* Ritzi wanted to say, but she forced herself to keep a neutral expression beneath her mask of stage makeup. Then she turned and walked away. Once their gaze was broken, Ritzi rushed toward the dressing room.

The twenty girls in the chorus line shared a large room backstage for makeup and costume changes. Shorty guarded the door. None of the stagehands made it in or out without his knowledge. For good reason. It was a scene of mass nudity.

"What's the rush?" Shorty asked as Ritzi pushed by him.

She knocked the bowler hat off his head with two fingers and darted through the door.

Elaine Dawn, one of her fellow dancers, laughed as Ritzi pushed the door shut. She was a busty blonde with powder-blue eyes and full lips. She had the look of a Ziegfeld girl and a permanent spot at the front of the chorus line. "You'd think being so close to the ground, he could get that hat a little quicker," Elaine said.

"He's so strange," Ritzi said, resting one arm against the door. "I don't know why Owney keeps him around."

"Need help with your costume?"

Ritzi turned so her friend could release the small clasp on her back and slip the tail feathers off. "God, that hurts. Why'd we sign up for this again?"

Elaine fluttered her eyelids in an expression of mock surprise. "For the fame and fortune, of course."

"Really? I signed on to this gig so Shorty could get his jollies peeking through the keyhole." Ritzi smacked the door with the flat of her hand.

He cussed on the other side of the door.

Ritz peeled her headpiece off and hung it on the doorknob. Now that her plumage was gone, she shrugged out of the bodice and stood topless, letting the cool air dry her wet skin. Half of her companions did the same. They walked around the room in varying stages of undress. One by one, the girls slid out of their costumes, collected the pieces, and set them on hangers. The ensembles then went on three long garment racks arranged by number.

"You look awful," Elaine said.

"Gee, thanks." Ritzi wiped an arm across her forehead. It came away slick with sweat.

"Seriously. Do you feel okay?"

"I just want to go home."

Elaine eased into her slip and pulled a snug cocktail dress over her head. "Suit yourself. I'm off to Club Abbey." She wiggled her eyebrows for effect. "I hear Owney's in a good mood tonight."

"How'd you hear that?"

Elaine pushed up her breasts and shook them a bit so they settled into her dress. "I have my sources."

"June?" Ritzi asked, looking toward the far wall, where June Brice, the vixen of the group, rolled stockings onto her legs and secured them with a black garter belt. "I thought she was with Owney?"

"She's moved on to some uptown guy. A lawyer or something. Which means"—Elaine turned around so Ritzi could zip her up—"there's a job opening."

"You don't want to mess around with him," Ritzi said.

Elaine's eyes narrowed. "You jealous?"

"No. I want you to be safe."

"And I want off this chorus line." She looked at the three racks of plumage. Leaned in and whispered, "I'm following your lead. Owney's my ticket to something better."

He's your ticket to the morgue. Ritzi winced at the thought. "Not a good idea."

"You've had him, right?"

Ritzi caught a flash of shame as she saw her reflection in the mirror. "That was a long time ago."

"Well. It worked for you." She gave an impish grin. "And Mae West. Look where she is now."

Until recently, the very mention of Mae West would have made Ritzi quiver with hope. Four years earlier Owney Madden had financed her highly controversial Broadway show *Sex*. After 375 performances and ticket sales of over three hundred thousand, the show had been raided by the police and the entire cast and crew charged with obscenity. West spent ten days in a prison workhouse and emerged a legend. Since then, her star had only continued to rise. She'd already abandoned New York for Hollywood.

"So," Elaine said, undeterred. "Any pointers?"

"Stay away from Owney. Find yourself a decent guy."

Elaine looked in the mirror and applied a coat of deep red lipstick. She smacked her lips twice, assessing her reflection. "I think I'll give him a shot. Wish me luck." She kissed Ritzi on the cheek and then left the dressing room.

The knot in Ritzi's stomach tightened as she watched Elaine leave. She pulled on her undergarments and stepped into her dress. Fumbled with her shoes.

Her cheeks were clammy and her palms damp. She felt dizzy. Ritzi grabbed her purse and ran down the hall to the public bathroom. A line of women waited, but she pushed by them and darted into the first open stall and vomited right into the toilet bowl.

MARIA unlaced her fingers from Jude's. "I need to use the ladies' room."

She had spent the entire three-hour performance searching the chorus line for Ritzi. She appeared in each act, but never so prominently as in the opening. Maria paid little attention to Jude as he commented on this number or that, or even when he jumped to his feet along with the rest of the theater after a particularly elaborate routine. Instead, she kept her gaze on the young woman, mesmerized by her poise and grace. Nowhere could she detect the panicked and embarrassed girl she'd surprised in Crater's bedroom or the desperate woman at the doctor's office.

"You should have gone at intermission," Jude said, "with everyone else."

"The lines were too long. Besides, I didn't need to go then."

Jude led her from the balcony and down the stairs into the lobby. "There." He nodded toward a sign. "That way. But be quick. I want to get you home." He traced the curve of her jaw.

"You're insatiable," she said, and gave him a peck on the cheek. "Be right back."

Maria took her place at the back of the line and searched the faces around her. It took five minutes to get inside the restroom itself and then another five for a stall to empty. No sooner had she gotten situated than she heard a rumble of discontent as someone cut in line. And then the door of the stall next to hers crashed open. Angry comments ricocheted around the bathroom until the poor girl began to vomit. Several toilets flushed at once, followed by the rush of faucets, as women hurried on their way. Those remaining in line tried to ignore the retches, and the bathroom hushed into an awkward silence.

When Maria left the stall, the girl was bent over the sink, splashing water on her face and rinsing out her mouth. Maria plucked several paper towels from the nearest dispenser and held them out to her.

"Thanks." The girl lifted her face to offer Maria a wan smile, but it quickly slipped away. As she reached to take the towels from Maria's hand, her face twisted with concern. "What are you doing here?"

They stood elbow to elbow at the sink, Ritzi drying her hands and Maria primping her hair. They looked at one another in the mirror as women swirled behind and beside them, adjusting makeup, necklines, and stockings. Ritzi, no longer in costume, with smeared makeup and tangled hair. Her street clothes and pallid skin went a long way to mute her role as the temptress she'd been in Crater's bed and on the stage that evening.

"My husband brought me to see the show," Maria said.

"He brought you to my show. Just because?"

"I asked him to."

A smudge of crimson lipstick marred Ritzi's chin, and she rubbed it away. Her eyes were heavy and tired-looking beneath the stage makeup. The false eyelashes and glitter did little to hide her exhaustion. "Why?"

It was a simple question. And Maria had prepared for days to answer it. But she found herself unable to utter the words in this place, surrounded by strangers. She took a deep breath. Shook her head. Closed her eyes. "I—"

A toilet flushed behind them, and when Maria looked up, she saw Stella Crater swinging a stall door open. Ritzi stiffened beside her.

Ritzi let out a huff of air and bent her head toward the sink. She did not watch as Stella approached the mirror, pale eyes on her own reflection, but rather swayed for a moment and then clapped a hand over her mouth and darted back into a stall to retch again.

"Mrs. Crater." Maria forced her eyes away from Ritzi's hunched form and nodded at her employer in deference. Whatever rules of etiquette applied in this situation were unknown to her.

Mrs. Crater's expression shifted from fatigue to recognition to relief when she saw Maria. She took in the familiar embroidery of her gown. "You look lovely in that dress."

"Thank you," Maria stammered. "You gave it to me."

"I remember. Joe hates"—she paused, a note of uncertainty in her voice—"*hated* it on me. Always said I didn't have the bosom to fill it out. Clearly a deficit you need not worry about."

Maria turned her eyes to the tiled floor, self-conscious. Crossed her arms over her chest and then dropped them to her sides. She eased her question out without ever meeting Stella's penetrating gaze. "How is Mr. Crater?"

Stella shifted closer as a patron sidled up to the empty sink and ran her fingertips beneath the faucet. "I was hoping you could tell me. Have you seen him?"

Maria stared at Stella, trying to word her response. How to tell her that she'd seen more of Mr. Crater than she ever wanted to? That she knew more than she could speak aloud? Especially in this place, with so many within earshot. But as she struggled with her words in the brief silence, Ritzi returned to the sink. She washed her mouth out again, spitting politely into the bowl.

"Disgusting," someone muttered behind them.

A number of women hurried from the restroom without looking at Ritzi. Some whispered on their way out.

"I really know how to clear a room." Ritzi offered a shaky laugh.

Stella pulled a box of mints from her purse and offered one to Ritzi. "Are you all right?"

"Just dizzy." Ritzi twirled her finger in the air. Took the mint. Placed it on her tongue. "All that *spinning*."

"I only saw the last number," Stella said. "It was quite impressive."

"I wasn't properly trained," she explained. "As a dancer, I mean. The others know how to balance and keep a point of focus. I just muddle my way through." Ritzi sucked on the mint and then hesitantly met Stella's eyes in the mirror. "You'd think I'd have a stronger stomach by now."

"Strong enough for what you need to do, though, right?" Stella asked.

"For my part. Yes."

"You do put on a good show." Stella nodded, approving. The clasp of her necklace had slid down, and she moved it back to the nape of her neck. "If you'll excuse me, ladies, I have business to attend to."

"Will I see you this week," Maria asked, "at the apartment?"

"I'm leaving Sunday. No need for me to stick around, given the current *circumstances*." She glanced at Maria and then at Ritzi. It seemed as though she wanted to say more but felt vulnerable in that small room with so many others around.

"I'm sure they'll find Mr. Crater," Maria said.

"Let's hope so. It would be nice to know where he is. For certain."

Maria lingered as Stella swept out of the bathroom. Ritzi gave Maria a desperate sort of look and, lacking anything else to say, grabbed her purse and left. Even in this, the pecking order remained intact. Wife first. Then mistress. Leave the maid behind to clean up the mess. Without thinking, Maria wiped down the counter with a paper towel and then stepped into the stall to flush the toilet Ritzi had forgotten.

STELLA climbed from the cab shortly before midnight. There was no sign for Club Abbey over the set of concrete steps that descended below street level. She paused and looked around. The location of this establishment was strictly word of mouth, considering its numerous illegal proclivities. The street was lined with cars and the sounds of jazz. Laughter rose from the bar below, but she was the only person in sight. Stella smoothed the creases from her dress, pulled her gloves up, and squared her shoulders. She gripped the rail in one hand and her purse with the other and began her descent. Eighteen steps. Each slow and measured, the heel of her shoe pressed against the riser. She took a deep breath at the bottom and reached out to push the heavy wooden doors.

"Password?" A man stepped from the shadows. He was a good foot shorter than Stella. Stocky. And had the heavy brow ridge of an Eastern European. "No one gets in without a password."

She snorted and drew a five-dollar bill from her purse. Waved it in front of him with two fingers.

"Works for me." He took the money and swept one arm toward the doors.

They parted easily beneath her hand. Stella had expected resistance, but instead she almost stumbled into Club Abbey. The bar smelled of smoke and whiskey and floor polish. Perfume. Sweat. It was intoxicating. So immediate, even with one foot still on the threshold.

Laughter.

A ruckus somewhere in the back.

The ceiling was low and dark and warm, with its embossed copper panels and mahogany trim. The speakeasy beckoned her to come in, come closer, get pulled into the fray. Stella stepped inside.

The doors eased shut behind her, and with them went the last hint of fresh air. She almost turned and left. Almost. Instead, she steeled herself and took a step forward, then another, purse clutched in front of her as though she were afraid it would be stolen. With each inch of movement, Stella felt a little bolder, a little more purposeful. Intent on her cause.

A jazz quartet played in the corner, massaging their instruments, almost impervious to the crowd. Notes floated up and around and mingled, cohabitating in the air. She could practically taste each chord change, that little pause in the air before she inhaled and then the new swell of music. The piano player sat tall and straight, his elbows at right angles. So serious. So intense. On the bass was a short black man, barely taller than his instrument but almost as wide. He plucked at the strings with intention and feeling and a sort of reverence that she could feel twenty feet away. Drums and saxophone lifted and bled between the notes, an instrumental game of tag. For years Joe had told her that he visited Club Abbey for business purposes, but she now understood his reasons were far more varied than that. This was a place he must have loved.

In the middle of the room was a large dance floor filled with couples leaning into one another and swaying to the beat with slow, sensuous movements. Stella could feel the heat coming from them. Women with their arms slung over men's shoulders. Men with hands dangling low in the small of a back. A face buried in a neck. Heads tipped back in laughter. All of it beneath the swirl of cigar smoke and dim light.

Booths lined the wall, and the dance floor was circled by tables of men with loosened ties and women with flushed cheeks. Stella pushed her way through the crowd and slid up to the bar between two men. She did not sit down. The bartender, a young man with startling red hair, poured a drink for a woman who leaned forward a little too suggestively, almost begging him to look down her dress. How did he do it? she wondered. How did he look at her eyes, so clouded with booze that one drifted off to the side, instead of taking her up on the offer of a free peep show? The bartender's gaze shifted to Stella, and he threw a towel over his shoulder and made his way toward her. The bawdy woman almost fell off her stool as she leaned after him, and the men beside Stella stepped over to catch her. They positioned themselves on either side, each with an eager hand to steady her. They flashed glares back and forth. Marking their territory. Marking their prey. Stella halfway expected one of them to pee on the poor woman and make it official.

"What can I get you?" the bartender asked.

"My husband is a regular."

"Ah. One of the wives."

Stella lifted one neatly plucked eyebrow in question.

"We get your type in occasionally. Uptown girl looking for her low-brow husband." He lifted a glass from the shelf and set it on the bar in front of her. "You want a drink, or do you want me to rout out your man?"

"My husband isn't a tosspot." Stella recognized Stan from their phone call, that voice with the faintest trace of puberty still audible. "But he is in here a lot."

"Name?"

"Joseph Crater."

She enjoyed the discomfort that swept across the bartender's face as he made the connection. His youth showed then in his embarrassed smile. "Which would make you the judge's wife?"

"Hello, Stan."

"I know Joe. Good man. Good customer." He motioned to the barstool. "Have a seat. We don't bite. Most of us, anyway. But you might want to stay away from that one," he said with a wink, and nodded at some unidentified patron behind her.

Stella gave him a closer look. Baby face. Probably couldn't grow a beard if he tried. His voice had solidly changed, but likely it still broke if he got excited. "How old are you?"

"Not old enough to serve liquor." He poured a shot. "Much less drink it." He knocked back the glass and shuddered a bit as the whiskey went down.

"You can't fool me. Bravado aside. You're a virgin."

He choked.

"With liquor, I mean! Liquor."

Stan shifted a little closer, one corner of his mouth twisted into a cockeyed grin. "Neither, miss. But don't tell Owney. He'd have me fired. Or shot. It's my job to protect the booze and the girls."

"So that's the trick, is it? The way to keep a joint like this in business? Liquor and women."

"We take a head count every night," he said proudly. "How many broads you see in here?"

She gave him a scolding look before she turned and rested her elbows on the bar. "I see fifteen *women*. Maybe twenty. Hard to tell. They won't sit still."

"And men?"

"Two or three times as many."

"Try five. For every gal that comes in that door, you can bet five men will follow her. All of them eager to buy her a drink. And it's not even midnight yet."

"I imagine the number will go up significantly?"

"Owney hired a bouncer. He only lets in the ones with looks or money."

"Well, it cost me five bucks. So I guess I know my category."

"You ain't the usual customer, I'll concede that. But I'd have to argue with the looks issue. You've already got admirers. I count seven making eyes at you right now."

A few men did have their eyes on her. Some looked confused. Others intrigued. "Drunk. Every one of them, I'd wager."

"Only three." He raised the bottle of whiskey. "I do keep count, after all."

Stella looked over Stan's shoulder at the bottles of whiskey behind the bar. It occurred to her that very little probably got past his keen eye. "Did my husband come in recently?"

He didn't respond.

"I'm not trying to get you in trouble. I just need to know where he is."

Stan leaned over the bar. "Joe comes in, right? But he's not all that regular. Not an every-nighter like some of these guys. I'm not sure the last time I saw him. It's been weeks."

Stella chose her words carefully. "Does he come in alone?"

"I don't see them come in, Mrs. Crater. My job is to watch what they do while they're here."

"What about when he left? Was he alone then?"

Stan shook his head. "No good's gonna come of you being here."

"If you won't tell me what I need to know, then I'll talk to your boss."

"You're a pretty lady. And you seem smart. But this"—he motioned around the room—"is not the place for you. Owney don't cater to your type. The only things you'll learn here will lead to heartbreak."

"You think I don't know about heartbreak?"

"There's a lot of things you don't know." He looked at the clock. "The first of which is that in about fifteen minutes this place is going to get rowdy. The dancing girls have let out. I doubt you have the stomach for that."

"I'm not a prude."

"Go home, Mrs. Crater."

"Where's Owney Madden?"

Stan took his dish towel and began to dry a set of lowball glasses. His eyes were warm and brown, and he looked uneasy. "See that guy back there in the corner booth?"

She looked to her left. A large booth sat on a riser, tucked into the corner. Its occupant was an arrogant-looking man with flinty eyes and a scar on his upper lip. "Yes."

"That's Owney. When Joe comes in, it's to talk to him. That's all I know."

"I'd bet you know what my husband has to drink when he comes in here."

Stan didn't answer.

"He doesn't drink tap water. I know that much."

He slid the whiskey bottle across the bar. "This," he said. "On the rocks."

"Pour me one of those, if you don't mind. Just the way Joe takes it."

"This is stout liquor, Mrs. Crater."

Stella set her elbows on the bar and leaned forward a few inches. Her smile was firm and cold. "Who the *hell* do you think taught me to drink?"

He dropped six ice cubes into the glass and covered them with whiskey. Slid it across the bar. Stella took her drink and walked toward the corner booth, where Owney Madden sat alone. She didn't turn around when Stan called her name, a clear note of warning in his voice. Poor kid. She'd leave him out of this.

Owney didn't notice Stella until she was a few feet away. He sat up a little straighter when she stopped in front of his booth and set her glass on the table.

"Mind if I join you?" she asked.

"Looks as though you've a mind to do just that."

Stella forced the amused look from her face. Such a ridiculous accent, Scouse. *Lewks as though yeh've a meend to do just thaht.* None of the dignity of the English or the passion of the Irish. Truly a stew of dialects, just as the name implied. Scouse: named for the lamb soup so favored by the citizens of Liverpool and Merseyside.

She smiled. "I won't intrude where I'm not wanted."

Owney spread his arm out. "Be my guest."

She stepped onto the riser and scooted across the seat until she was opposite him. She set her purse in her lap. "You're not drinking tonight?"

"I never drink while I'm working, Miss . . . ?"

"Mrs. Crater."

"Ah," he said. "Joe's wife."

"I assume you know why I'm here?"

Owney laughed. "Don't start assuming anything. We don't know each other."

Stella wrapped her fingers around the glass. The condensation soaked through her gloves, and she steadied herself. "You got my message?"

"Contrary to popular opinion, I do not have a secretary. Only a pubescent bartender who is highly unreliable when it comes to communicating details about the opposite sex." Owney plucked a cigarette from an open pack on the table. He propped it between crooked front teeth and struck a match. After he'd taken a long drag, he asked, "This message you left, was it important?"

"Do I look like the kind of woman who would be in a place like this otherwise?" Stella took a sip of her whiskey. She cupped it in her tongue, controlling every drop as it slid down her throat to avoid the cough that threatened to roar through her body. She took another sip.

"No, you do not. Liquor aside."

"Joe was a friend of yours?"

"I'd call him a customer."

"Your customer has gone missing, Mr. Madden."

Owney blew smoke out his nose. It clouded in front of his face and then drifted toward the ceiling. "So they say. But I don't see what you want me to do about it."

"Joe's gone. So I want you to return the deed to my lake house."

"I don't know what you're talking about."

"Sure you do. During Joe's *campaign* to get on the court, he sold a number of properties to raise funds. But the deed to the lake house is in my name. Not his. Something he failed to recall when he sold it to you. And I want it back."

Owney dropped his air of nonchalance, eyes tightening around the corners. "And what do I get in exchange?"

Stella undid the clasp on her purse and pulled out the business card she'd found in Joe's coat pocket. She placed it faceup on the table. "You get this. And a promise that I won't tell the police that you were the person who insisted my husband come back from Maine."

STELLA made it back to her apartment well after one in the morning. She stepped from the elevator and saw an older woman by the door. She glanced up as Stella approached.

"Where have you been?" the woman demanded, all nerves and sympathy.

"Honestly, Mother." Stella dug for the keys in her purse.

"A hello would be appreciated. Especially under the circumstances. I had to take the *night* train." Emma Wheeler had taken up sentry outside the apartment, sitting on her suitcase, a small purse clasped in her hands. Legs crossed and spine plumb-line straight.

Looks like she swallowed a walking stick in one gulp, Joe often said, marveling at her mother's posture. It made Emma look severe and uncompromising.

"You could have let me know you were coming."

"I called from the train station. Five times."

Stella reached out a hand and helped her mother to her feet. "I was out."

Emma wrinkled her nose. "Have you been *drinking*?"

"Only to prove a point."

"I raised you better than that. Women of decent reputation do not drink."

"Neither do they have missing husbands. Yet here I am, liquored up and fully abandoned. Now, would you like to come inside, or would you rather lecture me in the hall?"

"I've been waiting here"—she looked at her watch—"three hours."

Stella swallowed her retort and unlocked the door. She held it open. Emma swept into the entry, keen eyes searching for a point of criticism on which to land. She left her suitcase in the hallway for Stella to fetch. From the weight of it, she guessed her mother had packed half her wardrobe.

"I am your mother. It is my duty to comfort you in times like this."

"How did you know?"

"Your sister called. Said you'd come back to the city to look for Joe. Why didn't you tell me?"

She lied. "I didn't want to worry you." In reality, she hadn't wanted her mother to interfere.

After Stella set Emma's suitcase in the hall closet, she found her in the living room, running one finger along the bookcase. She inspected the tip of her glove. "You ought to fire your maid."

"Maria does fine work. Stop criticizing." A single lamp was on in the living room, and Stella switched the others on to lighten the room.

"What are you doing?" her mother asked.

"I'll be up for a while. I have some calls to make."

"But it's almost two in the morning."

"I can't sleep."

"Don't you think it would be wiser to go to bed? You've been out half the night." Emma peeled her gloves off, one finger at a time, and lifted her hat from her carefully set hair. "Doing God knows what."

"I was taking care of business. Why don't you go to bed?"

"You'd think a grown man would know how to look after himself."

"Mother!" The word was sharp, and Stella winced at the sound of her own voice. Her next words were kinder, though unwavering. "Did you come to help or chastise?"

Emma stared at her daughter, face turning to granite. They shared the same startling blue eyes and propensity for saying exactly what they thought. Mother and daughter regarded each other, unsure of the protocol in this situation.

Stella asserted herself. It was her home, after all. Her missing husband. And she'd not asked her mother to come. "I would drink some coffee if you made it."

Emma did not look up as she made her way to the kitchen, but Stella heard her mutter, "This trauma has addled her senses."

When Emma was out of earshot, Stella pulled a slim white envelope from her purse and retreated to Joe's office. She knelt in front of the bookshelf behind his desk and pushed against the lower panel. It swung outward to reveal a small safe built into the wall. She fumbled her way through the combination three times before getting it right. The door opened with a click, and she set the deed to the lake house inside.

JUDE hadn't moved from a supine posi-
tion by the time Maria finished dressing for Mass. She brushed a knot
of tangled hair away from his forehead and kissed his temple. He lay
stretched across the bed, arms and legs askew, and she stood back to look
at his half-naked body. The sheet was wrapped around his waist, his head
beneath one arm. Maria ran her finger over his parted lips, feeling the
warmth of his breath and then the stubble on his chin. Any other day she
would have crawled back into bed and made love to him. Instead, she left
a note—*Gone to Mass, be back soon*—and slipped out the door.

The sun had scarcely risen over Midtown as Maria walked toward
the spired Gothic beast that was St. Patrick's Cathedral. She had given
up her dream of a wedding there when she married Jude, but she still
adored every marbled, gilded inch of the place. It was the church of
her childhood: confirmation, confession, First Communion. Her father
had insisted they attend the elaborate cathedral instead of their smaller,
humbler parish in Queens. In time, she learned that his decision had less
to do with piety and more to do with business. The wealthy went to St.
Patrick's. Maria's father secured a job as a tailor at Smithson's within six
months of their first Mass. Irreverent as it seemed, Maria could never
argue the wisdom of his decision. The church had been kind to them. It
was the place where she first understood that prayers were holy and that
God wasn't some *other* thing out there, but the most important thing
anywhere.

She tugged on one of the ornate handles attached to the double
doors and stepped inside. Mass would not start for an hour. The sanctuary was filled with silence and splashes of indigo light from the sun

filtering through a stained-glass kaleidoscope above the altar. She kept to the shadows and slid into a wooden pew at the back of the church to wait.

The confessionals on each side of the nave were discreetly tucked behind towering marble columns. None of them were occupied. The repentant had not yet risen, apparently. Except for Maria. And she made no move toward the red-velvet-draped booths. Instead, she watched a handful of parishioners light candles at the side altars and kneel, whispering over clasped hands, filling the church with the scent of prayer: incense and candle smoke. Some settled into the pews. Others tiptoed from St. Patrick's, their business with God tended for now.

After several minutes, a small door creaked open inside the chancel and a weathered priest limped out. Maria relaxed in her seat. She watched him shuffle toward the altar and down three steps into the sanctuary. She was struck by his ruined body, how he took a step and then lifted his other leg, dragging a crooked foot along the floor—a dilapidated man in vestments. The priest lowered himself into the front pew and sat with his back to her, head bowed in reverence.

Maria took a quick breath through her nose. The scent of wood polish, floor wax, and the cracked leather of old Bibles gave her the courage she needed to rise and walk down the nave toward the confessional nearest the waiting priest. She cleared her throat as she slipped behind the red curtain and drew it shut.

The booth was small and oddly comforting. She sat, back straight and eyes on the cloth-covered ceiling. After several moments, there was a rustle of fabric on the other side of the screen partition. The click of wooden rosary beads knocking against one another. A whispered prayer in Latin. Then silence—her invitation to begin.

"Forgive me, Father, for I have sinned," she said, her words drifting away as it occurred to her that she did not know how to say what she'd come to confess.

More silence.

"It's been many months since my last confession." Maria wiped her sweaty palms across the fabric of her dress. "I don't know how long."

A melancholy sigh, and then the partition slid back.

Startled, Maria looked at the priest and saw the familiar face with its kind gray eyes and tender smile. She smiled. "Hello, Father Donnegal."

"Maria."

She looked at the wedge of partition tucked into the wall between them. "This is . . ."

"One friend speaking to another."

Finn Donnegal had taken the cloth five years before Maria was born, when her parents were still newlyweds living in Barcelona. He'd always been a staple in her life. Family friend. Counselor. Adopted uncle. He had secretly defied her parents to attend her wedding to Jude at City Hall—his support for their union stopping short only at performing the ceremony himself. She hadn't had the heart to ask.

"I came here to confess," she said.

"Did you, now?" A skeptical twitch of his eyebrow.

Maria opened her mouth and then snapped it shut again, abashed. She sank farther into the seat. "I've done something I shouldn't have."

Father Donnegal leaned back against the wall, allowing space for her confession. A note of doubt laced his voice. He would always believe her to be a wide-eyed innocent. "What have you done?"

When Maria could see just the edge of his profile, she said, "I stole money from my employer." It was more than that, of course, but the story was not entirely hers to share.

She was absurdly pleased to hear the surprise in his voice.

"Why?"

A complicated answer. She sighed. Maria wanted to tell him about that day in the apartment and about Jude and the envelopes. Her raging curiosity. Yet she'd come that morning to hear secrets, not to tell them, so she offered only a thin slice of the truth.

"Mr. Crater is missing," she said. "A reporter came to his home while I was cleaning and told me. And I thought . . . I don't know . . . that there might not be any more paychecks. The last one is three weeks late already."

"Many of God's children have been tempted by less."

"But I don't *do* that kind of thing."

"Apparently, you do." Finn clasped the gold crucifix that hung around his neck. "Does he know what you have done?"

"No."

"Do you still have the money?"

"Yes."

The booth settled into a solemn hush. Finn seemed perfectly comfortable in the silence, but Maria squirmed beneath its weight. "What is my penance?"

"You must return the money."

"Should I tell him what I've done?"

Finn tipped his head to one side. "Do you know the difficult thing about God, Maria?"

At the moment, everything about God seemed difficult. "There's just one thing?"

"He can only deal with the truth."

"What does that mean?"

"It means the truth is more important than protecting yourself. Regardless of the consequences."

Maria groaned. "I will lose my job."

"Perhaps."

Never one to rush the repentant, he waited while she considered that possibility. Only when she shifted her weight and sighed again did he say, "This is the first time you've ever come to me for confession. Why now?"

"It's awkward. You're practically family. It's like a brother reading your diary."

Father Donnegal pressed her with silence.

"You're the one I need to speak with," she finally said.

"Why?"

Maria wanted to give a different answer, but she couldn't lie to him. "Jude came to see you a few weeks ago."

"So now we get to the truth of your visit."

"I'm not here under false pretenses." Not completely, at any rate. She had wanted to confess her theft.

His face settled into a look of patient disbelief.

"He told me that he came," Maria continued. She played with her purse strap, coiling it around her fingers, wishing for her rosary and suppressing a sudden rage at Jude. She wouldn't be here if not for him. "I was hoping you'd tell me what the two of you spoke about."

"You know I can't do that." Finn gripped the edge of the partition with knobby, arthritic fingers and slid it shut. "Not even for you."

She winced. "But—"

"Let us pray."

Maria leaned forward, straining to hear his quiet absolution. She cleared her throat, ashamed. "Amen."

"Give thanks to the Lord," he added.

"For his mercies endure forever," she answered in a whisper. Maria pushed back the curtain and hurried from the church. The heat of embarrassment was still bright on her cheeks as she fled St. Patrick's.

GRAND STREET, LOWER EAST SIDE,
WEDNESDAY, MARCH 5, 1930

Maria laughed. "Careful, that's the curb."

She wrapped Jude's arm around her shoulders and dragged him back onto the sidewalk. He struggled to find his balance, as though it were the ground that spun.

"I'm drunk."

"No," she said, "you were drunk hours ago. Now you're outright pickled."

"Rotgut."

"I warned you not to drink that stuff."

Jude didn't so much slur as stumble over his words, each syllable seemingly independent of all the others. "Had. No. Choice."

Maria wedged her shoulder into his rib cage and pushed against him at an angle. One block left. Her only goal right then was getting him back to the apartment before he fell unconscious to the pavement. Jude outweighed her by fifty pounds and was a good six inches taller. There was no way she could lift him if he went down—she would have to fetch a blanket and stay with him until dawn. A miserable prospect for both of them on such a cold night.

Eight hours earlier, he'd been promoted to detective, and the two of them had been coerced into joining the boys from his department at some lousy gin mill near Chinatown. Bad hooch, cigar smoke, and lewd jokes had filled their evening. Maria abstained from all of it, while Jude, growing ever more uncomfortable at what she had to endure, kept a protective arm around her shoulders. He had a perpetual flush of embarrassment on his cheeks, but he didn't refuse the liquor—felt it would be rude, considering his new partner, Leo Lowenthall, bought the rounds. So he'd knocked them back, one after the other, until he could barely stand and would have lost a bet on his mother's maiden name.

Only after he'd gone to the bathroom and left her at the mercy of Leo's roaming gaze had she convinced him to leave. At three in the morning, Grand Street was deserted. Even the streetlamps looked exhausted, dim and sputtering in protest, as they shuffled back to their Orchard Street apartment.

"What's that?" Maria asked in response to a long string of mumbling. She peered up at the distressed look on his face.

"Said he'll bleed me."

"Bleed?"

"Pay up. Earn my keep." Jude tried to laugh but only produced a strangled bark. He pointed his finger at Maria's face in some forced imitation. "'Job comes with strings, you know. One day they'll be pulled. Prepare to dance, Pinocchio. Or your family pays.'"

He went on like this for several minutes before she realized he was trying to relay some conversation he'd had. "Who said that?"

"Mooney," he said, and shook his head. "Rooney." Jude tried again, forcing tongue and mind to communicate. "Mulrooney."

"The police commissioner?"

He belched in affirmation, and she stopped right there in the middle of the sidewalk, turning him to face her, a steadying hand on each of his shoulders. "When?"

"Tonight."

At six o'clock, Jude had stood on a platform with ten other offers during a promotion ceremony. She'd watched Commissioner Mulrooney hand him the detective's badge that finally got Jude off the vice squad. They both gave wooden smiles amid the press flashbulbs. Maria had been overwhelmed with pride, imagining how she'd seek out the papers the following day to save the headlines and show them to their children years from now: A CROP OF NEW YORK'S FINEST!

At one point in the evening, she'd noticed Mulrooney ease Jude away from the crowd. They'd had a private conversation at the back of the room. Jude had looked so serious, so stoic. And she'd assumed that he was overcome by the opportunity, humbled to be singled out by such an important man. But now she wondered if she had misread the exchange. Perhaps it was not congratulations but stipulations that Mulrooney imparted to her husband.

Jude crushed her lips flat with the same finger he'd pointed at her earlier. "Shhhh," he said. "'S'all off the record."

Her mind lit on one thought after another, realizations so scattered and erratic she felt drunk as well. The favor she'd asked of Joseph Crater. Jude's promotion. Mulrooney's warning. Jude drinking himself under the table.

This was her fault.

She'd opened Pandora's box. He was no better off as a detective than he was on the vice squad.

It was March and still cold enough for both of them to be in long coats. And though their breath had been swirling before their faces the entire walk home, Maria only then began to feel truly cold.

She reached up and set her hand against Jude's cheek. "I'm so sorry."

He leaned into her palm and rubbed against it like a kitten. The movements made him stumble forward, and she had to throw her weight against him to stop him from flopping to the ground. "Home it is," she grunted.

Maria steered him down the street, around the corner, and into the entrance of 97 Orchard Street, one of the nicer tenements in the highly populated immigrant section of Manhattan. She did not undress Jude or yank back the covers, merely deposited him as gently as possible onto their bed. She did take his shoes off, however, and then lay beside him, fretting until both mind and body surrendered to exhaustion.

When Jude woke at noon the following day, he remembered nothing, not how much he'd had to drink or who had been with them at the bar or their conversation on the way home. Maria would have been tempted to write it all off as the intoxicated ramblings of an inexperienced drinker were it not for his reaction when she asked about his conversation with Mulrooney at the ceremony.

"It looked like he was saying something really important," she said.

That conversation, he clearly remembered. Jude's face settled into the controlled, emotionless expression he reserved for her mother and her repeated attempts to convince him that converting to Catholicism was the only way to save his soul. "Nothing to worry about," he said. "Mulrooney was only making sure I fully understood the obligations of this new job."

EMMA occupied herself with cooking breakfast while Stella thumbed through Joe's address book, searching for any associates who might know his whereabouts. Most didn't answer so early on a Sunday morning; those who did couldn't tell her where he might be. As Stella left Joe's office, a swift knock rattled the front door.

"Shouldn't you freshen up before answering that?" Emma called from the kitchen.

"Why?" Stella glanced down at the wrinkled navy dress and the stockings that sagged a bit around her ankles.

"You look rumpled."

"Would you prefer to answer it?"

Emma turned back to her poached eggs with a sniff.

Stella peered through the peephole, breathed a sigh of relief, and opened the door.

Leo Lowenthall stood in the doorway, hat in hand. "I heard the news, Mrs. Crater. I'm so sorry." He motioned to a second detective. "This is my partner, Jude Simon."

Stella led them into the kitchen.

"Mother, this is Detective Lowenthall with the NYPD. And his partner, Jude Simon. Gentlemen, my mother, Emma Wheeler." They shook hands.

"Simon Rifkind called me yesterday and asked me to look around," Leo said. "I've checked out all the hospitals and morgues, but there's no trace of him."

Detective Simon took off his fedora and ran his fingers along the brim. He glanced around the apartment expectantly, as though looking for someone.

"I don't know what to do," Stella said.

"There isn't much you can do. Except wait." Leo offered her a patient smile. "When did you get back?"

"Friday night."

"And have you found anything here that might shed some light on where he went?"

"No. But I haven't looked around much." Stella had a hard time keeping her voice light and wondered if the truth was written across her face.

"Mind if we look around?"

"Please do."

The detectives led Stella and her mother through the apartment, opening closets and checking coat pockets. They rifled through drawers and inside cupboards but found nothing. After a while, their interest turned to the bedroom.

"Quite the clotheshorse, isn't he?" Leo asked, thumbing through Joe's closet.

Emma stood in the doorway, nodding her approval. "My son-in-law is a well-tailored man. Every bit the judge."

"Does everything look in order, Mrs. Crater?" Detective Simon asked.

Stella joined them at the closet and took stock of Joe's summer suits, mostly lightweight cotton and linen. She lifted a brown vest that seemed to have misplaced its companions. "There's a brown pinstriped suit that's missing. His favorite."

All of Joe's traveling bags were in place at the back of the closet, and most of his personal items sat on top of the bureau: a monogrammed pocket watch, a fountain pen, and a card case.

Leo wandered over to the bureau and inspected each of the orphaned items. "Does he usually carry these with him?"

"Yes."

"Any idea why he'd leave them behind?"

"I have no idea about any of this," Stella said as she watched Leo lift the edge of the bureau scarf.

He motioned to the small gold key that stuck out from the lock. "May I?"

"Certainly."

His eyes crinkled at the corners. "No personal items in there?"

"My underwear is well hidden, I assure you."

Stella sat on the bench at the foot of her bed as they moved toward the bureau. She feigned disinterest and plucked at the tassels on a throw pillow. They stared into the empty drawer. Leo tapped a squared-off fingernail against the wooden bottom. Jude popped the knuckles on his left hand one by one. Emma rummaged through a shelf at the back of the closet. Stella noted all of this in the silence that filled the bedroom.

"I'm a little puzzled," Leo said after a few long seconds, "that Joe didn't leave anything behind indicating his whereabouts."

"I've spent the last month puzzled about a great deal more than that," she said. Her voice broke on the last word, but no one seemed to notice.

An uneasy glance passed between the two detectives, and then Leo shut the drawer. "Here's the situation," he said. "I don't think anything should be done for the time being. Maybe you should go back to Maine? Let us look around a bit more."

Stella tossed the throw pillow onto the bed. "Joe's already been missing almost a month. And all I've done is sit up there and wait."

"What if he comes back and you're not there? Besides, I can keep you informed if anything happens here."

Jude rested against the bureau, unease etched across his face. He watched the exchange but offered no input.

"Perhaps that *is* best," Stella said.

Emma led the detectives to the door, Stella trailing behind. "If you don't mind, I'm going to lie down. I don't feel well," she said. "Good day, gentlemen. Thank you for checking on Joe."

Emma clicked her tongue. "But you haven't eaten breakfast."

"I'm not hungry anymore."

While Emma saw the detectives out, Stella returned to her bedroom and locked the door. Joe's Victrola stood beside the window, and she turned it on low. The room filled with jazz music and the faint rustle of static. She peeled the stockings from her legs and tossed them in the hamper, along with her dress. Stella lifted her slip above her knees and knelt on the hardwood floor. She reached into the darkness below the bed, her back stretching with the movement, and fumbled around before pulling out the leather satchel. Inside lay the four manila envelopes she'd found in the bureau drawer. Each addressed to her in Joe's handwriting. Each containing something that she could not let anyone discover.

"OWNEY Madden is sending a car to fetch you, Mrs. Simon."

Maria glanced up from her stitching. Donald Smithson stood beside her station, inspecting the work she'd begun on one of Owney's suits. He nodded in approval.

"Why?" Maria never stopped sewing, but kept her eyes on Smithson. The mention of Owney's name made her careless, however, and she pricked the tip of one finger with her needle. She jumped at the tiny surge of pain. "Is something wrong?"

"On the contrary. He's very pleased with you. Requested that you do a custom tailoring job for him."

"Sir, I don't think it's appropriate for me to be running around the city with a client. Why doesn't he bring the work in, and I can do it here?"

Smithson did not look up from her work. He turned it over. "Because the clothing is currently attached to the bodies of several chorus girls. We can't very well ask them to accommodate our schedule, can we?"

"What does that have to do with Mr. Madden?"

Exasperated, Smithson set down the material. "Our client is a financial backer of several Broadway shows. This one in particular is having an issue with a few costumes. And when a client is willing to pay double the going rate for custom work, we say yes. Understand?"

"Of course."

"Good. Get your things ready. His driver will be here any moment."

While she was debating whether to call Jude and let him know, a black Cadillac pulled to the curb, driven by a jumpy little man in a bowler hat. Smithson shooed her out the door before she could argue further.

The driver stuck out a hand. "Shorty Petak."

"Maria Simon." She shook it in reply.

Shorty helped her into the backseat and rushed around the car. He lurched into traffic as soon as his door was shut. "Hold on tight. Show starts in an hour, and several of the girls are having trouble with their tail feathers."

She spent much of the ride gripping the door with her eyes closed. The massive Cadillac roared through the streets of Manhattan, swerving around vehicles, ignoring traffic signals, and blaring its horn. When they finally ground to a stop in front of an alley, Maria felt ill.

Shorty hurried to open her door and then escorted her across the alley and into the employees' entrance.

"This way." He led her down a broad hallway crammed with stage props: artificial trees, an assortment of rowboats, a dining table, and a stuffed grizzly bear. She felt as though she were passing through a storage room for bizarre dreams.

They ducked between a set of leafy palms and stepped into a large area backstage. He pointed toward a door. "In there."

"I just go in?"

"They're expecting you."

Maria grasped her sewing bag and slipped through the door. A crowd of showgirls jostled for a spot in front of a long mirror rimmed by lightbulbs. Blondes, brunettes, and redheads laughed and elbowed one another. Most of them were topless, and Maria let out a small gasp of surprise. She looked away, but the room was filled with bare skin.

She watched the women prepare for the show. They helped one another into sequined tops and towering feathered headpieces. The costumes, though skimpy, seemed to take a great deal of dexterity to get into, and the women had a system in place that was fascinating. She wanted to examine the outfits to see how they were stitched together for such flexibility What kind of fabric allowed for that kind of movement? The dancers bent and stretched and kicked their feet above their heads as they warmed up, all of this in three-inch heels.

Maria cleared her throat.

A busty redhead looked up from her place at the dressing table. "Who are you?"

"The seamstress."

She turned toward her friends. "Hey! Who needed their tail feathers fixed?"

A show of hands, and then several women went to grab costumes from the long racks against the wall. While they were gathering their things, Maria looked for another face.

"I thought you were a maid?" The quiet voice betrayed a hint of anger, and Maria spun around.

Sally Lou Ritz had her arms crossed over a blue satin robe, a lit cigarette dangling from the fingers of one hand.

"In the mornings, yes. It helps pay the bills. But this is what I do best." Maria unpacked her sewing bag on the table and looked at Ritzi, uncertain. "Am I working on your costume as well?"

"Mine? No. At least not *yet*." She shrugged off her robe and hung it over the back of a chair. Her undergarments were small and sheer and expensive, revealing the hourglass suggested beneath her robe. She cleared her throat. "I might need your help later."

"Might?"

Ritzi dropped a hand to her stomach. Patted once. "Depends on how these costumes fit in a few months."

So cavalier, that movement. As though getting pregnant were as easy as catching a cold. Maria counted the years she'd been trying to conceive a child. How she often lay on her back with her feet on the wall after she and Jude made love. He laughed at her for that. But she heard once that it worked.

"It's simple enough to let out a garment, make more room in the midriff," Maria said.

"The costumes run small. The producers do it on purpose to keep us little. Nothing like the fear of popping a seam midshow to ensure you don't eat. Needless to say, they are not accommodating to certain *situations*."

Maria rearranged the pins on her pincushion. "I'm at Smithson Tailors in the afternoons. Let me know when you're ready."

"Thank you." Ritzi put the cigarette to her lips and inhaled. She blew two long streams of smoke out her nose. "It took the costume designer three months to make these things. But some of the girls are losing their tail feathers on the high kicks. It's embarrassing."

"Shouldn't be that hard to fix. I just need to reinforce the clasp." The dancers lined up in a row, and Maria knelt beside them, a seam ripper and a needle pinched between her lips. "Stand still," she said. "I don't want to nick you." She sliced into the first costume with the small hooked blade until the clasp was exposed.

The costume designer had used the wrong thread. Maria dug around in her bag for a topstitch-weight polyester thread. By the time the girls were needed onstage, she'd replaced the clasps on all five costumes.

As the girls bustled from the dressing room, Maria grabbed Ritzi's arm. "I can help you. Please let me."

THE drawer was empty. Where there had been four envelopes only days earlier, she saw nothing but wood grain and a film of dust. Maria slid the drawer shut and then reopened it, as though expecting them to magically appear. She pressed the stack of bills against her forehead and squeezed her eyes shut, lips moving in fervent cadence. She thought of Father Donnegal and his prescribed penance. "Count not my transgressions, but, rather, my tears of repentance. Remember not my iniquities, but, more especially, my sorrow for the offenses I have committed against you . . ." she whispered, palm resting on her heart.

A stillness wrapped around Maria, and what sounds reached her ears did so as though heard apart from her own body: her desperate exhale, water dripping in the bathroom sink, the rattle of a delivery truck on the street below, the creak of floorboards beneath her feet, the ding of the elevator down the hall, the metallic whir of the ceiling fan. She shuffled backward a few feet and dropped to the edge of the bed. Maria heard herself swallow.

On the bureau sat a small clock. It ticked away in the silence, and she watched the second hand move around the clockface. Once. Twice. Three times.

Maria was supposed to meet Jude for lunch. But after the shock of seeing that empty drawer, she struggled to remember when. Or where.

As a child, Maria had once stolen a piece of candy. Her father made her spit it out and carry it back to the store in her hand. She'd cried when telling the clerk what she had done. Her father hadn't let her wash the stickiness from her palm for the rest of the day. *That's what it feels like to steal,* he'd told her, closing her fist in on itself. *You wear it like a stain.* Indeed, her skin was tainted pink the following day, when he took her to confession for the first time. She'd begged him not to see Father Donnegal. Any priest other than the one who sat at their table for dinner on Monday evenings.

"Forgive me, Father, for I have sinned."

Maria stuffed the cash back in the inner pocket of her purse and went to collect the cleaning supplies. She made quick work of the apartment. She straightened the bed. Mopped the bathroom floor. Scrubbed the toilet. Brushed lint from the drapes. The bookshelves in Mr. Crater's office were dusty, so she took the books down one by one, wiped them, and cleaned the shelves. She tidied the room, turned off the lamp, and set the ceiling fan on low to circulate the air. Before leaving, she put Mrs. Crater's favorite potpourri in the pewter bowl on the dining room table so the room would smell of lavender and bergamot. Then she grabbed her purse and went to meet Jude for lunch.

MARIA found Jude beneath the memorial arch in Washington Square Park, his gray fedora obscuring his face, and two small packages, wrapped in newsprint, in the crook of one arm. He tapped a rolled-up newspaper against his thigh.

"Sorry I'm late," she said, and flicked the brim of his hat with her finger.

Washington Square Park sat at the foot of Fifth Avenue. From where they stood, Fifth Avenue yawned open before them, a broad swath of pavement rimmed by skyscrapers, a canyon of glass and steel and stone.

"I hope you're hungry." He waved the packages in front of her face. "Fish and chips. Fresh from O'Malley's Pub."

Maria hadn't felt at home with Jude since she saw him plant those envelopes. Everything he said and did now made her wary. And the worst part was that Jude was so preoccupied with his secrets that he hadn't even noticed the change. She kept waiting for him to ask what was wrong, but the question never came. Maria had to consciously tuck her hand beneath his arm and let him lead her around the fountain and down one of the side paths into the park. She forced herself to relax, to lean against him and inhale the mild air. It was a relief after a month of near hundred-degree temperatures. Brown-tinged leaves fluttered above them, a few falling to the ground and cartwheeling across the path, making little scraping noises as they went.

"This used to be a potter's field, you know. Twenty thousand people are buried in this park," Maria said. She pointed at a tall elm near the path. One of its branches stuck straight out like an accusing finger, while the others slanted upward in search of fresh air and sunlight. "That's the hanging tree. It's the oldest tree in Manhattan."

"What is it with you and graveyards?"

"They fascinate me."

"Dead people fascinate you?"

"No. The stories they leave behind." She peered up at him. "Don't you wonder who they were? What kind of lives they lived?"

Jude glanced up at the English elm—over a hundred feet tall—as they passed beneath its branches. "Not very good ones, if they were hanged to death."

"Not *all* of them were hanged. Just the worst offenders. The rest were normal people. Like us. Mothers and fathers. Children. Sometimes I wonder if they came here on ships or if they were born in the tenements. This was the public cemetery, a poor man's graveyard."

Jude stepped off the path and led her toward a bench. He pulled her down beside him and set one of the packages in her lap. It was still warm, and the heat pooled on her legs. "Eat your lunch before it gets cold."

The smells of fried fish and potatoes mingled with that of cut grass and browning leaves. She unwrapped the package and licked the salt from her fingers.

"Isn't this sacrilegious?" Jude asked. "Eating in a graveyard?"

Maria paused, a potato inches from her mouth. She winked. "Let us not mourn the departed, but rather thank God that such men and women lived."

"Is that a prayer or a benediction?"

"Both."

"In that case"—he tapped his potato against hers—"amen."

She grinned. There was the Jude she loved. Maria leaned over and planted a kiss on his cheek. It was cool against her lips, and she felt the beginning of stubble. "Thanks for lunch."

They slipped into a comfortable silence as they ate, enjoying the call of birds and the feel of sun on their cheeks. After a moment, Jude tipped his head backward and looked up through the heavy oak branches that stretched over the bench.

"I got a new case," he said. He unrolled the newspaper and pointed to the front page: JUSTICE J. F. CRATER MISSING FROM HIS HOME SINCE AUGUST 6TH.

There it was, the news of Mr. Crater's disappearance in black and white. She scanned the article so quickly that she couldn't fully make sense of the words. They registered in pieces, small details lodging in her brain: *last seen on August 6th . . . assistant says he cashed large checks earlier that day . . . bought a ticket for a Broadway show . . . acquaintances fear murder.* The byline was the last thing she read, but her eyes stayed on the name for several long seconds: George Hall.

"It's him," Jude said.

"Who?" She dared a glance at Jude, as though she'd been caught in her omission of the facts.

"Your boss. That judge."

Maria couldn't stop the hint of fear from slipping into her voice. "Yes."

"Did you know he was missing?"

"No, I . . ." She took a deep breath and spread the paper flat on her lap, trying to remain calm. "I didn't know this."

"What *did* you know?"

"People were looking for him. That's all."

"What people, Maria?"

"A reporter." *And his wife,* she thought, but didn't say.

Jude took the newspaper from her and reread the article slowly. It ran thirty-three column inches and was heavy on the details. He settled on a section of the story and brought the paper a little closer to his face. He read out loud: "'The Craters' maid, Amedia Christian, saw the judge early on the morning of August fourth and was told to come back on the seventh, after he returned to his vacation home in Maine. She noted that when she arrived that morning the bed had been slept in recently and his suit was left on the floor but there was no sign of the judge.'" Jude's face tightened into a stiff look of panic. "Did you talk to this reporter? Did *you* tell him this?"

"Not exactly. He embellished a bit. I didn't mention the suit." She played with a loose thread on the cuff of her blouse. Gave him a half-hearted smile. "He knocked on the door one day and started firing off questions. I talked to him for a couple minutes."

"Why didn't you tell me?"

"I didn't think it mattered."

"Your boss goes missing, and you don't think it matters?"

"Because I thought he was in Maine. With Mrs. Crater."

Jude scowled at the paper. "Listen, you don't need to talk to these people. None of them."

"What people?"

"Anyone to do with Crater. His associates. His friends. You tell me if they start nosing around, understand?"

Fifteen minutes ago she was famished, but now the sight of all that food made her stomach turn. "Why? What's going on?"

He held the paper in front of her face so the headline was only inches away. "'Justice J. F. Crater *Missing from His Home* Since August 6th.' *Home*, Maria. Not Maine. Not work. *Home*. You work for him. You're in his home all the time. I don't want anyone thinking you're involved."

What little she'd eaten of her lunch sat like a brick in her stomach. "Why would anyone think I'm involved?"

"They won't. Unless you give them reason to. I don't want you near this case." He waved a hand over the *New York World*. "And I sure as hell don't want your name in the papers."

"I didn't give that reporter my real name." She pointed to the article, where her mother's name was printed in black ink. "When he asked, I lied."

Jude gave his first real smile since they'd met for lunch. "Good!"

"It's not good. I don't like lying." Not that it mattered now. Owney had figured out that she worked for the Craters. So much for discretion.

"It's better this way," he said. "Trust me."

Trust had never been a question between them. It was natural and understood. But for the first time in ten years of marriage, they sat together offering half-truths and hidden meanings, neither going so far as to lie outright, but both certainly skirting the edge.

Maria picked at a potato with one thumbnail and chose her words carefully. "It's a weird coincidence, don't you think? You get this case, and I work for Mr. Crater?"

Jude stared straight ahead, into a thicket of trees on the other side of the park. It was several long seconds before he answered. "*Coincidence* is an understatement."

"Does anyone else at work know I'm the Craters' maid?" She searched his face for signs of deception.

"Leo."

"What does he think about you getting the case?"

Maria was certain he spoke the truth when he turned to her with a pained expression and said, "Leo recommended me for the case. Commissioner Mulrooney agreed."

"Why?"

"They said it would be a good test for me, a way to prove my commitment to the job." He crushed her against his side and buried his face in her hair. He held her tighter than usual. "I have to go to Maine and get a statement from Crater's wife."

Maria pulled away. "Please don't."

"I don't have a choice."

FIVE thousand dollars. That's how much the New York Police Department offered in reward for information leading to the whereabouts of Joseph Crater. Stella glared at the missing persons circular, studying the black-and-white photo of her husband. Joe, with his pursed lips and high collar and severe part, stared right back at her from the page. She sat on the edge of the pier, toes in the water and hands stuffed into the pockets of Joe's dinner jacket, fiddling with the half-empty pack of cigarettes and matchbook she'd found weeks earlier. Stella had taken to wearing the jacket when she retreated to the pier—always in the late afternoon and usually for hours at a time. It still smelled of his aftershave, and the satin lining felt cool against her bare arms.

A copy of the *New York World* was spread on her lap, along with two letters that had come by post that morning, and she switched between the front-page article, the letters, and the missing persons circular, as though each new reading would explain the mystery of Joe's disappearance.

The letters were the most distressing of the lot. The first, written in startling blue ink on cheap white stationery, was a clear attempt at extortion. When she'd read of kidnappings and ransom notes as a child, she imagined things along the lines of Robert Louis Stevenson. It was, in truth, far less romantic when she held the clichéd note demanding $20,000 in exchange for the safe return of her husband. *Have money small denominations. The quiet way is best. Cooperate fully or you will not see your husband again.* She stuffed it back in the envelope.

The second letter was from Commissioner Mulrooney and stated that he would be sending a detective to question her.

As far as the newspapers went, it had been a big week. A reporter by the name of George Hall had written both front-page articles. Above the fold was the now-staple face of Joe and more curious details of how he vanished. Below the fold was a picture of Al Smith at the construction site for the Empire State Building. "Eighty years ago, a very short time when one stops to think, this land was part of a farm," Al had said in his speech. "More recently it was the site of one of the great hotels in the world; and soon it will be the location of the tallest structure ever built by man." Stella found it ironic that the two men shared the same newspaper page. It was Al, after all, who had pushed so hard for Joe to get into politics, and then Al again who had helped arrange the details of his appointment to the court years later. She wondered if he'd paused at all that day to publicly acknowledge her husband or if he'd been too obsessed by watching his own dream rise into the New York skyline.

Stella had almost memorized the tersely worded announcement that went out to law enforcement around the country. Fred had brought her the circular, along with the morning papers, after he returned from the village earlier that day, and she'd worn them thin with anxiety.

$5,000.00 REWARD

MISSING SINCE AUGUST 6, 1930

JUSTICE OF THE SUPREME COURT, STATE OF NEW YORK

THE CITY OF NEW YORK OFFERS $5,000 REWARD TO ANY PERSON OR PERSONS FURNISHING THIS DEPARTMENT WITH INFORMATION RESULTING IN LOCATING JOSEPH FORCE CRATER

Description—Born in the United States—Age, 41 years; height, 6 feet, weight, 185 pounds; mixed gray hair, originally dark brown, thin at top, parted in middle "slicked" down; complexion, medium dark, considerably tanned; brown eyes; false teeth, upper and lower jaw; good physical and mental condition at time of disappearance. Tip of right index finger somewhat mutilated due to having been recently crushed.

Stella stopped reading and wadded the circular in her clenched fist. She loathed the words they used to describe Joe: *missing, time of disappearance, presumed alive.* Commissioner Mulrooney had signed the circular himself. One comment in particular drew her attention: "If we could find some of his papers we might learn something about the cause for his disappearance."

She could only guess that Mulrooney was hinting at the envelopes she'd found in the apartment, but she couldn't fathom how he knew about them. His name hadn't been on Joe's list of illicit business dealings. Stella hurled the newspaper and the circular into the water. Propelled by her anger, they fluttered in midair, pages spreading out like a fan, and then landed with a plunk and turned gray as water soaked them.

"That's not a statement," she said, "it's an obituary."

"The neighbors will think you've gone strange, talking to yourself like that."

Stella turned to find Emma standing above her, hands clasped at her waist in that infuriatingly polite way of hers. She hadn't heard the screen door snap shut or Emma's purposeful stride down the wooden pier.

"Look around. I have no neighbors."

"They boat. And they talk. You must maintain propriety. Appearances are important, you know." Emma pointed back toward the house. "One of those detectives from the city is waiting inside to ask you a few questions."

"I know." She held up the letter from Mulrooney. "I'll come in a minute."

"You're going to make that detective wait while you sit out here and talk to yourself? That's hardly a way for the wife of a missing judge to behave."

"I'm going to gather my thoughts," Stella said. "Besides, I don't really give a damn about appearances right now."

"Your language is appalling."

"No. What's appalling is that Joe's face is all over the front page."

"How else will they find him?"

"Those papers are a diversion, Mother. They're not looking for Joe. They're looking for ways to capitalize on his disappearance."

"You can't mean that."

"Every politician in New York just got carte blanche for as long as Joe is the headline. Tammany Hall will be a political free-for-all for months."

"What on earth are you saying?"

"As long as the headlines are filled with juicy tidbits about a missing judge, then no one will read about the grand juries meeting this month.

Or the voter fraud. Or the bribery. We won't read about the informants and the prostitutes that are disappearing every other day."

Stella pulled out a cigarette. She ran it beneath her nose, inhaling. It was a bit stale, having sat open so long, but it reminded her of Joe and dinner parties and the few wonderful things that had come with being his wife.

"Since when do you smoke?" Emma eyed the cigarette as though she would yank it from Stella's hand. But she glanced nervously back at the house instead.

"Since now." It was easy to rip out a single match from the book and strike it against the strip of sandpaper. Stella tipped the cigarette into the flame just to watch her mother's eyes widen.

"You've been out of sorts since New York. Is there something you need to tell me? If so, do it now, before you go in and talk to that man."

"No. Should there be?"

Stella never made the conscious decision to inhale. But she did nonetheless. It was sand in her throat and fire in her sinuses. Her lungs forced the smoke out in rapid-fire bursts, and her eyes went slick. Emma laughed. Stella inhaled again. Ashes on her tongue. The taste of soot. Another lungful of smoke, deep into the core of her body, and she held it long enough to grow dizzy. Then she let it out in a sputter. Stella coughed and wiped her eyes. She took a deep breath of clean air and lifted the cigarette to her lips again. This time she took a cautious drag and rocked back and forth on the pier, controlling the tingling new sensation that flooded her body.

"Here." She handed the second letter to Emma.

"What is this?"

"A fake ransom note demanding twenty thousand dollars for Joe's safe return."

"What?" Emma held the envelope away from her body as though it would burn her. "How do you know it's fake?"

"Read it. Whoever wrote that thing copied the text from a dime-store novel. It's a scam."

"Are you sure? Who would do such a thing?"

"Someone who wants to make a quick buck off the grieving wife of a missing judge."

"Well, what do you want me to do with it?"

"Give it to that detective." Stella drew her feet out of the water and slowly stood up. Dizzy and nauseated, she reached out to steady herself on Emma's arm. "And have Fred bring the car around."

"Why?"

"I'm going to Irv Bean's store so I can officially report my husband missing."

"It's all over the papers."

"Exactly. I can't have people wondering why I never reported it." Stella threw the half-smoked cigarette into the lake. "I must keep up *appearances,* after all."

"Pull yourself together, Stella. You're not going anywhere until you give that detective a statement."

Stella glared at the house. "Just send him out here."

BILTMORE HOTEL, NEW YORK CITY, OCTOBER 27, 1927

The crystal vase crashed to the floor, shards spinning across the wood parquet in every direction. An elaborate tulip arrangement lay tangled in the mess, buds broken and stems bent at unnatural angles.

"What in God's name was that?" Joe struggled with his bow tie as he stumbled from the bedroom in the high-rise suite.

"The cat." Stella pointed to a bushy-tailed orange tomcat that raced back and forth along the wall. His hackles were raised, and he hissed and spit as though batting away a predator.

"*Your* cat," Joe said, correcting her with a stern glance. "I suggested we board him."

"Chickie is *our* cat. And two weeks in a kennel would have killed him. Besides, it's that stupid parrot next door. Can't you hear it?"

Joe had arranged for them to stay in a suite adjoining that of Governor Al Smith and his wife, Catherine, while their new apartment was being finished. As a political move, it was genius, but it had proved a test of patience when it came to Chickie. The Smiths' green parrot squawked so loudly it made their eyes throb and had a laugh so eerily human-sounding Stella often couldn't tell whether she heard the bird or Catherine on the other side of the wall.

"Look at him," she said. "It's a wonder he hasn't dug right through the wall to get that bird."

"Put him in the bathroom, then. We need to get downstairs. Cocktails started ten minutes ago."

It took several minutes before Stella cornered Chickie between a set of purple velvet drapes and a large armoire in the sitting room. She held him at arm's length so he wouldn't shed orange hair onto her black dress and chucked him into the bathroom.

"That cat is a menace," Joe said, holding out his bow tie to her.

"He's a darling."

"He shit on the rug. Had to clean it up before the maid found it and complained to management. We'd be evicted."

Stella flipped Joe's collar up and ran the tie around his neck. She knotted it with nimble fingers. "The governor would never let that happen. Besides, I can only imagine what their place looks like. They don't keep that bird caged. And Catherine told me the other day that Al feeds it straight from his fork."

"They're waiting on us." He gave her dress careful scrutiny before finally offering his approval. "You look nice."

Stella spun in a small circle, seeking his approval. But as usual, his gaze didn't linger. "It's Chanel," she said, following him to the door. "Destined to be a classic, the salesclerk said—"

"I don't care," Joe interrupted, "as long as it was expensive."

It *was* expensive. The latest version of the swing dress, it was long sleeved and sat low on the hips, with a pleated skirt and a hemline that hovered midknee. The dress was perfect for that night's fund-raiser—sure to involve champagne and the Charleston. Stella dressed it up a bit with pearls, a small netted hat, and a sequined clutch.

Al and Catherine were waiting for them on the first floor in one of the smaller ballrooms adjacent to the Men's Bar.

"Get ready, dear," Catherine whispered in Stella's ear, "they'll end up in the bar before long."

Bright and charismatic, Governor Smith had taken a liking to Joe years earlier. That interest had not waned since, and Joe could easily trace his meteoric rise in the political world to the near-constant attention given him by the governor. Al Smith was, at times, almost alarming with his penetrating wit and leprechaun eyes. But Joe had received his blessing and, for the time being, that was all that mattered.

Catherine took Stella by the elbow and steered her toward a small crowd of political wives that stood by the window and nibbled hors d'oeuvres. Shrimp cocktail and stuffed mushrooms. Rolled prosciutto and Brie. A cornucopia of cheese and crackers. Caviar and grapes. Most of it sat untouched on the buffet. Every now and then, a woman plucked a grape from the bunch or ate half a shrimp.

"Aren't they hungry?" Stella whispered to Catherine.

Catherine laughed and bent close to Stella's ear. "They're waiting for us, dear. Grab a plate. Start a trend."

"Us?" Stella understood why the women would wait to eat until Catherine arrived. She and Al were hosting the fund-raiser, after all. But she couldn't grasp how she fit into the equation.

"You are my special guest tonight." Catherine lifted a delicate saucer from the stack and made her way down the buffet table, taking a small sample of each offering.

Stella followed her lead, and one by one, the political wives of New York City fell into line behind them.

That night, like so many that came before, was a blur for Stella. Champagne and music and robust speeches punctuated by periods of dancing. Joe worked the crowd, never attending to her for more than a few moments at a time, and then only to introduce her to this politician or that. And always the wives. They traded names of boutiques and designers like business cards, weighing one another's social status against the labels they could afford.

"Is that the new Chanel?" Stella was asked on more than one occasion.

"It is," she said, giving the same little spin she'd practiced for Joe earlier. She let the skirt flare just enough to elicit approval and, in a number of instances, envy.

"It looks lovely on you. You have the right sort of boyish figure to wear the flapper cut."

Narrow hips and a flat chest, they meant. A backhanded compliment. Occasionally Catherine took pity on Stella and whisked her away for another glass of champagne.

"You'll get used to it," she said. "They're only testing you."

"I'm not the one running for office."

She straightened the angle of Stella's hat. "Of course you are. Haven't you figured that out yet? Everything Joe says and does reflects on you. And you'll have to answer for it. In public and in private. Best you make peace with that now."

Shortly after midnight, the men abandoned their wives in favor of the bar. The women watched them retreat in pairs through the mahogany doors of the male-only establishment.

"Come along," Catherine said. "They won't be long."

The wives had rituals of their own. They scattered around the ballroom in groups of two and three for coffee, cigarettes, and gossip. The band quieted, and Catherine led her to a table in the corner, where Stella slipped off her shoes.

"Do you smoke?" Catherine asked.

"No."

"You might want to reconsider. Eases your nerves. Makes the time pass quicker." Catherine lifted a pack of cigarettes and a long cigarette holder from her purse. She lit the cigarette smoothly and set it inside the six-inch tortoiseshell holder.

"I'll never learn all these rules."

"Sure you will. It takes time. And practice. But you carry yourself well. And Joe couldn't be prouder of you. We've all noticed."

"How do you handle these long nights? I'd rather be home in bed."

Catherine looked at her wristwatch. "They're like little boys, you know. Give it fifteen minutes and they'll all begin to crash. Children and politicians have two speeds: running and asleep. But they haven't gotten loud enough yet. It gets obnoxious just before they wind down."

Sure enough, the ruckus in the bar began to grow until Stella and Catherine could hear them singing out in chorus:

The suckers will vote in the fall, tra-la;
The suckers will vote in the fall!

"Five more minutes and they'll come stumbling back in here, red eyed and dizzy." Catherine tapped the cigarette holder against her bottom lip and smiled, then pulled a long wisp of smoke between her thin lips. Fine lines were etched around her mouth, and Stella saw the telltale signs of age brought on by a hard political life.

True to Catherine's prediction, the husbands began to trickle back into the ballroom, sedate and exhausted. They collected their wives and ushered them home.

Before parting, Catherine kissed Stella on the cheek. "You'll do just fine."

It wasn't until Joe and Stella were back in their suite that she realized Catherine's attention that night had been placed on her singularly. It was her statement as the governor's wife to the other women that Stella was to be respected. And taken seriously. Had she known that earlier, she might have cried with gratitude.

Stella jumped when the bathroom door banged open. Joe stumbled out, stark naked and belting the lyrics to a profane drinking song:

There was a young lady named Lou
Who said as the parson withdrew,
"Now the Vicar is quicker,
And thicker, and slicker,
And two inches longer than you!"

His cheeks were flushed red from whiskey, and he roared with laughter when he saw the horrified look on her face.

She took a step backward. "You've been learning a few songs from Al Smith, I see."

"Meaning what?"

She looked at the wall to avoid Joe's raunchy gyrations. "That blasphemous song. And the one down in the bar."

"It's just a song, Stell. Something silly to lighten the mood." She flinched but didn't move as he grabbed her and flipped up the back of her dress. He ran his palm up her leg and tugged at her garter belt. "And that business down in the bar was just party high jinks. The boys were simply letting off steam with a harmless little parody."

"If your voters heard that, they certainly wouldn't consider it harmless."

"My voters," he said, yanking at her stocking, "would hardly be in a place like this. They're on the docks. And in the garment district. So don't you worry your pretty little head about it." Joe pinned her against the wall. His breath was sour and his hands rough, and Stella stared at the ceiling while he wrestled with her designer dress.

She tried to slide away from him. "You're drunk."

He grabbed her shoulders and pushed her back. His stubble was rough against her neck as he kissed it. "So?"

"You know I don't like to make love when you're drunk."

"I don't give a shit about making love, Stell. I want sex."

Stella pushed her skirt down away from his probing hands. "I'm not in the mood."

"You better get in the mood. Quick. Considering that I'm giving you a fourteen-thousand-dollar apartment tomorrow."

Joe's dark eyes were heavy lidded, and the beginning of each word was slurred. He groped her clumsily and grunted with the effort. Beads of sweat settled along his upper lip. Stella was sure he wouldn't remember this tomorrow, unless she angered him to the point of sobriety. She tensed between Joe and the wall and grappled with her decision. She could push him away—he'd never forced her, after all—but there would be retribution. Or she could submit to the indignity and he'd likely be asleep before finishing.

Stella sighed and slid out from under his arm. She took his hand. "Let's at least go to the bedroom."

"I want to do it here."

"I'll get the lights, then."

"Leave them on. I like to watch."

STELLA heard Jude walk down the pier, but she ignored him. She leaned out over the lake, eyes focused on some distant point, as he came to a stop behind her. Stella didn't turn around until he cleared his throat. Back in New York, she had been terrified that he would discover the hidden envelopes and hadn't noticed how handsome he was. Dark hair. Steel-blue eyes. A strong, square jaw and broad shoulders.

"Detective Simon," he said, extending his hand.

It hovered between them for a several seconds before she gripped it with cold fingertips. "We've met."

"I wasn't sure if you'd remember. Do you have a few minutes? I've come to take your statement."

"You could have done that when you came to my apartment." She could not keep the irritation out of her voice.

"That visit was unofficial."

"Meaning unsanctioned?"

"No. Meaning off the record until my superiors were certain how to proceed."

"You mean until another headline in the *New York World* forced them to proceed?"

"Should we sit? No point making this uncomfortable."

Stella motioned to two Adirondack chairs at the end of the pier. The white paint was peeling and the wood splintered in places, but they were comfortable. She settled into the one closest to the water and tucked her bare feet beneath her legs, wrapping Joe's dinner jacket tight around her chest. One hand wandered into the pocket. She lifted a cigarette from the pack and fumbled with the matchbook. Stella didn't want to smoke it—was sick from the last one, in fact—but she needed something to hold. Detective Simon pulled a silver lighter from his pocket and held it out to her. The flame was tall and immediate, and she passed her cigarette through, eyes watering at the acrid smell of singed paper and burning tobacco.

"I'm sorry about your husband," Jude said. "But I need to ask you a few questions."

"Are you? Sorry, that is. You didn't know him."

"I met him a few times, actually."

"Did you like him?"

"I didn't know him well enough to dislike him."

"Fair enough." Stella laughed. She drew on the cigarette but didn't inhale; rather, she held the smoke in her mouth until her tastebuds tingled and then spit it out.

"When was the last time you saw your husband?"

"August third. We had dinner at the Salt House."

"What happened that night?"

"When we arrived, Joe went to make a phone call. He was gone about twenty minutes, and when he came back to the table, he told me that he had to return to New York first thing in the morning to 'straighten a few things out.'"

Jude scratched at his notepad in shorthand as she spoke. Each stroke was deliberate and thick, indenting the page. "What sort of things?"

"The sort you don't discuss with your wife, apparently." Stella flicked the cigarette and then jumped to brush the hot ash from her lap.

"Do you know who your husband phoned that night?"

"No, I do not." She put Owney Madden, and their agreement, out of her mind as quickly as possible so the lie wouldn't register on her face.

"Judge Crater has been missing a month. Why didn't you report this before you returned to the city?"

"I was told not to."

Jude stopped writing and looked at her. "Please explain."

"He left here on the third. My birthday was that next Saturday, the ninth, but he didn't show up, even though he'd promised to be back in time. So I phoned Simon Rifkind—an associate of Joe's—and he told me Joe had been seen around town and not to worry."

"But you did worry?"

"About the wrong thing."

"Meaning?"

"Meaning that 'He's been seen around town' can sometimes be jargon for 'Your husband has picked up a skirt on the side and you need to keep your nose out of it if you want to protect his career.'"

Jude's pen whipped across the page in a frenzy. "Did your husband have a history of infidelity?"

Stella shifted away from him. It took too long to sift her answer. "I've learned not to question Joe when he has *business* that needs tending. That's why I didn't argue with him when he went back to the city. And that's why it took me so long to go after him."

"And that doesn't bother you?"

"There are things you learn to live with." Stella thought of Joe's bandaged hand. "More or less."

Jude watched her but said nothing.

"Are you married, Detective?"

"Yes."

"And do you cheat on your wife?"

His face twisted in offense. "Of course not."

"All men cheat on their wives. If not with a woman, then with work." She gave him a sideways glance. "I wonder which method you prefer."

"I beg your pardon, but I don't—"

"I'm not the one you need to convince." Stella finished her cigarette and then tossed the butt into the lake.

"If you knew my wife, you'd understand that infidelity is something I'd never consider." A spark of anger lit up his eyes but was replaced with an emotion she couldn't identify. He quickly transformed his face into a look of indifference.

The flash of intensity in his eyes convinced Stella that he was serious, that she'd assumed too much. But at least she'd found his weakness. This pleased her immensely, and she waited for him to continue.

He struggled to segue into his next line of questioning.

"Does Judge Crater have any enemies? Someone who would want to harm him?"

"Joe was only on the bench four months. He didn't have time to make enemies."

"What about from his days as a criminal attorney?"

"You must understand that my husband was"—she paused, searching for a generic label—"a man of ideals." Stella refrained from adding that most decent society did not share his particular brand of ideals. "He taught law for many years at New York University—that's what he did before getting into politics. I heard him tell his classes, on more than one occasion, that every man, though he be found guilty, is entitled to a defense. I suppose he could have upset someone during that time. But if he did, I never heard about it."

"How many guilty men did your husband defend?"

Stella stiffened at the insinuation. "A few made the papers."

"And he made money?"

"We were comfortable."

"You must have been, for him to get into politics. That takes deep pockets."

"Joe was highly respected for his legal skills. He was encouraged to get into politics because of his talent and charisma. People were drawn to him, even the ones that didn't particularly *like* him. That's a rare commodity in politics."

Jude tapped his pen against the small notepad. "Do you have any idea who your husband may have gone to see when he returned to the city?"

"None whatsoever." Stella felt dizzy, both from the cigarettes and from the growing list of lies she would have to remember if Detective Simon came calling again.

"What about his activities? Any associates that he might have talked to?"

"Joe's business was his own. He kept definite lines between his professional life and his private life." Stella settled her cold blue eyes on

Jude. "I only had access to one of those lives, Detective. I do not know why he returned to New York City."

Stella unfolded herself from the chair and faced the lake as Jude scratched the information on his notepad. The late-afternoon sun warmed her cheeks, and a deep weariness wrapped itself around her.

"My chauffeur will drive you back to the station, Detective. You wouldn't want to miss your train."

Chapter Fifteen

FIFTH AVENUE, FRIDAY, SEPTEMBER 12, 1930

MARIA didn't answer the door. She turned, considering, and then thought better of it. Her experiences at the Craters' apartment in recent weeks had taught her to leave well enough alone. No more covering for her boss. No more reporters. No more surprises. So she stayed where she was, teetering three feet off the ground on a wooden step stool, wiping dust from the top of Mr. Crater's bookshelves with a rag.

She'd taken to lingering over her work in recent days, trying to earn her paycheck—assuming Mrs. Crater actually mailed it. With Mr. Crater missing and Mrs. Crater hiding in Maine, there was no grocery shopping to do or fancy dinner parties to cook for. There were no trips to the cleaners or ill-fitting clothes to return to the high-end department stores they frequented. No laundry. No dishes. Maria was forced to get creative with ways to make up her time.

The front door rattled again with an insistent pounding. A short silence. And then a key turned in the lock.

Maria leaned forward to see the front door swing inward, followed by Jude's partner, Leo Lowenthall. She climbed down from the stool and slipped back into her shoes. "Hello?"

Leo stepped into the office, accompanied by three NYPD officers. "You didn't answer the door," he said, offended.

"It isn't my home."

"No." Leo eyed her uniform. "It's your *job*."

She looked at the key in his hand. "Where did you get that?"

Leo gave her a smug grin but didn't answer the question. He strode across the office and thrust a piece of paper in her face.

"What's this?"

"A search warrant."

Maria plucked it from his hand and read the court order.

"We'll start in here," Leo said, pushing her aside.

She stood back as they began going through the papers on Mr. Crater's desk. Drawer after drawer was opened, but not shut. They hauled books from the shelves, flipped through the pages, and tossed them to the floor until an entire library of legal volumes lay with cracked spines across the Oriental rug. At first she trailed behind them, protesting and attempting to keep the chaos at bay, but as Leo and his men spread across the apartment, Maria shrank back, appalled.

"Does Mrs. Crater know you're here?" she demanded when she found him in the master bedroom, pulling clothes off the hangers and digging through the pockets.

Leo didn't answer. He turned a red evening gown inside out, dropped it to the floor, and then kicked it out of the way. It landed in a crimson heap beneath the window. "How often do you work here?" he asked.

"Every morning when the Craters are in town. A bit less now that they're in Maine." Maria crossed the room and snatched the dress off the floor. "Can't you be more careful?"

"Has anyone been here recently?" Leo lifted a pile of silk stockings from a blue satin bag and ran them through his fingers, searching for hidden objects.

How to answer that question? *You. My husband. A naked showgirl.* "Only a reporter," she said. "And Mrs. Crater came back for a weekend."

"You haven't let anyone in?"

"No."

"But you talked to that reporter?" Leo left the closet door open and clothing piled on the floor and moved toward the bed.

"Briefly."

He yanked the coverlet right off the mattress. "Why?"

"Stop that!" She reached out and grabbed it from him. "You're destroying the place."

Leo swiftly turned on her, and Maria found herself shoved against the wall, staring up into his wide, dark eyes. His jaw jutted to the side, and he searched her face, appearing to relish the fear he saw there.

"Did he pay you?"

"Who?"

"George Hall."

"Of course not!"

"Then why give him those details? You wouldn't even open the door for me, but you tell secrets about your employer to the first newshound that drops by?"

Maria tried to slide away from him, but Leo blocked her with an arm. She grasped Mrs. Crater's red dress and the coverlet to her chest like a buffer, but he ripped them out of her clenched fists and threw them to the floor. He inched closer and tugged at a stray curl that had slipped loose beneath her cap. She jerked her head away.

"You're very pretty, Maria," he whispered. "No wonder Jude is always in a rush to get home."

Maria turned her face from the warmth of his breath.

"Or should I call you Amedia? That's the name you gave the reporter, right?"

The other detectives were spread throughout the apartment, opening cupboard doors and pulling things from shelves. She glanced at the bedroom door—only two feet away—but Leo forced it shut with the heel of one hand. He flipped the lock and turned his carnal gaze back to Maria. He blocked her in with both arms.

Maria pushed at him, panicked and angry, but he didn't budge. "Let me go."

Leo dropped one hand to her thigh and slid it around to grab her backside.

"Stop it!" She thrashed against him, but he pinned her to the wall with his torso.

"Word around the office is that you *begged* Crater for Jude's little promotion. Did you do anything else for him? You look like his type."

"Of course not!"

"Jude would have never gotten the job otherwise, you know. Too many damn scruples. You must have really made an impression on Crater."

Maria could hear the pounding of her heart and the blood rushing through her ears. She tried to bring her knee up into his crotch, but her entire body was pinned by the length of his. The more she fought against him, the more her dress bunched and rose up her legs.

Leo's fingers found her hemline.

"Don't touch me."

"What did you do with those envelopes?"

"I don't know what you're talking about."

"You're lying."

"I'm not. I swear to God I'm not." Maria's voice broke, and she tugged at the bottom of her dress. "Leave me alone, please."

Leo's breath was hot against her ear. "You think I didn't know you were here that day? That I didn't see you between the slats, hiding in the closet?" He wedged his elbow into the soft spot between her shoulder and breast. "What do you think Jude would say if he knew you were spying on him?"

Maria let out a sharp gasp of pain and tried to wiggle away.

Leo laughed. "You didn't tell him, did you?"

"No."

"Those envelopes are gone. You must have told someone. That reporter, maybe?"

Maria wanted to spit at him, to scream that she wasn't stupid. That she'd been married to a cop long enough to know that people who ran their mouths didn't last long in this city. "I didn't."

Leo lowered his elbow and studied her face. "And you're not going to tell anyone, are you?"

"No."

"Because if you do, you're going to end up just like your employer. Missing. Or worse. Understand?"

Her answer rushed out in a panicked breath. "Yes."

Leo stepped away and she stumbled forward.

"You talk about this to anyone, and *poof*!" He made a vanishing gesture with his hands. "You disappear. Owney can make it happen."

"I believe you."

"The thing is"—Leo reached out and patted her cheek—"Owney needs that husband of yours to do what he's told. And if Jude finds out about our little chat, he might not want to take orders anymore. Do you see how that could be a problem?"

Maria stepped away from his touch. She wrapped her arms around her chest and blinked furiously against the tears that burned her eyes.

"So you keep this conversation between us. Because if Jude becomes a problem, I can make sure he gets the kiss-off as well. Got that?"

"I do."

"Good girl. Now clean up this mess." Leo unlocked the door and jerked it open. "C'mon, boys. Let's make tracks. There's nothing to find here."

She heard them kicking things out of their way as they tromped toward the front door. It creaked open and then slammed shut so hard the wall rattled.

Maria waited for several long minutes, listening to her heart settle, and then tiptoed into the living room. The apartment was in shambles. Furniture overturned. Drawers emptied. The contents of every closet, cupboard, and cabinet jettisoned across the hardwood floor. Although they were careful not to actually break anything, it looked as though the apartment had been burglarized.

Maria closed her eyes and slid down the living room wall. She crumpled to the floor with a choked sob.

CLUB ABBEY

GREENWICH VILLAGE, AUGUST 6, 1969

Club Abbey was frequented by such like-minded criminals as Jack "Legs" Diamond, Dutch Schulz, and Vincent "Mad Dog" Coll. Judge Joseph Crater visited the club at least twice, and likely quite a bit more often than that.

—*Richard J. Tofel*, Vanishing Point

"I was sorry to hear about your wife," Stella says, but the lines around her eyes do not fill with sympathy. She is a woman impervious to grief.

Jude turns from her platitude, picks at a splinter in the table with his thumbnail. He could tell her the number of years, months, and days since he laid Maria to rest beneath a white marble headstone, BELOVED engraved above her name. He could tell her this, but he doesn't.

After a moment, he clears his throat. "She has a name."

"I haven't forgotten. I liked Maria."

It's been a long time since he has heard her name spoken aloud. It unsettles him. "I don't want to talk about my wife. Especially with someone who has no regard for her memory."

"What do you want, a eulogy? She was the maid."

Jude's fist lands like a hammer on the table. "She was my wife!" And a gifted tailor. His best friend. His lover. His conscience. He counts the roles she played, lays them out in his mind, innumerable, invaluable.

All eyes in the bar turn toward the commotion. Stan goes rigid and overfills a stein of Meister Bräu Lite. Suds slosh onto his hand, and he wipes it on his apron, but he never looks away. He gives the drink to his customer without a glance and leans over the bar, elbows resting on the varnished surface, straining to hear their conversation.

"Pity I didn't tell you back then that I knew," Stella says. "It would have been fun to watch you squirm."

"You're lying."

"You think I'm stupid? That I didn't know you two were married? She practically danced through the apartment when you made detective." The corner of Stella's mouth twitches with a repressed smile. "Maria was my insurance policy. I figured if you got too close to the truth, she would be handy collateral. Fortunately for her, I never had to play that card."

"You couldn't have used her, if that's what you're getting at. Maria wasn't for sale."

She snorts. "Like you?"

"Being for sale and being under duress are two different things."

"A convenient distinction after all these years, don't you think? It was my understanding that you volunteered for those little errands. Pocket a little extra cash. Grease the wheels for Owney. Everyone's happy, right? Except your wife. I imagine she didn't take kindly to realizing her husband was on the payroll of a gangster."

Jude recoils at her words. "I didn't volunteer for anything."

"That's right, it was Maria's doing."

"What do you mean?"

"She came to us. Asked Joe to put in a good word for you. Ambitious, that wife of yours."

"No."

"There's no way you would have ever made detective without a little help. I'm the one that pushed Joe to do it. For Maria." A small admission of affection, tossed at him like a bone before a starving dog.

Still, he can't accept this, shakes his head, argues. "I don't believe you."

Stella runs her fingers down the rope of pearls around her neck. Small, seedlike pearls at the top grew larger until the centerpiece: a grape-size saltwater pearl in the middle. Stella spins it around the string with her thumb.

"No one got anywhere those days without help. Everyone owed favors. And there were always layers of corruption. Hell, the well-oiled machine of Tammany Hall ran on bribery. You want a place in the club? You pay your dues to Owney Madden, and he puts in a good word with whatever politician he has in his pocket. But now you're beholden to Owney, and he has an agenda of his own. So when your indiscretions upset the balance, you go missing and the middlemen blackmail a gumshoe to leave some discreetly hidden envelopes in your apartment." Stella gives him a sharp, wicked smile. "I am curious to know which bothers you more: that you planted evidence in my home or that your wife couldn't keep her sticky fingers away from it?"

Jude whips his head back and forth in short little bursts of anger. "You don't get to talk about her—"

"Five hundred dollars. I wasn't expecting to find our life savings drawn in cash and tucked in a bureau drawer, but I did know how much was missing. Down to the dollar. What'd she do with it, anyway, Detective? Go to Coney Island and blow it at the craps table?"

Jude swallows the rage that simmers at the back of his throat, calms himself by pressing his hands onto the wooden seat. "It's a funny thing about that money," he says, when he's sure there won't be a growl in his voice. "You'd be surprised how many hands it went through before reaching its unsavory end."

"Nothing surprises me anymore. Especially when it comes to money and corruption and Joe's disappearance."

"There was this showgirl that your husband knew. Went by the name of Sally Lou Ritz."

"Ritzi," Stella says. Her expression is ambivalent, a subtle shifting around the eyes and mouth between anger and hurt. "What of her?"

"I interviewed her a few days after Joe made the papers. She was a real firecracker." It's Jude's turn to be cruel, and he flings the words at her like shrapnel. "No wonder your husband was so fond of her."

"What does Ritzi have to do with that money?"

"When it comes to this case, Ritzi has to do with everything. But you already knew that, didn't you, Stella? I imagine you've spent a whole lot of time thinking about Sally Lou Ritz. And hating her."

Stella drops the pearls back to her chest, considers her lack of curves, the way her dress hangs limp where it should be stretched over the fullness of breasts. "Joe had a thing for brunettes," she says at last, as though this admission explains everything.

RITZI slipped into the dressing room in search of a bandage. Two hours of rehearsal on swollen feet resulted in a dime-size blister at the back of her heel, and she'd taken the opportunity to skip out early and have a few minutes to herself. She kicked her shoes off and shrugged out of the skimpy rehearsal dress, digging around the supply cabinet until she found a bottle of Gold Bond and a bandage large enough to cover the back of her foot. The powder stung as it settled into the raw blister, and her face twisted in pain. She recoiled at her own reflection: stretched, gaunt. Wrung out.

Her rehearsals for *The New Yorkers* had begun a month earlier, turning an already busy schedule into a grueling merry-go-round of rehearsals in the day and live performances of *Ladies All* at night. Two different theaters. Two different plays. And a world of things to remember each time she stepped onstage. To make matters worse, *The New Yorkers* required a double role: the supporting part of May the prostitute and a filler in the chorus line. The Ritzi of the chorus lines was seductive and coquettish. But the Ritzi who played May in Cole Porter's musical was sad and lonely and appealing for entirely different reasons. Of the two roles, she much preferred May.

Once the ache in her foot dulled, she covered herself in a satin robe and tied a loose knot at her waist. Ritzi dragged one of the stage chairs up to the mirror and stretched out her legs until both feet rested on the dressing table. She lit a cigarette and listened to the not-so-distant sounds of rehearsal. The orchestra. The steady rhythm of tap shoes against the wooden floor: *turn, turn, touch down, back step, pivot step, walk, walk, walk.* She imagined the other girls linked at the arms, artificial smiles spread wide, as they cascaded across the stage in formation. Each woman strained in concentration to match the movements of those next to her. *Must. Keep. In. Step.*

Ritzi was relieved not to be out there. The thought startled her. And she might have pondered whether to feel guilty about it had a sharp knock not sounded on the door. Shorty Petak didn't wait for her to respond. He pushed the door wide open. Grinned. She shifted the robe to better cover herself.

Ritzi tapped her cigarette on the arm of the chair. "You're not supposed to be in here."

"You have a visitor." Shorty stepped aside to reveal a clean-cut, attractive man in a fedora and gray pinstriped suit. "Detective . . . ?"

"Simon."

"That's right. Detective Simon wants to have a few words with you."

"That so?" Ritzi stared. He was the sort of man who could make a girl lose her place in the chorus line if she saw him from the stage. A couple years ago she would have been flustered at the sight of such a man. But now she smiled and wrapped her lips around the end of her cigarette, drawing smoke into her lungs. She left her bare legs stretched out on the dressing table and flicked a hand at Shorty. "Go on. I don't need a chaperone."

Shorty seemed reluctant to shut the door, but he stepped away and gave them privacy.

The detective was young, maybe early thirties, with dark hair and bright blue eyes. The shape of his mouth hinted at dimples, but she couldn't tell with his stern countenance.

"Do you have a first name, Detective?" Ritzi asked. "I hate formalities."

"Jude."

"And is there something in particular I can do for you?"

"I'd like to ask you a few questions about Joseph Crater."

"What about him?"

"You know him?"

"Sure."

"How?"

"Everyone knew Crater. You could hardly go fifty feet in the theater district without seeing him."

His eyes narrowed a bit, and Ritzi immediately regretted her word choice.

"Knew?"

She puffed on her cigarette and then waved it around. "Sure. All the papers say he took a ride."

"Last I checked, they said he was missing."

Ritzi shrugged. "Same thing."

Detective Simon pulled a notepad and pen from his suit pocket. He flipped it open and walked through the dressing room, scanning the costume racks and piles of clothing discarded by the girls. Makeup. Trashy magazines. Cigarette butts. Stockings and high heels and underwear. Elaine had left her diaphragm on the counter, probably so she wouldn't forget to use it later. He pushed it aside with the tip of his pen.

"Not the classy place you were expecting?"

"I had no expectations, Miss Ritz."

"Sit down, Jude." She nodded at one of the other stage chairs. "And call me Ritzi. No one calls me Miss Ritz except my landlord, and he's a shyster."

Jude grabbed the other chair and set it a few feet away from her. He was careful not to glance at her bare legs or the plunge of her dressing gown, instead looking around the room while she smoked and waited for him to speak.

"My wife and I came to see your show a couple weeks ago. Maria was quite impressed with that opening number. And the one at the end. With the peacocks."

Surely not. "Maria? Pretty girl with big brown eyes? Bit of a Spanish accent?"

Jude tensed. "Yeah. How do you know her?"

Better than I should. "Met her in the bathroom after the show. I wasn't feeling too well. She helped me clean up."

"Maria didn't say anything about that."

Interesting. "She doesn't seem the type to brag on herself." Ritzi graced him with a disinterested smile and then drew on her cigarette again. "That all you came to tell me? That Crater's gone missing and you saw my show?"

"I'm afraid not Miss—Ritzi." He tapped his notepad with the end of his pen. "How well did you know Crater? Personally?"

Ritzi wished there were a window in the dressing room. The air was stifling and smelled of industrial cleaner and fresh paint and old cigarette smoke. She had to force herself not to twirl a piece of hair or rock her foot. Ritzi met his gaze and offered a small shrug. "Well enough. Crater's a regular. A real patron of the arts, you could say."

"You had dinner with him"—Detective Simon looked at his notes—"on August sixth?"

"Billy and I had dinner with him."

"Billy being . . . William Klein?"

"That's right." So he'd spoken with William Klein. The horrible, sticky memory of that morning in his office came rushing back, and Ritzi fought against the shiver that threatened to race up her spine.

Jude scratched a few notes, pen held at an odd angle in his left hand. "You and Mr. Klein are an item?"

"We spend time together."

"He said you were his girlfriend."

"Yeah. I suppose I am."

Jude tipped his head to the side.

"It's not good for me to seem attached," she explained. "Bad for business. You know, it ruins the fantasy. The producers like us to appear attainable. The regular Joes keep coming back if they think they have a chance."

He circled back to the question like a dog after its own tail. "But you were William Klein's date on the sixth?"

Ritzi nodded.

"What happened after dinner?"

"Crater went to see a show, and I went home with Billy."

"What can you remember about that night? It may seem trivial to you, but a random piece of information could be of huge import to this case."

She played with the belt on her robe. "We were having dinner . . . Billy and I. And then Joe showed up."

"Uninvited?"

"Late. And he plopped down at our table, ordered almost everything on the menu, then sent me off to powder my nose so they could talk business."

Jude scratched her answers into his notebook in some form of shorthand she couldn't read. "How long were you away?"

"I don't know. Ten or fifteen minutes?"

"Any idea what they spoke about while you were gone?"

She laughed. "Why do you think he sent me off, Detective? To redecorate the bathroom? When it comes to men like that, I'm not privy to most of what they discuss."

"I spoke with William Klein this morning, and he didn't say a word about having a chat with the judge that night. Why would he leave out a detail like that?"

"Don't know."

Jude seemed unconvinced. "They spoke privately. Then what?"

"They ate dinner, but I," she said, motioning to her figure, "am expected to survive on air and compliments. Jerks finished off my salad while I was in the powder room."

"Did anything else significant happen that evening? Anything you found odd? Then or now?"

"No. It was a normal night. Nothing unusual."

"What time did you part ways?"

"A little after nine."

Jude conferred with his notes. Eyes on the paper, he asked, "You said Judge Crater went to see a show. Do you know which one?"

Ritzi remembered the marquee lights as she waited in the cab that night. "*Dancing Partner,* I believe."

"Do you know if Mr. Crater reached his destination?"

"He got in a cab. We got in a cab. Everyone left. That's all I know."

"Where did you say you ate dinner?"

There were few things she agreed with William Klein on, but leaving Club Abbey out of their rehearsed story was one. "Billy Haas's Chophouse. It's a favorite in the theater district."

"And this *Dancing Partner,* where was it playing?"

"The Belasco Theater."

"That's odd, don't you think?"

"What?"

In that moment, Ritzi realized that she had underestimated the young detective. What she'd first taken as a sort of amiable nonchalance revealed itself to be a cunning interest in every word she said. His eyes were bright and focused. Lips formed into a barely suppressed smirk. Pen gripped firmly between two fingers.

"The restaurant and the theater are only about three blocks apart. Why would he take a cab on a nice summer evening?"

It was a good question. Logical. Especially if they had actually been at the restaurant that night. One she failed to consider. "I don't know. You'll have to ask him."

"Did you actually *see* him get in the cab, Miss Ritz?"

"Ritzi," she said, holding her breath and settling on the best lie she could deliver. "And no. I did not."

"Did you see which direction he went when you left the restaurant?" She shook her head.

"Can you tell me with any certainty that he even attended the show he'd purchased a ticket for?"

"I assume that he did," she said, drawing on the last of her cigarette and then stubbing it out on the arm of the chair.

"All trace of Judge Crater stops outside the Belasco Theater. Which means you are one of the last two people to see him alive. So I need to know everything—and I mean *every thing*—that happened on the night of August sixth."

Ritzi eased her aching feet down from the dressing table and set them on the cool floor. "I've told you everything I know, Detective."

They locked stares in a frozen challenge. Ritzi's thoughts tumbled over one another but she didn't voice any of them. Instead, she listened to the growing tremor of voices outside the dressing room. Rehearsal was over.

The door swung open and the showgirls flooded the dressing room. The sight of Ritzi wearing nothing but a thin dressing gown and seated in front of a young, handsome man instantly brought out the vixen in many of them. Jude was mobbed by a throng of half-dressed women who giggled and petted him as they walked by.

"Tough luck, girls," Ritzi said, giving Jude a victorious smile. "This one's married."

They booed and hissed and ran brightly painted fingernails along his jaw.

Jude jumped out of the chair, nearly knocking it over. The interview was done. He was outnumbered.

"Is there anything else I can help you with?" Ritzi asked.

"Not today."

"Then, if you don't mind, I have a show to get ready for."

Jude tipped his fedora and pulled it lower over his face, trying to hide the sudden rush of color in his cheeks.

"Will you be in the audience tonight?"

"No."

"Pity. We could have given you an eyeful."

"No offense, Miss Ritz, but you already have."

Ritzi remained in her chair until Jude ducked out of the dressing room. Then she stood and leaned against the counter, ignoring the curious—and, in some cases, jealous—glances of the others. She applied another layer of medicated powder to her blister and covered her heel with the bandage. Ritzi wasn't sure what bothered her more: that Jude had come so close in his questioning or that he was married to the only person who knew she was pregnant with Crater's child.

"I DON'T understand why you have to go back."

"This." Jude tossed an envelope onto the kitchen counter. "The district attorney wants this questionnaire hand-delivered to Maine. And I've got to supervise while Mrs. Crater answers. She's not exactly cooperating with the investigation these days."

Maria glared at the envelope. "Why can't they send Leo?"

"Because it's my case."

"Right. The case Leo *recommended* you for?" Her voice rose until Jude stared at her in disbelief, his diminutive wife raised up on the balls of her feet, straining with anger.

He set his hands on her arms and gently pressed her back to the ground. "What's wrong?"

"I don't want you to go."

"I have to go. It's important."

"For who?"

"For the investigation. Something's going on, and I've got to get to the bottom of it." Jude pushed the crocheted afghan out of the way and tugged her down onto the couch. Lifted her into his lap. "I interviewed the last two people to see Judge Crater today. A showgirl and a theater executive."

"Showgirl?" Maria forced herself to relax into Jude. She hid her face in his shoulder so he wouldn't see her panic.

"Some girl named Sally Lou Ritz. Goes by Ritzi. Fake name if I've ever heard one."

Maria wondered if he could feel her heart pounding against his chest. "And?"

"And she's lying."

"Why? What did she say?" Too eager. She could hear it in her voice.

"It's what she didn't say. I can't explain it. But there's something off. I just don't know what it is."

"What does she have to do with Mrs. Crater?"

"Apparently, fidelity wasn't one of Judge Crater's strong suits. And he had a thing for the theater. Wouldn't surprise me at all if he'd messed around with Ritzi at some point. Or that she knows who he was seeing. If he had a mistress, I need to find her." Jude pulled Maria tight against his chest. "You worked for the guy. Did you ever see anything?"

What hadn't she seen? And overheard? And been privy to? "No." She repented for the lie right there, even as she told another. "Mr. Crater is never around during the day. Mostly, I see his wife, and she's very private."

"If you remember anything, let me know. It's all important."

Jude shifted on the couch, preparing to stand, but she gripped him tighter. "Please stay."

"It's only for one day. You'll be fine."

Maria listened to the rise and fall of Jude's breath as he held her for a while longer. After several minutes, he stood and tipped her onto her feet.

His voice was muffled against her hair as he said, "I'll be back tomorrow night. I promise."

Maria watched her husband slip out the door, and then she turned all three locks after him.

RITZI sat before the mirror in her blue satin robe and stared at her face beneath the lights. Another show done. Only a million more looming before her.

The dressing room was empty apart from her. Cigarette butts and gum wrappers littered the floor. A metallic hum came from the lightbulbs around the mirror. An argument in the hallway outside—most likely Shorty Petak and a stagehand. The smells of sweat and perfume.

Ritzi arched her back and stretched her feet out in front of her. Her thighs ached and her ankles were swollen. A knock at the door made her jump. She pinched her cheeks and adjusted her dressing gown before approaching the door. "Yes?"

"Shorty. Let me in."

"No."

"Open up. Owney sent me."

Ritzi struggled to keep her voice steady. "Why?"

His voice lowered to a softer pitch, a warning. "This ain't a conversation we need to have through the door."

She unlocked the door and Shorty pushed in. He looked like a nervous animal, twitching, touching things, opening drawers. "Owney wants you at Club Abbey tonight."

She stiffened. "I'm going home."

"Ain't optional, sweetheart. He pays the rent, he calls the shots."

Ritzi tugged at her robe, pulling it tighter across her breasts. She resisted the urge to run a hand over her belly.

Shorty circled her, eyes roving, and she felt the heat of anger rise up the back of her neck. "So you enjoy taking orders? Doing what Owney tells you?"

He sniffed. "I'm my own man."

"Owney's the dog and you're the tail. Everyone knows that."

His dark eyes narrowed into wicked little slits. "I suppose that makes you the bitch? Get dressed." He flung the door open.

The door shook on its hinges when he slammed it, and Ritzi sat before the mirror for several minutes, preparing herself for what was to come.

RITZI hadn't been to Club Abbey since the night Crater disappeared, and as Shorty led her down the steps, she realized that she hadn't missed it. Something about the frenetic energy inside made her anxious. He held open the door and followed her through.

The place was packed. In recent weeks, Owney had broadened his vision to include a full band and a singer. Smoke hung low in the air, and smooth jazz rhythms vibrated through the dance floor, up her feet and thighs, and into her rib cage. It lured her with a serpentine motion, and she leaned into the music. For one brief second, Ritzi forgot her troubles in the seductive embrace of the singer's voice. Tall and waiflike and clearly not out of her teens, the black woman had a voice so full of emotion that Ritzi gaped.

She knew someone watched her as well. It was a feeling she'd grown accustomed to over the years. More often than not, it was harmless, some guy with more testosterone than courage eyeing her up from the other side of the room. The farther away they were, the more confident. Close that gap, though, and she could separate the men from the boys. Sometimes it was flattering. Usually, it was annoying. But tonight she had to choke the fear down and keep her back turned. Ritzi knew the feel of that dark stare. Owney Madden sat in his booth and watched her walk through the room. She slipped away from Shorty and headed toward the bar.

Stan greeted her with a shy smile as she eased onto a barstool. "The usual?" he asked.

"Not tonight. Just a glass of city juice."

He poured her water and dropped in a handful of ice cubes.

Ritzi nodded toward the stage. "Who's the canary? She's amazing."

"She goes by the name Billie Holiday. Rumor has it Owney found her in Harlem turning tricks for five bucks a pop."

Ritzi sipped her water and took a closer look at the singer. "How old is she?"

Stan seemed a little sad when he answered. "Not old enough."

"You're a good egg, you know that, Stan?"

"Nonsense. I'm a scamp like everyone else in here."

She reached across the bar and patted his cheek. "A regular cad."

"Don't you forget it."

"And what of your employer? What's his mood tonight?"

"Murderous."

"Figures." Ritzi winced and swallowed the last of her water.

She slid down the bar and looped her hand through the arm of a stranger. He was well dressed in a self-conscious sort of way, but he'd do. Ritzi's smile invited him to dance, and he stumbled from the barstool and onto the dance floor. Her partner—Harvey was the name—tripped over his words when he found out what she did for a living. A fan of Broadway. Always wanted to meet a real live showgirl. Damn good luck she found him at the bar. He tapped out the words like a jackhammer.

Harvey had an arm around her waist, and though he moved her around the floor, Ritzi was the one who led. Such a dead hoofer, the poor guy didn't even know when he'd lost control. She maneuvered her way to the other side of the room, and he fumbled in her wake.

"You're a great dancer," he shouted above the band.

They were at the farthest point from Owney's booth when she braved her first glance in that direction. He was hidden behind a swarm of people, and she breathed deep, letting the tension slip from her body. Her back and calves relaxed, and she settled into Harvey's arms enough to respond to his attempted leading. He prattled on, obnoxious but harmless. Ritzi nodded and smiled occasionally, but mostly ignored him.

Right when she imagined herself safe, she felt the firm grip of a hand on her elbow.

"This one's not available," Shorty Petak said. He wrenched her away from Harvey and shifted his grip so that her arm was pinned against his side, faux gentleman. "Enough of that."

"Hey, the lady was dancing with me."

Ritzi warmed at the term *lady*. She usually heard it in a derogatory way. Before Shorty pulled her into the crowd, she laid a palm on Harvey's arm, gentle. "Do yourself a favor and walk away, okay?"

He sensed both her warning and her fear and hesitated long enough for Ritzi and Shorty to fold into the dance floor, swept away by the crowd. Had she even hinted, poor Harvey would have come to her aid. And it would have been the last, worst decision he ever made.

"It's time for business."

"I was just having a little fun."

"Don't be a fool, Ritz. Stop avoiding him."

Shorty's arm was a vise, and she knew better than to fight him. Ritzi let him guide her toward Owney's corner booth. If it weren't for the black eye, Owney would look dapper. But he hid it well, hat tipped low over his face. Jacket off. Tan suspenders over a white shirt. Crisp. In control.

Ritzi sucked her stomach in and relaxed her shoulders. Shorty's grip on her arm loosened. "He lost a poker game this afternoon. Didn't take it kindly," he said out of the side of his mouth as they navigated through a pack of middle-aged men on the edge of the dance floor. "Beat the poor bastard bloody, but not before he took a solid left hook. Don't stare."

She nodded, and they stepped up to the booth. Shorty released her into Owney's care, and she slid into the seat across from him.

"You've been keeping your distance." It wasn't a question, merely a fact he stated with displeasure.

"You've got me busy with two shows." She met his gaze, smiled. *Damn Scouser.*

That wasn't good enough for Owney, though. Not intimidating enough. He walked around to her side of the booth and sat next to her, a barrier between her and everyone else. To those watching, it probably looked intimate. His thigh rested against hers, and she felt the heat through the satin of her dress. She was small. Vulnerable.

Without looking around the club, she could sense that the axis of attention had shifted toward them. Whom Owney spent his evening with was always of interest here, much to the chagrin of the politicians and mobsters who beggared themselves at the altar of Club Abbey. She could feel the glances of those in the room, their awareness.

"Drawing a lot of attention to yourself lately," Owney said.

She faked another smile. "Isn't that my job?"

Owney moved quick, like a viper. His hand was at her face, and she flinched, anticipating the bite of his slap. But he ran a finger along her chin, deceptively sensual. "You know what I mean."

"That's not my fault."

"How, exactly, do you mean?"

"I was at the wrong place at the wrong time."

"What place?" His breath was hot on her ear. That hand moved from her jaw and slid down her neck, thumb caressing her pulse.

"All that mess with Crater and Klein."

"A detective paid you a visit today. What did you tell him?" His palm cupped her throat.

"Nothing he can use. That I had dinner with Crater and Klein that night. And that I haven't seen Crater since."

"You mention the club?"

"Of course not."

He briefly considered this then changed the subject. "You didn't thank me for the new gig yet."

"I haven't had two minutes to myself. It's a lot to manage."

"What's stopping you now? Maybe you think I'm not generous?"

"No." She swallowed. Softened her look from fear to gratitude. "You are. Very generous. Thank you."

Owney laid an arm across the bench behind her, casual-like, and pinched the soft spot at the back of her arm. "You need to lose some weight, dollface." He squeezed until her eyes glassed over in pain. "You're getting fat."

THE second time Detective Simon came to the cabin, he wore a look of exhaustion along with his three-piece suit. He took off his fedora as he stepped through Stella's front door. "Good morning, Mrs. Crater."

She looked over his wrinkled suit and puffy eyes. "Up late?"

"I took the night train." He held a large envelope in one hand, and with the other he motioned toward the kitchen table. "May I?"

"Be my guest."

"Can I bother you for a glass of water? The walk is rather long from the station."

"If I'd known you were coming, I would have sent Fred to pick you up." It would have given Fred something to do. Stella didn't go out much these days, and he spent most of his time in the garage repeatedly washing the car.

Jude looked behind her, as though searching for something. "Short notice."

Stella led him to the table, where Emma worked a crossword puzzle. She gave her mother a look that clearly indicated her presence was not necessary. Emma collected her pen and newspaper and retreated to the gazebo so she could keep an eye on them through the kitchen window.

Stella went to the sink and turned on the tap. She let it run for several seconds before lifting a glass from the cupboard.

For most of the year, Belgrade Lakes maintained a crisp temperature, dipping into the single digits in winter. But during the summer, the earth softened, warming the waters. In late August and early September, the lake began to turn as the upper layer of water competed for dominance with the cool underbelly. This turning created a unique taste to the water. A bit muddy. The locals had long since learned that a few cubes of ice and a slice of lemon could disguise the flavor. Stella dropped both into the glass and set it on the table. She took a seat across from him.

Jude drained half the glass in one gulp and then slid the envelope across the table. "A special delivery."

She didn't open it.

"It seems you've been difficult to contact, Mrs. Crater."

She set her hands in her lap but did not respond.

"Don't worry, it's just a questionnaire."

"I'll be sure to fill it out and send it back to"—she peered at the envelope and read the name—"District Attorney Thomas Crain when I have a few moments."

Jude scratched the back of his neck. "It's not that simple, I'm afraid. My instructions were to supervise your answers."

"I am forty-three years old. I don't need supervision."

"That is a legal document. And it needs a legal witness. Seeing as how I'm an officer of the law, that means me."

After several uneasy moments, Stella picked up the envelope. There was no postmark. No stamp. She scratched the upper right-hand corner with a thumbnail. Inside were three sheets of Crain's letterhead. A total of twenty-nine neatly typed questions. She skimmed them quickly. The first few were questions she'd been asked already:

When was the last time you saw your husband?
Did your husband come in contact with anyone suspicious in the
days leading up to his disappearance?
Did your husband indicate that he was in any sort of trouble?

But halfway down the first page, they became more salacious, and she clenched her jaw.

Did your husband have a history of infidelity?
Was your husband involved in any illicit business affairs?
Were there any large cash withdrawals from your bank account
in the weeks leading up to your husband's disappearance?
Did your husband frequent any establishments of ill repute?

Stella threw the questionnaire on the table. "What is this?"

"I didn't write them. I'm only the messenger."

"They're insulting."

Jude looked at her, his pupils large in the dim light, and steepled his fingers. "Don't be so quick to dismiss them, Mrs. Crater. It may well be that you don't know your husband the way you imagine."

The tremor began in her shoulder and ran all the way to the tip of her index finger. She pointed it squarely in Jude's face. "How dare you."

He lifted a sheet from the pile and tapped one of the questions. "Take this, for example: 'Who would your husband be most likely to communicate with—aside from yourself, of course—if he were in distress or in trouble?'"

They stared unblinking at one another.

She was stingy with her admission, offering only a halfhearted shrug.

"I have to wonder, Mrs. Crater, how well you actually know your husband if such a basic question leaves you without an answer."

Stella's eyes itched with tears, but she resisted the urge to rub them. When her response came, it sounded hollow and dishonest. "Joe is a good man."

"Are you sure?" Jude slid his pen across the table.

It took some time before she had the courage to pick it up.

"I would remind you, Mrs. Crater," he prodded gently, "that the grand jury will regard any omissions or false information as cause for legal action."

"You threaten me in my own home?"

"Not at all. I simply mean to reinforce the seriousness of this matter." He took another long sip of water.

Stella plucked the cap off the pen and stared at its sharp point. "I haven't seen my husband in almost two months. Do you think that I have forgotten for one moment how serious this is?"

Jude's expression—the flinty blue eyes and hard set of his mouth—made her realize that he was far shrewder than he let on. "I doubt very much that you have forgotten anything."

Stella read the remaining questions, and her fury grew with each line:

Before this instance has your husband ever absented himself without letting you know his whereabouts?

*Did you notice anything strange about your husband's behavior lead-
ing up to his disappearance?*

Has your husband recently suffered from memory loss?

*Have you received any monies from anyone since August 5th, 1930,
which may have come from Judge Crater indirectly or which were
advanced to you on his account?*

*Who was the first person you communicated with when you sus-
pected he had disappeared?*

*Will you please list the names of your husband's most intimate social
friends, along with their addresses?*

On and on they went, questions about Joe's business dealings and
how he spent his spare time. Several others sought information on their
bank accounts and safe-deposit box. The district attorney wanted to
know who Joe's investment banker was and about any money that may
have gone unreported. It seemed no area of their lives was off-limits
from intrusion.

"None of this has to do with Joe's disappearance." She shook the
papers in Jude's face. "It's a waste of time."

"Please answer them to the best of your ability," he said.

That was the last Stella argued with him. She turned her full attention to the questionnaire. Of the twenty-nine questions, thirteen were
answered with a single word. To four she responded with *I don't know.*
Two she replied to with flat-out lies. And one she left blank altogether.
The rest she attacked with an acerbic wrath, pen imprinting the paper
so deeply that it almost cut through. No sooner had she signed her name
than she shoved the questionnaire across the table. "There."

Jude collected the three sheets of paper, tapped them on the table
until the corners lined up crisply, and slid them back in the envelope.
"Thank you for your time, Mrs. Crater."

"I'll thank you not to waste it again."

RITZI woke sometime after midnight and ran for the bathroom. She barely made it to the toilet before she threw up. Her stomach knotted and clenched and purged as she heaved forward, on and off, for fifteen minutes, and then she lay on the floor, her cheek pressed to the cold tile. When the spots no longer floated in her peripheral vision, she pushed herself up and knelt before the sink, cupping water in her palms. She rinsed out her mouth and splashed her cheeks. Then she sat with her back to the wall and pulled her knees to her chest. Ritzi laid her forehead on her arms and groaned.

"How far along are you?" Vivian stood in the doorway, a crimson robe cinched around her impossibly thin waist.

"Just sick. That's all."

"I'm not stupid, Ritz." Vivian stepped into the bathroom and sat on the edge of the tub. "You look like shit."

"Seems to be the general consensus lately."

"How long have you known?"

Ritzi wiped her mouth with the back of her hand. Debated whether to tell the truth. Relented. "Awhile."

"Crater?"

"Unfortunately."

"Does he know?"

She snorted. "Yeah. He took it *real* well."

Vivian's eyes narrowed. "How about Owney?"

"He'd kill me." The words were out of her mouth before she realized how true they were.

"You'll have to leave the show."

"No." Ritzi shook her head and immediately regretted it. Spots floated at the corners of her eyes again, followed by a throb in her temples. She squeezed her eyes shut and took a long breath through her nose to quell the nausea that tugged at the back of her throat. "The show wraps December thirteenth. I can make it until then."

"What about the next one?"

"I can hide it."

"Unlikely."

"I'm not showing."

"You look green all the time. You're dizzy. And from what I hear, you've been tossing your lunch in every alley and trash can around Manhattan."

"What do you mean?"

"You're not the only chorine I've placed, Ritz. And you're not the hungriest, by a long shot. There's a string of girls lining up to take your place. One miss. That's all it will take, and you'll be replaced."

"Then I won't miss." She forced herself up and stumbled back to her room. Vivian followed, unconvinced.

Ritzi reached for the cigarettes on her nightstand.

"How can you smoke those in your condition?" Vivian curled her lip in disgust.

She fumbled with the lighter. "Calms my nerves."

"Every smell turned my stomach when I was pregnant. Eggs. Ashes. Pee. You name it."

"You've got a kid?"

"Rose," Vivian said, settling next to her on the bed. "She's twelve now."

"I didn't know."

"I haven't seen her in seven years. Lost custody of her when I went to prison."

Ritzi lowered herself to the edge of the bed. Gave Vivian such a look of disbelief that she laughed.

"An asshole cop on the vice squad got me on a trumped-up charge. I worked for Polly Adler back then." She shrugged. "It was good money, but I like management better. Three years in a women's prison upstate taught me the nuance of extortion. Losing Rose was the worst part of it. Felt like someone ripped my soul out. I wasn't a perfect mom, but I did keep her away from the johns. No way I'd have let her end up like us."

"No. I don't guess you would." Had it come to that? Was Ritzi in the same category as the notorious madam Vivian Gordon? Vivian, with her client list a mile long and a little black book reportedly holding the names of almost every influential man in Manhattan.

In all the time they'd lived together, Vivian had never been so forthcoming with personal information. Her face softened, was almost kind, as she looked at Ritzi's stomach. "I'm getting Rose back, though. Soon. And when I do, I'm done with all of this. I suggest you make plans as well. It's going to get ugly."

"What are you talking about, Viv?"

"I've made an arrangement with Samuel Seabury to testify before his grand jury. Names and dates. I'm going to tell him about every bribe and every shakedown and every tip-off. The judicial scandal alone will keep him busy for months." Vivian picked at the quilt. "That's the trade. I tell him what I know, and he arranges for the state to return Rose to my custody."

"Are you *crazy*?" Ritzi hissed. "Do you *want* to get killed? Do you have any idea who will come after you if you testify for Seabury?"

"I've arranged my safety net with Seabury." Her smile was full of sympathy. "Listen. You're a sweet girl, Ritz. And I like you. But I don't plan on ever seeing you again after that. Make sure you have somewhere to go."

Ritzi took a long, shaky drag on her cigarette and closed her eyes. She set a hand on her stomach. Pulled it away quickly. "What do I do about this?"

Vivian motioned her to follow. "Come with me." She led Ritzi down the hall and into her bedroom.

Ritzi stood in the doorway, cigarette dangling from her hand, while Vivian rummaged through a small secretary desk in the corner. She had never been in this room. It was larger than her bedroom and decorated much more simply than she would have expected. Cream bedspread. Dark furniture. A hand-braided rug in the middle of the floor. Dark curtains. Not a single picture on the walls. Vivian never brought her Johns home and made sure that Ritzi didn't either. The apartment was a safe zone. No men allowed.

Vivian scribbled something onto a scrap of paper. "Here." She thrust it at Ritzi.

"What's this?"

"You'll need a corset. It's gonna hurt like hell. And they don't come cheap."

Ritzi looked at the address. "How long can I wear it?"

"If you can hold on until the end of February, I'll help you get out of this hellhole. But you've got to wait until then. I can't risk losing my chance to get Rose back."

RENAISSANCE CASINO AND BALLROOM, HARLEM,
THURSDAY, JULY 31, 1930

Ritzi had never seen anything like it. So many people in one room, laughing and gambling and huddled in groups at the bar, crowded around the craps tables cheering with each roll of the dice. She couldn't breathe for the smoke. Liquor on the breath of everyone within a three-foot radius.

Crater grabbed a lowball glass from the tray of a passing cocktail waitress and shoved it in her hand. "Here."

Ritzi sniffed the clear liquid. Her nostrils stung with the odor. "What is it?"

"Does it matter?"

"I'd like to know."

Crater gave her the look he reserved for the times he thought her especially unreasonable—lips folded in on themselves, eyes pinched. But he humored her and sniffed the glass. "Moonshine. Probably."

"It smells like piss."

"That's how they make it in Appalachia."

She handed it back to him. "I'd rather not, if it's all the same to you."

He lifted the glass out of her hand and took a swig. Didn't even wince. It must have gone down like pipe cleaner. "Let's go to the craps table. I feel lucky."

Joseph Crater was a terrible gambler. Bad with the money and mean when he lost. She, on the other hand, had remarkable skill with numbers—not that you could ever really beat the house, but all those years helping her father with the farm ledgers paid off when it came to taking a calculated risk. It was something Crater depended on her for.

"Which table?" Crater asked, waving a finger between the only two in the casino.

Each table could easily accommodate twenty-four people, with a much larger crowd gathered round if the dice were hot. That's what the one on the right looked like—a mass of bodies shoved up against the green-felt-covered table. Cheering. Jumping. Slapping backs and congratulating one another. The other, at the far end of the room, sat nearly abandoned, its dealer, boxman, and stickman glancing across the room with envious expressions, waiting for new players able to roll something other than the dreaded seven.

"That one." Ritzi pointed to the empty table.

Two years ago, Crater would have argued, would have said that she'd lost her mind and was intent on losing his money. But he'd learned better.

"Remember," she said, patting his arm. "It's always the player."

"Looks like it could be the dice this time. Lead weighted, I'd wager." He gave one last wistful glance at the crowded table and then led her to the open one.

"They're broke," she whispered. "And drunk. Now's the time to make our luck."

The stickman pushed the dice to the shooter and did his best to keep the tempo going. He looked grateful as Crater and Ritzi stepped up to the table.

"Comin' out. Bet those hard ways. How about the C and E? Hot roll comin', play the field! Any mo' on yo?"

"Don't forget your penny," she reminded Crater.

He found one in his pocket and tossed it under the table for good luck. In reality, it was a wasted penny, but the point was to appear knowledge-able. Never toss both dice in the air at once—only amateurs did that. But one made you look like a pro. It was all about looking the part. Raising the bets. And, ultimately, making money. Ritzi picked his numbers, blew on his dice, and gave her sultry smile to any man who made eye contact.

Within ten minutes, Crater was up twelve dollars. A buzz built in the air around them like static. Stragglers drifted to their table. The cocktail waitresses circled, making sure the booze was plentiful.

Crater foisted another drink on her. "Maybe you'll like the rum better."

She smiled and brought it to her lips. Dipped her tongue in the amber liquid. "Not bad."

Ritzi set the glass down on the edge of the table near his elbow. The next time he went to roll, it went crashing to the floor and splashed onto her feet.

"I'll get you another. Hold on to it better, though." He was enjoying himself too much to be angry. "Okay?"

"Sure."

Over the next hour, he tried to force a variety of liquors on her. It was their routine, the prelude to a raucous night in a random hotel room, where she would muster a faked orgasm, and then tears after he passed out. It was a routine she'd long since wearied of.

As usual, Crater could manage his drinking, hovering somewhere between a heavy buzz and being completely soused. Until he started losing. Then the liquor and the anger competed for dominance.

He started rolling sevens ten minutes before midnight and kept going until he'd lost over half his winnings. Left with only a hundred dollars and his wounded pride, he pushed her toward the whiskey.

Ritzi humored him, plucking out the ice cubes with her fingers and crunching them between her teeth.

Crater yanked the glass out of her hand. "Why so damned uptight? Drink it already."

Hurry up. Get drunk. Get easy. Don't make me work for it because I'm a lazy shit and I just wanna fuck and go to sleep, she thought. *That's what you really mean.*

Without giving a single thought to the consequences, she threw her answer at him. "Because, damn it, I'm pregnant!" Even though she screamed the words, they were lost in the din. He read her lips, though. And that was enough.

He waved the dealer away, stuffed his remaining winnings in his suit pocket, and grabbed her wrist. "Outside. Now."

She stumbled after him, one hand lifting the hem of her dress and the other trying to tug free of his pincerlike grasp. They stood together in the small glass chamber of the revolving door, and for that one suspended moment she saw murder in his eyes—a flash of pure hatred and disgust. But then the door finished its rotation and they were out in the open air and there was something else hidden beneath the dark glass of his eyes. Fear. Surprise.

"Say it again." He squeezed her tighter, fingers digging into the flesh of her arm.

"I'm pregnant."

"How?"

Such a stupid question. She didn't answer.

"Is it mine?"

"Of course."

"I've been married for thirteen years and we don't have children."

Something in the air that night made her bold. "Then the fault isn't yours."

"I don't care if I knocked you up. That's not my kid." Crater dropped her arm and stepped away. "You'll get rid of it. Soon. Or I'll tell Owney." He buttoned his dinner jacket and smoothed the lapel. "I'm going home. To my wife. Get your own cab."

And she did. It was after one in the morning when Ritzi got home. She was exhausted and furious, and for the first time she truly understood what Stella must feel like. Profound anger sat like a flame in her belly, radiating heat throughout her body.

She knew what she had to do.

Ritzi listened at Vivian's bedroom door to make sure she was asleep and then crept into the living room. She lifted the receiver from its cradle and asked the operator to connect her to the personal residence of George Hall.

THE loons retreated before dawn. Stella lay in bed, window open, listening for their early-morning chatter: a warbling tremolo or a frantic honk, perhaps the long clucking wail. Ears strained for the sound along the shore; she imagined a small pocket of loons tucked happily into the reeds. Safe. And together. Chicks beneath their mother's wing. Father standing guard.

She waited for the loons. But the lake was silent. The tip of her nose was numb, and she tasted autumn in the air. It was too chilly to sleep with the window open any longer. Stella pushed back the thin cotton blanket and rubbed her hands across her bare arms as she went to close it. She paused with her fingers on the frame. The lake, usually still this time of day, was peppered with dark spots. They seemed to float in the mist that hovered over the water's surface. Gray, oblong things. Denser than shadows, but still indiscernible from this distance. Then she saw the ripples spread around them, and she recognized them for what they were. Boats. At least a dozen. Maybe more. Headed toward the small inlet where her cabin lay. Not too many minutes later, she heard the whine of a small engine buzzing in the distance. Soon she saw the poles and the nets and heard faint voices call out across the water.

A search party?

Stella grabbed her flannel robe and tore off down the stairs, slamming the kitchen door behind her. Her bare feet padded across the deck and down the pier, right to the edge. With fists planted on her hips, she stood there as the sun lifted over the horizon and turned the mist into translucent gauze. Eighteen boats crept along the shore and sifted through the inlet. First one nest of loons and then another burst into the air as searchers thrust their poles into the reeds and jabbed along the shore. The birds beat the air with long, pointed wings and squawked in outrage. Stella heard an occasional comment shouted from one boat to another as the men looked under logs and in pools of shallow water. And all the while, they crept closer to the pier, closing in like a net. Soon Stella could make out faces. Beards. Deep-set eyes and broad foreheads. The stoop of a back and the hook of a nose. The foremost boat loomed closer, the man at the helm staring at her. Stella could not meet his eyes at first, terrified that she might see suspicion. But she could feel his gaze, and finally she lifted her eyes, only to recognize a man she knew and trusted. He was just twenty feet off at that point, prodding the shallow water with a long pole while the man behind him rowed.

Her question rushed out in a quiet breath. "Irv?"

The storekeeper motioned to the rower to stop. The small boat slowed and drifted to the side, pushing a wave of water toward the pier. It hit the beams beneath her with a melancholy sigh. Irv had not shaved that morning, and his stubble gave him a glum and drowsy appearance.

He kept his greeting to a bare minimum, shifting his eyes between her feet and the cabin behind her. Anywhere but her face. "Stella."

"What are you doing?" She pointed toward the flotilla around him.

Confusion was stressed into every syllable of Irv's answer. "They think you killed him, Stella."

"Who does?"

"Mr. Southard, the county attorney. And some of his friends back in New York. They're saying Joe came back to the lake after his trip to the city. Someone says they saw him on the train. They think he died here."

"And what do you think?"

"They asked for volunteers. I couldn't very well refuse."

Every head was angled her way, and the boats slowed to a drift, each of them bobbing on the surface as searchers turned to watch Stella flail her arms in anger. She should have been embarrassed or ashamed, but all she could evoke was rage.

"Well, I didn't kill Joe. So go ahead. Search. Poke your stupid poles into every square inch of this lake. But you won't find anything. Not a damn thing. You can come back to apologize when you're done."

Stella turned back to the house, and she saw Emma beckoning her from the kitchen door. Irv called out an apology, but she didn't acknowledge him.

"There's a man here," her mother said before Stella could voice her outrage at the invasion. "He wants to search the house."

"Surely you didn't let him in?"

"Of course not."

"Where is he?"

"At the front door."

Stella pushed her mother aside. She tightened the belt on her robe and charged through the living room. She yanked the front door open so quickly that the man on the other side stumbled backward.

He straightened his hat. "Mrs. Crater."

"Who are you?"

"Frank Southard." He extended his hand, but she didn't take it. "County attorney."

"You sent those men?"

"I did."

"Under whose authority?"

Frank Southard reached inside his suit and took out four sheets of paper, folded lengthwise. "District Attorney Crain asked me to look into your husband's disappearance. He doesn't have jurisdiction here." He paused to give her an incredulous look. "As you well know."

Stella glared at the papers before plucking them from his hand. By now she was quite familiar with Thomas Crain's stationery. A letter of introduction and the same three pages of questions that Jude had given her. The letter was verbose but she skipped to the end where Crain spelled out his request:

Some of Judge Crater's associates think that he has been the victim of foul play and that this possibility might have happened in your jurisdiction. I believe that Judge Crater disappeared after he arrived near his summer home the morning of August 7th. I would like to emphasize that any crime committed in that area would fall under your jurisdiction, and I expect that you will investigate the case with the possibility that there has been a crime.

I suggest you question Mrs. Crater concerning reports that she might have seen her husband after he left New York. A complete search of her Belgrade Lakes home would be prudent under the circumstances. In addition I'm attaching a list of questions I put to her in writing and request that you obtain more complete and definite answers than the ones she wrote for me. You may find it beneficial to question Mrs. Crater's mother, Emma Wheeler, and her chauffeur, Fred Kahler, as they are the two individuals most familiar with her whereabouts during the days in question.

Stella folded the papers and ran the crease between two fingernails. She handed them back to Mr. Southard. "You've come to search my home?"

"I have."

"I expect you brought a search warrant along with that offensive letter?"

Frank Southard rubbed beneath his nose with the edge of one finger. "I didn't think it necessary, you being a judge's wife and all."

"If you intend to step one foot over this threshold, I'm afraid it is."

"Now, Mrs. Crater—"

"Do not patronize me. I have already answered those questions in front of a witness. Thomas Crain makes serious accusations in that letter. And you want to enter my house without court approval or my attorney present?"

"It's a simple interview and a quick search."

"It's a violation of my rights. Good day."

Stella moved to shut the door, but Frank Southard propped it open with his foot. "Please be reasonable."

"Reason has nothing to do with this. Rule of law does. You may remove yourself from my property until you have a court order."

"Take a moment and consider how this looks. You'll heap suspicion on your head by refusing."

Stella kicked his foot out of the way, wincing as she stubbed her big toe against his dress shoe. "I am well versed in my Fourth Amendment rights . . . being a *judge's wife* and all."

Frank Southard took a step backward. "Very well, then. I'll be back. With papers."

Stella pushed the door shut so hard the glass rattled in the frame. Frank Southard stood there and they glared at one another through the pane. She waited until he retreated down the steps and got into his car before she ran up the stairs. Stella caught a brief glimpse of Emma, mouth carved into a disapproving line, as she bolted toward her bedroom. Once inside, she locked the door and crossed the room in three strides. Stella lifted one edge of her mattress, wedged a shoulder underneath, and then carefully tipped it onto the floor. In the space between mattress and box spring rested the four manila envelopes.

Had she let Frank Southard in, and had he found these papers, Joe's shifty business relationships would be front-page news, and her knowledge of them revealed. She couldn't allow that to happen. Not yet. She had to hide the record of those bribes until they found Joe.

Stella settled to the floor beside her bed and laid her forehead against the frame. The wood dug into her skin and offered a momentary distraction from the thoughts that tumbled through her mind. She sat there, eyes squeezed shut and hands limp in her lap, as she tried to subdue the reality that assailed her. It was no use. The townsfolk were dragging the lake for Joe's body, and she had refused entry to an official who wanted to search her home. To the casual observer, she looked guilty as hell.

THE letter was addressed to Amedia Christian, care of Stella Crater, 40 Fifth Avenue, and the sender was Thomas Crain, district attorney. Inside was a summons to appear before the grand jury regarding the disappearance of Joseph Crater.

Maria's contact with Mrs. Crater had been minimal since Mr. Crater vanished. One letter last week. It contained a check for her services and a request that she maintain the apartment on a minimal basis. She wanted Maria to stop by once a week to clean—dust, mostly—and collect the mail from her box in the lobby. Mrs. Crater was concerned about the pipes freezing once winter set in and the condition of the radiator. She included with the letter written permission for Maria to employ any handyman necessary should something need repair. She stated reluctantly that Maria would be paid less than half of her monthly salary because of her diminished responsibilities. She apologized for the inconvenience and made clear that she would not return to the city for an indeterminate amount of time. At the end was a postscript promising to make it up to Maria in any way she could.

Had there not been only one letter in the mailbox that day, Maria wouldn't have paid it any mind. It would have gone in the wire basket on the entry table with the rest of the mail she'd collected since August. But the fraudulent name she'd given George Hall—the one he'd used in his article—caught her attention. She lifted the envelope and held it for a moment, unsure. To the left of the address was a handwritten addendum stating that the registered letter had undergone repeated attempts for delivery and that the Postal Service had left it in the box as a last resort.

The instructions were simple: report to the United States District

Court on October 29 prepared to give testimony regarding the last time she saw her employer. It was worded, in no uncertain terms, that her appearance was mandatory.

Maria read the summons one time. Then she stuffed the letter back into the bond paper envelope and folded it into thirds. As far as she was concerned, Amedia Christian did not exist. Nor would she testify before any grand jury.

RITZI saw the postman sitting in the front row, his legs stretched out in front of him, tapping an envelope against the palm of his hand. He'd been watching rehearsal for ten minutes, a ridiculous grin smeared across his narrow face.

"Again!" the choreographer shouted. "Your timing is off, Ginger. What the hell are you looking at, Ritzi? Eyes on me, girls. One. Step. Two. Step. Kick. Kick. Kick!"

The entire company stood onstage, arms linked, practicing the last number, a rousing tune called "Take Me Back to Manhattan." High kick. Deep breath. And then they belted out the last two lines of the chorus: "So take me back to Manhattan, that dear old dirty town!"

"Okay. That's a wrap!" the choreographer shouted. He waved Ritzi over. "Since when did you start listing the Broadway Theatre as your primary residence, Ritz?"

"I don't."

He pointed to the postman in the front row.

Ritzi was not, in general, fond of sharing her address. Vivian's apartment was unlisted. As was the phone number.

"You got a registered letter."

She picked her way down the steps, apprehensive.

The postman jumped to his feet and thrust the envelope at her. "I need you to sign for this," he said, and handed her a clipboard.

Had she looked at the return address first, she would not have taken the letter from him. "What if I don't want it?" she asked after seeing the official seal of the New York district attorney's office.

"Too late now—it's yours. Sign right there."

Ritzi took the pen and scribbled her name. She tore open the envelope and read the letter as though it were an obituary. In thirty days, her testimony was required before the grand jury investigating Joseph Crater's disappearance.

"I'M very sorry about all this. You know that, right?" Simon Rifkind said.

Almost seven weeks after Stella placed that first panicked call to Joe's old business associate, he had finally shown up at the lake house to offer his condolences and bring her news.

They sat in the gazebo, backs to the lake, sipping mulled wine. Stella wrapped her palms around the ceramic mug and sank a little deeper into Joe's suit coat. After several moments of silence, she turned to Simon Rifkind. "I appreciate all you're doing to help."

"It was the least I could do." He had the slick look of a professional politician. Dark hair greased back and a part so sharp you could see the white of his scalp. Pencil mustache. Small wire glasses. When he smiled, his teeth flashed large and white.

"I lied to the district attorney," she said, "in the questionnaire he sent. Crain asked specifically if I'd received any money from Joe's account."

His shrug was indifferent. "You had bills to pay. And it was easy enough for me to collect Joe's paychecks."

Stella sipped her wine. Emma always went overboard on the cinnamon, but it was good nonetheless.

"This is a dicey situation, Stella." He leaned forward, expression somber. "You have to be so careful with the information you divulge."

"I just wanted you to know. That's all. For when Crain comes snooping around. And he will."

Rifkind tapped the edge of his mug with a fingernail. He plied Stella with a conspiratorial grin. "What do you know about Joe's safe-deposit box?"

"Nothing apart from the fact that he had one."

"Come now, Stella. You gave Crain permission to search it."

"He asked for power of attorney last month so he could open the box. I never even saw it, much less put anything in there. That was Joe's business."

"Do you know what he used it for?"

"Safekeeping." She dug at a chip in the mug with her thumbnail. "It gave him peace of mind. Like having a will. Or life insurance policies. Joe was that sort of guy. Cross the t's, dot the i's."

"Crain wasn't happy that you wouldn't turn over Joe's key."

"I don't have one. Never did. If I had, I'd have sent it back with the damned power of attorney. Crain would not believe me if I told him my eyes were blue. He'd argue that I had them dyed just to spite him."

"There is a standing belief in Crain's office that you'll exhaust yourself in the effort *not* to cooperate."

"Nonsense. I'll cooperate with anything that does not subject me to useless torture and notoriety."

"Well, it was fun to watch, regardless. He stood around for half an hour while a mechanic chiseled open the box—the manager at the bank was none too thrilled with that—and then stormed out cursing you and all your descendants when the damn thing turned up empty."

"Clearly a waste of breath, as I have no descendants."

"The fact that I was present as Joe's private attorney"—he gave Stella a sideways look and a small shrug, as if to say that he still considered himself to be so—"riled him even more. Almost wish I'd called the paper to photograph the entire thing." Rifkind eased back and draped one arm over the rail. "Couldn't have done that, of course. None of us had any idea what we'd find in that box."

Stella did not meet his curious gaze. She stared across the lake to the opposite shore, where the maple trees blazed red and gold. She knew exactly what Joe had kept in that box but had no intention of telling anyone. Especially since the contents were currently in her possession. "What were you expecting?"

"I can't say for sure. There are so many things left unaccounted for."

"Such as?"

"His will, for one. It's not been found in his office or at your home or in that safe-deposit box. I find that very odd. I know for a fact he had one written up a few years back. I signed as witness."

"He never mentioned a will to me."

"No reason to trouble you with those matters. Just be glad his legal house was in order."

Was. That word seemed to be settled among Joe's friends and the law and the papers. Dead and gone, Stella supposed they meant. A given assumption.

"I should have known more about our finances. But he was happy to take care of that, and I was happy to let him."

Simon Rifkind patted her shoulder. "That's just the way things are, Stella. You take care of the home, he takes care of the money."

She stiffened beneath his touch and would have liked nothing more than to throw the remainder of her wine in his face. She imagined how satisfying the purple stain would have been as it bled through and ruined what was obviously an expensive suit.

Simon stared into his mug, considering the dregs of cinnamon and cloves at the bottom, as he chose his next words. "There's an issue with Joe's finances."

"Meaning?"

"The court has stopped issuing his paychecks."

"They can't do that!"

"They can. And they have. Last week."

"No." Stella shook her head. "Isn't there something you can do?"

Simon placed his mug on the rail behind them and grabbed Stella's hand. "Joe hasn't shown up for work in weeks. It was only a matter of time. They won't continue to pay the salary of a man who isn't performing his duties."

Stella forced herself not to yank her hand away; she couldn't risk the offense it might give. "This is a special circumstance. Surely there's a law you can cite? Request an injunction? Something?"

"I'm afraid not," he said. "You'll have to make other arrangements."

She was about to argue that there was nothing else—Joe had supported them solely for thirteen years—when she heard the ring of a bicycle bell in the driveway, followed by a voice calling, "Western Union!"

Stella left Simon in the gazebo and slipped into the kitchen, grateful for the warmth and the reprieve. When she opened the front door, she was startled to see her regular telegraph boy. She peered down at him. His uniform was too large, cinched at the waist with a strap of leather with crude holes punched at irregular intervals, and the ends of his shoes were cut off, his toes dangling over the edge. But he was energetic and eager to please, and she couldn't help liking him even though his appearance at her door often heralded bad news.

"Shouldn't you be in school, Ezra?"

"School don't pay, miss. Western Union do."

"*Does.* Western Union *does.* And the fact that you're ten—"

"Twelve."

"—and don't know the correct usage of that word proves that you ought to be in school instead of running telegrams." She crossed her arms sternly across her chest.

It would probably take the child ten years to grow into his teeth, but when he did, they would certainly be one of his better features. Large and white, they stood in even rows on both top and bottom and were accentuated by a fetching dimple in one cheek. Right then, however, they gave him an impish look, a smile too big for his body, full of mischief. His bright blue eyes didn't help, and she suspected that Ezra found himself in trouble more frequently than he deserved.

"For you, miss." He handed her the telegram.

Stella unfolded the yellow paper and read as he waited for her reply. The message was short and blunt:

Mrs. Stella M. W. Crater
Belgrade Lakes, Maine

The New York County Grand Jury officially requests you to appear
for questioning on October 29th in the disappearance of your hus-
band, Supreme Court Justice Joseph Force Crater. This request will
be followed by summons sent registered mail.

District Attorney Thomas Crain

"Care to reply, miss?" Ezra asked.

"No," she said, and reached into her pocket for a nickel. "I do not."

He dropped the coin into a cloth pouch and stuffed it in his pocket. Small wages for a hard job. The boy couldn't make more than a few cents a telegram, but since he was over the minimum age of ten, the law allowed him to work. Ezra tipped his too-large cap. "Thanks."

Without thinking, she reached out and straightened his cap so it no longer sat cockeyed over his face. "If you were my child, I'd have you in school."

There was a flash in his eyes, the resentment of pity, and he jumped off the porch in one quick stride. Ezra tore down the driveway on his bicycle and grinned back over his shoulder. The words he flung at her were so spiteful she couldn't believe they came from such a young boy. "People say you can't *have* kids."

Stella wadded the telegram in her fist, angered by the cruel observation, and went back inside.

Rifkind had relocated to the living room. He crouched before the fireplace and stoked the dying embers. "Bad news?"

Stella threw the telegram into the coals and watched the edges of the paper gild orange and then ignite in a puff. "Is there any other kind these days?"

THE first snowfall crept in during the night. Stella woke to plumes of frozen breath clouding the air above her head. The chill settled across her cheeks and at the foot of her bed, where she'd tugged the blankets away from the mattress. She pulled her knees up and curled into a ball, dreading that moment when she would push the covers back and plunge into the cold air.

The kitchen door banged open downstairs, and she heard Fred's heavy footsteps and then the thump of wood dropping to the hearth. The metal grate slid across the fireplace. Paper crumpled. The strike of a match against sandpaper. And then another, followed by a muted curse. A whoosh of air up the flue as kindling ignited. Soon she smelled the acrid scent of burning newsprint and heard the crackling fire. Her room had not warmed so much as a degree, but the knowledge of a fire burning downstairs gave Stella the motivation she needed to climb from bed and find her clothes.

Gone were the days when she went downstairs barefoot. Before leaving her room, Stella fished a pair of Joe's heavy socks from the drawer and pulled on her hiking boots. In the eighteen years they'd been coming to the cabin, they had never stayed until first snowfall. She hadn't bothered to bring winter clothes. In hindsight, it seemed a terrible oversight, but Stella made the best of her circumstances, dressing in layers with her robe over top.

"Don't laugh," she said, catching Fred's raised eyebrow.

"I'm too cold to laugh, Mrs. Crater." He rubbed his palms together next to the fire.

"Thank you for doing that."

"I'd like to say it was for your benefit, but I'd be lying."

Emma shuffled into the living room and scooted one of the wingback chairs next to the hearth. "I didn't pack for this," she said.

"No need. We're leaving tomorrow."

Both Fred and Emma turned toward her, curious.

"What about the grand jury? I thought you didn't want to testify," Emma said.

They'd avoided the postman for a week, refusing to answer the door and sign for the registered letter. But he'd caught up with Stella two days earlier at Irv Bean's while she shopped for groceries.

Stella sat on the stacked-stone hearth. "We're not going back to New York."

"What do you mean?"

"I think a little vacation is in order. But first we have to close down the cabin."

For the remainder of the day, they packed and cleaned. Stella took the screens off the windows and put them in the hollow beneath the stairs. Emma set all the taps to drip so that the glacial air barreling down from Canada wouldn't freeze and burst the pipes. They stowed dishes in the cupboards and dusted while Fred oiled the door hinges and set mousetraps. Emma attacked the floorboards with an energy Stella didn't think possible for her eighty years.

After a lunch of soup and bread, Emma slipped back to her room for a nap while Stella sorted papers in front of the fire. Fred kept the fire going strong all afternoon in between running errands. He had not received his wages since the end of July. Nor had he asked for them. When Fred brought her the mail and that day's newspapers, she asked him to sit. He waited patiently as she sifted through the letters. At the bottom of the stack was another letter from the district attorney's office. Apparently, Thomas Crain was undeterred by her lack of response and was following up with a second grand jury summons. As if she could forget. Fred watched with alarm as she tore it into small pieces and fed it into the fire.

"Shouldn't you read that?"

"I already know what it says."

"Why won't you help them?"

"Thomas Crain doesn't need any help destroying my life. He's done a good enough job on his own."

Fred wouldn't meet her gaze. He watched the fire instead. "It seems like you're fighting against the people who are trying to find Joe. They're just doing their job."

Stella cleared her throat. "Those men aren't trying to find Joe. If they were, they'd be scouring New York City. They're trying to place blame. And they see me as an easy target."

"It doesn't look good, is all, you burning those summons and running from everyone who asks a question."

"Do you really think he's going to come back, Fred? That he'll walk through the door, give me that grin, and explain where he's been the last two months?"

His face plainly said that he didn't.

Stella tucked a wool throw around her legs. "Joe isn't coming back. I have to protect myself."

"Hiding up here won't make the problem go away. You need to talk to them. You got nothing to hide. I was right here with you when Joe was in the city. He never came back up here."

"Why don't *you* tell them that?"

"They're not asking me."

"You could go forward."

"It'd look like you put me up to it. Since I work for you and all."

Stella pushed the hair off her forehead with her palm. "About that—"

The smile he offered fell short of kindness and settled on resignation. "Don't worry about it, Mrs. Crater. I know you'll pay me when you can."

"That's just it. I can't."

He wanted to ask for clarification, she could see that. But he didn't. Instead, he sat quietly, waiting for her to continue.

"I *can't* pay you. Without Joe, without his salary, I can't pay anything." Stella lifted her purse from under the chair and dug around the bottom until she found the keys to the Cadillac. She tossed them to Fred.

He looked at them as though she'd laid an egg in his palm. Or a sunflower. Or some other random object. "Do you need me to run an errand?"

"I'd like you to take the Cadillac as payment for what I owe you."

He sighed, a desperate sort of thing, and said, "You don't have to do that."

"I owe you over two months' wages. And I don't have a prayer of finding the money. The court stopped cutting Joe's checks. It's this or nothing, Fred. I don't have anything else."

"What about Joe? You're just gonna let him stay out there? Missing?"

She turned back to the fireplace and stoked the embers. "It's better that way."

Fred looked at her, dark eyes narrowed. "Better for who?"

"Me. Everyone. Even Joe, at this point. Can you imagine the questions he'd face if he were to show up? The accusations? We'd be ruined."

Fred passed the keys from one hand to the other. They jingled in the silence.

"The title is in an envelope by the door. But there's one thing I need before you leave. Consider it your last act of employment." Stella wiped her soot-covered palms against her skirt. "I need you to drive Mother and me to Portland in the morning. It's my turn to disappear."

THE Hotel Eastland sat on the edge of Portland Harbor. It towered eight stories above the small fishing port and boasted an unobstructed view of the Atlantic Ocean. After checking in, Stella and her mother went to explore the famous heated observatory. Floor-to-ceiling windows and plentiful skylights made the dark clouds and choppy water feel less threatening. The women settled into wicker chairs in a corner and watched the fishing boats and private yachts slip in and out of the harbor far below.

"How long will we stay here?" Emma asked.

"As long as it takes."

She put down her knitting and looked at her daughter. "As long as *what* takes?"

"The grand jury to dismiss."

Emma looked around the observatory. "That could be months."

"Perhaps."

"This is a *nice* hotel, Stella."

She lifted a cup of steaming mint tea from the glass-topped table between them. "We wouldn't want to stay in a dump."

Emma shifted a bit closer. "You just let Fred go because you couldn't pay his wages. How will you afford this?"

"Fred was a nonessential luxury. And I more than compensated him for his work. I can find money when I need it. I just didn't need it for him."

Both women turned when they heard the steady tread of footsteps climbing the wrought-iron spiral staircase that led to the observatory. The concierge strode across the room, hands behind his back. "You requested me, Mrs. Wheeler?"

Stella laughed and nodded toward her mother. "*She* is Mrs. Wheeler. But I do need something of a favor from your staff."

"We are here to serve."

"My mother and I will spend the majority of our stay either in our room or right here. Is that acceptable?"

"It is."

"I do not anticipate receiving many phone calls over the next few weeks, but I would ask that only close friends and family be connected through to our room. May I provide a list of names to the front desk?"

His eyes narrowed slightly. "Of course."

"And anyone not on that list can be . . . *diverted*?"

"That will not be a problem. How long do you expect to stay with us?"

Stella lifted the porcelain cup to her lips and blew on the hot tea. "Let's just say we're all going to become very well acquainted."

If Joe had been found dead in an alley somewhere, it would have made headlines. But the fact that he had *disappeared* made news—national news, at that. Thankfully, it was his face splashed across newspapers from coast to coast. Had it been Stella's, she would have had nowhere to hide. As it was, the concierge acquiesced to her request, completely unaware of her identity. He gave a half bow and retreated down the staircase. Emma took up her knitting again in silence, and Stella tried to read a magazine. She tossed it on the table next to her after a few paragraphs and then spent the next two hours staring at the harbor below.

RITZI fumbled with her cigarette. She dropped it. Struggled to get it inside the silver holder. And dropped it again. "Shit."

"Need a light?" William Klein leaned against the wall a few yards away, watching her.

"No." Ritzi struck her lighter. It didn't catch, so she struck it again.

He sauntered toward her, hands in his pockets. "Give that to me. You'll burn yourself."

"I don't need your help."

"That's not what you said last time we talked." Klein took the lighter from her. A bright yellow flame hopped up, and he cupped it in his palm until it rose higher, and then he lit her cigarette.

"What are you doing here?"

"Same as you, I'd guess." He drew a registered envelope from inside his coat pocket and waved it at her. "Summons."

Ritzi tried to inhale deeply, but her ribs strained against the new corset. She coughed until her eyes stung.

"You gotta pull yourself together, Ritz. You go in there like that, and they'll see you for what you are."

"Which is?"

"Scared."

Ritzi moved away from him and sat on the bench. She crossed her legs and rocked her foot with a nervous twitch. "I *am* scared."

"They can't know that." Klein sat next to her and stretched an arm behind her on the bench.

"Don't touch me."

She gave him such a withering look that he shrank back. But after a moment, he lowered his voice and moved toward her ear. "Our agreement still stands?"

"Yes."

"As far as they're concerned, we're together?"

Ritzi nodded.

"Then you need to trust me."

She was about to tell him exactly what she thought of that suggestion when the double mahogany doors across from them swung open with a clang, revealing a large conference room filled with middle-aged men wearing expensive suits and dour expressions.

A clerk stepped into the hall. "Sally Lou Ritz?"

She straightened on the bench. "Yes?"

"We're ready for your testimony."

William Klein gave Ritzi a broad and deceptively kind smile. He cupped her face in his hands before she could protest and kissed her sensually in full view of the deposition room. "I'll be right here, sweetheart," he said, loud enough for all to hear.

Ritzi slid away with a blush and followed the clerk through the double doors. He pulled them shut and motioned toward a leather armchair at the end of a long conference table. "Have a seat, please."

Half of the men held cigarettes or cigars, and the room stank of smoke and musty aftershave. Ritzi settled into the chair, searching for a position where the corset didn't dig into her skin or make her light-headed. Effective as the contraption was, it wasn't made for sitting. She felt hot. And sick to her stomach.

"I'm District Attorney Thomas Crain," said a man at the other end of the table. At one time, he'd been tall and broad shouldered and most likely very attractive. But Crain now had the tired look of a man well past his prime. His eyes were glassy and his hair gray, and purple veins stretched across the end of his nose. His left hand trembled whenever he lifted it from the table. "I will be taking your testimony today."

A King James Bible lay on the table before her, and Crain instructed her to lay her right hand over it.

"Do you understand why you've been called before the court today, Miss Ritz?"

"Yes."

"And do you solemnly swear to tell the truth, the whole truth, and nothing but the truth?"

Ritzi felt the embossed letters of the Bible beneath the pads of her fingers. She pressed her hand against the leather and silently repented. Her father had a Bible just like this. So did her husband. She'd broken many promises made over those Bibles—why not this one as well? "I do."

"Very good. Will you please state your name for the court?"

"Sally Lou Ritz." She'd expected to give testimony in a large court-room under theatrical circumstances. Instead, the jurors sat along the wall in plush leather chairs and the magistrate and a handful of lawyers were spread along each side of the table beside her.

"Is that your true and given name?"

Like hell. "It is."

"What is your occupation, Miss Ritz?"

"I'm an actress."

Someone in the room snorted.

Crain consulted the file before him. "This says you're a showgirl in the production *Ladies All.*"

"I sing. I dance. I act."

Ritzi glanced around the room. She was the only woman present. The judge, the four attorneys, and all twenty members of the grand jury were male. All white. All in suits. All staring at her. She was suddenly aware of every inch of bare skin. Every curve. Her lipstick. Her perfume. She wished she'd worn a high-necked dress. She wished she hadn't come.

Crain sat with his hands folded together on the table. The skeptical slant of his eyebrows suggested that he was less than convinced about the legitimacy of her career. "Can you state for the court the last time that you saw Justice Crater?"

"August sixth."

"And what were the circumstances of your visit?"

"I had dinner with the judge and William Klein."

Thomas Crain inspected his notes. "How did you know Justice Crater?"

Instead of addressing Crain, she turned to the row of jurors. She gave them an innocent shrug and a few carefully chosen words. "Judge Crater was a regular on the theater scene. He often attended shows with his wife and with friends."

"Will you please walk us through the events of August sixth?"

Ritzi cleared her throat. "There isn't much to tell. William and I were having dinner at Billy Haas's Chophouse—"

Thomas Crain flipped through a stack of papers on the table. "William Klein, the attorney for the Schubert Theater Association? The two of you are romancially involved?"

"Yes. We're dating." The word felt wrong in her mouth, and she struggled not to curl her lip in distaste.

"Continue."

She told the story. Again. The same version she had recounted to Detective Simon. The same version she had silently rehearsed in the days after Crater disappeared. After that, the questions continued for some time. Thomas Crain grilled her on the minutest details of that evening. What Crater wore. What he had for dinner. Their conversation. When they parted ways that evening. She did her best to look relaxed. To smile. Ritzi shifted her gaze from Crain to the judge to the jurors. She did not swing her foot or play with her hair or pick at her fingernails. The questions were answered plainly and quickly, but she didn't offer additional information.

"Do you recall which direction Judge Crater's cab went?" Crain asked.

"No." Ritzi smiled. She wasn't so easily fooled. "As I told Detective Simon when he came to interview me—I'm sure you have a transcript of that conversation in your notes—I didn't actually watch Joseph Crater get into a cab. I assume he did, but I can't be certain."

"I see. And have you had any contact with him since?"

Not the sort I can discuss amongst men. "None whatsoever."

Crain consulted his notes. "Is there anything else you would like to add, Miss Ritz?"

"No, sir."

"Then you are free to go."

Ritzi pushed her chair back, picked her purse off the floor, and smoothed the front of her dress. She could feel the gaze of twenty-five men on her as she left the room. When she stepped into the long marble hallway, her hands began to tremble, and she clenched them to her side to steady them.

Klein stepped in front of the still-open door and gave her a quick hug, his face nuzzled against her cheek. "That was quick," he whispered.

"For you perhaps."

The clerk stepped into the hall and called, "William Klein."

"Looks like I'm up." He made a show of kissing her forehead and then followed the clerk inside.

Ritzi waited until the doors were closed and then rushed down the hall, away from the prying questions of Thomas Crain.

VARIATIONS of the Crater story were spread across the headlines of the *Sun,* the *Herald Tribune,* the *Daily News,* and the *Times.* It seemed as though every reporter in all five boroughs was scrambling for details about the judge's disappearance. While George Hall and a few other journalists maintained a sense of decorum, most dished out any article they thought would sell papers. Many of the stories were outlandish—sightings of Joseph Crater riding a donkey in Ecuador or giving safari tours in Africa. According to multiple unnamed witnesses, he'd been seen in Canada, Mexico, Europe, Africa, and Australia.

Maria scanned the papers at the newsstand, then turned away, shaking her head. The truth was far simpler than people would believe. She pushed through the crowded sidewalk, leaned into the street, and waved her arm vigorously for a few minutes before a cab drove up.

"Where to?"

"The Morosco Theatre," she said. "Hurry."

Having lived her entire life in New York City, Maria could navigate public transportation without giving it a second thought. But she could count on one hand the number of times she'd ever ridden in a cab. She felt high class, sitting in the backseat of that car, watching pedestrians scamper across the sidewalk. For a few brief minutes, she was removed from the vastness of her city. And then the cab rolled to a stop in the theater district, at 217 West Forty-Fifth Street.

Maria pulled a dollar from her purse and tucked it in the driver's meaty palm. She turned to look at the massive stone building. Somewhat blockish and plain, it stood three stories tall, with a scalloped green awning that stretched across the front of the building, MOROSCO glow-ing in red lights on the façade above. Maria tugged at the sleeves of her coat and ran her fingers through her hair to tame a few unruly curls.

Three double glass doors graced the front of the building, but Maria did not go through them. Only a few stragglers wandered the sidewalk. Mostly couples, an occasional drunkard. Lights from the marquee above her reflected onto the concrete in bright yellows and reds, and she stood in their glow for a few seconds, summoning her courage. According to the playbills plastered across the front of the building, there were only ten minutes left in the show.

Maria walked to the side of the theater and looked down the narrow, dark alley between it and the Hotel Piccadilly. If not for the trash bins, a car could have passed through. Halfway down the alley, Maria saw what she was looking for. A red exit sign above a metal door. The stage door where Shorty Petak had taken her two months earlier.

She picked her way around the garbage, careful not to step in the puddles of squalid liquid or paper bags filled with rotting food. The alley smelled of damp brick, stale cigarettes, and urine. The solid walls of the theater could not entirely muffle the raucous applause that came from within, and she guessed that the final number was drawing to a close. Maria sat on the edge of the wide stoop outside the door and waited. The voices and shouts and laughter grew louder on the other side of the door.

Several minutes later, the audience began to trickle from the theater and flood the street. Some walked away hand in hand, while others hailed one of the waiting cabs. A few gathered in groups to critique the performance.

The door behind Maria opened with a rusty groan. She jumped to her feet as three showgirls skipped down the steps, whispering to one another and laughing. They were at the bottom before any of them saw Maria.

"No autographs, lady. Sorry."

"I'm waiting for a friend."

They shrugged, looped their arms together, and sauntered away. Seconds later they were lost in the crowd.

Another stream of girls in eveningwear rushed down the steps. They sounded like a flock of geese flying down the alley, their voices bouncing off the tall buildings and echoing across the brick. That's how it went for the next fifteen minutes, showgirls and stagehands slipping from the building, off to the next part of their evening. She pulled her coat tighter around her shoulders and shifted on the stoop as her legs and face began to chill.

Just when Maria was starting to think that Ritzi had forgotten their meeting, she pushed open the door, gripping the handle to a small wardrobe trunk. Her dress was every bit as red as her lips, and her fur coat almost reached to her knees. She looked like an heiress stepping from an ocean liner, and as she compared her own plain dress, low heels, and navy peacoat, Maria wanted to shrink into the shadows, to disappear.

"Thanks for coming. And sorry it took me so long. I had to wait until everyone left the dressing room." Ritzi set the trunk down. "Would you help me with this?"

Together they lugged the trunk down the steps. Maria grabbed the handle and tipped it toward her, testing the weight. It wouldn't be any problem to get home on her own. "How many costumes?"

"Five. And you're sure you can alter them by tomorrow?"

"Yes. It's just a matter of letting out the bodice seams." Maria looked at Ritzi's stomach. "You don't look pregnant."

Ritzi closed the gap between them in one quick movement. She set a hand over Maria's mouth. The stage door was shut tight behind them, but she looked over her shoulder to check anyway. "Shh."

Faces only inches apart, they stared at each other beneath the red glow of the exit sign.

"I have an idea. An arrangement of sorts," Maria said, easing away from Ritzi's hand.

"What kind of arrangement?"

Maria tried to control her voice, but the hope leaked through anyway. "You don't want your baby. And I don't think I can have one." She wanted to reach out and touch Ritzi's stomach but restrained herself.

Ritzi's laugh was cold and cruel. "There won't be a baby soon. This is a temporary fix."

The emotion rushed up Maria's throat, and she had to swallow the sob that threatened to erupt. "I can take it. Give it a home. That's not such a bad solution. We both get what we want."

Ritzi snorted. "You're a fool if you think it would be that easy."

Their breath rose in frozen clouds between them, and Maria shifted from foot to foot, growing colder by the minute. "When the show ends next month, take a break. Long enough to have the baby."

"My next show starts three days after this one wraps. There is no time. And I have no choice."

"No one is holding a gun to your head."

She leaned in, a feral look in her eyes. Growled. "Yet."

"I can pay for it. Everything. Your rent. The medical bills."

"Have you lost your mind?"

Maria stepped closer, her face so filled with zeal that Ritzi flinched. "Five hundred dollars. Cash. You keep whatever's left."

Doubt swept over Ritzi's face, and Maria struggled to hold her ground. It would have been easy to back down, to give in to the guilt that tugged at her conscience. But she forced herself to stand toe to toe with the showgirl and wait for her answer.

One moment passed, and then two. Just as Ritzi opened her mouth to respond, Maria heard footsteps in the alley. The silhouette of a tall, thin man in a fedora crept closer, but she could not make out the details of his face. As he stepped into the small sphere of light, Maria took a step backward.

"Well now, ain't this a coincidence," said George Hall.

RITZI flinched. One side of George Hall's mouth twisted upward into a grin. There was no mistaking the fact that he remembered her from the park. His eyes flashed away from hers and settled on Crater's maid. Ritzi expected an immediate dismissal but was surprised to see George's eyes narrow. When she turned to Maria, she recognized the look of dismay on her face. *They know each other.*

George slid one hand into his coat pocket in search of a small black notepad. He looked back and forth between them, rubbed his nose with an ink-stained finger, and then flipped open the notebook. He tapped the blank page with his pen. "Fancy seeing the two of you here. Together."

"George," Ritzi said.

"You"—he pointed at Maria—"are Joseph Crater's maid."

Maria did not respond, simply gripped the trunk handle with one hand and inched back toward the shadows, her glance shifting to the sidewalk and the crowd of people that loitered in front of the theater.

George walked around Ritzi in a wide circle. "Thanks for the tip," he said. "Turned into one hell of a story."

"You doubted?"

"A mistake I won't make again."

"You might not get the chance, pulling stunts like this. You were supposed to wait for me to contact you."

"So you are the infamous Sally Lou Ritz?"

"Ritzi."

"One of the last people to see Crater alive."

"Lucky me."

"Pity I didn't put that together sooner." He leaned in, a hound on the scent of an irresistible trail. "How well do you know Joseph Crater?" His voice echoed loudly in the alley.

Better than I'll ever admit.

The stage door swung open with a clang, and the three of them turned to see Elaine Dawn skipping down the steps. She looked resplendent in a flirty black dress with a low neckline.

Elaine looped her arm into Ritzi's and looked at them, expectant. "Did someone say Joseph Crater? Have you seen the papers? God, that's a mess."

"Elaine," Ritzi said, "I thought you were already gone?"

"Bathroom." She took note of the reporter, his pen and notebook ready. "Who's this?"

"George Hall. He broke the Crater story."

Elaine smiled at George. She reached up and straightened his tie. Patted his chest. "You've caused a lot of trouble for the girls. Reporters are crawling all over this place. The director's been pissing and moaning about it for days. And all for a shit like Joseph Crater?"

His eyebrows lifted, eager. "You knew him?"

Elaine smiled, and her voice filled with innuendo. "Oh, I *knew* him. Period."

George lifted the notepad and wiggled it. "Mind telling me a bit more? On the record?"

"There's nothing I enjoy more than being on the record."

Ritzi gave Maria a desperate look and whispered beneath her breath, "I'll give you what you want, okay? Somehow. I'll find a way. But no one can know about this, you understand? Especially George."

"I promise."

"Do you know Grant's Tomb? On Riverside Drive?"

"Yes."

"Meet me there tomorrow at noon. Bring the costumes and the money." Ritzi gave her a gentle shove down the alley. "Now go. Quick."

George looked up as Maria hurried away, the trunk rolling behind her. "Hey! Not so fast!"

"Let her be," Ritzi said, placing a hand on George's forearm. Her grip was firm enough to prevent him from trotting down the alley after Maria.

"'Night, Ritz," Elaine said as she passed. Was it anger that flashed across her face? Or jealousy? No, Ritzi decided, it was the relentless spark of competition.

"'Night. Be good."

"Oh, I'm good." Elaine patted George's cheek.

George couldn't hide his smile as she walked away, all hips and legs. He twirled his pen. "Is she always so . . . ?"

"Yes."

Ritzi spun around to face George. "Why are you here?"

"I came to talk to the girl who saw Crater the night he disappeared. Lo and behold, it happens to be my informant. Not that you were exactly forthcoming with that information a couple months ago."

"I told you there was more to the story."

"Clearly." He scratched something into his notebook. "How do you know the Craters' maid?"

"I know a lot of people, Georgie."

"That's one hell of a coincidence."

"You like breaking a story, right?"

"Of course."

"Have you ever stopped to think what happens after you splash someone's name across the front page? That it can really mess up a life?"

"That's not my concern. I find the truth and report it. Besides, you don't really care about messing up someone's life when you call in the middle of the night with a tip. It took weeks to convince my wife that I wasn't having an affair." George tucked his notebook back inside his jacket and then stuck his hands in his pockets. He nodded toward the street. "Can I hail you a cab?"

"Sure." Ritzi followed him down the alley.

"So you gonna make good on your promise?"

"You'll get your story."

"When?"

"The moment I know talking to you won't land me in the morgue."

"That where Crater is?"

"I don't know where he is."

"I don't believe you."

"You don't have a choice. I'm the best source you've got."

"Not the best. Just the prettiest," George said. "What does that maid have to do with this?"

"Nothing."

He snorted. "You're a terrible actress."

"And you're a shitty reporter. I give you the story of a lifetime, and you're hung up on Crater's maid? If you want to find him, spend a night or two at Club Abbey." Ritzi straightened her coat and clutched her purse as they stepped onto the sidewalk.

"Where are you off to?"

"Home," she said. "And no, you're not invited."

"Don't worry," he called after her. "I know better than to mess around with a gangster's moll."

Ritzi halted midstep and turned around. She glared at George but said nothing. He crossed the short distance between them.

"I'm not stupid," he said, "despite what you think. I talk to people. I listen. And I know that you're with Owney Madden. Unless, of course, he gives you orders to be with someone else. Say, a New York State Supreme Court judge?"

The insinuation shook Ritzi, and she took one faltering step backward. "I'm not with Owney," she hissed.

"Good night, Ritzi." George tipped his fedora and gave her a cunning smile. "I'll be expecting the rest of that story real soon."

THE tan city cab took Ritzi on a zigzag-
ging route through the one-way streets of Manhattan. She stared out the
window, watching people and buildings and vehicles blur into a kaleidoscope of gray sky and sidewalk and wool coats and bright scarves.

"Wait here," she told the driver when he rolled to a stop before Liberty National Bank on Broadway.

Ritzi lifted her chin and opened the bank door. It was cool and dark
inside, and her heels clacked against the tile as she approached the first
window. The teller was about her age, but she looked as though she'd
been wrung out and left to dry.

"Can I help you?"

"I'd like to make a withdrawal, please."

"Certainly." She slid a withdrawal slip across the counter. "Fill this
out. Name?"

Even though she'd used the name for three years, the fabrication still
felt strange on her lips. "Sally Lou Ritz."

The teller stepped away from the counter and ran a finger along the
black-spined ledgers that lined the wall behind her. Three of them were
labeled *R*, and she pulled the last from the shelf and heaved it onto the
counter.

Ritzi's account was filed toward the front of the ledger, and the teller
took the withdrawal slip and checked her name and account number.
The tip of one index finger rested beneath the amount Ritzi wanted to
withdraw and the other on the balance of her account.

"Are you closing your account with us today?"

"No."

"But you're emptying your account."

"Yes." She did not explain further.

"I'll have to get the manager since it's over two hundred dollars."

"That's fine."

Bill Watson, general manager of Liberty National Bank, was far less amiable than the girl he'd hired to tend customers. It would seem that Ritzi's desire to leave with $250 in cash was considered a personal affront. He thumbed through the bills with a twitch, glancing at her occasionally as she counted along with him.

He tapped the stack of bills together and evened them into an orderly pile. "This is a considerable amount of money, young lady."

"Yes."

"Are you sure that you can handle it? Would you like me to hold it until you've brought your husband in?"

She bristled at the questions and clenched her left hand into a fist where it lay on the counter. The words were like sawdust in her mouth. "He's not around."

"Your father, perhaps?"

"Just an envelope. And a receipt."

He snorted his disapproval and then explained that the bank would not be responsible for anything that happened to this money once she left the premises. Did she understand that?

Ritzi propped her elbows on the counter. "Is there a problem, Mr. Watson?"

"What do you mean?"

"You seem awfully reluctant to give me my money."

"I am not."

The teller offered Ritzi a smile over his shoulder, her crooked teeth beaming a vindicated thank-you.

"Great. On second thought, I'll take it tied in one of those little black fabric bags, if you don't mind."

He cut a small piece of twine and tied the bills before slipping them into the bag. "Not responsible, hear?"

She put the money in her purse. "That's what all the men tell me."

"FIRED?" Jude asked.

Maria handed him the letter she'd taken from the Craters' mailbox several hours earlier. "I believe *let go* was the phrase she used. That's my last paycheck. A whole twenty-eight dollars."

Jude led her toward a small table at the back of the diner. He pulled out her chair and then sat across from her, anger stretching his mouth tight. He pressed the letter flat, smoothing out the wrinkles with the palm of his hand, and read the two-page apology. "How can she be out of money?"

"I think her definition of broke is vastly different from ours."

"That's not what I mean," Jude said, pointing at the postmark on the envelope. "She sent this from Portland, Maine."

"So?"

He tapped the logo printed on the linen envelope. "So that's a resort town. And she's staying at the Hotel Eastland, no less. Right on the god—" Maria gave him such a look that he snapped his mouth closed. Cleared his throat. "Right on the water. You tell me she can't afford to pay her bills?"

She wiped a few stray crumbs from the table and onto the floor. "Don't be so hard on her. She just lost her husband."

"Why are you defending her? The woman just fired you!"

"I've still got my work at Smithson's. Things will be a bit tighter. But we aren't destitute."

Maria watched him lift Stella's letter from the table. He folded it in thirds and tucked it in his suit pocket. "What are you doing?"

"Her little act of cowardice is an unexpected gift. She let me know exactly where she's hiding. It seems your boss skipped out on her grand jury summons and didn't bother to let anyone know."

Unease seeped into her voice. "So did I."

"That's different!" The couple at the next table looked up in alarm. Jude cleared his throat again. Lowered his voice. "You can't get involved in this. And they can't know my wife worked for the Craters. There's no way I would have let you testify." His smile was conniving. "Amedia Christian will have to do that, but since no one can find her, I guess the district attorney is out of luck."

Maria let it go, but she looked at his suit pocket where he'd tucked the envelope. "What are you going to do with that letter?"

"Flush her out of hiding."

"Jude—"

"Let me take care of it." He handed her the menu. Smiled. "Why don't you order something?"

"I'm not hungry."

"You hardly eat anymore. You're tired all the time. I'm worried about you."

It was true. The fear had gotten to her, eating away at her appetite and her energy. Maria glanced at the menu but didn't take it from him. She shook her head. "I can't. I'll eat later. Smithson wants me to come in early today. I'm making the final adjustments to Owney Madden's wardrobe."

"Has he been any trouble?"

"No. I'm invisible." She smiled through the lie. "Just the girl who sews his suits."

Jude ordered pastrami on rye, and Maria dutifully ate a few bites when he forced it on her, all the while watching the clock above the cash register. At eleven, she stood and kissed his forehead. She lifted her paycheck from the table.

Jude gulped down the rest of his sandwich, paid the bill, and walked her to the nearest subway station. "I'll try and get off early tonight." He looped his arms around her waist and buried his face in her neck. The warmth of his breath tickled the skin beneath her ear. "How about I cook for you?"

"Sounds perfect."

Maria wanted to linger in his embrace, but she would be late. So she settled for a hasty kiss and the promise of a meal together later that night. But instead of going to Smithson Tailors, Maria caught a train at Fulton Street, made a quick detour by their apartment for Ritzi's trunk, then went north toward Grant's Tomb on Riverside Drive.

FIFTH AVENUE, TUESDAY, MARCH 25, 1930

Maria reached under the bed, straining forward on her knees, chest brushing the hardwood floors. It was dark beneath the bed, and she could see nothing but dust and the heavy bed skirt. "I don't see your watch, Mr. Crater."

"Look again."

She realized this was a game to him when she felt the sharp pinch on her bottom. Maria lurched sideways, out of his grasp, with a startled scream.

"You didn't do Jude any favors by not telling him how you meddled to get him that promotion." Joseph Crater stood behind her, eyes bloodshot and belligerent. "He's under the impression that he earned his place on the unit."

Maria scrambled away from him. Stood up. Folded her arms across her chest and pressed her back to the wall. She looked over Mr. Crater's shoulder.

"Don't bother. Stella left five minutes ago. Shopping. Or some such foolishness. Pity she can't buy a new pair of tits. That's what I'd really like her to wear around the house."

"Mr. Crater, I don't think this is appro—"

"I don't care what you think. I care that your husband doesn't make me look like a fool. Ever again. When the police commissioner comes to me and says that my recommendation questions orders, that looks bad on me. Do you understand?"

"I'm sure he didn't—"

"So protect his ego if you think it's that fragile, if he can't handle the fact that you had to pull strings for him. But hear me on this." Mr. Crater lifted his jacket from the bench at the end of the bed. He slid his arms into the sleeves and shrugged it over his shoulders. Smoothed the lapels. All the while, he stared at Maria, seeming to delight in her discomfort. "He's expendable. A detective who rats out my friends is better off dead. And that's a call I won't hesitate to make if he doesn't learn—and I mean quickly—to follow orders when they're given. Even if they're orders he finds distasteful."

Maria was reluctant to look away for fear he would assume she didn't take him seriously. She could not find her voice, so she tried to communicate with her eyes and a short, panicked nod that she understood.

"I'm a generous man, wouldn't you agree?"

A hoarse whisper. "Yes."

"I didn't have to give this warning. Could have called in a favor and had the problem taken care of. But I didn't think that would be fair, considering how long you've worked for us."

"Thank you."

"See to it that he understands. Because my associates are not as patient as I am, and the next warning will be the last."

He asked the impossible. Maria knew she could never tell Jude how he had gotten his promotion or ask that he accept the strings attached. She would find another way to undo this mess.

Mr. Crater adjusted his cuff links, collected his money clip and hand-kerchief from the bureau, and stuffed them in his pocket. Then he crossed the room and set his hand under Maria's chin. Ran a thumb over her lips. "I wonder what would happen to a pretty girl like you if there was no one around to protect her?"

RITZI sat on the marble steps of the mausoleum that held the remains of Ulysses S. Grant. Her ankles were crossed and her hands were folded in her lap. She turned her face to the sun and drank in what little warmth November had left to offer. She kept her eyes closed as the timid footsteps and rattle of the wardrobe trunk approached.

"I've never been here before." Maria settled on the step next to her, breathless.

"Me either."

"Then why here?"

"It was the first place that came to mind." Ritzi opened her eyes and turned to the side, taking in Maria's nervous expression. She was perched on the edge of her step, like a bird ready for flight. "I was going to tell you no."

"Why didn't you?"

"George Hall showed up."

Maria fiddled with the clasp on her purse. "I'll make sure to thank him for the interruption."

Ritzi stiffened. "You can't."

"I wasn't serious. I just . . ." Maria paused. She wouldn't meet Ritzi's questioning gaze. "This is hard. I'm sorry."

A shipping barge inched up the Hudson River, and the two women watched it with exaggerated interest for several moments.

"It won't be as easy as you think," Ritzi said after a long stretch of silence. "Especially when I really start to show. But I'll try."

"The adjustments I made to your costumes will buy you at least three months. Longer with a corset."

"I've got one already. It hurts like hell."

Maria lifted a white envelope from her purse. She placed it on the step between them. "Five hundred dollars. Just like I promised."

"Where did you get that much money?"

"You don't want to know."

"Listen, I don't need any more trouble, okay? If that's dirty, I'm not taking it. Deal's off."

Maria did her best to smile. "It's not dirty. But it's not exactly mine either."

"What's that supposed to mean?"

"Let's just say the owner is missing."

Ritzi lifted the envelope and felt the weight in her hand. "Crater?"

Maria shrugged noncommittally.

Somehow that knowledge made the exchange feel less like extortion. More like poetic justice. "Did you ever imagine yourself doing something like this?"

Maria gave a short, startled laugh. "No."

"For what it's worth, I never thought I'd be the kind of woman who'd sell a bastard child. Because call it what you like, that's what I'm doing."

"I never thought I'd have to buy one."

"We're quite a pair, then." Ritzi stuffed the envelope in her purse. "I'll do my best."

"Will you let me know?" Maria asked. Her eyes were round and hopeful, and it hurt Ritzi to look at them. "When you feel the baby moving? My phone number is on the envelope."

"Yes."

Maria stood and wrapped her dark wool coat around her chest. She angled the trunk handle toward Ritzi. "Thank you."

Ritzi worried that Maria would reach out and try to touch her stomach. But she kept her fists balled at her sides, as though restraining herself. Maria nodded once in that polite way of hers and then walked away. Ritzi watched her walk down Riverside Drive until she was out of sight.

Chapter Twenty-Six

PORTLAND, MAINE, SATURDAY, NOVEMBER 15, 1930

STELLA slammed the phone down on the bedside table. "How could you be so *foolish,* Mother?"

Emma glanced up from her knitting, startled. She sat in a high-backed chair next to the window. The curtains were open, and she leaned toward the natural light for help with the intricate pattern. "What?"

"There was a reporter asking for me just now."

"I didn't give this number to any reporters. You know that."

"That was the concierge. George Hall was *here.* They just found him nosing around the observatory."

"Why are you angry at me? I had nothing to do with that."

"That letter you mailed for me, did you put it in a hotel envelope?"

"That's all they had downstairs."

"It led him right to us!"

Emma dropped the knitting to her lap and pressed her fingers against her eyelids. "I'm sorry. I didn't think about that."

"Obviously not."

A defensive note crept into her voice. "How did he come by that letter, anyway? It went to the maid. Why did George Hall have it?"

Stella let out a long, defeated breath. "Detective Simon must have taken it from Maria."

"Why would she do that?"

"They're married."

"You can't be serious?" Emma looked stricken.

"Joe and I helped him get the promotion to detective earlier this year."

"And you just now *remembered* this?"

"Of course not. I thought it was very convenient that he got the case, and I didn't want him removed. Which is exactly what would have happened if I'd told the NYPD that his wife worked for us. It was best to omit that particular detail."

"Clearly he knows. And said nothing."

"Protecting his wife, most likely."

Emma squinted at Stella over her half-moon glasses. Her bright blue eyes narrowed into slits. "What game are you playing at?"

"It's not a game, Mother. It's self-preservation."

"How do you know Maria didn't give that letter to George Hall?"

"No," she said. "I'm certain Jude intercepted it. Besides, we wouldn't even be having this conversation if you hadn't used the hotel stationery."

"I don't plan on apologizing a second time. I didn't intend that error, but I can't keep secrets I don't know about. Take care of the details yourself next time."

Stella threw herself on the bed and rolled onto her back. All the pieces of her carefully constructed plan were being pulled apart by centrifugal force, disintegrating into chaos. She was losing control. "Joe has ruined me."

"The fact that you're in a hotel with a concierge proves that you're not ruined. You have a perfectly good home—no, make that *three* perfectly good homes—you could go to. But you chose to come here."

"Both apartments are in Joe's name. I show up there and I'll be slapped with a subpoena before I can unlock the dead bolt. The cabin is mine, of course, but it's not made for winter residence." Stella glanced at her mother and wondered if that's what she would look like in thirty years. Silver hair and watery eyes and thin frame. "Did you know Joe tried to sell it?"

Emma's jaw clenched. "The cabin? You love that place."

"He wanted the money for his political *campaign.*"

"Please tell me you didn't let him?"

"I walked into his office one morning in April and he was on the phone with Owney Madden, negotiating the price. Twelve thousand dollars. I stood there, dumbfounded. He'd never so much as asked me."

Emma said nothing, merely waited, her knitting piled on her lap.

"It was the worst fight we've ever had. We've been married thirteen years and he'd never called me names like that before. I can't even repeat them to you, Mother." A frost settled into Stella's eyes. "But he forgot the deed was in my name. It took some maneuvering, but I got it back." She glanced at Emma.

"Why the cabin? You have the apartment on Bank Street. And it's empty."

"We needed that apartment to keep his voting district in Tammany Hall, and we needed the Fifth Avenue apartment to live in. You know how he was about appearances. In the end, he emptied every savings account, cashed in every stock and bond, and collected life insurance policies and investments for his campaign. And every bit of it is in a brown leather satchel right here in this hotel. I found it all in the apartment when I went back in August."

Emma's knitting needles fell to the floor with a tiny clank. "And you couldn't bother to tell me this?"

"It's not something I'm proud of."

"Nor should you be. But still, I deserve that much for gallivanting around the countryside with you."

Stella swung her legs over the edge of the bed and met her mother's bold gaze. "If they find Joe, it ruins everything."

"Ruins *what*, Stella?"

"My life! Everything we built. Every night I spent alone. Every compromise I made for him. Every one of Joe's affairs. Not to mention every penny we have. All for nothing!" Stella flung the words at her mother.

Instead of recoiling, Emma moved closer. "Your life—this life you're screaming about—doesn't exist. And if you don't wake up and salvage the life you really do have—the one loaded with debt and scandal—you're not going to have anything at all."

Stella arced her back, the tendons in her neck drawn. She could feel the trembling in her spine and the tips of her fingernails digging into her clenched fists. "I have to *try*, Mother. I have to wait this out. If they find out I knew about Joe's business dealings, they will freeze every asset we have and they will prosecute me. I will spend the rest of my life in prison for something my corrupt, philandering husband did. So you'll have to pardon me for being unwilling to take the fall for him. I'm not leaving this hotel until Thomas Crain has finished his grand jury investigation. Only then will I go back to New York and attempt to clean up the mess Joe left behind."

"WHO'S that?" Ritzi asked Lola, one of the girls on the chorus line.

Lola stepped closer to the mirror and applied a coat of fuchsia lipstick. It made her black hair and green eyes stand out in lovely contrast. "Name's Mary Anne."

The new arrival hung toward the back of the dressing room and tried to get into her costume without help—a hazing of sorts from the regulars, how they broke in the rookies. Her skin was pale and her hair typically blond. Large blue eyes. Cute smile.

"Who's she filling in for?"

"She's not filling in. Elaine didn't show last night. You know the rules."

Ritzi peered at the girl suspiciously. "That's not like Elaine."

"Maybe she spooked. She's been in the papers a lot lately, poor thing." Lola pointed at a column on the day's front page. "It's all anyone in this city can talk about. That judge."

Oh, I knew him. Period. George Hall quoted the exact words Elaine used in the alley that night. The innuendo was clear. She'd been intimate with Crater and was willing to talk about it. A stupid lie just to make the paper. Elaine had been harassed by reporters for weeks after that, her name paired with their seedy theories in every paper in New York.

"Did Shorty say anything about Elaine? She's been around Club Abbey a lot lately."

"He's the one that brought in Mary Anne. I doubt he cares. She's one of Owney's new *discoveries.*"

Ritzi took a seat next to Lola in front of the mirror and pinned her hair back with a pile of bobby pins. She set the feathered cap on her head and did not mention Elaine again. She had her theories, but they weren't something she would share with Lola. Instead, she set herself to work getting ready for that night's performance.

Ritzi's corset hung on the back of her chair, and she was about to ask Lola to help lace her up when the door to the dressing room swung open and slammed against the wall. Owney Madden loomed in the doorway, and behind him the stagehands and crew gaped at the women in various stages of undress as they shrieked and ran for cover.

"Good God, Owney. Can't you knock first?" Ritzi crossed her arms over her swollen breasts.

"I've seen it all before."

"Well, they haven't, okay? No need to give everyone a free peek." She looked over his shoulder at a row of young men craning their necks at the view.

He shut the door and leaned against it. "Don't be such a prude, Ritz. Everyone knows what you are."

The chorus line stilled to a hush. Those still in a compromising state slid into dressing gowns or tugged clothing over their heads. They stared at Owney and Ritzi.

"What would that be, exactly?"

"Cheap."

There was a stir of gasps behind them. Ritzi saw Lola plant her hands on her hips and stare daggers at Owney. But she did not come to Ritzi's defense.

"Everyone out," he said, and pointed at Ritzi. "Except you." He opened the door and held it for the chorus line. The girls filed out one by one. A few gave Ritzi a sympathetic look, but most rushed to escape Owney's wrath.

His hands were stuffed deep in his pockets as he circled the dressing room, looking for something.

Owney lifted her corset from the back of the chair. He motioned her over. "You really think this fools anyone?"

Ritzi cinched the belt of her dressing gown a little tighter. "I'll get Lola to help me."

"It wasn't a suggestion." He unlaced the back of the corset and held it out with both hands, elbows stiff.

When her robe landed on the floor in a light puddle, she sensed his eyes on her, white-hot. It wasn't the first time that Owney Madden had seen her naked body, but she felt vulnerable nonetheless. Her center of balance shifted to her stomach and the bulge between her hip bones. Owney said nothing as she walked across the room, stark naked, and snatched the corset from his hands. It took every ounce of self-control she possessed to step into the stiff fabric without shaking. She turned away from his furious gaze so he could lace up the back. But she saw him in the mirror, staring over her shoulder, watching her face.

"Where's Elaine?"

"Got rid of her."

"What do you mean?"

He snorted. "You know damn well what I mean. But if you must have details, I put a bullet in her skull. Then I had a couple of my guys wrap her in a sheet, stuff her in the trunk of my car, and drop her off the Brooklyn Bridge two nights ago." He grinned at the horrified look on Ritzi's face. "Or was that *too* much information?"

His words ran together in a blur of lilted syllables, and it took Ritzi a moment to make sense of what he said. A sudden rush of heat overwhelmed her when she finally understood. Ritzi willed herself not to throw up. "*Why?*"

"Because Elaine couldn't keep her name out of the papers. And I don't want people asking any more questions about Joseph Crater."

Ritzi blinked back tears, unwilling to dignify his admission with a response.

His hand dropped to the mound between her hips. Squeezed. "This was a dumb-ass thing to do."

Something inside her rose, and then coiled, eager to strike. The unfamiliar protective instinct surged, and she struggled to force it into submission. Her voice was blasé even as the blood pounded in her temples. "It's early. No one knows."

"I thought you knew better than to let this happen."

She laid her palms flat on the dressing table, an anchor to steady herself. "I did everything I could. It was an accident."

"A mistake. You'll take care of it, hear?"

Or else. That was the threat he'd left off, but she could feel it dangling in the air. She would end this problem. Or else she'd wind up like Elaine.

His fingers were quick and nimble as he laced up the corset. He'd done this before, likely in reverse, but at least he was familiar with the mechanics. Ritzi didn't complain as he jerked the strings and pulled them tight. He stopped at the point of discomfort.

"Take a deep breath," he said.

She tried to fill her lungs but couldn't quite expand them all the way.

Owney wrenched tighter and forced the air out in a sharp gasp. The face reflected in the mirror was cruel.

Ritzi's eyes stung. They began to water, and she blinked, determined not to cry.

Owney gave the corset one last tug, and Ritzi felt her pulse at the back of her eyes and a tingle in her lips. They stared at one another in the mirror for several long seconds.

Please, she mouthed.

Owney loosened his grip on the corset, and she took a wild breath.

"Better?" he asked.

She nodded, unable to speak.

He tied her off and then resumed his prowl around the dressing room. "Got a smoke?"

Ritzi didn't answer him. She rested a hand on her heart and took one deep breath after another. When his back was turned, she quickly ran her palm over her belly. The first tender act toward the child held captive inside her body.

Owney's gaze settled on her purse. He knew she always kept a pack in there. He grabbed it off the dressing table before she could protest and dumped everything out. A pack of cigarettes tumbled to the floor. He snatched it up and tapped it against his palm.

Inside the lining of her purse was the black bank bag containing every dollar she had—both what she'd withdrawn and what Maria had given her. If Owney found it, her escape plan was ruined.

Desperate to distract him, she flung the words out, heedless of the consequence: "I did what you told me." Ritzi stepped forward, bold. He couldn't do anything to her here. Not with so many people around. "Every bit of it was on your orders. I slept with those men because *you* made me do it. I spied on Crater because *you* told me to. Every lie. Every time I stole something from a wallet or an office or an apartment, it was *you* who made me do it."

"You were paid accordingly."

She waved around the dressing room, furious. "This? You think this was worth what it did to me? You can keep your damn shows. I don't want them anymore."

"Too late for that, Ritz. You work for me. And I don't accept resignations." Owney chose a cigarette from the pack. Lit it. Inhaled and then blew his insult at her with a mouthful of smoke. "Like I said, cheap."

"Get out."

He opened the door. "Be ready after the show. You've waited long enough to take care of that problem."

THE waiting room in Columbia Presbyterian Hospital's obstetrics unit was empty, all those expectant mothers most likely at home, feeding their growing families. As the last patient of the day, Maria had been ushered through the long gray hallway and left to wait inside Dr. Godfrey's exam room. The nurse informed her that he was on the floor above, assisting with a difficult delivery, and would be with her as soon as possible.

That was an hour ago. She'd gone back to the waiting room twice in search of an update, only to be reassured that Dr. Godfrey knew she was there and would be down any minute.

She was stretched out on the exam table, deeply asleep, when he finally arrived. Maria jerked awake at his touch. "What time is it?"

"Seven o'clock. I'm very sorry to make you wait so long. My patient delivered breech, and that's always"—he pinched the bridge of his nose—"a hard time for everyone involved."

Maria almost asked about his patient but decided not to. Perhaps she didn't really want to know. "I got your letter," she said. "I didn't realize I'd have to come in for another appointment."

"I didn't either. When I thought your case was straightforward."

There was a look of such sadness on his face that Maria sensed the heartache coming. Her first instinct was to avoid it, even if it meant hearing someone else's tragedy. "Your patient—"

"Will be fine," he interrupted. "As will her son. After a great deal of rest."

Maria wanted to be relieved but couldn't quite summon the emotion. "What about me? Am I going to be fine, Dr. Godfrey?"

"I have news for you, and I wanted to give it to you in person."

"What do you mean?"

"I know why you are unable to conceive."

All the hope rushed out of Maria. She wilted into the exam table. "Does it really matter why?"

"I'm afraid it does," Dr. Godfrey said. "It matters very much."

RITZI'S toes tapped against the stage in time with the orchestra as she spun in a tight pirouette. The music swelled, the audience roared, and then she was gone, running backstage. She jumped the gun a bit, ducking behind the curtain a few seconds early, but the crowd wouldn't notice.

"Hey!" one of the stagehands yelled as he stumbled backward, dropping a coil of rope after she pushed him out of the way. "Watch out!"

His voice was drowned out by the audience. They'd moved on to the next scene. The other girls would naturally fill the gap in the chorus line and buy her a few minutes. She fled into the dressing room and locked the door behind her. There was no time to get help with the corset, so she cut it off with a pair of scissors they used for trimming lose threads. When it fell to the floor, she bent over her chair panting, expanding her crushed ribs.

One last number and the show would be over. She would be expected onstage for the final bow. Perhaps an encore.

Not tonight.

Not ever again.

Owney and *The New Yorkers* be damned. It had never been worth it. She knew that now.

The elaborate headpiece took a chunk of hair with it when she ripped it off. She tossed it in a corner and grabbed her dress from a hook on the wall. Ritzi was in and zipped up in less time than it usually took to put on her shoes. She buckled her heels and grabbed her purse and reached for the dressing room door.

For one moment, that split second it took for the door to swing inward, she thought she might make it out of there.

And then she blinked.

Shorty Petak filled the doorframe, arms crossed. "Going somewhere?"

. . .

IT was almost midnight when she heard Jude's key in the lock. It turned and clicked and the door swung open on rusty hinges. She sank a little lower in the bathtub, the water lapping at her ribs. Maria squeezed her eyes shut as Jude's feet scraped over the hardwood floors in a weary shuffle. She pictured him on the other side of the wall, eyes half closed and head slumped in exhaustion.

What would he think, standing beside their empty bed? Would he see an impression on the left side—her side—little more than the suggestion of shoulders and hips recently pressed into the mattress? Perhaps run his hand along the shape of her? Maria imagined him rummaging through the cool sheets, searching for the warmth of her body, wondering at her pillow wadded into a ball on the floor. A moment later, Jude eased the bathroom door open.

The bathroom had the hot, damp smell of a summer afternoon, and steam hung from the ceiling. It clouded the mirror and ran in uneven lines down the wall. She'd been soaking long enough to pucker her fingers and toes. Maria rested her head against the edge of the porcelain tub, her arms draped over the side, limp. Wet curls clung to her neck.

Jude crossed the room and sat on the edge of the toilet. She pulled her knees up to her chest and shrank away.

He inhaled deeply and ran his thumb along her forearm. "It smells like you in here."

Every Christmas, Maria's mother gave her soap imported from Spain. The box held twelve bars, one for each month, and she made them last all year, whittling each bar down, never wasting so much as a sliver. It was made of olive oil, lemon peel, and lavender that grew on the hills outside Barcelona. It was her scent. It settled into the strands of her hair and the pads of her fingers and the soft patch of skin beneath her earlobes. She smelled of earth and citrus and rain, and Jude often leaned into her when she stroked his face and when she lay across his chest at night. The perfume clung to her clothing and her side of the bed, and it hung so heavy in the air right then that she could taste it when she took a long, slow breath between parted lips.

Maria heard him strip off his clothes and dump them in a dirty pile beneath the pedestal sink. The claw-foot tub was deep but not long, and she couldn't pull away from his touch as he climbed into the water at her feet. It wasn't their usual position, but she couldn't tolerate *that* at the moment. Jude slid his toes along her shins, tentative, then stretched his feet until they rested at the end of the tub, on either side of her waist. Their knees rose from the water like mountain peaks from mist, and she was locked between his legs.

"I thought you'd be asleep by now." Jude set his palm on the top of her knee, and she stretched her legs, pushing against his rib cage with her feet.

Maria shrugged, sending a wave across the tub. "Couldn't sleep." Her voice quivered with repressed tears.

"What's wrong?"

She looked at him with swollen, bloodshot eyes. "I went back to the doctor today."

"Ah, shit. Your appointment." Jude pulled himself under the water and stayed there so long the surface stilled. When he came up for air, Maria was chewing on the corner of her bottom lip, tears dripping off the end of her nose. "I forgot."

Evidence of Maria's anguish was plain: the bruise-like circles beneath her eyes and the chapped skin under her nose.

"What did he say?"

Maria pushed the heels of her hands into her eyes. She choked on the words like a hard-to-swallow fact. "That some women can't. And I'm one of them." And worse. Dr. Godfrey said much worse. But she could not bear to speak those words aloud right now. How he explained that sometimes a woman's ovaries failed to work correctly. How they became diseased.

Jude collapsed beneath the news. "Come here."

She lifted her feet off his chest and wiggled in the tub until she was in his lap, her body limp, emotions spent. Maria stared at the ceiling and let him draw her close. She didn't return the embrace.

"We don't have to do this anymore," he said. "It's okay that we . . . can't."

"No. It's not. Not for me." She thought of Ritzi and their agreement.

Jude tried to hold her together. Her bar of precious soap lay dissolving on the bottom of the tub, unused. He chased it around with his free hand and dropped it to the floor in a softened lump.

"You are the best thing that's ever happened to me." His hands explored the small of her back. "A baby could never top this."

She took a long breath, air catching in her throat, and let it go, exhaling years' worth of hope. "I'm going back to bed."

Maria crawled from the tub, dripping water. She stood there naked, all arms and legs and breasts. Jude reached for her, but she stepped away. Maria pushed at the tears with the back of her hand and shook them at him like an accusation. "It's not fair."

"I know."

Maria wrung her hair out on the bathroom floor, then shoved a towel around with her toes, soaking up the water. She grabbed her cotton nightgown off the towel rack and slipped it over her head. It clung to her wet skin.

Jude stepped from the tub and ran two fingers through the vines of wet hair that hung against her neck. She ducked her head and laid it against his collarbone.

"I should have been there with you." Jude scooped her up and carried her to the bedroom. He retrieved her pillow, tucked her in, and slid beneath the covers beside her. They lay like spoons, separated by a thin film of cotton and years of infertility. He was asleep before she had even lost the edge to her grief.

OWNEY was waiting when Shorty pushed her through the stage door. They each took an arm and forced her down the alley to the Cadillac.

"You can't do this," Ritzi said.

"You are not in a position to tell me what I can and can't do." Owney shoved her into the backseat. "I don't appreciate you trying to skip out on me."

"I don't appreciate being kidnapped."

"Escorted."

"Coerced."

Shorty didn't look at her, even though she stared at him in the rearview mirror. His eyes were locked on the windshield, hands lazy on the wheel.

Owney patted the space next to him, inviting her to slide over.

Bloody scally! Ritzi tried to think of every insult for someone from Liverpool that she'd ever heard. *Scouser!* She scooted against the door and glared at him.

"Don't look so sour, Ritz. We have to do it this way."

"I can take care of myself."

"Sure you can. Like you been doing all this time? Paying your own bills? Earning your spot on the stage? Yeah, you've done one hell of a job taking care of *yourself*."

"Can't a girl have some dignity?"

"Not your sort. Not on my dime."

They drove through the theater district and then Midtown. Through the money and the glitz, heading toward the West Side Highway and the Chelsea Piers. And all the while, Ritzi stared at the three inches of Shorty Petak's face that she could see in the mirror. Daring him to look at her. To acknowledge his part in this.

After threading the Cadillac through a maze of backstreets, Shorty rolled up to a five-story brick warehouse. There was no sign on the door, but the lights on the top floor were on.

Owney swung his door open. "This is costing extra. After hours."

"I never asked you to pay."

"My property. I pay."

The street was empty, darkness punctuated by a single puddle of light cast by an anemic streetlamp. Owney was at her door, tugging her from the car even as she gave Shorty one last stare. Pleading. For what, she didn't know. But anything was better than what awaited her inside.

Owney didn't knock; he simply shoved the door open and steered her down the narrow hall. There was an occasional door off to one side, marked with numbers but no names. No elevator, just a dark stairwell. Owney motioned her to go first. They climbed all the way up, Ritzi looking over her shoulder at the malicious grin on his face, and her heart pounding by the time they reached the fifth floor. The lights were on in the long, dirty hallway, but they felt sinister, flickering in the stillness and sending sputtering shadows across the faded linoleum floor. She grasped her purse strap with both hands.

"You're on the end, room twelve." Owney gripped her elbow, gave her a shove. "Let's get this over with."

Her thoughts raced, desperate for some argument that would change his mind. "*Ladies All* wraps in three days, Owney. And then *The New Yorkers* starts. You set that gig up. You wanted me to do it."

"They already found your replacement. A Hollywood actress named

Kathryn Crawford. Maybe you've heard of her? She's a real talent, Ritz. Not a whore like you."

Ritzi stumbled before him, shaking with fear and hatred and trying to match his stride. The door to room 12 creaked open, and a man stepped into the hall. He wore gloves and a stained medical coat. His skin was pale, his nose flat, and his voice an emotionless monotone. "You're late."

"This is John. He'll take care of you."

Not Dr., just John.

"I ain't got all night." John held the door open and motioned her in.

Ritzi tucked her purse under one arm and wrapped the other around her stomach.

Owney pushed her into the room.

"I don't want to do this," she said as he shut the door behind them.

John unrolled a white towel filled with surgical implements. He lay them on a side table, one by one.

"You don't have a choice," Owney said. He whispered something to John.

"I'm not your property anymore."

"Don't be a fool, Ritz. You can't go back on our arrangement. You came to me, remember? You wanted this. Time to pay up." If Owney had ever planned to let her walk away, she had missed the chance. Now she'd angered him to the point where he wasn't willing to pass the job to one of his thugs. He would see this through himself.

"I know what you did to Crater!" she shouted in desperation.

He stopped.

"I was there," she said. "In that hotel in Coney Island. Stuffed under the bathroom sink. I heard everything. Heard Crater begging for his life and heard you and your guys beating the hell out of him."

"I don't believe you." Owney's eyes narrowed.

"You asked him about the safe-deposit box and then you dragged him out of there. I wrote it all down, you know. Every detail goes to a reporter if I disappear."

Owney tugged at the end of his tie and looked at John. The man ignored their conversation. "No one would believe you, Ritz. Say what you want. Can't be proved."

"I'm ready to start." John nodded toward a long, bare table.

"Make it quick." Owney tipped his hat. "Let me know when it's done."

He turned and walked out the door, leaving them alone in the makeshift operating room.

Ritzi stepped away from John and backed up to the wall.

"Listen, he's already paid me. So no matter how long you stand there, this is going to happen. It would just be a hell of a lot easier if I don't have to come after you." He rested one hand on a stainless steel scalpel.

She blinked hard, pushing the tears back in, forcing herself to gain control. Ritzi looked around the room, searching for a way out. Two tables, a chair, and a pushcart piled with towels and surgical equipment were the only furniture visible. Behind John was a second gray metal door.

"Don't even think about it," he said, following her gaze.

She made her way to the operating table and leaned against it to steady herself. She had one chance. "What was the deal?"

"Deal?"

Ritzi pushed aside her fear. Took a deep breath. Summoned every ounce of charm and composure she possessed. "Did you tell him you'd sever an artery? Or maybe something a little cleaner? Like suffocation?"

He laughed. Unkind. "Listen—"

"I'm not stupid, you know." She lifted herself onto the table and crossed her legs. "People assume that. Girl works on Broadway, she must not have brains. Let's cut the bullshit, okay?"

John stood back and surveyed her. He crossed his arms. "This is new. Got a little fight in you, eh?"

She waved an arm around the room. "I'm curious how he told you to kill me."

"He left the specifics up to me."

"What'd he pay you?"

"None of your business."

"Oh, come on. I'd like to know what I went for. A cool hundred? Did that do the trick?"

"Three."

"And what would it cost to let me out of here? Alive."

"I work for Owney."

"How 'bout I double what he paid you?"

"A two-dollar whore like you ain't got that kind of cash."

She was surprised at the sharp edge to her laugh. "John, I cost a *hell* of a lot more than two dollars. Besides, I've been saving up."

He shrugged, uninterested, and finished removing the tools.

"Six hundred cash and we both win. Owney's none the wiser." Ritzi opened her purse and pulled the bank bag from its spot in the torn lining. Counted out six hundred dollars. She fanned the bills with her thumb, noting the greedy look in his eyes.

"Owney wants proof."

"I imagine you can arrange something."

"Or I can take his money and yours and not run the risk of you blabbing."

"Maybe I got someone waiting for me on the outside."

"Maybe when they come looking, I tell them you were just another slut that got knocked up and wanted an easy out. Happens all the time with your lot."

"Hardly the kind of thing you want to go around admitting. Since you run an illegal operation."

"No wonder you didn't make it in this business. You can't act worth shit."

Ritzi scratched her neck. "You like killing babies, John? Sometimes women too, by the sound of it? I think that maybe you'd like to go to sleep tonight without blood on your hands. Add some extra cash to the deal, and I don't see any reason why you shouldn't take me up on my offer."

A wicked grin spread across his face. "Take your clothes off."

CLUB ABBEY

GREENWICH VILLAGE, AUGUST 6, 1969

Crater's casual relationships with numerous showgirls and his visits to places such as Club Abbey and similar clubs in Atlantic City make clear that frequenting a house of prostitution would hardly have been out of character for him.

—*Richard J. Tofel*, Vanishing Point

Stella slides the envelope across the table with the tips of her fingers. She seems offended by its presence, despite the fact that not two seconds ago she took it from her purse. *Stella Crater* is written across the front in faded black ink, the letters a fine, feminine script. The corners are torn and bent—as though it's been crammed in a drawer for years— and a water stain across the front renders the postmark illegible. There is no return address.

"What's this?" Jude asks, staring at the red two-cent stamp of George Washington's profile.

"Your long-awaited confession."

He reaches for it, but Stella swats his hand, her movements alarmingly quick for one so ill. "Not yet."

"Why?"

"I don't plan on being here when you read it."

"You can't be leaving already?" Jude asks. "We were just starting to have fun."

Stella is limp and tired, and a bit of truth slips through her hard veneer. "I don't want to *see* you read it."

"Then close your eyes."

She puts a fingertip on the envelope and brings it back toward her an inch. "A few more minutes won't kill you."

They sit, bent over the table like two greedy children competing at slapjack: palms flat, fingers twitching, waiting for the next jack to land faceup on the table. But Jude isn't certain he's quick enough. And he doesn't want to lose this particular card, so he draws his hand away and drops it to his lap. Stella doesn't budge.

The early-August humidity has seeped down the stairwell and under the door, making Club Abbey smell like a wet ashtray. Someone wastes a perfectly good dime at the jukebox on John Lee Hooker's "One Bourbon, One Scotch, One Beer," the clichéd last call. Not like they need the reminder. Stan shuts the joint down promptly at midnight. It's been years since anyone protested.

Jude inspects the crumbling envelope. "How long have you had that?"

"Thirty-eight years. Give or take."

He grunts. "Ever heard of guilt by omission?"

"No."

"Means you can be found guilty of a crime by failing to report a felony. Withholding evidence being an obvious example."

Stella barks out a laugh and thrusts her hands toward him. Her wrists are like knobs on a twisted tree root, bones pressed against the loose paper of her skin, fingers little more than arthritic twigs. "Go ahead. Arrest me."

"I'm not interested in sending you to jail, Stella. Not anymore. I just want to know what happened to him." In four decades, they have never touched, but Jude cups her hands in his and lowers them to the table. They are tiny and frail and splayed open. "You've kept this up for a long time. What could possibly be worth all this trouble?"

Stella spins her watch to face upward. She notes the minute hand inching closer to midnight, regards Stan behind the bar as he washes the glasses and tips them upside down on a rack to dry. It's half past eleven, and there are only two other melancholy souls in the room—human dregs. One watches Johnny Carson on a grainy television above the bar, and the other is asleep at his table. She looks at the letter, still on the table between them, and is finally ready to tell the truth.

"This ritual is all I have left." The corners of her mouth flicker into a smile. "You couldn't have told me back then that things would go so wrong. We were right there on the edge of having everything. The trouble started in Tammany Hall, but it ended with the theater. Truth be told, I didn't much care for Broadway, but I liked to be there with Joe. Liked that it was an event every time we went out: the heels and the pearls and the chauffeur and the attention—attention that only doubled once he got his appointment to the court. Joe was a magnet for the stuff, and I lapped up the excess, intoxicated.

"This"—she swirls her hand above her head, indicating the whole of Club Abbey—"is my penance."

"For what?"

"For enabling Joe's corruption. For ignoring his infidelity. For helping him broker our future so he could buy a seat on the New York State Supreme Court. I thought we could have it all. Wealth and social standing and respect. And all I had to do was turn a blind eye. Keep the status quo. Show up at the right events in the right dress and smile pretty like a proper political wife. But it doesn't work like that, you know. There's always a price to pay. And, in Joe's case, a paper trail. Word got out the judgeships were on the block to the highest bidder. The wrong people started asking around, and one day Joe got a summons to appear before the Seabury Commission. Needless to say, there were people who had a vested interest in making sure he never testified." Stella eases the envelope back across the table. "You'll find the rest of what you need to know in there."

Jude sits quietly through all of this. He doesn't write in his notebook or interrupt or reach for the letter. For thirty-eight years, she's treated this like a shell game, shuffling the truth with sleight of hand, and he marvels at this revelation. Stella has tipped the cups over, shown him the ball. There is only one question to be asked.

"Why now?"

"Because I won't be here next year. This isn't the kind of thing one relishes taking to the grave." Stella glances upward. "Just in case."

"I can't absolve anything."

"I'm not asking you to. I just wanted you to know that I chose, all those years ago, to hide the truth. That it's eaten me from the inside out. Cancer has nothing on guilt, let me tell you that much. Shit. Forget the cigarettes. The guilt probably caused the cancer." Stella's hands tremble as she searches for another smoke. They're all gone. "So go ahead. Tell the story. Take it to the papers, for all I care. Consider this your victory." Stella's mouth is twisted wryly, as though she suspects he won't do it in the end.

There is a sudden emptiness within Club Abbey, and Jude and Stella realize that they are alone with Stan. He wanders through the bar with a broom, sweeping under tables and picking beer labels off the floor. They sit beneath a halo of dim light. Intense. Mournful.

"So now you know. Most of it, anyway." Stella lifts her glass from the table. She draws on the silence, summoning the ghosts of Club Abbey for support. "Good luck, Joe, wherever you are."

She tips back the glass of diluted whiskey and drains it in three wet gulps. A shudder runs through her body, and Stella presses the back of her hand to her mouth. Squeezes her eyes shut. There are no good-byes for her. No formalities. She gathers her purse and slides out of the booth, setting one unsure foot to the floor and then another. Stella straightens her dress. Nothing but habit keeps it from sliding right off her wasted body. She doesn't grace them with a parting word or a nod, simply crosses the bar and leaves Joe's drink untouched on the table behind her. As always.

Jude wonders if she has enough strength to pull the doors open. And then he remembers that only fools underestimate the strength of Stella Crater.

Chapter Twenty-Eight

THE State of Maine Express idled at Portland Union Station, sending sheets of white steam into the frozen air. The few passengers milling about did so with the slow shuffle of exhaustion. Absent was the usual grumbling of commuters as they jostled for position in the coach cars. No honking horns or whistles or delivery trucks rumbling down St. John Street. Those distractions would come in an hour or two, when civilized people went about their business. Five o'clock in the morning was too early for all but the fishermen, and they were already a mile offshore in Portland Harbor, lobster pots on the line, ready to set. But the hour suited Stella perfectly fine. She would slip away from her hiding place in the still of the morning and return home with no one the wiser.

Emma stood beside her on the platform; they waited as the porter gathered their luggage and placed it in an unsteady pile on the trolley. He led them toward one of the private cars and helped first Emma and then Stella aboard.

They followed an attendant through the narrow corridor, with its high windows and emerald carpet, toward a compartment at the back. The young man unlocked the frosted-glass doors and slid them open. Stella shed her outer layer and handed the wool hat, scarf, and gloves, along with a knee-length coat, to the attendant so he could put them on the luggage rack above her seat. Emma did the same.

"Don't touch it!" Stella snapped when she saw him reach for the brown leather satchel she'd placed beside her. "That stays with me."

"My apologies," he said. He waited awkwardly before ducking from the compartment without a tip.

Once the door snapped shut, Emma said, "I swear to God, if the contents of that satchel bring more trouble to your life, I will never forgive you."

Stella tapped one finger on the strap and stared at the dark circles beneath her mother's eyes. "There is no trouble. Except what Joe left me." She turned to the window and pressed her cheek against the headrest. She closed her eyes and listened to the rumble of the engine, aware of Emma's piercing gaze on her. Though wide awake, Stella remained in that position when the train jerked forward and when she heard the click of Emma's knitting needles as they worked their way through a mound of purple yarn.

Sometime later, the steward knocked with an offer of hot coffee and pastries, and Stella pulled yesterday's newspaper from an outside pocket of her satchel. She tucked the leather bag beneath her seat while Emma skeptically perused the stale selection of breads.

Once situated in front of the window with steaming coffee—heavy on the cream and sugar—and a glazed croissant, Emma asked, "When did the grand jury dismiss?"

"January ninth." Stella unfolded the newspaper and pointed: DISTRICT ATTORNEY THOMAS CRAIN SUSPECTS JUDGE CRATER'S WIFE COMPLICIT IN DISAPPEARANCE. "He's quite clever, actually. He waited until the grand jury was released. There was no evidence to proceed legally, so he took his argument to the papers. I'm on trial before the court of public opinion."

"What are you going to do?"

Stella took a gulp of her coffee. She winced as it scalded the back of her tongue. "Clear my name."

"And what of Joe?"

"He can fend for himself."

"Except that he can't."

She sniffed her croissant and set it back on the tray. "That is convenient, no doubt."

Stella turned her attention to the view outside the window. Hills and trees lay muffled beneath a coating of week-old snow. Little fissures spread out over the ground as the upper layer hardened to a crust and split open. Stella imagined the weblike cracks connected together in intricate patterns all the way from Maine to New York.

Just after noon, the train huffed to a stop at the 125th Street station, where an unusually large group of people waited on the platform, jostling for position. Emma was the first to understand their purpose.

"Lean back, Stella." She nodded toward the window. "Those men have cameras strung around their necks."

Stella drew away from the glass and counted. Fifteen reporters spread out along the platform, each wound up like a jack-in-the-box, ready to spring through the doors as soon as they opened. A particularly eager reporter had positioned himself right in front, knees bent and arms spread.

Emma heaved the kind of sigh that used to make Stella cringe as a child, tossed her knitting onto the seat beside her, and crossed the compartment. She locked the doors and returned to her spot with a grim expression.

The reporters filed in, and a few minutes later the train slid away from the platform toward Grand Central Terminal. Splurging on a private compartment suddenly seemed the wisest investment Stella had made in months.

"When this train stops, collect your things and walk straight out that door with your head held high. Hail the first cab you see. I'll get the luggage." The look Emma gave her was so fierce that Stella had no choice but to comply.

Three times during the short ride to Grand Central, someone knocked on the compartment door. And each time Emma answered with a dry and unconvincing Midwest accent. No, she did not care to give an interview about the condition of city transit. No, she did not wish to purchase a subscription to the *Herald Tribune*. And no, for the love of God, she did not have an opinion on the plight of workers in the garment district, certainly not one she'd care to share publicly, and would you mind leaving her alone to finish her coffee, she did pay extra for peace and quiet, damn it.

Not once in her life had Stella heard her mother utter a *gosh darn*, much less a full-blown *damn*. Her lips parted in shock.

"What?" Emma lifted one eyebrow in amusement and stuffed her knitting into her overnight bag. "We're here."

They collected coats and scarves and hats and bundled themselves until their faces were mostly hidden. When they stepped from the train, neither turned to see if they were being followed. Stella ducked around a crowd of rowdy tourists and hurried up the steps to the main terminal. She resisted the urge to run or to whip her head around and search for the reporters. Instead, she kept walking until she stepped onto Forty-Second Street. She tugged her scarf over her nose and frantically hailed a cab. Her knuckles stretched white as she gripped the handle of her satchel, waiting in the backseat for her mother. Not long after, Emma exited the station with a porter pushing a trolley full of luggage, and the cabbie hopped out to help. As he slammed the trunk shut, a handful of reporters made their way onto the sidewalk. They craned their necks and peered through the crowd looking for Stella.

She turned away from the window. "Forty Fifth Avenue, please," she said, and they slipped into traffic.

Fifteen minutes later, Stella was home. She tipped the cabbie generously after he unloaded the bags and hauled them into the elevator. It took them longer—without his help—to shuffle the bags down the fifth-floor hallway and into the apartment.

"I'll give you some space," Emma said once they'd deposited everything inside the apartment. "You settle in. I'll go find dinner."

No sooner had the apartment door clicked shut than Stella dropped her coat on the floor and went straight to the bedroom with the satchel. She pulled out the envelope with the cash. Her little retreat to Portland had cost almost a thousand dollars. But she'd need much more than that to stay afloat for the next few months. Stella chose five stacks of cash from the envelope—a thousand dollars each—and set them on the bed. The other six stacks she put back in the envelope. Then she turned the bureau key, yanked the drawer open, and stuffed the manila envelopes right back where she had found them months earlier. Stella took the cash she'd set aside to the safe in Joe's office.

MARIA and Jude strolled through Washington Square Park and kicked at the few remaining leaves. She stuffed one hand inside his pocket and the other inside her own. Jude found her fingers in the deep fold of his woolen coat and cupped them in his hand.

"Are you warm enough?"

"I'm fine," she lied, squinting at the dark clouds above them. "But it's going to rain. We should go home."

"Not yet. Walk with me for a while."

She wore her navy peacoat and a red scarf wrapped high around her ears, but they did little to ease the sting of cold on her cheeks. After twenty minutes of aimless wandering, she finally looked up at him and asked, "What's wrong?"

"Stella Crater is back in New York." He peered at the gray sky. "I regret taking that case."

Maria's dark eyes pooled with sadness. Enough. She was done with secrets and hidden meanings. She missed the marriage they used to have. And she loved him enough to speak the truth. Maria only hoped he would do the same. "Then you regret the wrong thing."

"What's that supposed to mean?"

"I was in the apartment that day, when you and Leo Lowenthall put those envelopes in the bureau drawer. I saw everything." Maria stared at the new growth of stubble along his jaw, at the red patch of skin rubbed raw by the wind, at the angry set of his mouth. She was too tired to lie any longer. "I looked in them."

"What?" The word came out strangled. "Why didn't you tell me then? Why are you telling me *now*?"

She thought of Leo Lowenthall in the apartment that day. His whispered threats. The way she'd choked on her own fear at the mention of Owney's name. "I've kept a lot of secrets lately. I'm sorry."

He tugged at the brim of his fedora, forcing it lower. "Since when do we keep secrets from one another?"

"You tell me."

Jude recoiled as though she'd slapped him. He pulled her hand out of his pocket and stepped backward to better see her, to understand this strange new development. He was unable to summon a response.

"I know they make you do things, Jude. Leo and Mulrooney. Others maybe. You told me the night of your promotion. You were so drunk." The smile she gave him was absolution. "And scared."

"I'm *still* scared." Jude scooped her into his arms, crushing her face against his chest. He held her like she would be ripped from him then and there. "I'm going to fix this. I promise you."

"There's more." Her voice was muffled by the wool of his coat. "That showgirl, Sally Lou Ritz?"

"Yes?" He tilted Maria's face up to see her.

"I found her in Mr. Crater's bed before he disappeared. That's the mistress you're looking for. She's pregnant with his child." Maria paused, letting him take that in before she continued. "And she said we could have the baby if I didn't tell anyone."

Jude's mouth hung open, but he couldn't speak. Anger and betrayal and surprise fought for control of his face. "Please tell me she doesn't have anything to do with those envelopes." Every syllable landed like a hammer.

The pleading look she gave him clearly explained that was not the case. "I took some of the money. I regretted it right away. But when I went to put it back, the envelopes were gone."

"What did you do with it?"

"I gave it to her."

"*Why?*" His voice echoed across the park, startling a group of pigeons nearby and sending them skyward.

"So she wouldn't get rid of the baby. Enough money for her to live on and pay for the delivery. Enough to let her get back on her feet after it's born."

Jude had the look of a man about to be violently ill. "Sally Lou Ritz disappeared over a month ago, Maria. That money is gone. And so is she."

STELLA would have welcomed snow—it had a soothing feel—but the rain made her angry. It came in a steady swell the night before, driving in from the North Atlantic, and seeped through the walls of the apartment, smelling of salt and despair. Cold gray clouds settled over the city, and she could see little but the glow of streetlamps and taillights out her living room windows. The streets below were filled with the honk of horns and the splash of water as cars veered into the gutters and sprayed puddles across the sidewalk. Pedestrians cursed in response.

Stella had debated her decision in the middle of that sleepless night but was dressed and ready before eight o'clock. The moment the hour hand settled on the Roman numeral, she picked up the phone.

"District Attorney Thomas Crain," she said after being connected to his office.

"He's not in. May I ask who's calling?" The young woman on the other end stifled a yawn.

"This is Stella Crater. Please leave an urgent message for him saying that I have found important evidence in the disappearance of my husband. I'll wait for his arrival at my home. He knows where I live."

Emma stood in the kitchen, plaid apron tied around her waist and a whisk in one hand. Her eyes widened in surprise.

Stella set the phone down and joined her mother in the kitchen. She filled the teakettle with water and set it on the stove. "When they ask, you'll tell them that I was bewildered when I opened that bureau drawer. That it's the first I've seen of Joe's will." She dared a glance at Emma. "Or his money."

Chapter Thirty

RITZI woke to the sound of rain. *Strange in winter,* she thought as she dragged herself from a fathomless sleep. She did not know the day or time, only that she was hungry and that her back ached with a dozen pea-size knots. For twenty minutes, Ritzi lay in the single bed, staring at the cracks in the ceiling above her—lines on a road map that stretched in seemingly random directions, crisscrossing, colliding, and widening into highways or thinning and wandering off like dead-end dirt roads. The tiny room smelled of wood polish and old curtains. She burrowed deeper into the covers and peered at the rivulets of rain sliding down the window. From where she lay, Ritzi could see pale gray sky, broken by the stark, naked limbs of an elm tree that hung low over the window. Teardrops of frigid water clung to the tips of each branch.

Ritzi ran her tongue over her teeth, cringing at the taste, but didn't push up onto her elbows until her stomach growled. She heaved her legs over the side of the bed and marveled at the size of her belly. She'd been a fool to think pregnancy was something she could hide. No corset could conceal this. Ritzi arched her back. Stiff muscles howled in protest, and she kneaded the heel of her hand against her spine, rubbing until she relaxed enough to stand. She eased into the small bathroom and brushed her teeth, relishing the taste of mint. Ritzi climbed into the shower and stayed beneath the hot spray of water for ten minutes, allowing it to soften the ache in her body. Never again would she take for granted what it felt like to be clean.

She remembered the filth of the lab coat against her skin as she fled the warehouse that night. She had bartered for the coat and her freedom, and John took every dollar he could find in her purse, far more than the six hundred dollars she offered. Her life savings, and Maria's bribe money, gone to a back-alley butcher. Ritzi slipped from the building barefoot and smelling of stale body odor and rancid chemicals. But she didn't even make it around the building before Shorty Petak found her. He clamped a hand over her mouth, fingers digging into the soft skin of her cheek, as she peered around the edge of a trash can. His palm muffled her scream.

"You think Owney didn't guess you'd try to escape?" he whispered, tucking her tight against his chest.

Ritzi tried to thrash her way loose, but his arms were locked immovably around her.

"Shut up," he hissed into her ear. "Unless you really do want to die."

And that's when she heard the voices farther down the alley. Owney and John.

"What took you so long?" Owney asked.

"She's a fighter," John said.

Ritzi stilled in Shorty's grasp, her heart beating wildly. She forced herself to relax, to breathe—slow, steady, consistent—through her nose. She strained to make out the conversation.

Owney sounded unconvinced. "You know I need proof."

"Here. Her clothes. Shoes. Purse."

"Why so much blood?"

"Like I said, a fighter."

Could that be regret in Owney's voice? "I told you to make it *clean*. Quick." His voice rose and echoed off the narrow walls of the alley.

"There's a reason they call this dirty work. Be glad I'm willing to do yours."

They strained to hear Owney's response, but the alley grew quiet.

Shorty's mouth was pressed next to Ritzi's ear, and she could feel the warmth of his breath against her temple. "This is the second time I've saved your sorry ass. I won't do it again."

Ritzi turned her head to the side, tried to see his face, to understand what he meant.

"In Coney Island," he whispered. "You think I didn't see your dress sticking out of that cabinet? That I didn't know you were in there? Shit. I'm not an idiot, Ritz."

Why? She mouthed the word against his palm.

She felt his shrug. "I like you. Always have. You're better than this."

It took Owney a long time to respond to John, but when he did, Ritzi felt herself go limp in Shorty's arms.

"I want to see her body," he said.

"No. You don't."

"You don't tell me what I want. This is a special circumstance."

"Suit yourself. It's at the bottom of the garbage chute. But you'll have to dig through two days' worth of trash to find it."

Ritzi imagined Owney looking at his new custom suit, his Italian leather shoes, his silk tie, deciding whether she was worth the trouble. Apparently not.

"Shorty!" Owney called down the dark alley.

They both tensed, and his hand lay fast over her mouth. Shorty cleared his throat. "Yeah, boss?"

"Is there anything I need to know?"

"No sign of her."

"Let's go, then."

"You sit here." Shorty's voice was barely louder than a breath. "You don't move. As far as I'm concerned, you're dead, and I don't ever want to hear different. Best you disappear. Forever. Got it?"

Ritzi gave her head the slightest nod, nothing more than the hint of affirmation.

Shorty didn't look at her or say another word, simply stepped from behind the trash can and ambled toward his boss, hands thrust deep in his pockets. Somewhere down the alley, doors slammed. And then Owney's Cadillac roared to life. The glow of taillights washed red against the warehouse as they drove away.

She stayed crouched there until her bare feet went numb against the frozen concrete. Once certain that Owney was long gone, Ritzi went in search of help. Freezing and queasy and paranoid, she stumbled upon a Jewish baker raising the shutters on his shop at four in the morning. She begged to go in and sit in the heat, and though he seemed disinclined at first, her tears won him over. He asked no questions but gave her a day-old loaf of sourdough. Ritzi fell asleep beside one of the ovens and slept until noon. Upon waking, she called the only person who could help: Maria Simon. The envelope with her number on it had fallen out of Ritzi's purse when John ransacked it, but she'd snatched it from the floor as he dragged her from the room.

Ritzi pushed the memories aside and selected a dress from the small closet in the sparse room. She stepped into the plain shift and tugged at the zipper, willing it to close. These days her clothing options were limited to one of two dresses. Both of them uncomfortable and belonging to Maria's mother—her kind benefactor in this self-imposed exile. How Maria came from the loins of a woman who willingly wore olive plaid was beyond Ritzi. Such stern material. Unyielding. And scratchy. A bit like its owner. But she was in no position to complain.

Ritzi's hair had grown, and the uneven tendrils brushed against her chin. Most days she tried to ignore the rolling of arms and legs inside of her. But she could not overlook the changes in her body: the swelling feet and the itchy skin and her already large breasts now profound in size. It seemed as though her entire body expanded in effort to make room for this strange person inside her. The change was unwelcome. And alarming.

A gentle knock sounded at the bedroom door.

"Come in."

Vivian Gordon slipped in and shut the door behind her. "I got your message."

Ritzi practically threw herself into Vivian's arms. "You came!"

Vivian's purse dangled from one elbow, and her copper hair and green eyes lit up the room. Just the sight of her in a periwinkle dress and pearls made Ritzi feel dowdy. She gazed longingly at Vivian's small waist and wondered if hers would ever be the same again.

"You look ill," Vivian said. She pecked Ritzi on the cheek.

"It's not my color. That woman has terrible fashion sense."

"What? This?" Vivian asked, tugging at the sleeve of Ritzi's dress. She laughed. And then looked as though she would cry. "It's good to see you, Ritz. Sorry I thought . . ."

"I know." Ritzi dropped to the bed and looked at her stomach, suddenly overcome. "I'm sorry. I had to wait awhile. It wasn't safe."

Vivian settled on the bed beside her. The mattress was old and soft, and their combined weight created a dip in the middle. They leaned in, shoulders brushing. "Owney got me a new roommate."

"Oh yeah?"

"He came by the apartment one day and hauled all your stuff away in garbage bags. I asked him where you were and if you were coming back, and he just laughed, said you'd moved on to a more *permanent* location." Vivian dug around in the bottom of her purse and found Ritzi's knotted gray sock. She set it on Ritzi's lap. "I would have never believed the message was from you if you hadn't asked for this."

Ritzi heaved a broken little gasp and clutched the sock to her heart. She could feel her wedding ring, firm against the skin of her palm. "Thank you."

"I took it from your closet that night you didn't come back. Just in case." Vivian gave her a half smile. "What are you going to do?"

It had taken weeks for Ritzi to find the courage necessary to make her decision. Nightmares and cold sweats and sudden panic attacks in the middle of the night assaulted her after her encounter in the warehouse. She'd wake screaming and clawing at the air. There was only one place she would ever feel safe, only one place she wanted to be. She could at least thank Owney Madden for that. He'd given her the certainty she needed. Ritzi smiled. "I'm going to have this baby. And then I'm going home."

"I thought you said he wouldn't take you back?"

"He probably won't." Her lip trembled. "I wouldn't."

"What if he doesn't?"

"Then that's the end. I've got nothing after that." Ritzi untied the tattered gray sock and dumped the wedding ring into her hand. She forced it over the swollen knuckle of her ring finger, ensuring that she would not be able to get it off again. She didn't want to.

CLUB ABBEY, FRIDAY, AUGUST 1, 1930

Ritzi knocked back a shot of whiskey. She wiped her mouth with the back of her hand and did a little curtsy at the bar as a small crowd of men clapped and cheered. Stan rolled his eyes. What these men really wanted was to see Ritzi get drunk. Get naked. Get loose. But that wasn't going to happen. Not here. Not tonight.

"Dance with me?" someone asked.

"Sorry, boys. I'm off duty." She gave them a winsome smile and patted a few cheeks as she walked away.

"What about me? Do I get a dance?" Owney. Just the man she'd come to see.

"Of course." She could feel a tingle at the tips of her fingers from the whiskey, and she forced herself to relax.

"Nice dress." Owney appraised the midnight-blue satin gown. Low cut with spaghetti straps, it clung to all the right places but didn't hinder movement on the dance floor.

"Thanks." She gave a half twirl, like a child showing off a church dress. "Crater bought it for me."

Owney gripped her around the waist, pressed in close, and effortlessly spun her onto the floor. "And where is he tonight?"

"In Maine. With his wife."

"That's a first. He hasn't been up there all summer."

"I guess he prefers my company."

"Good. Do you think his wife suspects anything? I can't afford to have her causing trouble."

"Don't mind Stella." Her hand lay flat on Owney's shoulder. She didn't protest when he pulled her closer, but neither did she wrap herself around him. "It's Crater you need to worry about."

She felt the muscles in his shoulders tighten.

"What do you mean?"

Ritzi relaxed in his arms. Picked her words carefully so she would sound concerned but not too eager. "He got a summons to testify before the Seabury Commission. Said people have been sniffing around, asking questions about his appointment to the court."

Owney's voice constricted with anger. "He didn't mention that to me."

Ritzi moved her hand along Owney's neck, played with his shirt collar and then his earlobe. "He avoids you. Says he's just biding his time until he can get out from under your thumb."

"Crater says that?"

"Occasionally. Mostly, he talks about his plans for higher office. I guess the deal you got for him wasn't big enough. Calls it a 'stepping-stone.'" Ritzi could feel the heat beneath Owney's skin, the strain in his neck as she spoke.

"Joseph Crater's a fool."

"Maybe. But he's ambitious."

"That makes him dangerous."

When the song ended, Owney maneuvered them to the edge of the dance floor. He stepped away with the last note.

Ritzi pouted and set her hands on her hips. "I thought you wanted to dance?"

"I've gotta make a call."

"Now?"

"I think maybe Crater needs to cut his vacation short. He and I need to have a chat." Owney disentangled himself from her arms and stalked off to the telephone hanging on the wall beside his booth.

Ritzi's eyes were bright and her smile barely suppressed as she collected her purse from the cubby behind the bar and walked out the double wooden doors and up the stairwell into the calm, clear evening.

MARIA could not bear sitting in the confessional again—not with Father Donnegal—so she waited in a pew four rows back from the altar. She knew he saw her, and that he waited for the church to empty. She'd chosen a slow time—two o'clock in the afternoon—to better her chances of speaking with him alone. Maria sat there for almost an hour, breathing in the stillness, listening to the cathedral settle beneath the weight of decades. As the sun shifted diagonally through the stained-glass windows and flooded the nave with pools of blue light, the last parishioner rose from one of the side altars. The old woman looked at her watch and seemed startled at the time. She blinked into the shadows and hurried from the church, jacket buttoned up to her neck. Once they were alone, Finn lurched his way toward Maria.

He dropped into the space beside her. Nodded. Waited for her to speak.

Maria wrapped her arms around her chest. She rocked back and forth in the pew. When the words finally came, she choked on them. "I can't have children."

Finn sat still for a long time, eyes on the altar, and Maria was afraid he would give her some religious platitude, that he would try to comfort her. But he didn't.

"I'm sorry." His voice was a whisper, and Maria heard the shared grief of a true friend. "I've always thought you would be a wonderful mother."

"It's a fitting punishment. For what I've done."

Finn controlled his voice, dropped it lower. "What kind of God do you believe in? He didn't give you cancer."

She jerked her head to the side. "How do you know about that?"

"Jude told me."

"He came to see you?"

"Many times."

She snorted. "I thought you didn't share what's spoken in the confessional?"

"He wasn't confessing." Finn patted the smooth surface of the pew between them. "He was crying. Right here."

Maria turned away. Blinked. Swallowed the hard lump of remorse that rose in her throat.

"A man's sorrow is different than his sin, yes? My calling makes me privy to both." Finn wrapped his hand around hers. It was cool, and the tips of his fingers were rough from worrying his rosary. "Cancer is not some divine currency, Maria, meted out as punishment."

"I've done more than you know."

"You've done nothing to earn this."

Maria made herself small in the pew, lowered her shoulders, and hung her head. She was hollowed out, flesh and bone wrapped around emptiness. "I manipulated that promotion for Jude and never told him because I wanted him to think he'd earned it on his own. Then I found Mr. Crater in bed with a showgirl and I kept the truth from his wife. That money I stole from the Craters? I saw Jude plant it there—forced to do so because of *my* meddling—and I told no one about it. When his partner came to threaten me into silence, I kept that from Jude as well. And then"—Maria gave Father Donnegal a desperate look—"I used that money to bribe Mr. Crater's mistress to let me have her baby. At this very moment, she's hidden at my parents' house until she gives birth. This too I have kept from Jude. I have lied. Stolen. Bribed. And manipulated my way for months. So please do not tell me that I have done nothing to deserve a barren womb. I deserve far worse."

Finn laid his hand on top of her head. They sat long in the pew as he whispered prayers in Latin, fervent, desperate, and somehow more powerful in their foreignness, as though he spoke God's own language. Maria rested beneath the weight of his hand, gathered the words into her heart. Believed them, though she did not understand them, because they were too abundant for her.

The front doors creaked open behind them, and Finn pulled away. Footsteps rang hollow down the side of the nave. Someone struck a match. Coughed. And then the murmur of divine supplication.

"What is my penance, Father?" she whispered.

"You have punished yourself enough already. God wants nothing but your repentance. And that you have freely given."

"There is more," she whispered. Maria picked her last secret from the darkest corner of her mind. She readied herself to speak it, to rid herself of its terrible weight. "But you will not believe me capable of such a thing."

CLUB ABBEY, SUNDAY, AUGUST 3, 1930

Maria picked her way down the steps, her hand on the brick wall for balance. She shifted a little to the side, unsteady in the high heels and fitted black dress. Her small black hat had a netted veil that covered her eyes, good for anonymity but bad for vision in the dim stairwell. Her ankles wobbled as she descended, and her breath caught in her throat when she reached the bottom. In the shadows, next to the unmarked door, was a short man in a bowler hat, one leg propped on the wall behind him, chewing on a toothpick.

"Whatcha need, dollface?"

She nodded at the door. Nervously rubbed her lips together. The extra coat of ruby lipstick she'd applied in the cab felt like grease on her lips.

He looked her over, assessing the hand-me-down designer dress, her full lips, her bare calves. Rolled the toothpick from one side of his mouth to the other. "Gotta password?"

Maria kept her eyes averted. She repeated the password she'd learned earlier that day. "Gold digger."

He grinned. Pushed the door open with one hand. Tipped his hat as she walked through.

Ten o'clock. She'd timed it carefully. Late enough for all the right people to be here but not so late that it was rowdy. She'd been warned. It got rowdy at midnight. Besides, Jude might be home from work by then. His hours had gotten erratic since the promotion. Sometimes home by dinner. Sometimes home in the middle of the night. Maria went out of her way not to make a fuss, to welcome him home regardless of the hour. She'd taken Mr. Crater's warning to heart.

Maria didn't have a purse to match the dress. No fancy beaded clutch or velvet shoulder bag. Only her old canvas purse, tucked against her side.

She pulled the sealed envelope out as she approached the bar. *Owney Madden* was carefully printed on the front.

The bartender was redheaded and freckled and seemed far too young for the job. He lined up three glasses, dumped a handful of ice into each, and ran a bottle of liquor over the tops without so much as a slosh. With an experienced flick of the wrist, he sent them sliding down the bar to a group of men huddled at the end.

Maria laid the envelope flat on the bar. She didn't sit.

"What can I do for you?" he asked.

"Take this to your boss." She pushed the envelope toward him.

He squinted at her face, trying to make out details.

Maria lowered her eyes.

"Take it yourself. He's over there."

She was careful not to look, showed nothing but her back. "I'd rather not."

"You sure? He's watching you anyway."

"My only business with your employer is in that envelope. I'd be grateful if you would deliver it for me."

"I'd be grateful to know your name. Seeing as how he's gonna ask."

"My name," Maria said, taking a step backward, "is not important."

Stan lifted the envelope from the varnished mahogany bar. Tapped it a couple of times. "Suit yourself. Just know Owney don't like secrets. Has a way of figuring things out."

STELLA followed Simon Rifkind into the Surrogate's Court. Their meeting was on the first floor, down a long hallway off the main atrium. Rifkind led her not into a courtroom, as she'd expected, but into a small conference room off the main corridor.

"Thank you for doing this," she whispered as he pulled out a dark wooden chair. She settled into the green velvet seat and scooted closer to the table.

"It's the least I could do," he said.

"I wish I could pay you."

"There's no need. Joe was a friend. I'm just sorry it's come to this."

The room was formal but not intimidating. A long table and no windows. Wood paneling. Burgundy carpet. Two bookshelves filled with leather-bound volumes of archaic legal texts. An oversize portrait of John Adams, attorney and founding father. The air tasted stale, and she shifted away from the heavy musk of Rifkind's cologne. She looked at her watch. "How long will this take?"

"Shouldn't be more than a few minutes. The letters of administration will only give you access to the money in your bank accounts. Joe's life insurance policies will have to wait." His voice settled into a legal monotone, but he did give her one apologetic glance. "To cash those in, his body would need to be found. Otherwise, he will have to remain missing for seven years before he can be declared legally dead."

She hadn't accounted for that. "So long? Isn't that what a life insurance policy is for?"

"It's the law, I'm afraid. In theory, the wait stops insurance fraud and other criminal activity. But it's hell on widows, if you ask me."

"I've grown accustomed to hell."

Rifkind set his briefcase on the oblong table and began sorting his notes. As they waited, an attorney entered and heaved a stenograph machine onto the table across from Stella.

"Ralph Gutchen," he said, extending his hand. "I'm the law assistant to Surrogate James A. Foley. I will conduct the proceedings."

Ralph looked weary and restless, as though he were used to phone calls in the middle of the night and depositions that lasted days. He would have been a handsome man apart from the dark, puffy eyes and the limp set of his mouth.

Stella watched as he slid paper into the stenograph machine and tested the ink ribbon with a few random strokes.

"Are you ready to begin?" Ralph formally asked.

"We are," Simon Rifkind answered.

Ralph took a deep breath, his hands hovering above the keys. "What is your purpose here today, Mrs. Crater?"

"To obtain temporary letters of administration," she said, "so I can execute my husband's estate."

"Anything else?"

Stella looked at her hands. Cleared her throat. She tried to speak but could not. After a strained silence, she reached into her purse and chose a cigarette from the pack of Camels. She lit it with a trembling hand.

"Please excuse my client. I'm sure you can imagine how difficult this is for her." Simon Rifkind shot her an uncertain glance and reached across the table for an ashtray. He slid it in front of Stella. "In addition to the letters of administration, Mrs. Crater would like to file a death certificate for her husband."

Ralph lifted his head from the notes beside him. "You realize the complications with that request?"

"We do. But it is my client's wish that legal proceedings toward that end begin immediately."

"Very well, then," Ralph said. "We will attend to the letters first. Can you list, in detail, the assets Mrs. Crater is requesting?"

Simon Rifkind slid two pieces of paper across the table. He read from one of them: "'Twelve thousand dollars on deposit in the Empire Trust Company; a balance of fifteen hundred dollars in Judge Crater's brokerage firm; the lease on their cooperative apartment; six thousand dollars in cash recently found in their apartment; and assorted fees and commissions owed to Mr. Crater, a list of which he left in his own handwriting, along with the will. And, of course, the life insurance policies, which have premiums due.'"

Ralph took the papers, glanced them over, and handed the second to Stella. "Mrs. Crater, are you agreeable to the verbiage in this affidavit?" She took it from him and read:

Petitioner knows of no reason why her husband should have left her or abandoned his career. Petitioner does not believe he would have done so if he were of normal mind, nor believe that he would remain away, if still alive, save by reason of mental infirmity or constraint. Petitioner concludes that he may be dead, or has become a lunatic or has been secreted, confined, or otherwise unlawfully made away with.

Stella wrapped her lips around the cigarette and inhaled until her body went cool. She closed her eyes, relishing the control it gave her. Joe was dead. That was true enough. The details in that affidavit were wrong, but irrelevant. "I am," she said.

"The court grants Mrs. Crater the letters of administration. You are free to deal with your husband's affairs as you see fit. However, before attending to the request for a death certificate, I must ask you a few questions. Is that agreeable?"

"Of course."

Ralph looked at his notes and then at Stella. He typed without a glance at the stenograph machine. "Since the third of August last year, have you had any contact—physical, verbal, or written—with your husband?"

"No. I have not."

"Have any monies from his accounts or debtors been delivered to you, either directly or indirectly?"

Stella felt Simon stiffen beside her. The checks he'd deposited on her behalf had long since stopped coming. She tapped her cigarette on the ashtray and brought it to her mouth. Breathed in. Her answer was firm and convincing. "No."

"As a matter of procedure, I am required to ask if there is any reason you would not want your husband found? Fiduciary? Relational? Legal?"

The question caught her off guard, and Stella felt short of breath. There were plenty of reasons. "That's a rather absurd question, don't you think, Mr. Gutchen?"

He ducked his head.

"My life was *ruined* when Joe disappeared. I can think of no reason why I would have ever brought that on myself. And I am appalled at the suggestion that I might."

"No one is suggesting anything, Mrs. Crater. This is simply a legal matter that we must get through."

"Then, by all means, let's get through it."

Ralph paused. He flexed his hands. "Have you exhausted every effort to try and find Mr. Crater?"

"Yes."

He struck the keys a few more times. They waited for him to continue, but he yanked the paper from the stenograph machine and blew on the wet ink. "That will be all, Mrs. Crater. I will file your request for a death certificate this afternoon. I wish you luck but do not expect you to have any."

MARIA read the letter first. She found it on the bed in her parents' spare room, along with a copy of the *Daily News* from the day before. Vivian Gordon's picture was on the front page next to the headline NOTORIOUS MADAM FOUND STRANGLED IN VAN CORTLANDT PARK! She'd been murdered two days earlier, on the eve of what would have been her testimony before the Seabury Commission. Her frozen, garroted body was found by a truck driver walking along Mosholu Avenue and was identified later at the city morgue. The article was clear in its implications, and Maria couldn't have missed it even if Ritzi hadn't gone to the trouble of underlining it for her: "Miss Gordon was the center of the seething fires of graft, bribery, shakedowns, and judicial corruption."

But none of that mattered to Maria. She lay, curled up on the bed in a fetal position, grappling with the reality that Ritzi was gone, and the baby with her. She had felt it moving in Ritzi's belly on her last visit. It was the first time she'd had the courage to ask, and she'd sat there for ten minutes, marveling at the tiny elbows and knees so active beneath her hands. Maria had considered names on the train ride back to the apartment—some charming combination of American and Castilian. She still did not know how to tell Jude that Ritzi was alive and that the child would be theirs. There was time, or so she thought. But now the fantasy came crashing down.

Ritzi hadn't signed her name, had simply explained that with Vivian dead, she had to leave. That she was afraid. That she couldn't risk endangering Maria or anyone else. And that if she remained, it was only a matter of time before Owney found her. Then Ritzi had scratched two words into the paper that ended Maria's only hope of ever becoming a mother. *I'm sorry.*

Chapter Thirty-Four

THE letter sat in the basket on the entry table. It was buried in a pile of bills and catalogs and looked as though it had been wadded in someone's pocket for days. This wasn't the first letter Stella had received since Joe disappeared. There had been a handful of opportunistic ransom notes. Condolences. Accusations. Requests for money. Sales pitches. A bit of voyeurism here and there as people offered their theories on his disappearance or wondered what it was like to be her—god-awful, if they really wanted to know.

But never a confession.

Dear Stella, it began, and her hands trembled as she read the letter. She dropped into a chair next to the fireplace and laid the pages on her lap so they wouldn't rattle. She read the sender's name—Sally Lou Ritz—and then started over.

Two pages. Nary a crossed-out word and only one ink blot, as though her pen had hovered over the page as she sought the right words. Clean and simple and direct. And so very final. Her husband dead. His killer named. And details about Joe's murder that no one could ever learn.

"Oh. God." Stella clutched the letter in her fist and crumpled it into a ball.

She stood up.

Then sat down.

Stella repeated this a few times, once even stepping away from her chair. After a moment of uncertainty, she sat again and smoothed the letter on her lap. Then she folded it and slid it carefully back inside the envelope. Distasteful as it was, the letter provided a certain amount of insurance. She took it to the safe in Joe's office and tucked it inside one of his beloved legal tomes—a first edition of *Commentaries on the Laws of England* by Sir William Blackstone—a place she was certain no one would ever think to look. A place she could easily forget.

Ritzi pulled herself tight inside the bathroom cabinet. Her only goal was not vomiting or coming so unglued that the men less than ten feet away became aware of her presence. By force of will, she stopped her teeth from chattering and her muscles from spasming. Even as the sweat dripped down her spine and the smell of fear overwhelmed her nostrils, she did not move.

Owney Madden's voice shifted to a calm, measured tone, almost all trace of Scouse gone. This frightened Ritzi more than his previous rage.

"From what I hear, people owe you money, right?"

Crater's voice broke. "Yeah, sure. Lots."

The rustle of paper. "Names, see. That's what I need. Who owes you and how much. Start writing."

There was a long silence as the desperate judge scratched a pen against the paper. Five, ten minutes. Even in the bathroom, she could hear the pained wheezing of his breath.

"Here."

"Good. Your handwriting is shit, but it'll work."

She heard the banging of drawers and the sound of someone rummaging through the closet. "You keep a safe-deposit box, right?"

Crater's voice, almost a whisper. "Yes."

"And the key? Where do you keep that?"

"On the ring. In my pants pocket."

"Which bank?"

"New York Bank and Trust."

The jumble of keys on a ring. "That where you're keeping my money?" A silent affirmation, and then, "What else is in the box?"

"My will. And the remaining life insurance policies that I need to cash out. You know I'm good for it, Owney. I wouldn't stiff you." Crater coughed twice and spit on the floor. "That what this is about? You think I wasn't going to pay?"

"I don't want your money."

"What?"

"If I don't collect my fee for getting you on the court, Seabury can't trace the deal back to me. The trail dies with you."

"You know I wouldn't talk to Seabury."

Owney's voice lowered, and Ritzi had to strain to hear it. "You won't be talking to anyone. Ever again." The sound of a kick in Crater's rib cage and a furious bark of pain.

The nausea that Ritzi had fought since Crater rolled off her rose to the back of her mouth. She swallowed and breathed and prayed. In the dark coffin of that cabinet, her heart raced so loud she could hear the rush of blood in her ears. Ritzi saw Crater in her mind, naked and bruised, crouched on the floor with a pen in his trembling hand. And as much as she loathed the touch of that hand on her skin and the taste of his kiss, she felt pity for him. She knew what it was like to look in the eyes of the man who stood over him and fear for her life. She wouldn't wish that feeling on anyone.

"Get up. Get dressed," Owney said. "You're taking a ride with us."

Ritzi didn't move when the light went out or even when the hotel room door clicked shut. For over an hour, she huddled there, fist rammed in her mouth to muffle the scream that boiled in her chest, drawing blood from her knuckles.

RITZI kept to the side, where the country road softened to dirt, and walked along in a pair of new patent leather shoes that pinched her toes and rubbed a blister on her heel. As a girl, she ran down these gravel roads with bare feet toughened to leather and wind in her face. There wasn't a swimming hole or a rope swing within ten miles that she hadn't befriended. It seemed like another lifetime. Another woman, really.

The fields were wrapped in snow, and the sky was a clear cornflower blue. Beneath the frozen soil lay a crop of winter wheat, planted after the corn was harvested. Ritzi could see the gentle rise of each row, dormant, waiting for the warmth of spring before it would send tender green shoots skyward. She scanned the fields, peering into the horizon, and then tilted her head up and drank in the sight. No skyscrapers to block the view. No exhaust or smog. A cathedral of sky above her.

She'd been walking for almost an hour, and stiffness rose up through her calves and into her lower back. Her entire body felt strained and heavy, cracked at the seams. At the train station, a kind farmer had offered her a ride, and she'd allowed him to bring her as far as the turn onto Rural Route 79. She took the rest on foot, and with each step her courage waned. For the last twenty minutes, she'd been walking slower and slower, looking for opportunities to stop and ponder this or that.

When Ritzi came to the last rise in the road before the Martin farm, she stopped. There was no way to count the number of times she had traveled this road, both as a child and as an adult. She knew its curves and dips. That pothole a quarter mile back that no one ever bothered to fill and everyone swerved to avoid. She knew where the split-rail fence buckled over the culvert and how that ditch always overflowed in spring when the rains came. The fields, whether newly planted, bursting with wheat, or stripped bare, were intimate friends. She had lived within two miles of this farm for all but three of her twenty-two years. Yet Ritzi was not prepared for the terror that filled her as she stood atop that knoll and looked down at her old home.

Ritzi stared at the thin gold band on her left hand. She rubbed it with her thumb, took a deep breath, and made her way toward the gate at the bottom of the hill. Ritzi had all the courage of a newborn calf. She would have turned and run, but her belly weighed heavy and her lower back groaned with the strain. This was the end for her. She had nothing left. And so she limped across the yard and up the front steps. They sagged in the middle, same as always, and the porch rail still needed painting. Everything looked the same as it had the morning she left, only sadder, emptier.

There was a hush in the air, as if the farm held its breath, as she reached out, hand curled into a fist, and rapped on the screen door with her knuckles. It was the first time she had ever knocked. Ritzi locked her knees and waited. Seconds later, she heard boots thumping down the hall. The rattle of a hand on the knob, and then the door opened. Ritzi looked at her husband.

"Hi, Charlie."

He pushed the screen open and filled the doorframe, shoulders broader than she remembered. Chestnut-brown hair flipped out in curls above his collar. His eyes were still kind and blue, but he'd gotten the sort of lines around them that only sorrow could bring. He hadn't shaved in days. Charlie stood there, clenching and unclenching his fists. She watched as his face contorted from shock to rage to sadness to relief. He looked her up and down, over and over, wincing every time he glanced at her swollen abdomen.

Finally, Charlie took a deep breath and looked straight in her eyes. His voice cracked. "That ain't my baby."

Ritzi stepped backward and dropped her chin. "It is if you'll have it."

He flinched as though she'd slapped him, and she saw that look on his face, the one he got when trying not to curse. Charlie couldn't look in her eyes any longer, so he stared at her feet instead. His arm twitched like he wanted to slam the door shut in her face.

"You been gone a long time, Sarah."

The name was a blow. Her name. Coming from Charlie's lips, it sent a shudder through her body, and she reached out to steady herself against the side of the house. But there was no stopping the tears. They were a flash flood, coursing down her face. "Nobody's called me Sarah in years."

"That so?" There was a long pause as he stood there, one arm propping the door open.

She wiped her cheeks. "Mostly, they call me Ritzi these days." She'd tried to say it with nonchalance, but all she could muster was embarrassment. It was the stage name she'd picked for herself as a child, when she dreamed of being something more than a farmer's daughter.

Charlie barked out a mirthless laugh. He shook his head there in the doorway like he'd never heard anything so ridiculous in his life. Her breath clouded between them in the cold, and she rubbed her arms, shivering.

"That's a right stupid name." He turned and walked back into the house.

The tears came even though Ritzi fought against them. She stood on the front porch of the home she had once shared with Charlie and stared at the door. He'd left it open.

Five months later . . .

STELLA stood across the street from Club Abbey on the first anniversary of Joe's disappearance. She'd dressed for the occasion in black satin, pearls, and two-inch heels—enough to be dressy but not celebratory—and carried a simple black clutch. Her hands were bare except for her wedding ring. It was almost ten o'clock. The girls of the evening sauntered from the shadows and into the bars of New York City near midnight, but the respectable women did their drinking before then. Especially when swilling for two.

She made her way down the steps and through the double doors without hesitation. The band played a subdued tune, and half the tables were occupied, despite the early hour. Stella found a seat at the bar and made eye contact with Stan.

Stella, he mouthed, and she nodded, oddly pleased at being remembered. He threw the bar towel over his shoulder and made his way toward her.

"What are you doing here?" He flashed his boyish grin.

It was an easy question. Nothing invasive. But when Stella went to answer it, she couldn't find the right sequence of words. She swallowed her first attempt. She shrugged and said, "A year ago. Today."

Stan needed no further explanation. "You'll be drinking, then?"

"Who's to say I haven't started already?"

He shook his head. "You're not the type. I'd wager you've saved up a year's worth of liquor for tonight."

"I hate being predictable."

"I believe they call that classy."

"Is that the term now? I thought it was stodgy." Of all the people in the world, an underage bartender in a seedy Greenwich Village speak-easy seemed to be the only person who could put her at ease.

"What'll you have tonight?"

"Same as last time. Whiskey on the rocks. But make it two."

"Where do you want to drink?" He spread his arm out across the bar. "I'll clear any table in the place."

"Don't bother. Here is fine."

"No way. You came to drown your sorrows, and you'll do it in style." He pointed to Owney's booth in the corner. "Over there?"

"Looks like it's taken."

"Not for long." Stan stuck his thumb and middle finger beneath his tongue and let out a sharp, high whistle. A few seconds later, Shorty Petak stepped behind the bar.

"Who's that in Owney's booth?" Stan asked.

"Some prick."

"Does the prick have a name?"

"Harris, I think."

"Well, you tell Harris to take his sorry ass to another booth."

"Why?"

"This lady here needs a seat."

"Looks like she's sitting. And that guy"—he pointed at Harris, who was busy whispering in a young woman's ear—"is a paying customer."

Stella suspected that the woman, not the alcohol itself, was the commodity Shorty referenced.

"This here is Stella Crater." Stan grinned, clearly enjoying himself. "I believe you are familiar with her departed husband?"

Shorty's eyes filled with knowledge. He nodded.

"A little respect for the dead, then."

"Shorty Petak." He stuck out his hand. "I knew your husband. Good customer."

Stella tried to smile, but her mouth drew tight at the corners. "You saw him often?"

He backpedaled. "A few times."

"Often enough to think highly of him as a *customer*? Like Harris, perhaps?"

Shorty played with the brim of his bowler hat. "Your husband was a good man."

"So they say." Stella hadn't been in the place five minutes and had already grown weary. "Stan, can I get my drinks? Then I'll be out of your way, and you gentlemen can continue with your *business.*"

Abashed, he turned to Shorty. "You clear that table for Stella. Send Harris and his . . . lady friend . . . to me."

Stella watched Shorty approach the booth. He said nothing to the middle-aged man, merely cocked his head back toward the bar, and Harris slipped out, tugging on the woman's arm.

"Don't you think it's a bad idea? Me sitting in Owney's booth?"

"He won't be in tonight. You've earned the spot, I think." Stan picked up the glasses. "Follow me."

They skirted the edge of the dance floor, and she followed close behind, eyes away from the growing crowd. She could feel them watching. Recognizing. The bartender leaving his station and escorting a woman through the room was a flare for attention, and the crowd responded. Heads turned. Eyes narrowed.

Stan set his palm on her elbow as he guided her onto the riser that held Owney's booth. "Mrs. Crater," he said. "Your drinks."

Those nearest her booth began to whisper.

"Thank you." Her words came out stiffer than she intended. Colder.

Stan stepped away with a wink. Somehow the little charade had become a spectacle. The band played on, oblivious, but half the room stared at her. Stella met as many glances as she dared, unafraid. She would make certain they remembered this.

On the other side of the room, at a small round table, sat Detective Simon. She wasn't sure if he'd been there when she came in or if he was a new arrival, but he seemed intent on her every movement. Stella matched him blink for blink, then turned her attention to the two glasses on the table. She took a deep breath and lifted the first glass. Sniffed the pungent whiskey. Took a long, slow sip and let it roll around her tongue before she swallowed.

"Good luck, Joe." Stella said it loudly. Clear. Then she lifted the glass a little higher so that the amber liquid was eye level. She could almost imagine him, amused, on the other side of the booth. That arrogant, lopsided grin on his face. "Wherever you are."

She drank the rest of the glass in three slow, measured gulps. Stella felt the whiskey rush through her system. She blinked hard at the ice cubes in the bottom of her glass. Her usually thin frame had shrunk considerably over the last year, and she could feel the tingle in her veins.

Stella pushed the other glass to the middle of the table and stood, steadying herself with one hand as the edges of her vision blurred. Stan watched her from the bar. He wiped up a spill and grinned. She gave him the hint of a smile and then wove her way across the dance floor with uncertain footsteps, toward the doors of Club Abbey.

When she reached it, Detective Simon stepped in front of her.

"Stella." He pulled the doors open. "May I have a word with you?"

She looked to the street above. Eighteen steps. It may as well have been eighteen stories for the way her head swam. "If you hail me a cab."

Jude followed her up the narrow concrete stairwell. "What are you doing here?"

"What does it look like I'm doing?"

"Putting on a show."

Stella flicked a stray curl out of her eyes. "I am honoring the memory of my husband."

"Interesting choice of venue."

"Joe was fond of the place."

"Was he fond of the owner?"

Stella looked over Jude's shoulder as two city cabs drove by. She watched them idle down the street and turn the corner. "Is this an interrogation?"

"As I recall, you don't care for those. Just trying to get at the truth while I can."

"You think I'm going somewhere?"

"You've been known to wander away for long stretches of time."

Stella unclasped her purse and lifted out the now-standard pack of unfiltered Camels. She held the cigarette out to Jude, and he fished around in his pocket for his lighter. "What does it matter to you? I hear you resigned from the case."

"It'll always be my case. Officially or not."

Stella Crater smiled at the young detective. She considered laying her secrets into the silence between them like playing cards. She'd turn them over, one by one, and expose the full house she'd carried all this time. It would be a relief. That freedom tempted her, but only momentarily. Instead of telling Jude the truth, she raised the cigarette to her lips and let the nicotine flood her lungs. She held it. Savored it. And decided that she would keep what she knew to herself. Stella could never let anyone know that she helped Joe buy his seat on the New York Supreme Court. Or that she was partly responsible for his death. That wasn't the sort of guilt she could shake off with a simple confession.

"Are you going to hail that cab, Detective? Or are we going to stand around all night and stare at each other?"

Jude slipped the lighter back in his pants pocket. He looked as though there were many things he'd like to tell her. But he too kept his silence. Jude stepped into the street and waved down the first cab he saw. When it eased to the curb, he opened the back door for her.

"Will I see you back here next year?" Stella asked.

"Is there any reason why you should?"

"Feels as though I started a tradition tonight." Even as she said the words, Stella knew she'd found her penance.

"Go on and torture yourself. I don't care to be a witness."

She gave him a wry smile and slipped into the cab. "I think you get a lot of satisfaction out of watching me suffer."

"Good night, Stella." He shut the door.

"Next year." He shook his head as the cab rolled into traffic, but Stella felt certain he'd be back. If not next year, then the one after that. She would not be alone in this misery. Even if it meant baiting him to keep her company.

FIFTH AVENUE, MONDAY, APRIL 7, 1930

Joe popped the cork on a bottle of champagne, and a cheer went up around the apartment. Stella had assumed that he would hire a band and send out embossed invitations, that he would make a big deal out of his appointment to the court. But Joe said there were people he needed to thank quietly and that a private cocktail party was more appropriate.

"To my friends." Joe raised a crystal goblet. "Whom I owe."

"And don't you forget it!" Senator Wagner shouted.

Laughter filled the room, and Stella watched her husband bask in the glow of success.

The only thing that upstaged the hors d'oeuvres and flower arrangements was the women. Wives mostly, but also the occasional showgirl or indiscreet mistress. As Stella glanced around the room, she couldn't help doing a quick comparison. She cleaned up well—tonight in particular, having spent the afternoon at the salon—and there were only two women in the room who made her feel uneasy. The first was to be expected: Sally Lou Ritz, the voluptuous showgirl seated next to William Klein. Ritzi's hazel eyes and seductive pout were envy inducing. It felt a bit odd to have her sitting a few feet away, quiet and demure and hardly the shimmering woman seen onstage. Her presence was unnerving. It was the closest Joe had come to admitting the affair, and the fact that he included her tonight was the height of hubris.

The other woman who stirred Stella's jealousy was the maid. She'd always considered Maria pretty. But tonight she realized that Maria, wearing the high heels and black cocktail dress that Stella had given her, was a great deal more than pretty. She was stunning. Glances followed Maria around the room as she served appetizers and champagne. Eyes appraised her curves, her full lips, and her warm skin—Joe's included. He seemed distracted every time Maria was near him. This unsettled Stella in ways she couldn't articulate—especially after three glasses of champagne.

Joe stood and draped his arm over Stella's shoulder. She stiffened beneath his touch, but he flashed the same confident smile he had the day they met. He planted a kiss on her forehead for the benefit of their guests.

"To the judge!" The chorus rose around the room. A few men whooped. The ladies clapped. And Stella grew angrier by the moment.

"I owe each of you in a different way," Joe said, nodding first at one man and then at another. "Robert, I thank you for hiring me as your law secretary ten years ago."

"Worst mistake I ever made. Lazy bum. Look where it got you."

More laughter.

"Indeed, it got me a seat on the New York State Supreme Court. And for that appointment, I thank *you*, Governor."

Governor Roosevelt had been silent most of the evening, listening to the chatter, sitting a few seats away from Joe. He'd come alone. Trouble with the wife again, most likely. At least he hadn't shown up with his mistress this time. No one could dampen a dinner party like the pious Lucy Mercer. "Had to fill the hole, my boy," he said, "and you looked like a decent plug."

Joe looked at Martin Healy and Owney Madden. They were seated together near the fireplace. "Marty, Owney, I'm grateful for your invest-ment in my career. I wouldn't be here apart from you."

"To Joe!" shouted Martin after a swig of champagne, and the cheer was repeated around the room.

Owney met Joe's glance and gave him a single quick nod.

Once Joe made his public acknowledgments, their guests began to collect jackets and purses. Stella couldn't remember the names of half the people she walked to the door. Fifteen minutes later, the apartment was almost empty. Joe made his way toward the office with William Klein, Owney Madden, and Martin Healy. Stella was about to follow when Ritzi set a hand on her elbow. She stopped short, glanced at her hand and then at her face. Back and forth.

Ritzi didn't let go. "You don't want to go in there."

"Excuse me?" Stella looked around the room for support, but there was only Maria, and she was busy gathering champagne glasses and ashtrays. "This is my home."

Ritzi gave her arm an amiable tug. "But it's their party."

"I—"

"Trust me." Her smile was genuine, and Stella struggled to dislike her. "They don't let the women in on business."

Stella could see the back of Joe's head through a crack in the door. He'd taken off his dinner jacket and draped it over a chair. His black sus-penders were stripes against his shirt. Cigar ends glowed like taillights in the dim room. The others, still clad in suit coats, were shadows against the mahogany bookshelves. Someone pushed the door shut.

"Business?"

Ritzi laughed. It was a charming sound, and Stella realized how much the young woman must have banked on it, among other things, to work her way up the social ladder.

"With those boys, everything is business," Ritzi said.

The heat rose in Stella's cheeks. She wanted to hurl accusations at Ritzi, to punish her. But she picked at the truth instead. "So you're with William Klein?"

Ritzi looked at the office door with an expression that Stella couldn't decipher. "I'm his date tonight, but I'm not *with* him." She lowered her voice and walked back toward the living room. "Truth be told, Billy is an ass."

Stella followed. "Then why come with him?"

"He works for the most powerful theater association in the city. Girls like me have to get a leg up wherever we can."

"Sounds like a sorry life."

"You have no idea." Ritzi pulled a cigarette holder out of her purse. "Do you mind?"

"Not at all."

Stella settled into a chair next to Ritzi as the office door popped open. Joe caught her eye and nodded toward the bedroom.

Ritzi snorted.

"Be right back," Stella said, and followed Joe to the bedroom. She gave him a frozen glare when he shut the door behind them.

"Are you all right?" he asked.

"Why wouldn't I be?"

"That girl. Ritzi. She's not exactly the kind of company you normally keep."

"*You* don't seem to mind keeping her company." She stuck a finger in his face. "Or bringing her into our home."

Joe squared his shoulders. Stiffened his mouth. "What have you two been talking about?"

"I didn't tell her I know, if that's what you're worried about. What good would it do? Humiliating the girl like that?" Stella knew Joe well enough not to hold Ritzi at fault for the affair. This was his doing.

The worried grimace on Joe's face smoothed out. He leaned against the door and grinned. "I'd call this a success," he said.

"If your goal was to end up in prison, sure."

"That won't happen."

"Twenty thousand dollars, Joe. It's our life savings. You drained every bit of it. What happens to me when this comes back to incriminate you? When we lose everything?"

"I'll make ten times that on the court. The salary is great. So are the *incentives*."

"Bribes, you mean."

"That's what it means to play at this level. It's a calculated risk."

"It's foolish. And criminal. And—"

Joe clapped a hand over her mouth. "We've been over this. It's done. If you don't like it, you can leave. Then you'll be a twice-divorced, penniless ex-socialite. See how you enjoy life then. Living in Queens. Working retail. That what you want?"

Stella knocked his hand away and took a deep breath. "I know how to keep up appearances. You taught me that."

Satisfied with her cooperation, Joe opened the door and started out of the room. He stopped to stare at Maria. In fact, bent over the coffee table, wiping up a puddle of Cuvée Brut from the dark wood finish.

"Who knew?" Joe said, eyes traveling down the dress that used to belong to his wife.

Stella cupped Joe's cheek in her palm and turned his face toward hers. "They are waiting for you in the office."

Joe shrugged away from her touch and returned to the meeting while she stood, hands balled into angry fists. Maria's face was flushed red; clearly she was not as oblivious to the attention as she'd appeared. Ritzi shifted uncomfortably at one of the tables overlooking the church garden, smoking her cigarette in silence as they waited for Joe to finish his business.

Ritzi and Maria jumped when Stella's seething voice broke the silence. Her eyes bored a hole into the office door. "I wish he were dead."

"So do I," the others answered in unison, their voices little more than a whisper. They startled. Looked at one another.

"Why do we let him get away with it?" Stella asked, giving each of them a pointed look.

"It's just the way things are," Ritzi answered.

There was fire in Stella's eyes. "It doesn't have to be."

Maria could not hide the fear in her words. "What do you mean?"

"I've heard Joe talk about your husband. I know what he's threatened you with. He wasn't bluffing."

Maria dropped to the couch.

Stella turned to Ritzi. "Joe is a lousy lover. And he's using you. How long are you willing to fake it for him?"

"You know?" Horror flashed across her face.

"Do you really want to know the conversations he has with his friends about you? The things I've overheard?"

"No." Ritzi gulped. "I don't."

"We could end this misery," Stella said. "We could do it together."

The air stilled as the three women regarded one another, drew closer.

"It's wrong." Maria rubbed her neck, searching for her rosary. She glanced between them, conflicted. Guilty.

Ritzi smiled, calculating. "We would never get away with it."

"Perhaps," Stella said, "the reason we *would* get away with it is because no one expects women to do such a thing."

While Joseph Crater plotted his political takeover with a handful of the most corrupt men in New York City, the three women in his life began to whisper fifteen feet away.

"WHAT kind of name is Vivian, anyway?"
Charlie asked, resting against the doorframe.

Ritzi filled the tin cup with water and poured it over the baby's soft brown hair. Ringlets had begun to curl over her ears and at the base of her neck, and Ritzi toyed with them as she lay her down in the shallow tub.

"A pretty one."

"She looks like you." He was a bit closer now, standing over her shoulder.

"Yes."

"I'm glad." Charlie knelt next to Ritzi on the floor and rested his arms on the edge of the tub. "I didn't know what to expect."

"Neither did I."

She could feel the heat of his gaze on the side of her face. The nape of her neck. The rise of her breasts. Ritzi wanted to bury her face in his chest. She wanted to touch his cheek. Instead, they both looked at the baby, their forearms brushing lightly. If she moved her pinkie an inch to the left, she could wrap it around Charlie's. She didn't.

Charlie reached into the tub with his other hand and set one finger in Vivian's chubby fist. She curled her fingers around it and tugged. From the corner of her eye, Ritzi could see the dimples flash on Charlie's face.

"She needs a middle name," he said. "I've been thinking about Jane. After my mother."

Ritzi cleared her throat, and emotion filled her voice. "I didn't know you wanted a say."

"Sarah," he said, voice tender. "I hate the bastard who did this to you.

But she's your baby, and I could never hate *her*." He pulled his finger from her tiny grasp and set it against her little rosebud lips. "I think Vivian Jane Martin is a good name."

Charlie handed Ritzi a towel and left the bathroom.

Once Vivian was clean and dry and diapered, Ritzi lay her in the middle of the bed to kick her feet in the air. She stood next to the open window and looked out at the fields. The corn was ready for harvest, and in the darkness it looked like a black wave rolling from the house in all directions. A breeze gathered the long, rough leaves and rubbed them together. When she closed her eyes, it sounded like summer rain. The sky was clear and the stars bright, and Ritzi was overwhelmed with the simplicity and beauty of that evening. She hadn't seen the stars one time in New York City. Before shutting the window, she leaned out a bit and inhaled the scent of grass and wind. The earthy fragrance of geraniums drifted up from the porch below.

Ritzi slipped out of her shoes and pulled her dress over her head. She didn't notice Charlie in the doorway watching until she saw his reflection in the window. She could see his eyes trail down the curve of her back, the roundness of her bottom beneath her slip. He swallowed. She hoped he would come into the room. That he would talk to her. Touch her. But when he caught her eyes in the reflection, he turned and walked away. Ritzi flipped out the light and curled around the tiny form of her daughter. She lay in the bed wide awake.

The hall was dark, and she heard Charlie's familiar steps heading toward the linen closet. He grabbed a blanket, like he'd done every night since she'd come home, then picked his way down the stairs to the living room. His feet shuffled across the hardwood floor. In her mind, she could see him sitting on the edge of the couch and taking off his boots, the left one first and then the right. He would unbutton his shirt, fold it, and set it on the chair. Same with his pants. Socks laid neatly on top of the pile. Ritzi imagined him standing in the living room, moonlight grazing his face and chest, and longing crept through her.

The couch groaned beneath his weight in the room below. He fussed with his blanket and pillow. Slowly the house grew quiet, only the faint creaking of wind and the settling of old plaster walls.

Vivian whimpered in the bed beside her, and Ritzi laid a hand on her stomach, feeling the rise and fall of her breath. Then she sang a few lines from her favorite Gershwin song, soft and low, so as not to disturb Charlie: "I never had the least notion that I could fall with such emotion . . . 'cause I've got a crush, my baby, on you."

At the sound of her mother's voice, Vivian grew still, and her breathing evened. She stuck one fist in her mouth and sucked. The little smacking sound of her lips made Ritzi smile, and she closed her eyes as well. An owl hooted outside, and together mother and baby drifted off to sleep to the lullaby of cornstalks rustling in the wind.

Some time later Ritzi woke when the blanket lifted from her. And then the weight of Charlie on the mattress. She looked up at him in the moonlight. His eyes were dark and shone like obsidian, and the shadows chiseled the lines of his face. Without a word, he slid next to her, and the heat of his skin against hers quickened her pulse. He smelled of leather and soap and fresh air, and she could feel the stubble of his chin rest against her shoulder.

"I'm sorry," she said. It sounded like a gasp, full of apology and grief.

Charlie tucked his legs in behind hers and reached over to play with one of Vivian's curls. His lips brushed against her ear and he traced callused fingertips up her arm. Gooseflesh rose at his touch and she took a deep breath, inhaling the smell of his desire. "I'm glad you came home," he said.

MARIA listened to the sound of Jude's key in the lock. She lay on the couch, afghan spread across her legs, and waited to see the look on his face. He stopped in the doorway, breath balled in his throat. The apartment was transformed, awash in candlelight and floating in the sounds of Haydn's Third Symphony. It had taken them months to save up for the record player, but the splurge seemed reasonable, given the circumstances. The soft scratch of the needle traveling through the groove added texture and depth to the music. A faint blush of orange light painted the upper half of their living room window as the sun set behind the skyline.

"Welcome home." She smiled.

"Nowhere I'd rather be." Jude crossed the room and kissed her forehead. He joined her on the couch. "I got a really interesting cold case today."

She raised her eyebrows in question.

"Apparently, a New York State Supreme Court judge disappeared a year ago, and no one ever found out what happened to him." He cupped her face in his palms, kissed her deeply. It felt like the brush of apology against her lips. "So now I've got all the time in the world to make it right. I promised I would."

"I know." A flash of worry crossed her face. Every time Joseph Crater came up in conversation, she grew anxious.

Jude tucked her into the tender circle of his arm. "I have something for you." He pulled a small box from his pocket and set it in her palm. It was wrapped in brown paper and tied with a shoelace.

Maria glanced at his feet. One of his shoes had sacrificed a lace. She touched her smile with two fingers as her eyes glassed over with tears.

"Open it."

Jude tensed around her, eager, but Maria took her time, slowly unraveling the crude bow and peeling the paper off one edge at a time. She gasped when she lifted the lid. Inside, resting on a soft bed of cotton, lay her rosary. The silver chain was repaired, all fifty-nine glass beads were set back in place, and the crucifix dangled at the bottom, newly polished. He held it up for her inspection.

Maria ran a tentative finger across the chain. "It's even more beautiful than I remembered."

"Finn helped. I wasn't exactly sure how it all went." Jude placed it around her neck. He pressed his forehead to hers. "Forgive me?"

"Ages ago."

Jude stretched out on his side and drew her to him, her spine against his stomach. In the background, the symphony played on, dipping and curling around the silence. Her breathing slowed, softened, as their bodies melted together. She fought the sleep that tugged at her eyes, wanting to savor this. It happened often lately, a sudden exhaustion that swept her away from the moment, only to release her hours later to find that a chunk of time was gone—a blank spot in an increasingly precious number of days.

When she'd finally shared Dr. Godfrey's diagnosis with Jude, they had both wept, arms thrown around one another, knotted together in grief. Her lengthy battle with infertility was explained by two excruciating words: *ovarian cancer*. The life they'd always hoped for was replaced by an urgent need to soak up every minute they had left. All talk of cancer and dishonesty was abandoned. They allowed no room in their conversation for words acquainted with heartbreak. They spoke only of love and faith and hope. Of each other.

Haydn wound to a close, the record player humming, and was replaced by the symphony of New York. Cars and people and the never-ending rattle of the El. Their neighbors fought in Polish, indiscernible words drifting through the poorly insulated walls. Someone paced in the apartment above them, a cane tapping against the floor. Jude patted her back in rhythm. Pulled her closer. Breathed in the scent of her soap. She felt his lips smile against the nape of her neck. And she knew that she would rather have this than a baby. She would rather have Jude.

Chapter Thirty-Nine

FINANCIAL DISTRICT, MANHATTAN,
MONDAY, AUGUST 24, 1931

STELLA reported for work at eight. Unable to justify the cab fare, she'd taken the subway, and she was still unsettled as she walked through the intricately detailed lobby of the Transportation Building. One of the newer skyscrapers in Lower Manhattan, it had a masonry exterior with a charming stepped-back form. But it was the capped copper roof in the shape of a pyramid that set the building apart from its neighbors. It was lovely, and Stella was grateful to be there, as opposed to a retail store. Or, God forbid, the garment district. Her mother had objected, of course, had said she was too good for the job, that she should hold out for something more dignified. But Stella brushed aside the comment, noting that beggars couldn't be choosers. She had brought this on herself, after all. So she stood tall, lifted her chin, and resumed the role of working woman for the first time in fourteen years.

"Name?" the receptionist asked when Stella approached the sprawling counter in the lobby.

"Stella," she said.

The woman stared at her with an insolent expression, waiting for elaboration.

"Stella Clark," she added. "I'm one of the new switchboard operators."

She slid a long fingernail down a clipboard until she found Stella's name, then tapped it as if to say, *Here you are.* She jutted the clipboard toward Stella. "Sign in."

Stella scratched her name on the paper with a pen that was almost out of ink, then stepped around the desk and walked toward the elevator.

"Where do you think you're going? The switchboard is in the basement."

Stella pointed toward the ceiling. "I interviewed up there."

"Yeah, well, you'll be working down there." She pointed toward a hallway off the lobby. "Stairwell is at the end. Don't forget to sign out when you leave."

Stella turned away from the elevator and the bright lobby and walked down the narrow hallway. She wouldn't be working in a high-rise, after all, but in a dark, dank basement. The air seemed to close in around her as she nudged the stairwell door open and peered down the flight of steps. Flickering bulbs cast a cold gray light. Stella descended to the floor below, wishing she'd worn more practical shoes. She'd purchased the twenty-dollar heels two years earlier after seeing Joan Blondell wear them in *Life* magazine. They'd been a special order from Saks, and she'd had to wait three weeks for them to arrive from Hollywood. Stella had been so proud of the shoes, but since she'd left her apartment, they'd already rubbed a blister on her ankle where the strap buckled. She limped toward a solid metal door that read SWITCHBOARD. Stella pushed it open and stood, dazed at the chaos within.

Fifteen women sat on swivel chairs before a wall of lights and wires and plugs. Each wore a headset and a solemn face as she directed calls to the offices above.

An older woman with a brash voice and unkempt hair barreled toward her. Her name tag read LOIS, and she held a roster in the crook of her arm. "Are you Stella Clark?"

Stella winced at the fake last name she'd given when applying for the job. Her real name was too controversial. Too easy to reject out of hand. "Yes, I am."

"You're late."

"It's eight—"

"The Transportation Building opens for business at eight o'clock. Your *shift* begins at seven forty-five. Now get to work. The other girls have been covering your station."

Stella received a glare or two as she followed the floor manager down the row to an empty station at the end. "Go on, we don't have all day."

She sat, only to find that her swivel chair was broken and her headset was taped together in two spots. Stella held it in place with one hand to stop it from sliding off her head.

"What are you waiting for?" Lois asked.

Stella glanced at the massive contraption in front of her. With all the cables and bulbs and coils of wire, it looked as though its innards were spilling out. "I don't know how to work this thing yet."

"If you'd gotten here on time, that wouldn't be a problem." Lois lifted the roster and put a small mark next to her name. "You'll have to figure it out as you go."

Stella's throat tightened and her tongue felt dry. "How do I start?"

"Plug your headset in there." Lois pointed to a small opening. "It lets the switchboard know you're available."

She pushed the long metal prong into the outlet, and within a few seconds lights on her board went from black to red and began pulsing. The girl next to her sighed in relief as a number of her calls transferred to Stella's station. She stiffened in her chair, unsure what to do next.

Lois rattled off instructions for directing the incoming calls to their proper locations in the building. Stella tried to pay attention, but the rush of noise in her ears made it difficult. She could feel the panic rising in her chest. Her pulse quickened. The room suddenly felt warm and small, and she tugged at her lace collar.

"Take those stupid gloves off," Lois ordered. "It works better with bare hands."

Stella peeled the satin gloves from her fingers and tossed them to the floor. She tried to remember the instructions as she reached toward the closest blinking light. With a deep, rattling breath, Stella flipped the switch on her new life.

CLUB ABBEY

GREENWICH VILLAGE, AUGUST 6, 1969

It is a case which seems to have become the symbol of all men and women who have vanished. Every year on August 6, newspapers recount the story, often adding new touches or theories. Comedians use it in their acts. Many legends have sprung from it. A great number of them were, and still are, myths born of imagination.

—Oscar Fraley, preface to *The Empty Robe*

Jude is alone in Stella's corner booth with nothing but an overflowing ashtray, a letter, and a lukewarm glass of whiskey. He picks up the drink, downs it in a quick gulp, and grimaces.

Then Stan is at the booth.

Jude glares at him, skeptical. "You water this shit down?"

"Ice melted."

"Bull. What'd you mix it? Eighty-twenty?"

Stan grins. "Seventy-thirty. You saw her. She can't handle a Shirley Temple, much less straight whiskey. I'm just glad we didn't have to carry her up the stairs."

"How long you think she has?"

"Three months. Maybe. She's only lasted this long to piss you off."

Jude sets the glasses side by side on the table. "I'll miss that old broad." He laughs at Stan's sour expression. "Okay, maybe *miss* is a strong word. I'll be bored without her. How's that?"

"It's time to let this go." There is a deep sadness in Stan's eyes as he looks around the bar. He rubs a spot on the table. Shifts from one foot to the other. "I got an offer on the place last month. Told them that I'd call back with a decision tomorrow. I just wanted to see Stella one more time before I made up my mind. Is that crazy?"

"No," Jude says. It doesn't seem crazy to him at all.

When Stan returns to the bar, Jude picks up the letter. He's careful with the envelope, lifting the flap and easing out the pages with two fingers so they won't disintegrate on the table before him. His hands feel thick and clumsy as he unfolds them.

Dear Stella,

I like to think that maybe, under different circumstances, we could have been friends. And I'm sorry that's never going to happen. Accomplices will have to do.

I know we agreed that we wouldn't talk about this again after our final meeting at the Morosco Theatre, but I wanted you to know how it ended. You deserve that much from me, considering the role I played in destroying your marriage.

No one ever guessed that I tipped off Samuel Seabury, or that you told me he would be in Atlantic City that weekend. I burned your telegram when I got it. Owney never said a word about the investigation to Crater. His mind was made up the second I planted that seed at Club Abbey.

Crater never saw daylight after August 6, but he didn't die in the seats of the Belasco Theatre like we planned. He should have gone to see Dancing Partner *alone that night. He should have met his end at the hands of Owney Madden during intermission. I made sure that the letter Maria delivered to Club Abbey had all the information Owney needed.*

Jude's heart gives a violent shudder, and he grips the edge of the table with one hand. His eyes keep going back to Maria's name. He reads it over and over and tries to shake it from his mind. To refute what he sees. But he knows it is the truth as the letter continues.

After you went to Maine for the summer, Maria and I continued our monthly meetings in the restroom—just like we arranged that first night in April. We coordinated everything, down to what she wore and when to arrive that night. She wanted no part of this—you know that—but she was the only one who could have delivered that letter to Club Abbey. If either of us had taken it, Owney would have known it was a setup. He had to think it was a tip from someone who didn't want Crater to testify before the Seabury Commission. He had to think Crater was arranging a deal for clemency. And in the end, Maria understood it was the only way to protect Jude. Crater would have followed through on his threat to have him killed. Jude was becoming a liability. Knowing that was all it took for Maria to do her part.

Our plan would have worked if Dancing Partner *hadn't been sold out that night. Owney would have finished him off. We would have all gone on with our lives, and you would have gotten the insurance money. But when Crater couldn't get an extra ticket for me, he changed the plan and had the cabdriver take us to Coney Island. That's when everything went wrong. There was supposed to be a body and a scandal and headlines. His disappearance ruined everything.*

I'd like to say that Crater went quickly. Or that it was merciful. But that's not the truth. They beat the hell out of him that night. But he was still alive when they dragged him from the hotel room. My guess is that his body will never be found. Owney Madden doesn't leave loose ends.

The fact that I got pregnant was an accident. You never knew that, and I kept it from you. And I'm sorry. It just felt so cruel to throw that in your face as well. The only one who knew was Maria. She found out early on, and I would have given the baby to her—I swear I would have—if Owney hadn't killed Vivian Gordon before I could deliver. She was set to be Samuel Seabury's key witness. Viv would have blown the scandal wide open. Her testimony would have brought the whole racket down. We were fools to think Owney would have ever let it happen. We were fools to try this in the first place.

I've hated Crater since the day I met him. But now I hate myself for having a part in this. If I had the choice today, I wouldn't do it. Not for you or for anyone else. I don't know how to live an entire life-time knowing that I helped kill a man. I don't know how, but I have to try. The hope of a normal life is all that I have left.

Tell the cops if you want. But know that I don't plan on ever being found.

Sally Lou Ritz

Jude only reads the letter once. He presses against the booth and squeezes his eyes shut, only to see Maria's name etched against his eye-lids. The one piece of evidence he needs to settle this case bears the name of his wife. Reveals her part in this mess. Maria, now dead thirty-seven years and buried beneath a maple tree on the outer edge of Calvary Cemetery in Queens. She did this for *him*.

Jude tears the letter in half, then in quarters, and rests it on top of the ashtray. He pulls Maria's lighter from his pocket. It's scratched and tarnished, and the striker only works sporadically. Two flicks of his thumb, and a small mound of flame licks the air. He cups it in his hand for a moment and then touches it to the letter. Jude expects to feel regret as he feeds the paper into the flames, but it's relief that consumes him.

It's over.

Maria's lighter is warm, and he presses it to his palm, drawing her memory into himself. Then he sets it back in his pocket and watches the confession turn to ash, taking the truth with it forever.

Even though this novel is based on true events, it is a work of fiction. My attempt was to show what *could* have happened to Judge Crater, not necessarily what *did*. Though no longer front-page news, it is a case that once obsessed a nation and, out of respect for those who still follow it quite seriously (and believe me, there are *many*), I would like to note a few things about the story within these pages. I compressed some of the time frame and took creative license with a handful of dates and details. I did so for the sake of space and narrative drive. A few examples: *The New Yorkers* actually began rehearsals in November 1930, not August. *Ladies All* wrapped on December 13, not earlier in the month as I suggest. Stella's deposition for the letters of administration and the request for her husband's death certificate actually happened on two different dates. In neither instance was Simon Rifkind her attorney. Although a real character and associate of Joseph Crater's, he is presented here as a composite of the numerous lawyers Stella worked with over the years to settle her husband's estate. I believe that one lawyer in a novel is more than enough. Some of what you read here may be different from what you've read elsewhere. This account is nothing more than my own speculations, the fiction I created from the bits and pieces of truth Joseph Crater left behind. My personal interest in the story lies in the fact that *someone* knew what happened to him yet chose not to tell. My job was to ask who that person (or persons) might be and what they had to hide. That said, here is what I know for sure about Club Abbey and the people mentioned in this novel.

CLUB ABBEY no longer exists. The gathering spot for showgirls, mobsters, and corrupt politicians was owned by Owney Madden and was considered a "night club of sordid reputation" and a "white-light rendezvous." Though Joseph Crater told his wife that he visited it only for political reasons, there is sufficient evidence to suggest that his motives were more carnal. We know that Stella Carter performed her ritual for thirty-eight years in Greenwich Village, but we do not know exactly where. I've taken creative liberties in locating Owney Madden's nightspot farther downtown in the storied neighborhood where Stella's own memoir tells us she performed it.

JOSEPH CRATER'S disappearance remains a mystery to this day. For more than eighty years, amateur sleuths and armchair detectives have attempted to discover what happened to him. Most likely we will never be certain of the truth. However, we do know that a set of human remains was found beneath the pier at Coney Island in the mid-1950s when construction began on the New York Aquarium. Authorities were never able to identify the remains, and they were sent to Hart Island, the world's largest tax-funded cemetery, and buried in a mass grave. I like to think that he *was* found. We just never knew it.

JUDE SIMON is a composite of the many officers of the New York Police Department who have investigated Crater's disappearance over the past eighty-four years. These officers are discussed in Stella Crater's memoir, *The Empty Robe: The Story and Legend of the Disappearance of Judge Crater,* and in Richard Tofel's *Vanishing Point: The Disappearance of Judge Crater and the New York He Left Behind.* However, none of those officers were married to the Craters' maid. Jude's character, as represented here, is drawn only from my imagination.

VIVIAN GORDON, the notorious New York City madam, was found garroted in Van Cortlandt Park on February 26, 1931. A truck driver discovered her coatless body, a crepe dress pulled up around her neck. Her silk stockings were ripped at the knees, and one of her slippers was missing. An eight-foot length of clothesline was drawn like a noose around her neck. She was scheduled to give testimony the next day before the Seabury Commission, which, among other things, was investigating the connection between the NYPD and an unprecedented judicial scandal. Gordon was to be the key witness.

GEORGE HALL was the first reporter to learn that Joseph Crater had gone missing. He broke the story on September 3, 1930, in an article in the *New York World*. By that afternoon, the story had spread to the *Sun*, the *World*, the *Herald Tribune*, and the *Daily News*, followed the next morning by the *Times*. Afterward, hundreds of articles were printed about Crater, the vast majority of which were a salacious mix of conjecture and traditional reporting. Hall never revealed the identity of his informant.

STAN THE BARTENDER is a creation of mine, inspired by an article on the yearly tradition at Club Abbey. At the height of the excitement surrounding Crater's disappearance, a packed bar would join Stella in toasting her missing husband. They would raise glasses along with her and shout, "Good luck, Joe, wherever you are!" In later years, however, the tradition was forgotten, and she was alone in her penance. I thought it fitting to give her a sympathetic companion who remembered the glory days of Club Abbey.

DISTRICT ATTORNEY THOMAS CRAIN was denounced as senile and incompetent by the influential City Club of New York on March 7, 1931, after failing to get an indictment in the disappearance of Joseph Crater. Governor Franklin Roosevelt appointed a panel to examine the district attorney's record.

SAMUEL SEABURY led the investigation to determine whether any judges in the state of New York had purchased their seats on the state supreme court. Joseph Crater disappeared before he could give testimony to the grand jury, Vivian Gordon was murdered, and several other key witnesses invoked their Fifth Amendment right. Despite attempts over several years to convict him, Martin Healy was acquitted three separate times. Although Seabury was unable to get a conviction, he did manage to become an "implacable enemy" of Tammany Hall. His investigations brought to light the inner workings of that political organization and forced its members to testify before various grand juries and public hearings. Whatever else he may have failed to accomplish, in his battle with Tammany Hall, Seabury put an end to business as usual.

LEO LOWENTHALL was one of many NYPD detectives assigned to Missing Persons File No. 13595. The case was quietly shelved less than a year after being opened and has been only nominally investigated since. The possible involvement of the NYPD in Crater's death is a popular theory among those enthralled with the case. This theory gained credence in 2005 with the discovery of a letter written by a woman in Queens named Stella Ferrucci-Good. Found after her death, it claimed that Crater was killed by her husband, a former NYPD detective, and buried beneath the pier at Coney Island.

WILLIAM KLEIN was an attorney for the Shubert Theatre Corporation. He was, along with Sally Lou Ritz, one of the last two people on record to see Crater alive. There has been much speculation through the years as to whether Ritz was his girlfriend or Crater's mistress. In their statements to police, both Ritz and Klein claimed to have been an item— a convenient fiction had they been trying to provide each other with an alibi. Regardless, both were adamant that they were with Crater at Billy Haas's Chophouse—not Club Abbey—the night he disappeared. It is interesting to note that records show Crater and Klein visiting Club Abbey at least twice after the judge returned from Maine.

DONALD SMITHSON is a product of my imagination.

EMMA WHEELER arrived in New York City to comfort her daughter at the end of August 1930. According to Stella's memoir, Emma was a constant source of comfort and companionship in the years following Judge Crater's disappearance.

SIMON RIFKIND replaced Joseph Crater as a law secretary when he was appointed to the New York State Supreme Court. They were friends and associates. It is believed that he collected and deposited Crater's paychecks for several months after the judge's disappearance. It is not known whether he did this of his own volition or at Stella's request. Regardless, authorities suspected that there was much about the Crater disappearance that he never revealed.

FRED KAHLER worked as a chauffeur for the Craters for three years. In the weeks after Joseph Crater's disappearance, he was an invaluable source of information to Stella. She sent him to New York on at least one occasion to inquire after her husband's whereabouts; his report back to Maine detailed his conversations with Crater's associates and their insistence that he stop asking questions. Later that year, unable to pay him, Stella let Kahler go but gave him their car as payment for back wages.

FATHER FINN DONNEGAL is a another product of my imagination.

SHORTY PETAK was inspired by a good friend of mine. He knows who he is. And I hope he will forgive me for portraying him as such a lecher when he is, in fact, one of my all-time favorite people. I wouldn't have allowed him in my wedding otherwise.

OWNEY MADDEN was an infamous gangster and bootlegger of New York City's Jazz Age. He owned a number of speakeasies, including Club Abbey, and was a frequent financial backer of Broadway shows. He was exiled to Hot Springs, Arkansas, in 1935 after the murder of fellow gangster Vincent "Mad Dog" Coll. He died there, of natural causes, in 1965.

SALLY LOU RITZ, a popular showgirl and rumored mistress of Joseph Crater, was one of the last people to see him alive. She testified that she had dinner with William Klein and Crater at Billy Haas's Chophouse the night the judge disappeared. She vanished from the public record shortly thereafter. The Charley Project, a database of missing-person cold cases, officially lists her as a missing person. Most of what is written about her here comes from my imagination.

MARIA SIMON was drawn from a single article by George Hall in the *New York World*. While it is known that the Craters had a loyal long-term maid who was in the apartment in the days after Joseph Crater vanished, no one was ever able to question her on the record regarding his disappearance. When interviewed by George Hall, she gave the name Amedia Christian. It is uncertain whether that was her real name. Her character in this story is a complete conjecture.

STELLA CRATER'S picture was splashed across the front page of every paper in New York when her husband was declared legally dead in 1939. As a result, she was fired from her job as a switchboard operator at the Transportation Building for fear she would bring "bad publicity." Up until then, she had been known as Stella Clark. It has been speculated, but never proved, that she was in possession of information that would have led to her husband's killers. She published a memoir in 1961 chronicling her side of the story. *The Empty Robe,* written with Oscar Fraley and published by Doubleday, sold well but was widely criticized as naive and melodramatic at best and purposefully dishonest at worst. In the thirty-eight years after Joseph Crater disappeared, she never missed her annual ritual. Even in death, she could not escape the shadow of her missing husband:

FRIDAY, OCTOBER 3, 1969

Died. Stella Crater Kunz, 82, former wife of New York State Supreme Court Justice Joseph Force Crater, the central figure in one of the century's classic mysteries; in Mt. Vernon, N.Y. On the evening of August 6, 1930, the recently appointed justice stepped into a taxi after attending a Manhattan dinner party and vanished. A sensational manhunt followed, but failed to turn up a clue. Crater was declared legally dead in 1939 (Stella Crater remarried in 1938), but the case remains unsolved to this day.

ACKNOWLEDGMENTS

I once heard that in the ancient world men and women did not personally thank those who had done them a kindness. Instead, they went out in public, to the town square or the city gates, and they told *others* about the integrity of a friend or the promise kept by a brother or the kindness of a stranger. They honored their friends and family and neighbors by speaking well of them in public. It's a pretty image, don't you think? Well, I'm a modern girl so I tend to think that we ought to go about it *both* ways. But humor me for a moment while I publicly thank a few people for the book you hold in your hands.

This book would not exist if not for the following people:

Stella Crater. As fascinated as we are by the disappearance of her husband, Stella's was the *real* story. She had the courage to live her life in public. And the dignity to keep her head held high when the world was falling down around her. We will probably never know the answers to many of the questions she left behind. But who doesn't love a good mystery?

My early readers: Melissa Dick, Bonnie Grove, Joy Jordan-Lake, Christa Allan, Alli Fernberg, and Abbie James. They gave me sharp insight and treasured friendship. I would have quit a hundred times if not for them.

I won the literary agent jackpot with Elisabeth Weed. She's wise and funny and charming. I couldn't ask for a better guide to help me navigate the world of publishing. Thank you for the unlikely yes.

I owe so much to the publishing wizards at Doubleday. My editor, Melissa Danaczko, championed this book from the moment it landed on her desk. She continues to do so today and I'd be lost without her wisdom and insight. James Melia keeps me on track, on time, and in the loop. And he's always up for a round of witty banter. Bill Thomas, Publisher of Doubleday, came up with the title and has supported this book from day one. Emily Mahon designed the cover and I'm not sure if there's ever been a prettier book. My copyeditor, Amy Schroeder, has the patience of Job and the thoroughness of the IRS. She deserves a medal. And a vacation. Pei Koay designed the interior layout. She's an artist in her own right. Todd Doughty, Judy Jacoby, and the publicity and marketing teams at Doubleday—geniuses all. And finally, I am so thankful for the Random House sales team who always speak of this book with an exclamation point.

I wouldn't make it through a day without my friends at SheReads.org, Marybeth Whalen and Kimberly Brock. In truth, they are more than friends. They are sisters. The family I chose for myself.

And there were others who helped me along the way. My film agent, Dana Borowitz. Sarah Jio for introducing me to Elisabeth. My sister, Abby Belbeck, who isn't afraid to entertain my children (a.k.a. The Wild Rumpus) when I'm in the writing cave. My mother, Emily Allison, for teaching me that story is the shortest distance to the human heart. Dian Belbeck. Reggie Coe. JT Ellion. Paige Crutcher. Melanie Benjamin, Caroline Leavitt, Karen Abbott, Lydia Netzer, Kelly O'Conner McNees, and Julie Kibler for your kind and gracious endorsements. All my thanks to the Master Storyteller, without Him I would be lost.

And finally, for the men in my life: my husband, Ashley, and our four sons, London, Parker, Marshall, and Riggs. Never, in all the world, has a woman been so lucky. I love you. I love you. I love you.

ABOUT THE AUTHOR

Ariel Lawhon is cofounder of the popular online book club SheReads.org, and is a novelist, blogger, and lifelong reader. She lives in the rolling hills outside Nashville with her husband and four young sons.